DOCTOR WHO

DARK PROGENY
STEVE EMMERSON

BBC

For Ben and Shirley

Published by BBC Worldwide Ltd
Woodlands, 80 Wood Lane
London W12 0TT

First published 2001
Copyright © Steve Emmerson 2001
The moral right of the author has been asserted

ISBN 0 563 53837 6
Imaging by Black Sheep, copyright © BBC 2001

Printed and bound in Great Britain by Mackays of
Chatham
Cover printed by Belmont Press Ltd, Northampton

Your children are not your children.
They are the sons and daughters of Life's longing for itself.
They came through you but not from you
And though they are with you yet they belong not to you.
You may give them your love but not your thoughts,
For they have their own thoughts.
You may house their bodies but not their souls,
For their souls dwell in the house of tomorrow, which you cannot visit, not even in your dreams.
You may strive to be like them, but seek not to make them like you,
For life goes not backward nor tarries with yesterday.
You are the bows from which your children as living arrows are sent forth.

Kahlil Gibran 1883–1931
The Prophet (1923), 'On Children'

Part One

Through envy of the devil came death into the world.
– Wisdom of Solomon ch. 2, v. 24

11.9.2847 (Earth Standard)
Ceres Alpha

A scream exploded out of her as Veta Manni sensed the oncoming pain like a rapidly expanding storm. It hit. Ripped through her. Subsided and left her shivering and gasping for air. She chased rivers of sweat from her face and tried to prepare for the next giant wave. Her body was a wreck. Muscles and sinews torn apart by the tornadoes that struck one after another. A relentless, perpetual torture. She thought she must have experienced heights of agony well up there in the outer reaches of human tolerance.

And it was building again. She gritted her teeth and clenched her fists. The pain came with terrifying intensity. She lost her grip. Howled and screamed and produced animal sounds that weren't her voice. She was so entirely lost in the suffering now that she felt she'd left her body and was crashing around in a tumultuous sea of pain.

Josef watched his wife undergoing her private torment, and the fear tore at his throat. His insides were knots. He took her hand, feeling powerless to help. As the pain died away, she gripped his hand tight and gasped for air. He leaned in close and kissed her cheek, then found her eyes imploring him.

'More drugs,' she pleaded.

Josef shook his head sorrily. 'They won't let you. Too dangerous.'

'I can't go on, Joe.'

'Course you can,' he told her, forcing a smile into his face. But he wasn't so sure. She was visibly weakening now. Wet with sweat and quivering with a mixture of exhaustion and fear. Her eyes

7

were dark hollows, full of dread thoughts. He swallowed back the compulsion to sob and tried to force down inside him the feelings that were screaming to get out.

The past six months had been a huge strain on both of them. Even before today, and the panic of the baby arriving a whole two months early, Josef had long been gravely worried for his wife and their child. It had been one endless catalogue of terrors. The abnormal scans, the changes in Veta, the intense bouts of sickness. His wife had gone from being a blissful prospective mum to a physical and psychological wreck in the space of those six immeasurable months.

Sensing movement behind him, Josef turned to find Dr Pryce in the doorway, regarding them with a curiously absent look as if his mind were elsewhere. There were two nurses behind him, and a man in a suit whom Josef didn't recognise. Pryce's face abruptly broke into a disarming smile and he stepped into the room to look over Veta.

'Everything going all right?' Pryce asked, not bothering to introduce the nurses and suited man who'd followed him in and now stood observing Veta's naked bottom half with a keen scrutiny.

Josef threw the sheet over his wife's legs and nodded uncertainly. For a moment there was only the sound of Veta's coarse breathing as she prepared for the next contraction. Then she began to scream and Josef grasped her hand, this time feeling her squeeze so hard he thought she was going to crush the bones in his fingers. The scream lasted for ever, and all Josef could do was watch the suffering so obvious in her contorted face. This wasn't his wife. His wife was a pretty girl, not this snarling, screeching, crimson-faced monster.

The wave subsided and Josef was relieved to feel the pressure on his fingers release. Veta was sobbing gently now, and she watched him through her tears for a moment before recovering her voice.

'Next time,' she hissed, '*you* can have the baby.'

* * *

So, thought Fitz, this is panic stations. OK. Just maintain that cool and aloof exterior. Try not to appear too obviously fazed. And for God's sake don't look as though you're about to *scream*! Even though the TARDIS is shrieking through the vortex and the Doctor looks like he's gonna completely lose it any moment. This sort of thing happens every day in the TARDIS. Par for the course. Just another humdrum day in the life of a swashbuckling time gypsy.

The Doctor lay flat on his back under the half-dismantled control console. A mess of wires spilled out to engulf him, and as he worked he was forced to keep disentangling his arms. Fitz gazed anxiously at the TARDIS manual that was wedged open on the edge of the console. The Doctor had peered into it maniacally before plunging on his ridiculous little trolley into the tangle of wires. The baffled look on his face while he read the manual had not inspired in Fitz a very great deal of what might be termed 'confidence'.

The Doctor extricated himself with a chatter of trolley wheels.

'Pass me that sonic *wrench*,' he yelped as a small shower of sparks went off like a Roman candle at the side of his head.

Fitz didn't know what the hell a sonic wrench was among all that weird-looking clobber in the Doctor's toolbag. He plucked out a likely-looking gizmo and offered it over.

In return, he received a baffled gaze from the Doctor.

'The *sonic wrench*,' the Doctor repeated.

Sonic wrench. OK. Wrenches are big things, right? Something big with a big handle and some sort of futuristic soundy-looking thing on one end... As Fitz gazed in consternation into the bag, he saw the Doctor's hand reach across and grasp something that looked neither anything at all like a wrench, nor anything at all like a sonic thing. The Doctor swivelled on his trolley and disappeared smartly back under the centre console, knees stuck up and right foot tapping furiously as he worked.

'You haven't found the problem then yet?' Fitz asked the Doctor's legs.

The tapping foot increased the tempo of its tapping.

'Things are all under control,' the Doctor's muffled voice reassured him from inside the wire-spewing console.

'But you don't know what, exactly, the problem is, yet?' Fitz pressed.

The foot stopped tapping and the legs brought the Doctor back out on his trolley. Face smeared with greasy brown marks, hair wild and matted with what looked to Fitz like grey cobwebs, the Doctor regarded Fitz in silence for a short while before he spoke again.

'If I knew exactly what the problem was,' he said evenly, 'I would have fixed it by now.'

'Doesn't this TARDIS have some sort of self-diagnostic system?' Fitz demanded. 'A "fault locator" or something?'

'It does,' the Doctor muttered, apparently trying to keep the cap screwed tight on the bubbling irritation inside him.

'So why not use that to tell you what's wrong?'

'It's faulty.'

'The fault locator's on the blink?'

'*Everything's* "on the blink".'

Fitz paced about the console room, slapping a clenched fist repeatedly into the palm of his other hand. He felt like a jack-in-the-box with the lid nailed down. And some snotty kid shaking the box madly trying to get it to work.

'Can't *I* take a look at it?' he asked finally.

The Doctor sat upright on the trolley and wiped his forehead on the back of his sleeve.

'If there was anything you could do to help, Fitz, I would have told you.'

'This is ridiculous,' Fitz said in frustration. 'I feel like a spare –'

'Why don't you go check on Anji?' the Doctor suggested.

Anji! Probably dead by now. But sure – check on her. See how many of her life signs are still registering on that stupid little telly the Doctor had hooked her up to. With a resigned nod, Fitz swept across the cluttered console room. He threw himself through the doors and down the main corridor that led to their quarters. Steeling himself outside Anji's room, he entered to find her lying perfectly still on the bed.

Perfectly still. No rising and lowering of her chest. No rapid flickering of the eyes as if in dream-troubled sleep. No nothing!

He checked the monitor and noticed that the heartbeat had restarted, but now the electrical activity in the brain was flatlining extremely worryingly. Some of the other blips of light were way too high, most were way too low. He reached out to touch her wet face. It was red and coated in perspiration, but she was cold as an ice cube. Fitz pulled his hands away when he realised how violently his fingers were shaking and thrust them back into his pockets.

The screaming TARDIS he could stand. The Doctor's manic dancing about he could cope with. Against all the myriad hysterical provocations snapping at his heels today he had managed to sustain a brave face. But this inability to *do* anything was too much. It was breaking his resolve, crumbling his façade, cracking him up.

In vexation, he kicked the stand that supported the monitor and all the readings flared into life at once. His heart bounced about inside his chest, while he stood and watched the monitor return to its old, pathetic state. Her signs were all over the place. But mostly on the floor. So what now?

Fitz found himself scraping the bristles around his chin. He delved into his pockets for a ciggy but was irked to find them empty except for a slip of paper he'd picked up in one of the deserted corridors this morning. It looked like a sheet of paper currency, and he'd intended asking the Doctor how many packets of fags it would buy on whichever planet it hailed from. But that was before all this emergency stuff had erupted out of nowhere.

First, Anji feeling suddenly violently sick and throwing up all over the kitchen where they were all sipping orange juice together. Then the TARDIS lurching and spinning – throwing them, the crockery and the sick all over the place. Both Anji and the TARDIS had gone downhill fast from there. It was hard to believe that was only a couple of hours ago. It felt to Fitz as if he'd spent the last week in frenzy mode, and he wasn't sure how much more of this battering his composure could take.

He found himself patting his trouser pockets distractedly, then the breast pocket of his shirt. Nothing.

Anji made a low groaning sound and Fitz was abruptly kneeling at her side, grasping her hand and patting it nervously. Her eyes were moving again. For the first time in nearly an hour. But, when she opened them, Fitz was dismayed to see that they were completely black inside, as if the pupils had spread like an oil slick to fill her entire eyes. She gazed about blindly.

'Doctor?'

'It's me.'

'I can't see.'

'You'll be fine. Don't worry. The Doctor's got it all sussed. Don't worry. You get some rest.'

She tried to rise, but slumped back with a blast of air. Fitz watched her closely. The eyes were inert under their lids, but her chest was moving again now. He glanced at the monitor and realised that all her signs were almost back to normal except the bottom one, which the Doctor had said was something to do with her trace telepathic centres. That one was dancing about here, there and everywhere with a life all its own. Fitz waited for it to settle down, but when it refused he looked back at Anji and watched the nothingness happening behind her eyelids.

The thought struck him that she had quite a beautiful face. Her lips were sort of full and straight both at the same time, and they pouted at him without actually pouting, if that was at all possible. His attention strayed again to her chest, and he watched her breasts rise and sink slowly. He found it difficult to drag his eyes away, then mentally kicked himself for even considering staring at her like that.

Letting go of her hand, he jumped to his feet and marched from the room.

Back at the dismantled console, the Doctor worked furiously. Fitz squinted at the Doctor's fingers as they moved with ferocious dexterity among the remaining controls.

'So,' Fitz said chattily, trying to paper over the cracks he could feel developing, 'what's happening?'

'Don't worry,' the Doctor said in a reassuring tone without looking up for even an instant. 'It's all under control.'

'*What's* all under control?'

The Doctor's eyes met his for the briefest fleeting moment, and Fitz wished they hadn't.

'This is really bad, isn't it?' Fitz asked him straight.

'Bad-*ish*, yes.'

'You haven't got the faintest idea what you're doing, have you?'

Now the Doctor shot him a black look, dark curls violent above his brooding eyes. He pointed to a small monitor that jutted up out of the surface of the console.

'That's the problem,' he announced, and Fitz heard a trace of something akin to awe in the Doctor's voice.

Rounding the console, Fitz stared hard into the monitor. All he could see was a computer-generated 3-D image of a coiling multicoloured shape suspended against a black background. It could have been anything.

'What is it?'

'A virus,' the Doctor told him.

'A computer virus?'

'Rather more than that, I suspect. I think the TARDIS has contracted the same disease as Anji.'

For a good few moments Fitz said nothing. His pummelled brain threw the idea around and around and got absolutely nowhere with it. Then he heard his voice stuttering.

'How can the TARDIS catch a disease?'

'She's more than a machine,' the Doctor reminded him. 'In fact it's possible that Anji caught the virus *from* the TARDIS. I'm guessing here, but, going by the way it's affected Anji's telepathic centres, it could be that that's how it's transmitted.'

'So now you know what the trouble is, you can cure it, right? You *are* a doctor.'

But the Doctor was shaking his head. 'No no no no no. Not that simple. I've tried everything.' He flung his arms open in an expansive, defeated gesture. 'I've thrown the entire manual at it, but it's still very obstinately *there*. It's in everything. I'm not sure what I can try next.'

'Meanwhile Anji is dying and we can't land,' Fitz reminded him angrily, as if the Doctor might have forgotten.

He found the Doctor's eyes searching his again. This time they were those of a little boy lost. Perhaps it was his fear for Anji's survival. Perhaps it was something else. Fitz had often wondered at the depth of the bond the Doctor shared with his TARDIS. Maybe the same virus had affected him. Maybe *he* was disintegrating like his ship. Momentarily, the Doctor was not the man Fitz knew. Momentarily, he seemed almost too human.

Veta screamed. The machines they'd attached to her screamed. The medics dashed about the room checking readings and yelping information and instructions at one another. Dr Pryce was sweating now, not at all the calm and imposing man that Josef Manni knew.

Josef felt stupid, standing there in the corner gazing into the mayhem. He wished he could *do* something. Or get out and go haring down the corridors screaming himself. Watching the multitude of agonies his wife was being forced to endure, feeling so utterly useless to help, made him feel like a sick voyeur. He suddenly didn't want to be here any more. He needed air. He needed to be alone. But Veta's words of the last few months came back to haunt him –

'*I think something's seriously wrong, Joe. I think something really bad's gonna happen. I can sense it…*'

And Josef couldn't for a single moment take his eyes off his wife's agonies.

'The baby's heart rate's over three hundred a minute,' one of the nurses yelped.

'Blood pressure's way above safety parameters,' Pryce said, his voice tight and showing the strain.

The man in the suit had very quickly vanished when it looked like things were going wrong. Josef had watched him almost enviously as he walked away. The nurses and Pryce shouted, dashed about the room with equipment, pushed an oxygen mask over Veta's face.

Josef caught snatches of almost hysterical conversation.

'Moving to breach…' 'Severed umbilical…' 'In distress…'

Transfixed by the image of his wife writhing on the blood-gorged bed, screaming and crying and clawing and thrashing, Josef simply stood on the outskirts and the whole scene seemed to recede into a vast distance. As if he'd finally somehow managed to disengage himself from the trauma. The room went into slo-mo. Forms and images began to merge, colours swirling into one another, Pryce moved steadily around, walking through the nurses as if they were liquid things. The horror of the sounds also receded, becoming muffled and blunt. Josef felt as if he were floating around the edge of a glass bubble that contained the room in which his baby was being born.

He heard Pryce's voice, thick and slow, talking to him. It was made of sound as thick as treacle. Deep and evil and appalling. Josef saw one of the nurses looking anxiously at him, silent and faraway.

Then he was back and the room was filled with a screaming baby.

Veta collapsed on the bed, eyes closed and her whole body still.

Pryce vanished with the baby, and as the nurses followed him out into the corridor at a run, Josef was sure that the sound of the baby transformed into an animal yowl.

The console room was empty, except for the detritus from the Doctor's hysterical rampaging through his multitudinous toolkits. Fitz was pretty sure the Doctor didn't completely understand most of the gadgets and gizmos he owned. He seemed to have been trying them on the console in a state of sheer desperation. And nothing he'd tried had done any good at all. The TARDIS still screeched. It still buckled occasionally. It still felt as though it were on the very brink of exploding.

'Doctor?'

'Yes?'

A distracted head appeared from behind the console. The Doctor's hair stood on end, damp with sweat, and his face was blotched with dark, dusty stains.

'How's it going?'

A smile sprang into the Doctor's features.

'Fine,' he said brightly. 'No problem at all. Soon have her fixed.'

Then he was gone. There was another shower of sparks and the Doctor flew into the air briefly with a startled look. When he landed Fitz gave him a brooding scowl.

'*Fine?*' he asked.

The Doctor shrugged and sent a hand foraging through his rowdy dark brown curls.

'Well… I fixed the artron conduit… How's Anji?'

'Not good.'

'How "not good"?'

'Very "not good".'

'Oh…'

'I think the word you're looking for is "bugger",' Fitz offered.

The Doctor gave him a faraway look that disconcerted Fitz more than any of his dashing about like a thousand things possessed.

'Can't you get us down *anywhere*?' Fitz demanded.

'No good. Anji needs medical attention from a reasonably advanced culture. We're locked on to a set of co-ordinates that register signs of level-four civilisation but I just can't get the phase modulators to mesh.'

Great, thought Fitz. Technobabble. Not good. Very very not good when the Doctor starts spouting technobabble.

'Can't we bypass them?' he asked, hoping it wasn't too stupid a question.

The Doctor gazed deep into the space behind Fitz. His hands hovered very slowly over the console until his fingers settled around a set of switches and levers. Without looking down, he spoke softly to Fitz and his voice was an anxious whisper.

'Bypass them. Supremely dangerous. But we can try it.'

'How "supremely dangerous", exactly?'

'Supremely supremely dangerous indeed.'

'Are you sure you should try it, then?'

'How "not good" did you say Anji was?'

'OK,' Fitz agreed. 'If you're sure we have no choice.'

Out of the corner of his eye, Fitz thought he saw the Doctor's hands move slightly around the switches. Then the shrieking of the TARDIS took on a whole new set of dimensions and Fitz knew abruptly what it sounded like to skin a cat alive. The whole room pinwheeled about him and the floor swept up to smash him under the jaw. Then the fabric of time and space unravelled and Fitz felt himself being sucked inside out an atom at a time.

An immense silence stretched between them, like a cold dark ocean filled with fear. Veta glared at the clock, then back at the door, and the vacant corridor beyond. Josef slumped on the bedside seat and gazed off into empty air.

It had been twenty minutes since they had rushed off with the baby. One of the nurses had returned briefly to examine Veta, but she'd dashed off again without any indication of how the baby was doing. They'd left the bloodied sheets, and Veta still sat in a pool of viscera. Twenty minutes and not a word. With every passing moment the dread intensified. Veta trembled, although the room was unbearably warm. She sensed a void where there should have been a baby. Her arms ached to hold him and she tingled with milk.

She found Josef watching her with dull eyes. He looked tired, but there was no emotion in his face. Just a blankness, as if he'd finally stopped feeling anything at all.

They both looked up at the sound of scuffling down the

corridor. A shadow hesitated briefly, before Doctor Pryce appeared in the doorway. His face was grey and grim. His arms were empty.

Veta felt the tears trickling down her face before Pryce said a word. The emptiness bloomed outwards to engorge her, and the fear gave way to grief.

Pryce spoke softly, his voice a whisper like something half heard in a dream.

'I'm so sorry,' he said.

The room was full of shadow, the shadow was full of equipment. Veta saw curling pipes that ended in tiny masks, stands with small displays and wires spewing out of them. As she walked into the room with Josef at her side, the suffused milky light was swamped by their shared shadow. The only illumination came through the large window behind them, and that was a subdued light from the anteroom. It took a moment for Veta's eyes to adjust to the gloom. Then she saw the incubator. Then she saw the tiny, still thing inside it.

She froze – and felt a cold stab of panic thrust through her soul. There should be tears. Her mind churned the idea over and over. Where were her tears? Where were her cries of despair? Where was her reaction?

Feeling Josef grasp her by the arm, she gave way to the gentle pressure and he marched her slowly forward. They stood together and Veta felt Josef's grip on her arm like a communication of things he just couldn't put into words.

The baby was naked, arms outstretched, face turned slightly aside. His eyes were closed and his dark lips puckered. He looked as though he were sleeping, except there was no rise and fall of his chest, no spasm movements of his hands, no dreams at all in his sad little head.

And then the tears came. And a frightening kind of howl that emerged from somewhere so deep inside her that Veta couldn't believe it was coming from her own throat. She felt Josef's arms around her, felt him turn her face into his chest, felt him grasping her so tight that she was afraid she would crush. They sobbed together, lost in a crashing sea of emotions.

Finally pulling herself away, Veta turned to the incubator and reached out to touch it. Her fingers found the plastic wall and she was surprised how cold it felt. Her hand was yanked away and she found Doctor Pryce standing there watching her with concern.

'I'm sorry,' he said. 'Please don't touch.'

'Don't touch?' Veta's voice was thick with incomprehension.

'Besides all the birth traumas, there was a highly contagious infection.'

'Infection?' asked Josef.

'This is a sealed unit,' Pryce pointed out. 'I'm afraid we couldn't risk contact.'

The words floated around in Veta's head like wisps of smoke. Intangible things with traces of meaning she couldn't quite grasp.

'Can't we… touch him?' Josef asked. He was pleading.

'I'm sorry,' Pryce said.

The baby lay quite still. Veta watched it. Through the plastic walls of the incubator she felt her love probing. She felt the baby respond with a giant love of its own. And she felt her lips curl into a smile that sat strangely in her face before fading. Who said she couldn't touch?

Part Two

Save me, and deliver me from the hand of strange children:
whose mouth talketh of vanity, and their right hand is a
right hand of iniquity.

— Psalm 144, v. 11

9.11.2847 (Earth Standard)
Ceres Alpha

A strange new sensation gripped Anji Kapoor. She recognised it as fear, but it was strange because it wasn't her own.

Her head was full of passing thoughts. Far too many thoughts. Interloper thoughts that felt all wrong. Here and gone before she could assimilate them. The mental sensations were so overwhelming that it took her a while to realise she was moving, but not on her own legs. There was storm outside to match the storm in her head. Searing winds. Cutting sands. Freezing hail and rain. A curious odour of dank earth, different from any earth she'd smelled before. Her arms were hoisted up and held tight at the wrists either side. And finally, through the nightmare, she realised she was waking groggily and being carried between the Doctor and Fitz.

She tried to speak but her mouth refused to function. Still too many thoughts in her head. Tumbling around and falling back out again like stones thrown into an open washing machine. They clattered around making noise without sense. She tried to locate her own thoughts among them, and suddenly discovered a vast, all-consuming pain engulfing her. A white-hot iron plunged into the centre of her brain. The grey matter boiled. There was a bright white light that she knew wasn't real. Then a voice, soothing like an anaesthetic.

'It's all right,' the voice said. 'We're going to get help.'

She tried to look at the Doctor at her side, but he was shielding his eyes from the sands, forcing forward through the maelstrom. Again she tried to talk. Again failed to make a sound. What the hell was wrong with her?

'A disease,' the voice answered. 'I think it's Paxx-Sinopoli Syndrome. It's affected the latent telepathic centres. Not serious. You're going to be fine. Don't worry.'

'*Shit!* We're just not gonna make it,' another voice said. This one was spiky, not in the least bit soothing. And its source was the same as the fear she'd sensed.

'The problem is,' the first voice said, 'you have only the primitive centres stimulated and your brain isn't evolved enough to restrict the activity. You can't control what you hear. Fitz doesn't know what he's thinking about. Ignore him.'

'I want to sleep,' Anji said. She heard it come out of her mouth like a sound of animal suffering.

'Don't try to speak. The motor regions are busy with other things. Just try to relax.'

Relax! She felt as if she'd fallen inside the Internet. An Internet connection without the hardware to get in the way of the free flow. Myriad ideas and random thoughts crashed through her conscience without a net nanny in sight to control the content. Thousands of people. Millions of thoughts. She felt as if she were swimming in water and floating in air, weaving in and out of reality like a ghost. A constant clutter of feelings that were nothing to do with her own body. Pains and pleasures real and imagined worries and hopes for a future in a strange land real thoughts dream thoughts people and lives too many to count some thoughts almost familiar mostly jarring in her head mother father baby child sitting dancing calming wild –

'Relax,' the Doctor soothed. The word, or at least its sense, solidified to displace the noise. 'Try to focus in on yourself. What's the first prime?'

'Prime?'

'The first prime number. Come on!'

'Two.'

'Then what?'

'...city's too far... not going to make it... I can't walk much further...'

'He'll be fine. Don't listen to him. What's the next number?'

'Three.'

'Next?'

'Five… Seven… Eleven… Thirteen… Seventeen… Nineteen…'

'Jesus Christ!'

She felt Fitz's pain a split second before her own. An explosion in his right leg. They all collapsed and for one precious moment the noise was cut and she felt herself falling. There was a sharp crack and another fleeting explosion. This time Fitz's left arm. No! Not Fitz's arm. Her own arm. Her own pain. It shrieked through her brain, volume full blast. She tried to scream and it emerged from her lungs like a small cough.

Then the noise. A tidal wave of too much noise. The curious scent of earth intensified. Alien dirt. Somewhere at a deep, deep level she knew they weren't on Earth. The notion was whipped up in the spiralling tornado of other people's thoughts until she lost sight of it completely and there was only the noise.

Fitz was no stranger to pain since he had met the Doctor. It went with the territory, he understood that plainly enough. You have big adventures, you accept the downside that you're gonna get hurt now and then, in all senses of the word. No pain, no gain. You want a rich and fulfilling life, you get it full of all sorts of shit.

The alternative was more frightening. To remain at home selling half-dead shrubs to half-dead biddies, with only your jamming sessions and never-to-be-realised dreams for comfort. To get locked into a pattern of life that would age you just as quickly as running around the universe losing your head every now and then. He'd reached the conclusion long ago that, given the choice, he'd rather get old dying than get old dead.

But still he detested these moments of uncertainty, when you think you're a mere spit into your thirties and you're going to cop it in a vicious alien storm on a featureless planet a billion miles from London and not a slavering monster in sight to make your exit heroic. Fitz just wasn't a connoisseur of the anticlimax.

'It's bleeding badly,' the Doctor informed him.

'It's bleeding painful,' Fitz informed him right back, squeezing the words out through his teeth and his pain. 'You go on. Leave me here.'

But the Doctor was busy working, tearing Fitz's shirt to create a strip of material like a bandage. He set to work above the wound, using an old wooden ruler that came, impossibly long, out of his coat pocket to create a tourniquet. For a moment the agony intensified, then began to ease as the Doctor tore off another strip of shirt to dress the wound.

'There's a lump of material embedded in it,' the Doctor told him. 'It looks like a slice of rock. I'm going to have to leave it in there.'

'Great. I can grow old with buried shrapnel. Moan down the pub about me dicky leg. Probably worth a few free drinks. That's cool.'

Fitz tried to hoist himself up to see how Anji was doing. She had collapsed motionless in the mud. Her eyes were open but she was gazing at nothing at all. The hail and sand were hitting them but there was no blink, no reaction.

'Is she going to make it?' he asked.

'She'll be fine,' the Doctor assured him. But Fitz knew the Doctor well enough by now to recognise the difference between sincere confidence and blustering determination. 'We need to get you under shelter. Come on. Stand up.'

Easier said than done. Fitz struggled to his feet with the Doctor's help and a few well-chosen expletives. The next thing he knew he was being lowered again, this time into a hollow. Then he found he was being pelted with the broad-leaved, thick-stemmed growths that passed for vegetation on this world. They wouldn't win any major horticultural prizes in his book. But they did make good cover against the lashing sand and hail. The biting cold still had teeth, but they were blunted now so they could only gnaw rather than slice.

Fitz found the Doctor's face in front of his own.

'Don't move,' the Doctor ordered. 'I'll get back to you as soon as I can, all right?'

'Well, if I'm not here, I'll've just gone for a quick jog round the block to keep warm. OK?'

The Doctor smiled. Then frowned. 'I won't be long,' he promised, and vanished.

Trying to lift himself up to see, Fitz was stunned by an abrupt invisible kick in the teeth. He collapsed back and lay in his hole listening to the howl of the wind and the scuffling of the Doctor as he lifted Anji and continued on his way. A moment later there was only the sound of the wind. Fitz gazed up into the dark night sky, full of whisked-up phantoms and ghost shapes in the combined sand- and hailstorm. He was shaking now with fatigue. His leg thudded like a big bass drum. Since their emergency landing his head had felt as if it were filled with jelly and bizarre new aches that were and weren't headaches. He wasn't sure what exactly bypassing the phase modulators had done to him, but he wouldn't choose to put himself through that particular mangle again in a hurry.

He pictured himself lying here in his shallow grave, covered with the dank-stinking foliage, out in the middle of the lifeless plain on this godforsaken dead rock. He pictured the Doctor, Anji hanging off his arm like a life-size puppet with her strings cut, lifting the binoculars intermittently to keep his fix on the dim-glimmering lights of the invisible city he swore he could see out in the distance and the blizzard. Fitz closed his eyes, and allowed himself the luxury of anxious thoughts about Anji. His mind drifted back through the past hours since he'd emerged from scary darkness to find himself still in one piece following the TARDIS's emergency materialisation.

'She's going to be fine,' the Doctor had said. But he'd said it so many times that Fitz was sure he was saying it now only to try to convince himself.

They'd emerged from the sanctuary of the TARDIS into the humdinger storm and Fitz had instantly sustained a twisted ankle in the fumbling blackness and shifting ground. Anji was a dead weight between them, entirely lifeless for the first hour or so, then

27

starting to emit intermittent little sounds like those of a kitten coming out of deep anaesthetic.

'*We should wait out the storm,*' Fitz had argued.

'*We need to get help,*' the Doctor had insisted.

'*Get us in closer,*' Fitz had pleaded.

'*Can't risk a short hop,*' the Doctor had answered. '*We've already slipped two local-time months off target. We could end up anywhen.*'

'*We're not going to make it.*'

'*She's going to be fine.*'

She's going to be fine. The phrase echoed through his skull as his eyes closed lightly. *She's going to be fine,* he told himself again and again. *She's going to be fine. So why was he so damn scared for her?*

As Fitz began to drift in delirium, he became only vaguely aware of the vibration of the ground – a steady rumbling like an earthquake that just couldn't be bothered to get out of bed in the morning. He wondered what the hell it was, but that was only one worry in his overcrowded head as he lay there in a pool of human suffering and thankfully allowed the darkness to come in and consume him.

The clang of rattling metal was almost deafening when Aaron Pryce entered the holding bay. The clatter came from the twelve titanium doors, reverberating from inside the cells. As he stepped down between the doors, Pryce felt the hairs on the back of his neck bristling. He stood for a moment, trying to understand the reasons for his own fear. It was an irrational reaction, he knew, but one that he couldn't for the life of him fathom or prevent. It was something in the air. A kind of supernatural presence. He stood there feeling like a small child alone in the dark.

He wouldn't be sad to see the end of this particular cargo, and he'd counted the days since Dr Domecq had been summoned from Earth Central to deal with this little problem.

Pryce had always felt decidedly uncomfortable in this small

section of the city, and the physical attributes of the place didn't help. It was a short corridor with meagre light, and the only heat came from the nearby motor-cooler heat exchangers. The cells had been added as a makeshift solution to a bizarre storage problem – prefabricated boxes bolted hastily on to the side of the medicare block. The whole place was a patchwork flung together from previously discarded or damaged building units. He could see messy streaks of weld, like solidified gastropod trails on the bare metal, and there were regions of dull rust in the walls. Pryce always felt that the whole slipshod edifice might collapse at any moment.

But structural integrity was the least of his worries. There was a larger danger here, something deeply disturbing. And he sensed it most keenly at times like this, when the inhabitants of the holding bay were restless and frustrated.

Pulling himself together, Pryce thrust the chunky metal key into the lock of the first door. Instantly, the noise silenced.

Pryce sensed the rancour intensifying inside him. It was his way of dealing with the fear, replacing something he had no power over with some raw emotion that was under his own control. The door swung open in front of him and he stalked into the cell.

He found the small shape cowering in the opposite corner. The only illumination was a single pathetic bulb in the corridor, but the thing in the cell raised its spindly arms to shield its eyes from the light.

In the background, the rattling resumed, this time quietly, a begrudging but insistent clatter of metal doors in their frames. Pryce realised that the doors were banging in harmony, all of them thumping at precisely the same rate. And there was the sudden, dread realisation that the banging was exactly in time with his own heartbeat.

Pryce observed the round dome of the top of the thing's head, mottled with clumps of wispy, silver-coloured hair, before swooping down and grasping the thing by the arms. They felt like slender rods of soft cold metal in his hands, brittle bones covered with a uselessly thin layer of skin. He found the huge saucer eyes peering at him with what he took to be alarm. It was hard to tell with these strange faces. Pryce felt his lips curl with rage as he lifted the thing into the air in front of his face.

'Get them to stop,' he snarled.

The sound continued while the creature remained suspended in the air in front of Pryce. The tempo had increased, and Pryce felt the rate of his own heart accelerating as if to keep up.

'I'm not going to warn you again,' he told the thing.

But the sound persisted, now getting louder and just a little bit faster, until Pryce snapped and hurled the creature into the corner. It landed with a thud, a pile of twisted arms and legs, the ridiculous head bent awkwardly over to one side. The breath exploded out of its lungs and Pryce heard the soft low sound of its voice.

The door rattling endured, and Pryce swept across the tiny space to grasp the creature again, this time by the neck. The thing's eyes widened in terror, and Pryce sensed a huge loathing expand inside him, threatening to consume him completely. There was a moment of stasis, a stalemate when the doors clanged and boomed through his skull while the anger boiled through him.

Then all the pent-up rage escaped –

Removing a carton of synthogen from the fridge, Veta slit the top and slipped two taste caps into the package before she placed it in the oven. Not even checking the flavour of the caps, she scrunched up the foil pieces and dropped them into the waste. Her life these days seemed to be a hollow ritual of this domestic duty. A long series of empty days punctuated by the preparation of meals.

Not that she ate her meals lately, nor that she tasted them when she did eat. She'd made meals over the last few weeks where she'd forgotten to put in the taste caps and hadn't even noticed. She'd watch Joe's chin whirling uncertainly around the bottom of his face, then see him looking at her with a dazed expression.

The oven cut without warning, its gentle hum suddenly silent while the lights throughout the apartment dimmed and brightened momentarily. Veta watched as the oven restarted, only distantly annoyed at the inconvenience of having to recheck the program. Just a few months ago she would have been intrigued by such interruptions to the smooth running of the city-machine. But now nothing mattered any more.

Josef had droned on about the increasing workload. How the job of comptech had become a mindless chore recently, with the city comps suffering ever-multiplying instances of faults. As if the software were suddenly prone to those old-fashioned viruses that used to threaten their existence. Investigations were monotonous, fingertip searches through measureless reams of data, no sort of job for a human being. And ultimately the problems turned out to be minuscule glitches in the core programming language. Problems that should be instantly self-rectifying. Failures so elementary that nobody should notice even the slightest hiccup.

Coming out of the kitchen into the apartment, Veta stood amid the mess and sighed. She really ought to get some work done. She really ought to tidy up. She really ought to give Joe some kind of home to come home to.

She really ought to.

Then she sensed the movement nearby. Then she saw him standing there. A small boy, perhaps three years old, with a large oval head and big dark eyes pleading with her. She caught her breath and found she couldn't move. Gripped in a kind of numb inertia, she reached out for him. His face was full of fear. She could sense it in the room. Feel it in her heart. Impending darkness rushing in –

Then she heard the buzz of the door and found Josef watching her from across the room, a puzzled look on his exhausted face. She turned back to the child, but the room was empty. She looked back at Josef and felt the tears trickling down her face.

'What's up?' he asked, rushing over to hold her.

But Veta couldn't find the words to explain. She couldn't tell him what she'd seen and what she felt. There was no language in the universe that could articulate her pain. She could only cry. And he could only grasp her tight in his arms and wait for the grief to subside.

Dr Mij Perón peered into the globe of gathering static that was supposed to be showing her the events of holding cell one. She could make out only chunks of almost meaningless dark and light, colourless streaks flaring sporadically through the image. Perón tried to refine the signal, instructing the software to hunt down the interference and eradicate it. The sound had already degenerated into a constant incomprehensible cackle, and now the picture was following close in its tracks.

Analysing the readouts that streamed through the air below the hologram, Perón could find no reason for the breakdown. The system checked fine and there were no extraneous signals to cause the problems she was experiencing. The transmitter was only next door, for God's sake.

Amid the grey fuzz she could just make out the shape of Pryce. He seemed to be flinging his arms wildly but she couldn't see the creature at all now. There was a blaze of white light that could have been fluid splashing through the cell. A short pandemonium of motion. Then she saw the whole 'gram go black before finally collapsing completely, to be replaced by the WorldCorp logo.

Slamming the desktop to cancel the image, Perón leapt up and stormed from the office. As she marched towards the holding bay she realised that she was shivering. Then she realised that she couldn't get the final image out of her mind. The 'gram had gone absolutely black for an instant before it cut. Absolutely black, without a hint of interference or static, like a perfect sphere of glass in the centre of her room. It reminded her of something that had always troubled her deeply and inexplicably.

The creatures' eyes.

As she reached the holding bay, she found Pryce emerging from the storeroom door.

'Dr Pryce,' she said with a trace of sarcasm. 'Fraternising with the enemy?'

He was pale and a little out of breath, but his face was abruptly occupied by a tight smile. It was forced, of course. A mask to hide his real face, the one that was cracking up underneath.

'Dr Perón, how are you?'

His voice was quivering, but he was managing a half-decent job of keeping it under control.

'Very well. You?'

His white coat was filthy, covered in stains and dust. He realised with a small gasp of shock and began to brush himself down, doing his utmost to sustain the smile.

'Oh, I'm fine. Fine. Busy, but, you know...' The stains were proving just too much for him.

'Fine?'

'That's it.' He sent a hand into his hair and that was when she realised just how untidy it was.

'Are you having a little trouble?' she asked.

He shook his head, struggling now to support the smile he'd squeezed into his lips. 'No. No problem. No problem at all.'

Pressing his security code into the door com, Pryce watched her nervously. Perón had a sudden impulse to bark an order at him to pull himself together. She wanted to slap his silly face and knock some dignity into him. But with a magnificent force of will she instead insinuated a wry smile into her face.

'I take it you've had... words with them.'

'You could say that.'

'Are they back under control now?'

'Oh, yes. Quiet as the grave in there now.'

'It might be an idea to get yourself cleaned up, Dr Pryce,' Perón said. 'We don't want to worry the patients, do we?'

He nodded uncertainly, then turned on his heel and marched off down the corridor. She watched him vanish round the corner before inspecting the door com closely. There was a trace of liquid where Pryce's fingertips had entered his code. Just a trace, hardly glistening at all, but when she touched it with a tissue she realised it was red. His or the creature's, she wasn't entirely sure. Either way, it meant that Pryce was at the end of his tether.

And that Military One were probably near the end of their little experiment.

Danyal Bains sat alone in a room that would be big enough to house multiple families back on Earth. It was vaguely obscene that one man should command so much space. The desk in front of Bains was vast and empty. The room itself was almost clinically clean and barren of either pictures or ornaments of any kind. There wasn't even an image of Gaskill Tyran's immediate family and that, thought Bains, said a great deal about the man with whom he was currently supposed to be in conference.

The walls were constructed of grey panels with white edges that created the impression of radiating white strands spreading outwards from behind the big black seat at the head of the desk. The white lines intersected each other in such a way as to suggest a spider's web. The effect was obviously intentional, and Bains wondered if Tyran had actually designed the place himself. When he had first sat down to wait, Bains had imagined the black blob of the chair on the opposite side of the desk suddenly unfurling immense legs and opening a pair of giant, multifaceted eyes which fixed him with an emotionless stare. The longer he sat there, the more the image unnerved him. He suspected it was a deliberate ploy to undermine his confidence.

Checking his watch again, Bains jumped to his feet and began to pace about the room in a growing state of agitation. If he had better things to do with his time, he would be losing his rag by now. As things stood, however, what he *had* to do with his time depended entirely on the outcome of this meeting with Tyran.

The door opened with an unobtrusive swish and a medium-sized man swept in and stood farside of the desk, surveying his domain with a cultured, detached demeanour. What Gaskill Tyran lacked in physical stature he more than made up for in his calculating, understated intensity. Wearing black, with unnaturally dark eyes (which would probably cost a whole three months' wages for most people), and thick black hair swept back from his wide face, he was a man you immediately knew not to underestimate.

On Tyran's entrance, the walls of the room took on a pale-blue hue, splashes of the colour washing through the previously grey panels. The room seemed to have come alive in response to its new occupant.

'Sorry I'm late, Mr Bains,' Tyran said, waving vaguely towards the chair at the opposite end of the desk. 'Please take a seat.'

'I've been waiting nearly half an hour,' Bains protested, preferring to remain on his feet. He was still bristling with fury at the way he'd been left hanging about.

'Management meetings,' Tyran dismissed, plunging into his own seat at the back of his desk. 'Take forever.'

'Getting to *you* takes for-bloody-ever. It's taken me three weeks to fight my way through your bloody bureaucratic defences.'

'Defences?' Tyran was apparently amused. 'We're on a civilian, and *civilised*, operation here, Mr Bains. This isn't a military stronghold, it's a boardroom.'

'Well it's been like trying to talk to a bloody board.'

'But now you're here, Mr Bains. You've fought your bureaucratic battles. And now you have my undivided attention.'

Tyran eased back in his seat and clasped his hands loosely on the desktop. There was a scintilla of humour in his dark eyes, and the pale blue of the walls became tinged with dusky pink bursts that bloomed and faded like silent little fireworks.

'I know what you're playing at,' Bains informed him, trying to keep his voice level and his anger under control. He was only thankful that the room wasn't keyed into his own emotional centres.

'Playing at?' Sham perplexity now filled Tyran's eyes. He was putting on an act, still playing his stupid little games. Bains supposed it became an occupational diversion when you reached the pinnacle of power that this man enjoyed.

'Prevaricating. Messing me about for weeks on end. D'you know we're less than two days away from Grid 1123?'

'Are we really?' Mocking lines of concern appeared in Tyran's brow. 'No. I wasn't aware of that, as a matter of fact.'

'You're perfectly bloody aware!' Bains said, almost yelling but just about managing to keep control. He wanted to grasp Tyran by the scruff of the neck and beat some sense into his smarmy little skull. 'Don't kid me! The most startling archaeological discoveries in centuries and you're going to grind them into dust.'

'That's quite emotive language, Mr Bains.' Tyran fixed him with those immensely dark eyes. For a moment the playful glint was gone and Bains noticed that the walls were briefly spattered with patternless pinpricks of carmine. His voice hardened slightly and he tensed in his chair. 'Extremely subjective. We've reviewed the data and an executive decision has been taken on the matter. You'll find a full report logged on our scientific appraisal of your discoveries.'

'I've read your bloody so-called full report. It's a load of bull, if you don't mind my saying, Mr Tyran. A load of bloody bull.'

'You're entitled to your opinion, of course. However, the evidence has been weighed, and we can see no reason to change our planned course.'

'You think that once it's gone you can cover this up, don't you? Well I'll tell you something, Mr Tyran: you're not going to bloody well get away with it. I have friends –'

'I think you'll find, Mr Bains, that we all have friends. And, curiously, some of them may well turn out to be mutual acquaintances.'

Tyran touched the desktop and a hologram flared into life in the air above them. Bains was appalled to see that it was his own face, greatly enlarged so that he could see the lines of anxiety etched around his eyes. The hologram coughed and leaned in conspiratorially.

'Hello, Jahn. Danyal Bains. I am currently on Ceres Alpha. I have made astounding discoveries here that are about to be deliberately concealed. I fear that WorldCorp, for obvious economic reasons, would prefer that these discoveries had never been made. I believe my position as company archaeologist is a fraudulent sham. They employed me for my reputation in order to allay fears after WorldCorp's suspected involvement in the conspiracies on Reevis. It was hoped that nothing would be found and Ceres Alpha could be acquired without conscience. As it happened, a very many things *were* found, but nobody here is interested. I'm a virtual prisoner. My permit has been suspended and I'm not allowed off-city. I requested a leave pass, but it was rejected. They seem determined that nothing of this will get out until it's too late. We're less than a week now from destroying an entire site of invaluable finds. Concrete proof that a previous civilisation flourished on Ceres Alpha. There's so much to learn, but it's all going to be lost. I need you to help me. I want a temporary halt to development in the 1100 sector. I know it's a lot to ask, Jahn, but the rewards could be enormous. The knowledge we can secure from these finds is beyond any economic value. I just can't stress enough how important this is to human understanding. Please do what you can, Jahn. Danyal out.'

The image froze and Tyran allowed Bains's silence to stretch. When Bains spoke again, his voice was subdued, mellowed by the implications of the playback. If every single one of Bains's personal coms was being subjected to such close examination and decryption, then he'd gravely underestimated the security of his confinement.

'You've accessed my personal codes,' Bains said quietly.

'No,' Tyran admitted. 'Your message was extremely cleverly hidden. Encoded into a subroutine of an equipment order, triggered for separate release when the order was processed by Earth Central. Very cunning. I'm extremely impressed. I'd hate to play you at chess, Mr Bains.'

'But how –'

'As I said, Mr Bains, some of our friends are mutual. Jahn Morgan did receive your message. I believe he was quite moved by your plea, in fact. But money, Mr Bains, moved him more.'

'You bastard.'

Tyran didn't react to the word. The walls remained predominantly pale blue, with hints of pink and only sparse suggestions of the carmine. He was a man of impressive self-control. When he spoke his voice was calm and matter of fact.

'Contacting Earth Central about affairs here is no go. Do you understand, Mr Bains? The decisions about what happens on Ceres Alpha are made by me. Nobody else. This world is my responsibility. It's my domain –'

'You planted your personal flag here, did you?'

'I planted billions of my personal fortune here, Mr Bains.'

'You can't buy the right to destroy the past –'

'I think you'll find, Mr Bains, that if you've got enough money you can buy anything,' Tyran glanced at the frozen image of Bains's face suspended over the desk. 'Absolutely anything at all.'

'Not anything,' Bains told him flatly.

'You would have been well advised to accept our remuneration package and leave Ceres Alpha while you had the chance.'

'There are more important things than money.'

'And there are more important things than relics, Mr Bains.'

'They're a window on vast new knowledge. You're forced to conduct archaeological surveys on all worlds you consider for damn good reasons. Past experience shows how valuable these discoveries can be. When Earth Central learn that WorldCorp destroyed evidence of an extinct alien civilisation there'll be repercussions. You can't flout the law, however much you, or the human race, need Ceres Alpha.'

'The wheels of industry, Mr Bains, are an unstoppable force to be reckoned with.'

'You're planting human roots in unknown soil. There was a civilisation here before. Not too long ago in ecological terms.

Aren't you interested to know what happened to it?'

'All I'm interested to know is when we can get people moved out here.'

'Blinkered greed and glory…'

'Pragmatism.'

'Pragmatism weighs the facts…'

'The facts are clear in this case. Ceres Alpha is the closest planet we've ever found to Earth conditions. My God, we can even breathe the atmosphere. What that says to me is that those poor souls back on Earth need not spend their days in incarcerated squalor. We can give our children more than a box in which to live out their lives. We can breathe real air and see blue horizons. We could even have birds back in our skies again. Those are the *facts*, Mr Bains.'

'The race for space! A boom in room! You forgot the mantras, Mr Tyran. Don't forget the WorldCorp mantras.'

'Truths. WorldCorp truths.'

'The truth is that you don't know what the hell you're doing here.'

'We're building a bright new future for the human race.'

'Good God! D'you spout that stuff in your sleep?'

'Mr Bains!' The walls flared angry crimson for a wild split second. Tyran had to physically get a grip on himself before he continued. 'I'm afraid I'm going to have to cut this meeting short. I'm finding this exchange unconstructive and your attitude frankly unhelpful.'

'When am I going to get my permit back?'

'I thought it would be obvious by now that it is unlikely that you would recover your archaeological permit before our work in this sector is complete. There are certain procedures –'

'Procedures! You put my dig off-limits, put armed guards on the entrance to the find, you bring me here and imprison me in my quarters –'

'You are not a prisoner, Mr Bains. You are at liberty to move freely about the city. There are no restrictions on your activity whatsoever.'

'Don't make me laugh! I'm not allowed to go to the only place I want to be.'

'It's for your own safety –'

'Safety –'

'There were seismic disturbances. I can't risk the safety of my staff.'

'I'm perfectly responsible for my own bloody safety, thank you very much. Seismic disturbances? You recorded mantle tremors caused by your own bloody city-machines. You're talking out your bloody –'

'Mr Bains! Your permit is under review. When our people are certain there is no further danger, it will be returned to you and you can continue your work. If you wish to leave Ceres Alpha, you are perfectly at liberty to do so.'

'I don't want to leave Ceres Alpha. It'll take me two months to get back to Earth. A further two months to get back here. In four months' time there's not going to be much of Ceres Alpha bloody well left.'

'You wish to remain on Ceres Alpha, fine. You wish to continue your work on the surface, no problem. The moment your permit is returned, you can do so. I think we've covered everything we needed to. This debate is at an end. Good night, Mr Bains.'

'You can't –'

'*Good night*, Mr Bains!'

Passing his hand over the desk, Tyran pushed himself back in his seat as the door swished open to admit one of his assistants. He was a thickset man with a face hacked out of granite. His eyes were like oily small stones, and at his side he wore a firearm.

'Please show Mr Bains out, will you Zach?'

Bains stood up to leave, but as he headed for the door he turned back to the dark shape in the centre of the web.

'I'm sure we'll continue our conversation very soon,' Bains told him in a tight voice.

Tyran grinned, apparently delighted. The walls swirled with blue-pink clouds. 'I'd like that very much, Mr Bains. I do enjoy lively conversation. Thank you.'

Zach stood in the open doorway, and Bains allowed himself to be ushered through. Out in the corridor he called the lift and began to head for his apartment, but changed his mind halfway there and instead decided he needed a good strong drink. Over the last forty years, he'd grown out of the custom of being social, preferring to be alone with his work. Now it had become a deeply entrenched habit to shun any contact with others, but he headed nevertheless for the bar at For'ard Obs.

The apartment was a tip. It had been subjected to two months of neglect, and now it was getting hard to even sit down amid the piles of litter and heaps of unwashed plates. They didn't have the space to let detritus pile up like this.

Josef Manni picked his way through the mess in their living area to the door that led to their sleeping quarters. The lights were on all through the place, but their bedroom was empty except for more piles of dirty clothes and linen. There was a faint smell of sweat and something else he couldn't quite put his finger on. He was sure that if he hadn't been out at work all day he wouldn't have noticed it.

As he cleared enough space down his side of the bed to clamber out of his clothes and into his bedshirt, he felt the resentment spreading again inside him. And close on its heels came the guilt – the shame that he could resent her dereliction. He crossed to the bathroom and regarded his face in the mirror gloomily.

He'd aged twenty years in the last two months. They both had. The loss of the baby had taken a tremendous toll. So many unmanageable feelings ravaged them through wake and sleep. At least he had his work to throw himself into. Veta had only her grief.

The face in the mirror was almost unrecognisable these days. He had eyes that belonged to a much older man, dark with sorrow and glazed with fatigue. His hair hung limp and his cheeks were pale and sunken. He hadn't even had a workout for nearly five months. His body chemistry was probably saturated with oxidants. He was completely worn out, yet he wasn't sleeping at all.

After splashing water briefly across his face, he dried and returned to the bedroom, where he threw back the sheets and slumped with his head in his hands on the edge of the bed. For long moments he listened to the thud of his own heart and wondered how much more of this torment it could thunder through. For months his face hadn't entertained even the slightest inkling of a smile. He had become grey and insipid. There seemed no purpose to his existence any more. Nothing to look forward to. Nothing to drive him forward through the day.

Only his work. And even that had become a thankless drudge lately, starting early and working late in the intensifying battle against comp breakdowns. There used to be a time when he enjoyed his job. It represented such an unfathomable challenge some days that it would exercise his technical abilities as well as his imaginative skills to the point of defeat. Systems analyst was a career on a par with human analyst. He'd often compared himself to a brain surgeon being paid to remove single rogue worries from somebody's head. Subroutines within subroutines frequently pathed through bioconstructed subliminal gates. Reprogramming by means of intuition, it had been called. Comp systems infinitely more complex than the human brain, and programs that had evolved over hundreds of years, reconfiguring themselves to meet the new challenges constantly thrown at them by human beings.

A timeless debate raged about AI. Did systems have souls? Over the years, Josef had grown to believe that they did. He'd seen comps suffer all manner of breakdowns and quirks of personality, some so subtle that there was no traceable programming reason for them. Now he wasn't so sure. He'd never seen a comp suffer the pain of personal loss. Comps didn't have children. No. They didn't have souls.

Deciding it was long past time for bed, Josef stomped down the corridor to find Veta. She'd become ever more distant over the past eight weeks. He expected little from her by way of response, but he felt it was still his duty to go through the motions of getting her safely into bed at night. What happened in her dreams was out of his control, but at least he could still hold her in his arms.

Extinguishing the light in the living area, he headed for the room at the end of the short corridor opposite their bedroom. The light in there was subdued, as it always was. A pale orange glow, soothing, sleep-inducing, warm and cosy. He peered around the edge of the door to see Veta slumped at the comp, fingers flitting over the key panel, entirely lost in whatever she was doing. He briefly witnessed a monitor teeming with code, long strands of data scrolling faster than Veta could possibly read. But abruptly the screen went black, and he realised that she'd sensed his presence and cancelled the call.

'What you doing, love?' he asked.

She gazed at him from the other side of the room, haunted and pale, a ghost of the woman he knew.

'Nothing.'

He glanced around. Nothing had changed. Nothing ever changed in this room. The small lamp with its lamb-shaped cutouts, the cloudy-sky walls, and the little white crib in the corner. The empty crib.

'It's time for bed,' he told her.

She rose automatically and he accompanied her to their room, leaving on the nursery lamp as they left.

In bed he wrapped his arms around her and felt the shape of her body against his. Nuzzling her soft warm hair, he breathed her scent. Since their baby had died, they had rarely spoken in bed, bar the routine queries –

'Did Leanne come today?' he asked.

'She called on the comlink.'

'What did she say?'

'I don't know. I didn't want to talk to her.'

'She's here to help.'

'I don't want help.'

A long pause ensued, but she didn't relax in his embrace. Her body felt stiff and angular, refusing to yield. In the silence he could hear the steady grinding groan of the city-machine's progress. He felt the almost imperceptible jiggling motion that became such a part of your daily ambience that you mostly forgot it was there.

'What were you doing in the nursery?' he asked at last.

'Nothing.'

'If its something on the comp, I could help,' he offered.

'It's nothing.'

He let out a heavy sigh and felt his eyes begin to close. Over the last two months he'd felt increasingly that he was trying to impose on her emotions. That he was as unwelcome an intrusion into her grief as Company Therapist Leanne was. A pattern of alienation had been set up between them shortly after the loss of their baby, and that pattern had become ever more convoluted and complex, as if they were performing a dance of avoidance. They were excluded from each other's world now. Strangers in close proximity.

These thoughts he took into his dreams, as he did every night. And there they were put to rest by the dragons and monsters of his psyche.

For'ard Obs was a tumultuous mass of activity, with people jostling for precious space on the overcrowded tables. Bains had left his jacket over the seat next to him in order to stake a territorial claim, awarding himself a slice of view through the giant observation screen out into the dark storms of Ceres Alpha. But it was getting busy now and people were beginning to muscle in on the reserved chair. He'd successfully resisted a number of hostile bids. A young woman with severe features cut across his line of vision as he gazed out into the swirling blackness that was night on an angry planet.

'I don't think she's coming,' the woman said. She had a low feminine voice, the kind of voice that might have been produced by inexpensive larynx work.

'I'm sorry?'

'I think you've been stood up,' she said. 'Can I buy you a drink?'

Bains grinned. It wasn't every day he got an offer like that. The woman must have been about forty, still with her clear girlish complexion and sharp bright eyes. Bains wasn't exactly decrepit, but at a hundred and forty-nine he was advancing now in his middle years and the only interest he usually earned was that of slightly more mature women. Since he had left his teaching post back on Earth his opportunities for immature conquests had all but vanished. Obviously that worldly-wise casual charm of his had not deserted him while he'd been embroiled in his work for the last forty years.

'Any other time I'd jump at the chance,' Bains assured her, trying to sound earnest. 'But I'm waiting for a business colleague. Sorry.' A white lie, but Bains wasn't in the mood for talk, and he had his own good reasons for avoiding the company of women.

'Don't apologise.' The woman laughed and the severity of her features softened momentarily. Bains almost regretted his rebuff. 'Maybe some other time, eh?'

'Maybe.'

He took a sip of his drink and when he looked up the woman was still there. She scanned the room, then observed Bains coolly.

'Haven't seen you in here before,' she announced.

Ten out of ten for perseverance, thought Bains. 'Probably because this is the first time I've been here.'

'First time in For'ard Obs? What d'you do with yourself at nights?'

'I'm an off-city.'

'Really?' she moved in closer, depositing herself on the edge of his reserved seat. 'What d'you do?'

'I dig up dead things.' He was trying to be blunt. Trying to say 'piss off' without employing the actual phrase. But it wasn't going to work.

'Sounds absolutely fascinating.' There was irony in her voice.

'Well, I get a kick out of it.'

'Oo-ooh. Bit of a necro, eh?'

Bains found himself becoming distracted by the sparkle of her drink and the sparkle of her eyes. When she'd been in your face a few seconds, she wasn't as severe as you first thought. There was a kind of streamlined beauty about her that he suddenly found alluring. He smiled but left her question unanswered.

'I prefer to get my kicks with the living,' she told him, putting her drink on the table and leaning back, making herself at home in the seat.

As she moved, Bains couldn't fail to notice the exaggerated curve of her breasts straining against the thin material of her blouse. Everything about everybody seemed to be exaggerated these days. Too-dark eyes, too-large breasts, too-wide shoulders. Only a few generations ago you could tell those with the money. They looked different. They looked too good. Not just the clothes, but the physical features too. Now anybody with a handful of dollars could afford enhancements, and the whole universe seemed to be populated by beautiful people. The nice thing was, you could generally tell a lot about a working-class person from the enhancements they chose to buy. A forty-year-old girl with enhanced breasts, for example, might indicate a certain shallowness.

'I still don't want you to buy me a drink,' Bains told her flatly.

She raised her eyebrows at him. 'I'm sorry if I'm intruding. But I noticed you from over there and I said to myself, Carly, there's a man without a great deal to smile about. There's a man who looks like he could do with somebody to cheer him up.'

'I'm afraid I'm just not in the mood for being cheered up right now,' he told her. 'Like I said, maybe some other time, eh, Carly? Thanks for the offer, but no thanks.'

She sighed, took a sip of her drink, and finally came to a decision.

'OK, Mr Misery. I'll leave you to wallow. Maybe see you around, uh?'

He smiled but said nothing, and she left. At last the view became available again, and Bains settled to watch the swirling darkness outside. There was a slight movement, a kind of gentle oscillation as they moved over the surface of the planet, swallowing everything in their path. Huge sensonic dampers with living limbs cancelled most of the effect of the movement in the inhabited areas of the city-machine, but it was a motion that never stopped, was never neutralised completely. The city-machine worked night and day, claiming the planet in the name of the human race. Indigenous microbic life would be consumed to feed the humans' genetic microbes and the very chemical structure of the ground would be recombined to form the ideal soil for the growth of human genetically enhanced crops. Alien landscape in one end, improved earth out the other. The land was consumed to deep level. The original biosphere would be obliterated utterly. The wheels of industry, Tyran had said, are an unstoppable force.

Within the next forty-eight hours that unstoppable force would demolish irretrievable evidence of the previous inhabitants of Ceres Alpha. The past had so much to say, and WorldCorp were going to silence it forever.

'It's moving!'

Emerging out of a storm of colliding noises and notions, Anji tried to listen to what the Doctor was trying to tell her. There was shock in his 'voice', undisguised astonishment. She sensed herself being lowered and felt her first physical sensation for hours.

The ground was shaking.

The Doctor crouched at her side. She felt her head being turned but all she could see was storm. Black night and grey swirling sand. There was the sound of screaming winds, but it was soon lost again to the sound of screaming voices.

'What's wrong? What's happening?' She forced the questions into her mouth, but couldn't get them out through her lips.

'I thought it was a city.' The Doctor's voice filled her head. 'But it's a giant machine of some sort. It must be miles wide, a mile or more tall.'

'I can't see,' she tried to tell him.

So the image appeared. She realised that she was seeing through the Doctor's eyes. He was putting his sight inside her head. She tried to focus through all the other noise and the image became clearer. A vast darkness, covered in tiny lights. It was dull grey and black, filthy as the night, stretching off as far as they could see in all directions. The great structure was covered in irregular lumps and blocks, as if it had been built and repaired piecemeal over an age. Pipes and wiring conduits covered its surface, standing out like grey veins on a heap of dead grey bodies.

Then Anji heard the sound of the howling winds, and realised abruptly that there was also the sound of grinding machinery mixed in. All the songs of hell – screeching, bellowing, yowling. The vicious storm tore around the vast structure as it forced through the blizzard towards them.

At the base of the moving edifice the ground was being churned. They watched a rolling cloud of dust and debris being flung into the air. Anji knew suddenly that it was the biggest earth-cruncher in the history of the universe. And it was trundling towards them at a terrifying pace. She remembered Fitz in his hollow, badly injured and unable to run. And it was too late now to go back. She sensed the Doctor making furious mental calculations, trying to work out how long they could outrun it, whether or not they could make it back to Fitz before the machine. The ground was rumbling ominously now, and she became aware that the Doctor was struggling to remain on his feet.

Then the clutter of stuff in her head cut abruptly. She sensed herself falling, flung out her arms, found empty space, then a jolt. She hit with immense force and felt a great weight of rubble falling on top of her. The last thing she saw was an image of the moving mountain of metal rolling towards them out of the terrifying storm. Eating the planet.

Consuming everything in its path.

* * *

Gaskill Tyran gazed at the image of Danyal Bains suspended in the air above his desk. Tyran was lost in secret thought, eyes dark and fists clenched. Carly Dimitri wondered what dark notions were tumbling through that depraved head of his, what he had in mind for this poor man who had somehow inadvertently, most probably quite innocently, crossed Tyran's path.

Danyal Bains had seemed a nice enough man. God knew, there weren't many men in Carly's broad experience who had the strength of character to resist what she'd offered. She scrutinised the image of his face. He had tiny lines around his eyes that could so easily be removed. There were touches of grey appearing at his temples. He had a rugged, squarish face that Carly suspected she could find extremely seductive in the right time and place. Although he'd been quite blunt with her in For'ard Obs, she'd come away with the impression of a kindly man. A fatherly man. A man she could trust.

Unlike the man she sat opposite now.

'I can try again tomorrow,' she suggested, finding it almost impossible to keep the quivering out of her voice.

'You seem to be losing your touch,' Tyran said.

His words contained profound implications. And so did his eyes.

'I'm sorry,' she told him.

She wanted to say more, to fill the portentous silence with excuses and apologies, but she knew better by now. She'd let him down and that was a dangerous thing to do. In recent months, as operations on Ceres Alpha had proved progressively more difficult, as the city services had begun to crumble, Tyran had grown ever more unstable. She'd suffered his frustration, his escalating volatility. She'd spent increasingly long hours hitched to her personal accelerator, repairing the injuries he'd inflicted, soothing the bruises and healing the scars before she could show her face in public.

The suspended image of Bains flickered and crackled unexpectedly, twisting and coiling as the projectors dephased and struggled to correct themselves. The room lights dimmed and

Tyran's eyes flashed about in the dark. Cancelling the image, he slammed his fist on the desk and pressed back in his seat in silence. There were fires raging in him. They were going to tear through, and she knew she was going to get scorched.

As the lights flared back into life, Carly rose and made her way round to his side of the desk, taking her steps like a predatory cat, putting on an act of sensual self-assurance in an attempt to cover her dread. As she stood at his shoulder and sent exploratory hands down over his chest to test his reaction, she was shivering. After a while he grabbed her hands. With his free hand he reached into his pocket and drew out the squat black shape of the mind probe. She flinched at the sight of it. She saw him send a signal to the desktop and the walls came alive with images. They were so close up that she could hardly make out the detail at first. Then she realised they were pictures of Tyran lashing out. He was using the desktop comp to channel her thoughts, to project them on to his walls. Fierce dark eyes in a mask of spite. The walls were red, and the room pulsed with hatred. Carly pulled back her hands and brought them up to her face, an instinctive reaction to his assault.

'Turn it off,' she snapped.

He sprang from his seat to face her. She felt a fresh surge of fear, and found his sneering face close to hers.

'Don't ever tell me what to do.' he hissed.

'I don't want you inside my head,' she implored.

Flinging her aside, Tyran leaned over his desk to make adjustments and the walls continued to pulse with colour, spinning images flashing through a viscous red paint that looked like thickening blood. Memories of beatings. Memories of terror. The room was alive with her deepest fears, and they all contained this man.

'*Stop it*,' she screamed, clasping her hands over her ears in a desperate attempt to keep him out.

But the sound shrieked louder through her head, tearing at her mind. The intensity of pain rose to a swift crescendo until all she could hear was the screaming –

* * *

Surfacing from darkness and a kind of unfocused haze of sleep, Josef Manni found the bed empty at his side. Puzzled, he glanced at the bathroom to find it in darkness. He pushed himself up on to his arms and listened to the brittle silence of the apartment, disturbed only by the constant background rumble of motion.

There was a gleam of light in the corridor. The glow from the nursery lamp. But no other light at all.

Checking the clock, Josef saw that it was a little after three in the morning. Dragging himself out of bed, he plodded in his bare feet down the corridor to find Veta slumped in the nursery, cross-legged on the floor. She had her back to him, and this time she didn't sense his presence. She was oblivious to his watching her. Oblivious, it seemed, to all the world. She sat there apparently in a trance, completely still. Then he saw with a small shock that the crib had been moved from its usual place in the corner.

Nothing had been moved in the nursery for over two months. To touch anything at all in this room was sacrilege. It was a shrine to their lost child. Nothing less.

Josef stepped silently over the threshold, and now Veta did sense him there. She turned to face him, remaining slumped on the spot, and he saw her cheeks streaked with tears, her dark eyes haunted. And beyond her he saw what she was looking at.

A holographic picture of a baby, sealed inside a plastic incubator. There was no movement at all, just a long, sorry silence.

He recalled her furtive activities on the comp over recent weeks. Her refusal to accept his help or even tell him what she was up to. Abruptly, the anguish exploded inside his chest. A feeling of sickness spread through his soul. He watched her watching him with those big dark eyes, then glanced again over her shoulder at the holographic baby.

Veta was smiling at him. When she spoke, her words were a whisper.

'I got him out of the medicare computer,' she said softly. 'I just couldn't bear the thought of him left in there alone.'

Josef simply stared. It was an image of their dead baby, exactly as they'd seen it with Dr Pryce in the isolation room two months ago. He felt the tears trickling down his own face, and felt the familiar aching emptiness that threatened to swallow him up.

'Isn't he beautiful?' Veta said, her words as soft as the silence of the room. She turned back to him and he saw the smile jerking, a crazy animation of her lips. Her eyes were full of shadows and joy.

'Isn't he beautiful?'

De-ann Foley was about to climb into the shower when the hail came, and she was annoyed as hell because she was sweaty and smelly after a harsh workout in the gym. Although she knew it was just a comp call, she still grabbed a towel before she gave it permission to enter her bathroom.

'Yes?' she snapped, the irritation evident in her voice.

A hologram appeared in the air in front of her. The WorldCorp logo with its animated representation of birds flying off into an empty blue yonder and a sun beaming off to the right. The birds coiled in the air on their interminable journey, while the comp voice of Military One chipped out its syllables at her.

'We got company in direct path central.'

'Direct path central?' Foley repeated dubiously. 'Are you sure?'

'Life signs confirmed.'

'Nature?'

'Possibly human. Signals very weak and intermittent. This is code red. We're almost on top of them.'

Dropping her towel, Foley drove herself into her tunic and cancelled the shower program.

'Where the hell did they come from?' she demanded as she swept through her apartment with the hologram close on her shoulder.

'Unknown.'

Falling on to her bed, she slammed her feet into her combat boots. 'How the hell did they get into central region without being detected earlier?'

'Unknown.'

Grasping her com unit and shouldering her way deftly into the harness, she headed for the door and slapped the exit pad with unnecessary ferocity that just made her feel a tad better.

'Where the hell are Downs and Klute?' she demanded as she hurtled down the corridor to the elevator. The hologram, now routed through her com unit, continued to pursue her tenaciously.

'On their way to chopper pad four.'

As she soared upward in the liftpod, taking harness and systems through their standard checks, she continued to toss questions at the hologram.

'How could anybody get in so close without being detected?'

'The storms are severe tonight. Massive interference. They were lucky we picked them up at all.'

'They won't feel particularly damn-shit lucky when I get my hands on them.'

'Fifteen seconds to open level.'

'What the hell kind of klutz puts himself in the direct path of a world-devouring city-machine?'

'Unknown.'

'I mean – do these people have a death wish or what?'

'Unknown. Five seconds.'

Green lights flared across the com unit just as Foley felt the liftpod grind to a halt.

'Open level,' the hologram told her, rather redundantly, she thought.

The doors swept open and Foley hurled herself out into the churning, howling night. The chopper on pad four was already lifting itself into the storm as she pitched herself through the rapidly closing door. She landed hard on her shoulder, jarring the muscles in her neck and almost ripping the ear off the side of her head. The sidegate buzzed shut and there was a sound as close to quiet as you ever did get in these tin bees. Foley struggled on to her knees and fell into her bucket seat.

Klute was up front. He looked back at her with a big fat grin.

'Where the hell've you been?' he demanded. 'Seven seconds over drill.'

'I was just getting in the shower,' Foley informed him hotly as the chopper bounced around and she fought with the clip on her safety harness.

'You should've come as you were,' Downs smirked. He was already laced into the seat beside her.

'In your dreams, Downs.'

'Oh – every night,' he smiled.

Foley felt a rush of animosity as she failed and failed again to lock the catch on her harness.

'Every night, *sir*!' she barked.

The silly grin was wiped from his face when he heard the tone of her voice.

'And can't you keep this bone-rattle crate under control, Sergeant Klute?'

Klute stiffened abruptly, grasping the joystick and brawling with the storm.

'Yes, *sir*,' he snapped.

At last the catch snapped home and Foley gritted her teeth in an attempt to keep her rising hostility under control. The men remained silent now, and she felt the chopper pitch and dip as it reached the edge of the city and plunged towards the ground.

'When we land, Downs comes with me,' Foley ordered. 'Klute will prepare the med unit. The life signs are weak and intermittent. That could be the storm interference or it could be critical readings. We'll assume the worst since they're well inside the red zone. When we get them back in the chopper, you'll take us home, Downs.'

'Yes, sir.'

There wasn't a trace of smirk left in him now, and that was just exactly how Foley liked it when they were on a mission.

'Coming in now, sir,' Klute shouted.

She felt the chopper hit ground and level out with a jerk. The door swung down and their safety catches sprang open on auto-release. Foley and Downs spilled out of the chopper into the freezing hell that was Ceres Alpha. Downs already had a fix.

'Ten metres one o'clock,' he yelled above the wind, stomping off with the detector out in front of him.

But he was looking more at the detector than where he was walking, and Foley managed to grasp him by the shoulder as he was about to tumble into a small abyss that the groundworks had opened up.

'Hold on, Corporal,' she shouted. 'There's gonna be three critical if you don't watch where you're going.'

He might have looked embarrassed, but Foley wasn't really interested. Down in the hole she could make out a prostrate figure, upturned pale face just visible above the churned muck. The ground here was uneven, potholed with hollows. The leading edge of the city's awesome hunger was about thirty metres away now and it was difficult to remain on your feet under such conditions. More rubble dislodged from the edge of the surrounding precipice and fell into the hole. Foley watched it engulf the lifeless shape and suddenly she could see nothing down there except mud and dust.

Judgement. Risk two more lives or remove themselves to safety? These people were obviously suicidal anyway. Were they worth it? Decision…

Slapping Downs on the back, she led him down into the dip and started furiously digging in the dirt with her bare hands. Downs spun with the detector, his face a mask of concentration. She could hear nothing above the screams of the winds. The whole place was shaking enough to unearth the dead.

A face appeared in front of her, relinquished by the soil. It was a man. Dark hair. Quite good-looking in a curious sort of way. She could make out the collar of a dark-green coat. She managed to find an arm, and regardless of any potential spinal risk she grabbed hold and heaved the man out of the ground. If she killed him they could revive him when they got back to the chopper. And she wasn't about to let him get away with this idiocy, anyway.

She found Downs a few short steps away, digging furiously on his knees. Foley sensed movement, and turned to see a whole mountain of rocks and dirt plummeting into the hole behind them. Hoisting the man across her shoulders, she marched over to Downs and whacked him across the back, slicing her throat with her fingers to signal enough was enough. But Downs shook his head and continued to dig. He was nearly a metre down now and the soil here was loosely packed. Foley glanced back and saw the terrifying front face of the city towering over them, vanishing into the storm-filled turmoil that was the sky.

Again she punched Downs and again he refused to acknowledge. She spat abuse at him that was whisked up into the winds and lost in the night, before forcing her way out of the hole with the body a dead weight over her shoulder. As she ascended, the dirt beneath her feet collapsed behind her, but somehow she managed to get back on the level and pushed through the storm to the chopper.

Klute seized the man from her and she stalked back to the edge of the hole, where she found Downs clambering towards her with another body. He was about halfway up when the whole thing collapsed in a fluid slide of dirt and rubble. Foley saw both Downs and the body vanish swiftly under the torrent, and launched herself into the ditch after them.

Fighting the treacherous ground, which writhed like a blanket of snakes below her feet, Foley pushed her hands through the muck, trying to find something human to grab hold of. The ground in front of her exploded, and she was relieved to see Downs's filthy top half rising out of the dirt like something deceased returning to haunt her. She dragged him out, and found that he was still fervently holding the other body. Between the two of them, they scrambled with it uphill towards the chopper and safety.

Klute took the second body and Downs flung himself into the driving seat. While Foley proceeded to help hook the body to the med unit, the chopper rose steeply and noisily into the storm.

'You're on report, Downs,' Foley yelled as she worked, fixing wires to the temples of the girl they'd pulled out.

'Yessir.'

'Don't ever, ever disobey me again. Is that perfectly bloody crystal bloody clear?'

'Yessir.'

Switching on the med unit, she saw the readings flare into life. Then she found Klute watching her in puzzlement.

'That's not right, is it?'

The readings were all over the place. Some of them flat on the floor, some of them dancing in the sky. Foley reached out and thumped the monitor, but it didn't make any difference to the sense it was making.

'How's the other one?' she asked.

'More odd readings,' Klute informed her.

Shuffling across the floor of the bucking and lunging chopper, Foley regarded the monitor for a few seconds, taking in the information and shaking her head.

'There's an echo on the heart readings, and some of this other stuff is outside normal parameters, but my guess is that he's probably alive.'

Turning back to the girl, Foley wasn't so sure.

'Ever seen anything like this, Klute?'

'No, sir. She's dead and alive and a dozen shades of in between. Never seen readings like these before. Heart rate looks like zilch, but her brain's certainly getting oxygen from somewhere. Look at those cerebral peaks. Must be something wrong with the machine.'

'When was the last systems check on this thing?'

'Twenty-eight days.'

'No problems?'

'No, sir.'

'Well, let's just see what they make of this at Medicare Central, shall we?'

There was motion over the other side of the floor, and Foley shuffled over to help the man raise himself to his elbows. He looked bewildered, eyes unfocused, and he was muttering something but the words were almost unintelligible at first. Foley leaned in close to catch what he was mumbling.

'Fitz… Fitz… Must get back for Fitz…'

'It's OK,' Foley assured him. 'We got Fitz here. She's going to be fine.'

He appeared relieved, if still confused. Then she saw a haze of incomprehension come down over his eyes, before they rolled upwards, closed, and the man finally collapsed backwards in her arms. She lowered him to the floor and grasped the seat support struts as she felt the chopper veer suddenly to come in to land.

Dr Pryce found Mij Perón and Captain Foley already in med-ops when he arrived there. Perón was busy with a man who lay unconscious on one of the two beds that had been wheeled in, while Foley leaned over the unresponsive shape of a young, olive-skinned woman on the other.

'What have we got?' Pryce asked as he swept into the room, doing his best to project a businesslike air of confidence that he didn't feel at all.

He received a flash of smile from Foley, while Perón indicated the man.

'Some weird stuff,' she told him, making hand adjustments to the monitor. 'The systems check out OK, but I just don't believe these readings. This guy, unless I'm very much mistaken, has a dual heart arrangement, and there's some other very bizarre stuff here I've never seen before. I'm sure nobody's achieved biological revision of this magnitude. Metabolism, tissue composition, circulation, the whole cardiac setup, there are even unrecognisable antigen profiles. And just look at that electroencephalogram.'

'Did you run a systems diagnostic?' Pryce asked.

'I ran several. One of the heartbeats is erratic. I thought it must be some kind of data echo, another one of our little substructural glitches. But the system insists it's telling me the truth. Two hearts. Look for yourself.'

Pryce examined the information revealed on the monitor insets. There wasn't a single graph contour that he recognised. This man had quite obviously subjected himself to some very cutting-edge improvements. His internal make-up was no longer even remotely human. But he was obviously still no superman. He was as susceptible to injury as anyone, as evidenced by his extensive lesions and bruises. Dark blood streaked his face and pooled at the corners of his mouth, but the blood was still red.

'Any response from him?' Pryce asked.

'Nothing. But according to the ECG he's wide awake.'

The man appeared to be quite young, although it was impossible to hazard a guess at his age considering the enhancements he'd obviously undergone. He had a strong facial structure that may or may not be natural. Good-looking, certainly, but not conspicuously so. He had brown hair that curled at the fringe to lend him a rebellious look. Cursory examination of his hands suggested that his work certainly didn't involve any kind of manual component, although he was obviously keen on physical fitness, going by the muscle structure – not overheavy, but certainly robust. He must certainly lead an active life.

As Pryce took in the blood- and mud-gorged body, he suddenly noticed that the wrists had been locked into restraints.

'Who did this?' he demanded, outraged, knowing full well who'd damn well done it.

Finding Foley now attaching restraints to the girl's wrists, he stomped over and pushed her out of the way.

'What d'you think you're doing?'

'Securing the prisoners,' Foley informed him in a matter-of-fact way that tried to make him look stupid.

'They're *patients*, not prisoners.'

'Until we get ID they're military captives,' Foley argued.

'*I* apply the restraints in this department, Captain Foley,' Pryce seethed. 'Would you please remember that you're not in Military

One now: you're in *my* medicare unit.'

He saw Foley's jaw clench and the beginning of a snarl was only just kept from manifesting itself on her face. She stiffened as if to attention, then she caught Perón's eye and the temper passed.

'Yes, Dr Pryce,' she conceded, but there were distinct undercurrents of dissent.

Bristling with rage, Pryce set to the task of examining the girl. She was younger than the man. Trim and pretty, but again not excessively so. Pryce guessed that she was probably unenhanced, possibly a completely natural twenty-something. Foley was talking, pointing at the monitor.

'This one's strange as well,' Foley said. She managed to sound a little contrite, but he wasn't going to be taken in by that. 'Physically, no problems, but there's something extraordinary happening inside her brain.'

Bending over to examine the girl's eyes, which seemed to be locked open but entirely blind, Pryce could see clearly that there was substantial trauma to the eye-surfaces, presumably caused by the storm and her inability to blink or close her eyes. Removing a pack of treatments from the monitor's dispenser, Pryce set to work applying a layer of clear gel to the girl's open eyes before fixing tiny wires into the gel from the monitor.

While he worked, he saw Perón come over behind him to examine the ECG. Nudging the controls on the monitor, she projected a hologram into the air above them, a magnified map of the synaptic activity in the girl's brain. The areas were automatically colour-coded for rapid recognition, and Perón was able to delete levels of data to look at only selected zones. She moved slowly down into the image, cancelling chunks as she went and expanding other areas to get a better view.

'Ever seen anything like this in the deep mid-brain?' Perón asked.

Pryce shook his head. 'It's going crazy. I've never seen so much activity in any area of any brain. Have you?'

Perón nodded. 'I once saw the effects of a mind probe. A

military recording. The probe was turned up full blast and the man's brain was being literally fried. Thoughts and memories and nightmares sparking all over the place.'

Pryce was genuinely disgusted, and he failed to hide the fact in his expression.

'I didn't *make* it,' she said in her defence. 'I just watched it.'

Pryce hated these games they played. Perón seemed to derive a distorted amusement from teasing him with hints of just how ruthless the military could be.

'That's sick,' he told her.

'It was part of a course on cerebral dysfunction.'

'How to incinerate minds in one easy lesson,' Pryce said hollowly.

But Perón wasn't listening. She was gazing again into the colour patterns in the air above them. The image looked like a 3-D star chart, a chaos of swirling sparks of light. She began to think aloud.

'I wonder if this activity could be jamming up the other signals in the cerebral cortex. Overloading the nervous system.'

'Hijacking the motor functions...' Pryce chipped in.

'The question is, what's causing it?' Perón asked.

'Cranial trauma?' Pryce suggested.

'Never seen anybody act like this from a bump on the head before, have you?'

Pryce hadn't. Nobody had. The girl was a mystery, and one he thought they might explore a little easier once they'd tidied up her physical wounds.

He glanced begrudgingly at Foley. 'Where did you pick them up?'

'Direct path central.'

Pryce looked up sharply.

'Don't ask,' Foley said, shaking her head and shrugging her shoulders.

'Any papers?' queried Perón. 'Any ID?'

'Not a jot. Both a complete blank.'

'No incoming expected?' Perón asked.

'Only Domecq. But we haven't had his entry signature from the portal yet, so he's going to be a day or so away at least.'

'Come off it, Captain,' Pryce interceded. 'There's so much atmospheric turbulence these days that we don't get the signatures any more. Perhaps Dr Domecq has already arrived. I think it's altogether possible he crash-landed tonight right on our doorstep.'

Perón looked over to the man on the bed. 'Don't jump to conclusions,' she warned Pryce simply.

'So who the hell else could they be?' Pryce demanded. He hated the closed mindset of the military. No docs – no go. There was something just too damn automatic about their reasoning. He'd never understood why they needed people to fulfil that particular function anyway. Remote-droids could do a much better job, and they'd *cost* a whole lot less in the long run.

'Competition employees?' Foley suggested. 'Agents provocateurs? There's a limitless universe of possibilities, Dr Pryce.'

He perceived an overtone of patronisation that was barely disguised. He'd had run-ins aplenty with Foley, and he guessed she was a woman to nurture a grudge. Unless it was just a charming twist of personality that made her obsessively confrontational with everybody.

'Thank you for your input, Captain Foley,' he snapped. 'I'm sure we can manage from here.'

'I think I'll hang around,' Foley said, 'if you don't mind.'

Pryce felt his blood begin to boil.

'I think I'll have to insist that you leave,' he told her levelly.

'These people are under close military supervision,' she responded like a whiplash.

'These people are receiving emergency medical attention,' Pryce hissed. 'And you are in grave danger of overstepping your jurisdiction, Captain Foley.'

Foley watched him with undisguised hostility. Then he caught another hint of nonverbal communication between her and Perón. Foley backed down reluctantly, but her eyes were still burning with frustration.

'You will, of course, inform me as soon as either of these people awake,' she growled at Pryce.

'I'll let you know,' Pryce said, doing his utmost to keep his voice even.

Foley left her eyes on his for a good few moments too long. He felt uncomfortable under her intense, unflinching stare. At last she nodded curtly and marched from the room.

The door swished shut behind her and Pryce felt a rush of relief. He found Perón gazing at him from over the room with a detached, unreadable expression, and felt a fresh surge of animosity at their intrusion into his department. The military had arrived two months ago with the creatures, and since then he'd felt his authority here crumbling steadily. Foley's challenges were becoming ever more arrogant and blatant. And the support he'd received in the early days from Perón was fast turning into antipathy.

'I think I'll begin my reports,' he announced, making for the door after Foley.

'Yes,' Perón's voice followed him. 'You do that.'

At the door he turned on her.

'You'd be as well to remember who runs this department, Dr Perón,' he told her hotly. 'Military One might well be a powerful arm of WorldCorp, but there are far more powerful forces in the universe, believe me.'

She allowed a laconic smile into her lips.

'Oh, I know where the power lies, Dr Pryce,' she assured him, staring at him evenly until he had to turn away.

He stalked from the room, heard the door swish shut behind him, and felt ashamed at the fresh wave of relief that washed through him.

The dirt was a fairground ride. When Fitz awoke the adrenaline was already pumping, burning him up like a raging fire. There was pain and confusion, but through it all he knew he just had to run.

Throwing the cover of vegetation off, he thought he must have fallen into a television channel that was off air for the night. There was only meaningless static and a hissing, howling, rumbling sound that could well have been the Devil coming up to swallow him whole.

The ground churning and boiling around him, Fitz did his utmost to scrabble to his feet. But his legs were less than useless. He achieved a short-lived verticality before everything south of his belt decided to go AWOL and he collapsed back to the dirt with a thud. He tried to rise again but it was impossible.

There were lights in the storm. Little yellow dots that came and went in the winds and swirling sand. Fitz yelled for help but his voice was whisked up by the storm and torn to useless shreds like ribbons that spiralled, then were gone.

There was thunder and chaos and apocalypse. There were very probably four mounted horsemen on a nearby hill overlooking his doom, nodding sagely to one another as the ground below Fitz opened up and he plummeted to a place he didn't want even to think about –

Having tossed and turned for half the night, Danyal Bains lay awake at 4 a.m. feeling more than a little disgruntled. He dragged himself out of bed and into the bathroom to find a man in the mirror who was obviously suffering from severe sleep deprivation. He gazed into the reflected eyes, and for a long moment didn't recognise himself at all. The last four weeks had seen his determination eroded by the continual battle against petty bureaucracy. His meeting last night with the top man himself, Gaskill Tyran, had finally proved to him that he was never going to see his dig again. WorldCorp were absolutely single-minded in their pursuit of this planet, and last night's meeting with Tyran had only driven home the futility of his fight.

They were less than forty-eight hours now from Grid 1123. Less than two days from annihilating a past civilisation and all its invaluable knowledge. There might well be plenty of other significant finds left undiscovered beneath the surface, but, after all his efforts and Tyran's determination to destroy his work, he doubted very much if he'd be allowed to reveal them to anybody. If news got out to the right people in Earth Central, he was confident that works would be stopped, at least in this sector. What were a few square kilometres of dirt in an entire world? It was a potential delay to *all* ops on Ceres Alpha for perhaps as long as two or three years. And that was what terrified the likes of Gaskill Tyran.

Splashing cold water over his face, Bains heaved a giant sigh and turned from the sorry image in the mirror. He made his way back through his apartment and began to clamber into his work gear. If diplomatic channels had failed, he thought, then there was only direct action left. He'd been a prisoner for over a month and he'd managed to squander a lot of valuable time by his inertia. If he didn't make a stand now, today, then he knew he'd regret it for the rest of his life.

Fixing his com unit over his shoulders, Bains ran through the system checks with a casual familiarity while he slumped on the edge of the sofa to put on his boots. The unit rewarded him with a series of green lights, and he opened the door and poked his head out into the corridor.

Empty. Good start. Now all he had to do was get to chopper pad 26 without being seen, and that was only forty levels up and nearly a kilometre away. No problem.

Mij Perón was nodding off when Pryce returned. She'd spent the last few hours squatting on an uncomfortable chair in med ops, trying and failing quite spectacularly to make herself comfortable while the patients slept and the accelerators worked their small miracles.

'You look tired,' Pryce commented.

'I'm fine,' she lied, trying to straighten herself into an upright position, while her bones and sinews refused point-blank to co-operate.

Pryce leaned over the girl, carefully peeling away the eye gel.

'Healed nicely,' he said.

He poked and prodded the monitor, running through the total-body checks one at a time with a distracted fluidity, nodding all the while.

'Those internal lesions have healed OK,' Perón said.

'That cerebral activity's still all over the place, though,' he pointed out.

'Well hopefully we can make some sense of it all when she's physically recovered.'

Pryce examined the girl's face, his fingertips plying the skin of her cheeks, pressing tenderly to explore the bone structure beneath.

'Those zygomatic fractures have repaired nicely,' he noted. 'She'll thank us for that when she wakes up.'

A sudden furore behind them snapped their attention to the man. He sat bolt upright on the bed, staring at the wrist restraints that Foley had attached. His eyes were wide and incredulous, pale blue and gawking.

Then he glared at Pryce and Perón.

'How long have I been here?' he asked. The words tumbled out of him almost faster than Perón could recognise them. She watched Pryce dash over and grasp the man's shoulders.

'Easy,' he soothed. 'You're in Medicare Central. You're going to be fine.'

But the man's eyes were wild, glancing from Pryce to Perón to the girl and around the room with frantic motions of his head. His monitor readouts were everywhere at once, dancing a most strange and alien jig. A whole clutch of red warnings flashed in a frenzied fury on the screen.

'How long?' he demanded. He had a commanding voice that Pryce was compelled to answer.

'About five hours.'

'Fitz!' the man said. There was genuine pain in his eyes now. Realising there were sensors attached to his face, he swiped his head from side to side until they were all dislodged, lying useless on the bed. The med unit flatlined abruptly, and the air squealed with its shrill warning cry.

Pryce switched off the unit and pressed his hands on the man's shoulders.

'Calm down,' he said. 'Fitz is OK. She's right over there. She's going to be fine.'

'That's not Fitz,' the man yelled. Perón thought he looked about to burst into tears. He was yanking at the restraints. 'How do I get outside?'

'You have another colleague?' Pryce was asking.

'Yes, yes,' the man said, rocking on the bed in an attempt to break his bonds.

Pryce tried to force him back, but he sprang up again instantly. The bed crashed and rattled under his ferocious assault and Pryce tumbled back into the middle of the room.

'*Let me out!*' the man screamed.

'Calm down,' Pryce urged, maintaining a wary distance. 'You're in no fit state to go anywhere.'

The man fixed Pryce with his cold blue eyes. 'I can assure you that I am in a perfectly fit state indeed. Now will you kindly unfasten these... *things?*'

But Pryce remained exactly where he was.

'If there were anybody out there, the detectors would have picked them up,' Perón assured him.

She found the man's stare on her, saw how fierce his eyes were under his unruly brown fringe. Windows on the soul, she'd heard. She found herself gazing for a moment into a bottomless pit. When he spoke again, the words cascaded out of him in a quiet torrent, a waterfall of whispers gushing into the room.

'He was injured. I put him under cover. The storm was getting worse. You didn't pick us up until it was very nearly too late. There's a very strong possibility that you missed him completely. But there is also a very slim possibility that he somehow managed to get out of your path. I know where I left him. Let me go *now*.'

'The only way you're going to get out of here is with military co-operation,' Perón told him. 'And you're only going to get that if you can prove who you are.'

'I am the Doctor,' he said.

'Dr Domecq?' Pryce asked.

Perón noted more than a hint of hope in his voice. The creatures in the hold were Pryce's wards until Domecq arrived from Earth. As the weeks passed, Perón had watched Pryce gradually crumble under the strain as the creatures got the better of him. She knew how relieved he'd be to see the back of them, and Domecq was the man to take the baton.

There was a short pause. 'Yes.'

'How did you get here?' Perón asked bluntly.

Another caesura. 'We crash-landed.'

'Why didn't we get your signature?' she demanded.

'I don't know,' Domecq lowered his head. 'We hit some kind of severe turbulence.'

'A localised warp?' asked Pryce, doing his best to jolly the conversation along in his preferred direction.

'Yes,' the man said, a little too enthusiastically for Perón's liking. 'Exactly.'

'Where are your documents?' she asked him.

'Lost in the crash, I suppose. We didn't have much time to get ourselves ready. Everything happened in something of a confused rush, I'm afraid.'

Perón shot Pryce a sceptical look.

'We crawled through chaos to get here,' Domecq told them, his voice now completely calm. 'I have a friend out on the surface who may well have been chewed up in this infernal machine of yours.' He watched them both, one after another, and Perón saw fear in his face. 'For pity's sake will you please unfasten these straps?'

Stepping forward suddenly, Pryce slipped the bolts. The straps came free and the man grasped him by the shoulder.

'Thank you,' he said with obvious relief.

He jumped off the bed and proceeded to brush himself down,

showering the floor with clumps of dried mud that flaked from his clothes.

Pryce pressed his wristcom and a WorldCorp hologram ghosted into existence in front of him.

'Captain De-ann Foley,' he requested.

The logo mutated into Foley's head, the flock of circling birds migrating smoothly into her short dark hair.

'Dr Pryce.'

'Captain Foley. I'm afraid you may have missed one civilian on your rescue mission.'

The head shook. 'Not possible. We did a comprehensive sweep. Nobody else. I take it one of my prisoners is awake. There in five.'

Pryce was about to say something, but before he could speak the head snapped out of the air in a puff of sparkling static.

Perón realised that Domecq had moved and was now standing over the girl, peering fretfully into her face.

'She's going to be fine,' Pryce told him. 'Physically at least.'

There was a gentleness in his features that equalled the fury of only moments ago. Perón watched in fascination as the man stroked the girl's cheeks. He was obviously a man of extreme passions, this Dr Domecq.

'You scanned her brain?'

'Yes,' Pryce confirmed. 'Do you know what's wrong with her?'

'I'm not sure,' Domecq said, unable to remove his gaze from the girl. 'I think it had something to do with the turbulence we hit. There are regions of her brain working overtime and double rate. I think it might be Paxx-Sinopoli Syndrome.'

Pryce shook his head. 'Never heard of it.'

'I have,' Perón announced. 'But this isn't it. Paxx-Sinopoli is a parasitic disease. It's caused by a virus that attacks the brain. It resides in the mid-brain, uses synaptic bursts to energise itself, and meanwhile devours the cerebral cortex. There's a dissonance set up in human hosts that causes partial paralysis, and gradually the host dies of cerebral emaciation. There's no emaciation in your friend.'

Domecq reached out and stroked the girl's forehead, not for a single instant taking his eyes from her.

'But there's a short-term cure for the effects of Paxx-Sinopoli,' Domecq said. 'I understand the dissonance can be countered by harmonising feedback from a skullcap ECG.'

Perón shook her head. 'Never heard of that.'

'Something I read,' Domecq said, rising to face Perón. 'It's quite possible it was just a theoretical paper.'

Thumbing the girl's eyelids in an attempt to get some response, Domecq appeared disappointed at her total lethargy.

'We could try to program the ECG on the monitor,' Domecq suggested. 'That might give her some relief from the paralysis. Maybe if she gets some of her normal function back, then she can fight whatever it is herself. Sort of giving her psychological immunity a bit of a boost.'

'We could try,' Perón agreed. 'I'm not at all sure what the results will be.'

'Can you suggest anything else?' Domecq asked.

Perón couldn't.

'If you set up a secondary failsafe on a separate ECG,' Domecq said, 'and if you post somebody who knows what they're doing at the side of her bed to keep an eye on things, there can't be any harm in trying it, can there?'

'Do you always treat your patients in such an experimental manner?'

'I'm a man who thrives on improvisation,' Domecq said.

'I can quite believe that, having seen your bioscans.'

'Ah,' Domecq blustered, apparently embarrassed. 'Yes. Well, that's a long story...'

But he was saved from further exposition by Captain Foley, who arrived in the room with a furious mask where her cold, hard face should have been. She had adopted a belligerent stance before she even opened her mouth to speak.

'What's this man doing out of his restraints?'

Domecq rushed over and grasped her by the hand, much to

Foley's astonished animosity. He shook her hand warmly, a great fat grin occupying the entire southern territory of his face.

'Ah, Captain Foley, how good of you to come so promptly. I understand I owe you my life. I can't begin to express my gratitude.' He prattled on, apparently entirely oblivious to the dark scowl she was giving him. 'Now, if we can organise a search party I can show you where to start looking for my friend. Please – lead the way. We may well be too late already.'

With an unsure glance back at Pryce, Foley had little choice but to allow herself to be ushered to the door by Domecq. At the door she managed to halt his amiable advance.

'Just a minute. Who the hell do you think you are?'

'I'm Dr Domecq. Come on. Chop chop! Can't stand around all night chatting. We've got work to do, Captain.'

Perón saw a dubious look flash through Foley's features, but she allowed Domecq to propel her energetically out of the door and into the corridor. Domecq was still chattering ceaselessly when the door sliced shut. Perón found Pryce at her side looking aghast, unable to believe that he'd just witnessed a real-life taming of the shrew.

'Shall we get the ECG rigged up?' Perón suggested.

'I think we ought to do as he says, don't you?' Pryce agreed.

Having reached Upper Level without bumping into anybody, Danyal Bains was relieved to see the series of small doors that led out into the open roof area of the city-machine. He didn't have a plan, as such, but he knew he had to get back to the dig site and salvage as much evidence as he could. He hoped that the armed guards he'd seen posted there when he was quite unceremoniously ejected had not remained. He was pretty sure they were just for show, to put him off any idea he might entertain about sneaking back. He was sure they had better things to do with their time than stand around his dig for the past few weeks.

There was the problem, of course, of what to do with the material he salvaged once he'd got it. If he tried to bring it back here, he was certain Tyran and his cronies would obliterate it. Leaving the city-machine tonight like this meant going on the run, he knew that. It meant living off roots that tasted like old soldiers' boots. It meant taking scant refuge from the storms in caves. It meant evading Tyran's search parties and maybe even having to fight for his life.

But the alternative was to simply sit in his apartment and know that the priceless material at his dig was gone for ever. Not a choice, really. For forty years his work had been his life, and he'd never found anything quite like his discoveries on Ceres Alpha.

The exit area was entirely empty, as he'd expect at this time of day. Even the maintenance crews would be wrapped up in bed now. Bains slapped a door pad, and as the door swept open he lifted his hood to cut out the storm.

It was a short dash to chopper pad 26, and when he got there he was glad to see that his chopper had not been replaced by a military machine. Still a little dubious, however, he tried his code on the door com. The pad responded with a green light and as the door opened Bains heaved a sigh of relief. The thought obviously hadn't entered their stupid little minds that he might be so audacious as to make a run for it.

Having thrust his kitbag into the passenger seat and strapped it in, Bains sank into the cockpit and belted up. The dash lights flared into life in front of him and he attempted to release the locking bars. A new message flashed on the monitor in red letters.

SEC CODE?

What sec code? Release of the locking bars had always been automatic. The sharp pang of comprehension struck him. They hadn't replaced his chopper with a military one: they'd simply commandeered it. Incensed, he started the rotors and fired up the jets. The sounds of the wind were met by those of his own private storm as he grasped the joystick and prepared to attempt a vertical thrust that he hoped would snap the bars and fling him into the air and freedom.

Max thrust prep'd. Green light. Go.

The chopper shuddered but the bolts held firm. He was going nowhere fast, sitting there watching his precious liberty slipping through his fingers. Again he attempted to blast through the restraints. This time the chopper lurched violently and for an instant he was afraid he was going to topple and smash the rotors. He'd managed to break the portside bar. There was a flutter of hope. He cancelled the rotors and while he waited for them to retract to safety he noticed the large dark shadows bobbing around the bay and realised that they were after him. He heard the door com buzz as somebody on the outside tried to get in. He tried to lock the door but the query message flared again:

SEC CODE?

He slammed the monitor in frustration and peered up to see if the rotors were safe enough yet. Punched in instructions to fire max thrust on jets alone. A small inset on the monitor showed him that the blades were almost safe now, but they were stowing themselves with infuriating slowness. Risk blast? The side door was retracting and Bains could see a black-cowled shape appearing in the opening. He watched as the shape hoisted a rifle and took careful aim.

Bains glared at the readouts. He wasn't going to make it. The jets were ready but the blades weren't safe. He fingered the monitor. A warning screen overlay all the others, telling him he couldn't use the blasters with people so near. Bains punched in a manual disregard. Closed his eyes. Took the plunge. The chopper jerked violently, but slammed again back on to the pad.

When he looked, the man with the gun was gone, no doubt blasted by the jets in Bains's failed attempt. Red warnings flared angrily at him from the monitor. There was frantic motion at his rear as somebody scrambled on board. Above the noise of the wind and eager jets, Bains heard the tiny click of the cocking of a rifle. There was cold metal on the side of his face. He turned to see one of the black-hooded men shaking his head slowly at him.

Bains reached up cautiously, keeping his hands in plain view, and he was given just enough room to rise out of his seat. He scrambled into the back of the chopper, but when he began to make his way to the door he felt an explosion hit the back of his head and a bright white flare sent him falling blind.

When he opened his eyes again he was on his back on the chopper pad, the wind screaming in his ears and four burly men with guns towering over him. There was another explosion in his back, and he realised he was being kicked by one of the men. Raising his hands to protect his face, he received a brisk punch that rocked his head back sharply. He took a blow to his unprotected stomach, and when he reached down reflexively, they kicked him again in the face. Two of them reached down and Bains was dragged to his feet and slammed in the direction of the nearby doors.

As they entered the city, Bains saw two people rushing towards him on their way out. One was a curiously dressed man in a bottle-green coat. The other Bains recognised as Captain De-ann Foley, the woman who had led the raid on his dig a month ago. She'd treated him with undisguised malice and no respect whatsoever. She'd bulldozed him back to the city and incarcerated him for hours before the order came through for his release. He'd received an official apology for his 'processing', but Foley, he knew, had delighted in his mistreatment.

Foley saw him and there was a fleeting recognition, but she swept past and continued on her way without so much as a backward glance.

Bains was bleeding from the mouth and he'd taken a boot to the right eye. He'd obviously got on the wrong side of somebody. But Foley was finding it hard going keeping up with Domecq, and she had only the briefest impression of Bains's injuries.

'This one?' Domecq was asking, indicating the chopper on pad one.

'That'll do,' Foley snapped, entering her code while Domecq stood there being blown about in the storm.

They scrambled inside and she eased herself into the cockpit. Domecq knelt behind her watching every move with eager, childlike interest.

'You better strap in,' she told him.

'I'll be fine,' Domecq said. 'I'm one of those backseat drivers who want to see exactly where we're going.'

Foley punched in her code and watched for the green light that signalled release of the locking bars. By the time the light was given, she'd fired up and they were already lifting into the blizzard.

'Amazing that you can use this kind of transport under such terrible conditions,' Domecq said as they took to the air.

'You can't knock one of these out of the sky unless you got a multiphase anti-aircraft cannon,' Foley assured him. 'These things can fly through any planetary conditions you could imagine, plus a few you wouldn't want to think about.'

'What d'you think he'd done?' Domecq asked.

Foley was thrown by the non sequitur. 'I'm sorry?'

'That poor man we passed who'd been beaten up by your uniformed thugs.'

'That poor man could be a vicious outlaw,' Foley said, swooping them over the edge and plunging down into a steep planet-fall.

The air turbulence made it heavy going, and the chopper was thrown about like a toy. Foley gripped the joystick and disregarded the auto-override that was trying to cut in. Domecq defied all the laws of momentum to remain glued to her shoulder. He seemed entirely unperturbed by her shock tactics, and in fact he was shaking his head with his mind obviously elsewhere.

'I recognise the hallmarks of brutality,' he said simply, as she yanked the stick to level them out. Her stomach continued along the same trajectory and took a short while to get back in touch.

'You only saw him for a split second,' Foley argued, trying to compensate for some particularly bad-tempered near-ground currents caused by the unevenness of the terrain.

'Oh, it has distinct characteristics,' Domecq assured her. '*No!*'

The tone of his voice changed so suddenly that she had to glance back to read his face. He was peering out into the storm, now shocked into silence. Through the front screen, following his gaze, Foley could see very little. Visibility was down to a few metres.

'What?'

'The TARDIS.'

'The what?'

'Put us down.'

She did as he said and they clambered out into conditions that made Foley thank God she had her anti-sand-storm gear on. She pulled the goggles down over her eyes and dropped the flaps to protect her ears. Domecq wandered off, for all the world as if he were taking a ramble on a breezy summer's day. His hair whipped up above his head and his jacket flung itself around his shoulders, slapping him in the face and rising like wings about him.

Foley followed him as he strolled into the storm. The ground bucked and vibrated from the approach of the city, and there was so much noise she could hardly hear herself think. Domecq seemed oblivious.

Then she saw what he was looking at. It emerged from the storm and she glared at it in disbelief. A squat dark box apparently made of blue-painted wood. Incredibly, the slightly battered-looking colour had remained intact, despite being subjected to the sandblasting that sometimes passed for night on Ceres. Foley grasped Domecq by the sleeve.

'What the hell's that?' she screamed above the wind.

'My equipment,' Domecq told her, fighting with his flailing coat. He was looking back in the direction of the city, pointing. 'We set off in that direction,' he yelled. 'I left Fitz about a kilometre over there.'

Foley adjusted the goggles to try to penetrate the storm, and only fifty or so metres away she could make out the lights of the approaching city. She gazed into the ferocious night while she unhooked the detector from her com unit, then did a complete sweep of the vicinity, widening the range as she turned repeatedly.

She realised Domecq was scrutinising the readings at her shoulder. She shook her head.

'I'm sorry –'

Domecq grabbed the detector from her.

'You get back to the chopper,' he said. 'I'm going to take a look around.'

'Don't be stupid,' Foley hollered. 'You're not exactly dressed for these conditions. You need combat fatigues, a survival kit –'

'I *am* a survival kit,' he told her. 'Wait in the chopper. I won't be long.'

He was about to turn his back on her when she grasped his shoulder and clenched her fist angrily in front of his face.

'Now listen to me,' she shouted. 'I'm not going to let you go get yourself killed again. It's not gonna look too good on my report card if I lose you after risking my life to save your idiot skin in the first place.'

She started to drag him towards the chopper, but found herself holding an empty jacket that whipped around in the wind. She saw his white shirtsleeves briefly before he was devoured by the weather.

Foley considered pursuing him, but without the detector there was a real danger she could lose herself completely out here. She decided instead to return, fuming, to the chopper and give him a few minutes before abandoning him to his fate.

Back at the chopper the monitor was flashing in alarm. She scanned the readings and realised just how dangerously close the city now was. Out in the squall there was no sign of Domecq. She could sit here for a few minutes only, then she'd have to move. Slamming her fist into the monitor, she decided to practise her cussing techniques for the remainder of the time she had.

Bains was manhandled down a series of corridors until he

recognised the holding area of Military One. He'd grown accustomed to these walls when he was last forcibly brought back to the city a month ago, and he didn't particularly relish the idea of spending any more nights in these cells.

Tossed into a tiny room that contained a desk and two chairs, he slumped into one of the chairs to gingerly test his injuries while he waited. There was intense pain down one side of his upper trunk, but only when he tried to breathe. Broken ribs, maybe. There was the option of not breathing at all, but on balance he preferred to put up with the pain.

The men who'd captured him had spoken not a single word. There'd been no questions asked, no comment on his activities. He assumed they knew who he was and what he'd been trying to do. And he assumed they were acting under instructions from Gaskill Tyran.

So he'd finally proved what depths they were willing to plumb to stop news of his finds getting out. He thought back to the day he got the job on Ceres Alpha. The offer that came through a series of friends, a fortuitous invitation to apply for the post of official archaeologist on Ceres Alpha, the WorldCorp discovery that was a planet so close in conditions to Earth that people could even breathe the atmosphere. It was an opportunity too remarkable to decline. Initial surveys confirmed no intelligent life. The atmosphere was maintained by micro-organisms and elementary vegetation. Nothing toxic. The perfect environment for an earlier civilisation to have survived in. He'd never been offered such a chance in his life.

And now he was beginning to wish he'd never set foot on Ceres Alpha.

The door cracked open and a short woman entered. Bains noted that she wore a sidearm and that the holster was open. She was broad with the physique of a man. Short brown hair stuck up from her head in tufts. She regarded him with a shadowy scowl and he imagined that it was her customary expression, one that was set in stone.

The woman remained standing over him while Bains forced the breath in and out of his lungs, using the table for support. When she spoke, she had a voice to match her masculine appearance, deep and gruff with singularly unpleasant undertones.

'You were caught trying to steal a military chopper –'

'It's *my* chopper,' Bains started to argue, but the agony it caused was too much to bear and his sentence floundered in midair like a bird shot in flight.

'*Silence!*' the woman snapped. 'Furthermore, you deliberately overrode safety protocol to use your blasters when there were military personnel in the vicinity. I have a man badly injured due to your ruthless stupidity.'

She allowed a long silence to ensue and Bains opted not to punctuate it with anything.

'Before we've done with you,' she snarled, 'you'll wish you'd never set foot on Ceres Alpha.'

The chopper was lifting when Foley saw Domecq reappear directly in front of her. He was waving his arms, trying to catch her attention. She thought about leaving anyway, but changed her mind at the last moment and pressed the door com.

Domecq climbed on board, his shirtsleeves torn and filthy and his hair a scruffy pile of dark-brown curls above his pale face. For a passing moment he looked like a phantom, and Foley fancied that he'd got himself killed again after all.

'Nothing?' she asked.

He shook his head, peering down at the detector in his hands.

'Have we got lifting gear on board?' he asked.

'For that crate of yours?'

He nodded.

She gave him a rare and indulgent smile. You just had to give the man credit.

'I think we can manage that for you,' she said. 'But this time will you strap yourself in, *please*?'

* * *

79

Tyran's private apartments were vast. Great empty spaces with the bare minimum of functional furniture, rooms without warmth or any kind of human feeling. Places without a soul. Carly remembered being hugely impressed the first time she saw them, amazed that anybody could command such space. But over recent months these rooms had increasingly filled her with dread.

Struggling to overcome the trepidation she felt, she crossed the living area and made her way towards the bedrooms at the back. Outside Tyran's door she paused, listening to the sound of her own ragged breath and the thump of the blood through her head.

Slipping in silence into the room, she found Tyran fast asleep. Prone and alone. She'd seen him like this many times, of course, having shared his bed, on and off, for four years now. Shared his bed, and his sec codes. She gritted her teeth and began to search the room in silence, discovering the mind probe on the dresser near the door. It had been discarded casually, like his com and his watch. Such a vile thing, yet to him it was a trinket among his personal effects. She took it in her fingers and felt the tingle of absolute power that it represented.

The probe was sleek and felt comfortable in the palm of her hand. Formed from black plastic, it had unmarked controls along the side. Carly had no idea what the controls actually did, but the ergonomics of the thing suggested that the raised bump at the front, accessed by the trigger finger, was the business button. Levelling the device in front of her, she crept towards the bed, shaking so badly now that the probe jigged about in the air and she wondered for an instant whether she could finish what she'd come here to do.

But now she had no choice. He'd made it plain that she'd reached the end of her usefulness. He had tired of her company, and of her services. And she knew that people like her didn't get pensioned off by Tyran. People like her knew too much to be released.

Clambering on to the bed on her knees, Carly pointed the probe at his head and savoured this moment. With the probe he'd terrorised her. He'd effectively killed her many times over. The sweet justice of this vengeance was a beautiful thing to taste. She took a deep breath before pressing the button. The air was filled with the scent of ozone and Tyran flung up his arms as if in alarm. His eyes snapped open and he watched her in bewildered astonishment. She was gratified to see something akin to fear in his wide-open gaze.

But then his fear transformed. Lifting himself on to his elbows, he simply watched her out of the gloom. Feeling the tears pouring down her face, Carly frantically tried some of the other controls. But Tyran's expression didn't change and she shook the probe in frustration as he pushed himself up and reached out to grab it.

Blind fury consumed her. She lashed out, using the probe as a truncheon, and Tyran fell back with a grunt, dark blood splattering his shadowy pillow. Dropping the probe, she laid into him with her bare fists, beating and scratching and sobbing with fury.

Then she felt her arms gripped tight and she was hurled through the air. She hit a wall and the wind blasted out of her chest. Momentarily stunned, she found Tyran standing over her wiping the blood from his nose on the back of his arm. Then she saw he had the probe. It swung up through the air and she smelled again the scent of ozone. She glimpsed the loathing in his eyes, and the white light that exploded into her brain filled her with fires that raged and consumed.

And the last thing she ever knew was the look on his face as he killed her.

There were two long scars down the side of his face and blood smeared around his lips and nose, but a few minutes on the accelerator would repair all the damage she'd done.

After splashing his face with cold water, Tyran dried quickly and got himself dressed. Before leaving the bedroom, he bent briefly to peer into Carly's bright eyes. They gazed back at him out of an empty head that lolled back curiously on her shoulder.

'You shouldn't play with dangerous toys,' he admonished.

She didn't, of course, reply.

As he swept through the apartment, Tyran grabbed his jacket from the stand by the door. Not bothering to put the jacket on, he unclipped the com and put in a call to Zach. The apelike head of his guard appeared in the air nearby looking as if it'd just been pushed through a mincer.

'Morning, Zach,' Tyran said brightly as he left the apartment and paced down the corridor towards the elevators. 'Woman overboard, please. You'll find her in my bedroom.'

'You were very fortunate,' Perón told him. The words came out a bit dispassionately, but Domecq needed shaking out of his morose preoccupation. It was nearly six now and he'd spent the last hour at the girl's side simply staring off into space, completely oblivious to the comings and goings of Perón and the staff.

Emerging from his trancelike state, Domecq gazed at her for a moment like a startled cat.

'I'm sorry?' he said at last.

'You were very fortunate,' she repeated. 'Both of you.'

'I should have been there for Fitz,' he said.

'You can't blame yourself,' she told him. 'Forced landing at night on Ceres Alpha is a dangerous exercise. It's a miracle any of you survived.'

She heard the door open behind her and turned to find Pryce coming into the room. He looked tired and more than a little frazzled around the edges, as if he'd just come in from outside himself.

'Ah, Dr Domecq,' he said. 'I'm sorry to hear about your colleague.'

Domecq shot him a rueful stare. 'He was my *friend*.'

'Yes,' Pryce said, suddenly unsure of himself. 'Yes. Of course. I'm sorry.'

Floundering for a moment, Pryce looked from Domecq to the girl to Perón and back to Domecq. It was comical to see, this head of department lost for words and direction.

'Do you want to see the creatures now?' Pryce asked suddenly. 'Or would you prefer to get some sleep first?'

'The creatures?'

'Yes.'

Domecq came to his senses, jumping abruptly to his feet. 'Yes. Yes, of course. I'm sorry. I don't know what I'm thinking.'

'Don't you think it might be better to get some rest before you start work?' Perón suggested. She'd prefer to keep Domecq away from the creatures until she'd verified just who exactly he was. Foley had reported no trace of a wreck on the surface, and it was still possible that the man before them was not Domecq at all. She stared pointedly at Pryce before turning back to Domecq. 'You've been through a long series of quite traumatic experiences tonight.'

'No no no no no.' Domecq fluttered his arms about dismissively, and when they settled again Perón found his eyes clear and keen. He was a different man from the one she'd been speaking to only moments before. 'No time like the present, so they say.'

Pryce looked decidedly relieved, leading Domecq to the door and ushering him through with far too much eagerness. When the door sliced shut, Perón checked the girl. The accelerators were nearing the end of their task, and the deep brain activity was now only slightly erratic, due apparently to the jury-rigged skullcap that Domecq had suggested. He had said he was a man who thrived on improvisation. Perón was beginning to warm to him, despite the fact that he could yet prove to be an enemy spy. If that were the case, she thought, it could prove an exhilarating challenge to take this man down.

Shivering from the noticeable temperature drop when they entered the storerooms, Pryce led Domecq to the bolted door at the end of the short stretch of corridor.

'The mothers checked out perfectly,' Pryce was saying. 'No family history. No nothing. But the things they gave birth to... well, you'll see for yourself.'

'These creatures are *babies*?' Domecq asked incredulously.

Pryce gave him a dark look. 'These creatures are *creatures*. Can't you feel the atmosphere as soon as you come in here?'

'I can certainly feel the cold,' Domecq observed.

Pryce unbolted the door and waved Domecq through. The room beyond contained metal shelves stacked with detergents and a whole arsenal of cleaning equipment. Domecq looked bewildered, and Pryce indicated the floor-to-ceiling stack of swiftcloths at the back of the room. Domecq still looked blank, until Pryce grasped one of the rolls of cloth and tugged open the disguised door that led to the second, hidden door beyond.

Domecq was abruptly fascinated.

Pryce opened the door to reveal a further short corridor with six doors off to each side. This section was even colder, and Pryce sensed the danger here as soon as he stepped inside. It was a most tangible malice, even though the cells were entirely silent. Opening up the door to cell two, Pryce waved Domecq into the darkness. Obviously puzzled at first, and perhaps a little mistrusting, Domecq gave him a furtive look.

'Over there.' Pryce pointed. 'Behind the toilet.'

Peering into the shadow, Domecq finally saw the creature cowering in the corner of the cell, watching them with wide, terrified eyes.

'Careful,' Pryce warned, as Domecq stepped over the cell to crouch near the creature.

Watching from the door, alert for the sounds of the others, Pryce saw Domecq trying to offer his hand. The creature stared fretfully and Domecq edged closer, dropping to his knees in an attempt to shrink himself to the same size as the thing.

'Hello,' Domecq cooed. 'What's *your* name?'

'This is Number Two,' Pryce responded, stepping over to hunch beside Domecq.

The creature shrank back, and Domecq fixed Pryce with a peculiar look, his eyes twin fires in the darkness.

'They don't have names?'

Pryce shook his head. 'Why should they?'

Ignoring the question, Domecq returned to the creature, raising his hand again in a coaxing gesture. The creature simply gawked out of its great black eyes, completely unresponsive.

'I'm the Doctor,' Domecq said softly. 'I'm here to help you.'

'They won't speak,' Pryce told him.

'Quiet,' Domecq snapped. The creature flung up its arms in an automatic, useless gesture of defence.

'I'm sorry,' soothed Domecq. 'I'm not going to hurt you...'

Extending his hand towards the creature, Domecq positioned his fingers only centimetres from the thing. It gazed at his hand and, to Pryce's surprise, actually began to reach out to touch.

'That's better,' Domecq whispered. 'Are you going to come out of there?'

Wrapping its three spindly fingers around Domecq's outstretched hand, the creature allowed itself to be lured out from behind the toilet, but it remained wary. Domecq sat cross-legged on the floor so that his face was level with the creature's, and Pryce watched as he gazed at the slim pale thing as if he were under some enchanted spell.

'Now, Mr Number Two,' Domecq said, his voice trickling into the cold dark air like liquid compassion, 'would you mind very much if I take a closer look at you?'

The creature allowed itself to be turned for inspection, finally gazing back at Domecq with only the slightest trace of anxiety remaining in its huge eyes.

Domecq fumbled in his pocket, and a moment later Pryce saw a small white ball had appeared in Domecq's fingers. Clasping the ball in his other hand, Domecq left the clenched fist momentarily in the air while the creature watched in silent fascination. Slowly, Domecq's fingers spread to reveal an empty hand. The creature looked instantly at Domecq's other hand, only to find that empty as well. Baffled, Pryce watched as Domecq opened his mouth to reveal the ball. It fell into his open hand and he grinned at the creature. Pryce was amazed to see the small dark line that was the creature's mouth stretch into a tiny smile. The last vestiges of mistrust seemed to ebb from its eyes, and it extended slender fingers to touch Domecq's lips in wonder.

Apart from the continuous rumbling of the city's progress, Pryce realised abruptly just how quiet the holding bay was tonight. No restless shuffling in the cells, no agitated rattling of the doors. Pryce had never been able to enter this area without feeling threatened, but suddenly he sensed a new tranquillity in the hold. It seemed to Pryce that Domecq had accomplished in seconds what Pryce had failed to do in two months. He'd made contact with these things. But Pryce knew what they were capable of.

'I'd be very wary,' he warned. 'They can be unexpectedly vicious.'

Domecq looked doubtful. 'Vicious?'

'They use telepathy. Get into your head. They're like wild animals sometimes.'

'Mr Number Two here seems harmless enough to me,' Domecq observed. He was doing the trick again, this time making the ball vanish completely as the creature observed in amazement. It touched his lips and Domecq opened his mouth to show it was empty.

'Don't let them fool you. They change so suddenly. They're evil.'

'Evil? That's an odd word to use.'

Pryce nodded knowingly, watching the huge black eyes of the creature gleaming in the shadow. They watched him right back, entirely empty of human emotion of any kind.

'Oh, they're evil all right,' Pryce assured him. 'They've got the Devil in their genes.'

'Perhaps they're just cold and hungry,' Domecq suggested, eyes flashing around the desolate cell. 'How long have they been in here?'

'Eight weeks now, since they were born.'

Domecq appeared amazed, scrutinising the creature with renewed fascination.

'They're only eight weeks old?'

'How much did they tell you in the reports?'

'Very little,' Domecq admitted, reaching out unexpectedly to pluck the ball from behind the creature's ear.

'They wouldn't want too much information out in the open,' Pryce supposed. 'Daren't risk the wrong people getting to know too much.'

Domecq nodded, passing the ball for the creature to inspect. 'That's understandable.'

'We've got twelve of them,' Pryce told him, rising from the floor to squat on the edge of the creature's bunk. 'All born at the same time. The strangest thing was, they were spread right over the six continents. Pretty evenly distributed across the entire world. The med comps picked up abnormalities in foetal development so we knew there was something strange about them long before they arrived. They were all exactly the same, same developmental problems, same natal aberrations. Have you seen their hands?'

Domecq observed the creature as it turned the ball repeatedly in front of its face. 'Three fingers…'

'They were born two months premature,' Pryce informed him. 'Same cranial bloating. Big wide heads and those enormous, weird eyes. And they have some kind of telepathic link with one another. If you hurt one, they all feel the pain.'

Domecq looked appalled. 'You've been inflicting pain on them?'

'Of course. We've carried out exhaustive research. We've prepared detailed reports. I'm sure you'll find them fascinating'

Domecq was on his feet, pacing up and down the cell, plunging his fingers through his wild hair. He was talking fast and low, words spilling into the room like shards of shattered metal.

'You're torturing sentient beings to test their telepathic abilities? And you call *them* creatures? You label *them* evil? It never fails to amaze me just how conceited, egotistical and downright thoughtless human beings can be. You have such an unparalleled capacity for… *caring*… yet you seem totally inept at putting it into practice…'

'*Doctor!*' Pryce cut across his flow, and found Domecq glaring at him out of a deep dark shadow backed by the light from the corridor. The man appeared to Pryce for a moment like some kind of angel with a protective radiance. There was a long, outraged silence, then Pryce filled the cold air with consoling words.

'We were operating under strict instructions from Earth Central. *From your own people!* These things were developing much faster than anybody anticipated, racing through weeks' worth of growth in days. You were *two months* away. We couldn't just wait…'

Domecq shook his head.

'These children are not lab rats,' he said despondently. 'You can't treat them like this.'

'They're not children,' Pryce reminded him plaintively. 'They're creatures. Not human. Don't be taken in by a superficial similarity.'

Domecq plunged to his knees to take the ball form the creature, swiftly repeated his trick, produced the ball magically from his mouth, and the creature slapped its hands together and awarded him a grin of delight. Domecq handed over the ball and Pryce was stunned into silence by the look he received from Domecq.

'If that's not a child,' Domecq said, obviously struggling to keep his feelings under control, 'then I don't know what your definition is.'

Pryce abruptly saw something in the creature's eyes. As the creature inspected the ball clutched delicately between its three slender fingers, head tilted slightly and eyes completely engrossed in the magic of such an ordinary thing, Pryce recognised suddenly a childlike wonder at the world.

At that moment Mij Perón appeared at the door, watching them curiously.

'Mr Tyran is ready to see Dr Domecq now,' she informed them briskly.

As she ushered them out of the cell Domecq paused at the door, gazing back to see the small creature standing alone in front of the toilet, ball in hand, shoulders hunched in sadness. It regarded Domecq with big, dejected eyes. And then the door slammed shut.

* * *

Wallowing alone in a pool of pain and darkness, Danyal Bains had reached his second momentous decision this night. Badly injuring a military operative by blasting him with chopper jets was a capital offence, Bains decided. It wasn't written up as such, oh no, but he knew for sure that he wasn't going to get out of Military One tonight with his life. They were going to make him pay for his insolence. They were going to put him through hell, then send him there.

Bains was now a prisoner of war, and the codes governing his safe conduct were about to be violated in the name of a greater cause. It would be extremely convenient for Gaskill Tyran if Bains never made it back from his daring and highly risky attempt to make off with a military chopper. Bains had proved a very irritating itch now for far too long, and the information inside Bains's head was the most dangerous knowledge in the universe.

So, tonight, here in the cells of Military One, Danyal Bains was going, for his sins, to cop it. They could, of course, kill him and take him to medicare to be revived. But he doubted medicare figured in their plans. They'd probably kill him, leave him dead, and fake the circumstances of his demise to suit their purposes. Nice and tidy. Get rid of Bains *and* his discoveries all in the space of a day or so. Easy.

And that was why, when the door opened to admit the sour-faced woman from earlier, along with a rough-featured man who reminded Bains of Tyran's personal guard in appearance and in attitude, Bains felt he had absolutely nothing to lose.

The woman still wore her sidearm, and Bains was gratified to see that the holster was still unclipped. The gun was intended as a threat, but it was going to prove just the opposite.

They didn't waste any time. The woman sat stiff-backed on the seat facing Bains, while the man grasped his arms from behind and tugged them up so that Bains cried out in pain from his smashed ribs. He recognised a glint of satisfaction in the woman's eyes as she cupped her hands on the desk.

'Did I tell you how serious your offences were, Professor Bains?'

Bains couldn't get a reply out through his gritted teeth. The thug yanked his arms again, and he was forced to gasp –

'*Yes.*'

'And did I mention that you were going to regret ever setting foot on Ceres Alpha?'

'*Yes,*' he replied before the next explosion of agonies ripped through him.

The woman's eyes flicked up briefly, and Bains felt the pressure on his arms suddenly released. The woman fixed him with her little black stones-for-eyes. He was reminded fleetingly of the image of a grotesque pig. A filthy beast used for its meat before synthogens replaced the need for animal tissue completely. She watched him squirming in pain on the desk for a while before pushing herself back on her seat. It scraped across the floor with a thunderous growling sound.

The desk cracked suddenly as she slammed a truncheon down on it only a centimetre from Bains's face. The recoil from the desk slapped him in the jaw and he wondered if he now had a perforated eardrum on top of all his other troubles.

'I have a man down because of you,' the woman hissed. 'Get on your feet.'

But Bains remained where he was, biding his time, playing lame, saving every scrap of energy he had left in his battered body. The seat vanished from under him, presumably wrenched out by the bruiser at his back, and he crashed to the floor at the side of the desk.

'Get up!' yelled the woman.

She tried to encourage him with a fresh kick to his already shattered ribs. The agony filled his head to the exclusion of all else. When he regained his senses he realised he was being yanked up by the hair. Grasping the edge of the desk, Bains found the woman standing directly at his side, truncheon slapping impatiently into the palm of her hand.

That was when he made his move. The gun came out of its holster in a fluid motion and swung in the air until he saw the man behind him. He let out a single shot that exploded like a bomb going off in the enclosed space. The man collapsed to the deck with a blast of air and a sound like an animal cry, scrabbling in a pool of spreading blood as he clutched his knee.

The gun continued through the air and a split second later Bains was pressing it against the woman's forehead. Her piggy eyes froze and the truncheon clattered to the floor at her feet.

'Com,' Bains barked.

Removing her com instantly, she handed it over without a word. He left the gun exactly where it was and she floundered in uncertainty and approaching doom.

'Cuffs,' he demanded.

She handed them over and he nodded to the seat. She got the message loud and clear and let him fix her to the chair.

Bains knelt by the thug and yanked the com from his tunic. There was blood pooled around him and he grasped his knee in paroxysms of pain, spreading the dark liquid across the floor with his writhing. Bains unclipped the cuffs from the man's belt and trained the gun on him. The man offered one arm while he used the other to try to stem the flow of blood from his leg. Finally Bains clipped the second wrist into the cuffs and the man lay there blasting rapid breaths through clenched teeth.

Rushing back to the woman, Bains scrutinised the pouches that covered her tunic.

'You have tranquilliser pellets,' he said.

'Not part of civilian-duty rig,' she told him, managing to sneer the words.

He levelled the gun again at her head. 'More than one way to keep you quiet,' he said, trying to make it sound like an off-the-cuff remark. He needed her to think he'd have no compunction at all about killing her on the spot.

'Top pocket,' she snarled. 'Right side.'

Giving her an appreciative grin, he found the bubble foil where she indicated and released one of the pellets. Lodging it with great care inside the barrel of the gun, he placed the gun to her lips, still keeping up his ingratiating smile. She accepted the pellet and chomped, not for a second taking her vengeful eyes from his while he let the gun sway loosely in his grasp in front of her.

'Goodnight,' he said, stroking her cheek with the pistol. 'I can't say it's been a pleasure.'

Then he returned to the man and offered him the same choice. He swallowed the pellet without a word, while the woman prattled angrily in the background, spitting words at him with open venom.

'Don't think you're going to get out of here alive,' she seethed. 'You're a walking dead man, Bains.'

She used his name without his ever having told her what it was, which confirmed his suspicion that he'd been set up and they'd expected him to make a run for it all along. Bains prodded gently at his sides and winced from the fires they contained. 'You're probably right,' he told her, 'but I'm not going to go without a fight.'

'Well, you're gonna get that all right,' she promised. But her eyes were already growing heavy, and he realised she was using her anger to combat the oncoming drowsiness.

'Not from you I'm not,' he said, watching her eyes flicker reluctantly shut.

Dropping the gun, Bains proceeded to apply an impromptu tourniquet to the man's leg using a torn strip of the man's own tunic and the woman's truncheon. Satisfied the thug would survive, Bains swept to the door and carefully poked his head out to find the corridor empty. With a final glance at the two sleeping figures in the room behind him, Bains stepped outside and began to make his way towards the lifts and his freedom.

Taking a good deep breath, Gaskill Tyran swept into his office to greet the ambassador from Earth. He found Domecq slouched at the head of the desk in Tyran's own lavish chair. The man appeared completely at home fingering the desktop experimentally to produce various reports and records in the air above the desk. Tyran was thankful he'd protected the more personal areas of his comp with a complex series of shields.

'Dr Domecq, so very good to meet you at long last,' Tyran thrust his hand for the man to take.

Domecq sprang out of the seat and responded warmly, shaking his hand with vigour and awarding Tyran an intensely agreeable smile.

'Mr Tyran,' Domecq enthused. 'It's a very dubious pleasure to meet the man responsible for the atrocities I've witnessed down in your so-called medicare unit.'

The smile was up full volume, as if Domecq were genuinely complimenting Tyran on an exceptionally well-run operation. Tyran found himself momentarily disconcerted by Domecq's directness, but he somehow managed to sustain his own smile in the face of Domecq's assault.

'I'm very surprised,' Tyran retorted, 'that Earth Central feels it can suddenly afford that kind of supercilious indignation on such a matter, considering the immeasurable pressures currently faced by it. I take it you're voicing here your own *personal* views, and not trying to put across any official opinion?'

'Nothing can be worth the misery of those children,' Domecq told him, suddenly full of fury.

'I can see that you were very poorly briefed about the purpose of your visit here,' Tyran told him. 'The fact is, up to now we have been acting under very strict instructions from Earth Central in carrying out our... *tests* on these creatures. I understand your archaic idealism, Doctor, but this is neither the time nor the place to express it.'

Activating the desktop, Tyran offered Domecq a drink from the cabinet that he summoned out of the nearby wall.

'Whisky? It's a delicious, four-hundred-year-old malt from an ancient Scottish tradition. They used real white oak containers to age this stuff.'

Domecq shook his head, while Tyran poured himself a shot and took a delicate sip.

'It really is very good,' he told Domecq.

'How can you stand by and disregard the abuse of those poor children?' Domecq demanded.

Tyran perched on the edge of his desk and peered over his glass at the curious figure in front of him. The scent of the malt was spirited and ancient, much like the man he found himself facing over the desk. Domecq wore clothing like Tyran had never seen: a strange dark-green coat with grey trousers and a singularly anachronistic cravat at his neck. Domecq had riotous brown locks that invaded his face from all sides, giving him the appearance of having just come in from the storms. He had a strong face, possibly enhanced, and his eyes were a curious combination of green and blue, appearing to be either colour depending on when you looked at them. Tyran recalled the report he'd been given by Colonel Perón. Domecq had certainly spent a good deal of effort on his internal organs, and it was entirely likely that he had expended as much effort on his external appearance. The most curious thing, however, was the fact that when you first met him you didn't question that appearance at all. He seemed perfectly comfortable looking like that, and carried the eccentricity superbly.

'You saw one of those creatures for the first time only ten minutes ago. You spent a few minutes examining its responses. We've spent the last two months with those things, and I can tell you now that those creatures are extraordinarily dangerous. They may possess a passing likeness to human young, but they're volatile monsters with powers beyond our understanding.'

'If it's different, kill it, eh?' Domecq began to sermonise.

'Those creatures pose an unprecedented threat to the human race,' Tyran reminded him simply. 'The only points that matter here are – what caused them? How can we prevent such aberrations ever occurring again on Ceres Alpha? And how can we dispose of them? It is to answer those three questions that you have been called here. Keep those concerns at the front of your mind, Dr Domecq, and please do me the courtesy of keeping your personal moral outrage to yourself. We have a job to do.'

'You really think I'm going to help you destroy the lives of those poor innocents?' Domecq fumed.

'*Children? Innocents?*' Tyran stood and slammed his glass on to the desk. 'Why do you feel the need to use such passionate, obstructive language, Doctor?'

'Because I am a passionate, obstructive man, Mr Tyran.'

Tyran was tired of performing these diplomatic dances. Ultimately, he invariably got his way and in the end everything always turned out exactly as he'd planned. He hit obstacles time and again, but he never failed to achieve his goals. The power he wielded had a way of sorting things out in his favour. And if his financial might was to fail him, there were always more brutal arguments that would convince those who saw things differently. Everybody was perfectly aware of his power, particularly those in official circles.

'All right, Dr Domecq. You made your point. Now, what is it going to take to remove that obstruction?'

'Are you offering me a bribe?' Domecq asked.

'Are you not requesting one?'

'I am certainly not.' Domecq seemed doubly outraged at the suggestion, and Tyran found himself on unanticipated ground.

Who did this man think he was? Some kind of Lone Vigilante? The real Domecq would take the bribe at this point. And an agent would play the part. So why the hell was this man pushing his luck?

Could it be that Earth Central really had suddenly discovered some new capacity to moralise? Did they have an alternative contract to Ceres Alpha? Tyran's enquiries said not, but perhaps he could have been misinformed. Or was Domecq's resistance some kind of personal crusade? There was the possibility that the man was an impostor, of course, engaged by an enemy corporation to upset Tyran's plans.

Colonel Perón had expressed clear concerns about the legitimacy of the man's ID, and she'd provided Tyran with a recording of Pryce's absurdly impatient acceptance of Domecq's credentials. Tyran's gut feeling at this point was that the man was indeed a counterfeit, but that should make no difference to the outcome of events. An enemy agent would have to possess the expertise required to carry out his task or he would very soon be exposed. The man who stood before Tyran should be more than capable of doing the job he'd assumed. And right now Tyran needed answers to his questions far more than he needed to reveal an impostor. But Domecq would never get out again with his information. In the end his subterfuge would be 'discovered' and he and his employers would shoulder all blame at official levels. And at all other levels nobody would ever know the truth about Ceres Alpha.

That was the way of the worlds.

That was what made Gaskill Tyran utterly invincible.

'I'm not going to play games with you, Domecq,' Tyran told him flatly. 'You've got the opportunity to answer some fundamental questions here. I can give you access to all the data we have on the creatures if you're going to answer my questions. It's a simple choice. Co-operate or… don't.'

Domecq considered his options, perhaps aware now that he had pushed his luck too far. He regarded Tyran with a brooding expression before coming to a decision.

'All right,' he said. 'I'll do what I can to solve your little mystery, Mr Tyran. But I want your word that the children won't be harmed while the work's being carried out.'

'The creatures are under the custody of Dr Pryce in Medicare Central,' Tyran told him. 'You will work alongside Dr Pryce to carry out your research. He has all the records. He is the only man who's followed these things from the beginning. I'll leave it to your discretion how the creatures are handled. But I must tell you, Dr Domecq, that those creatures are extremely dangerous. Pryce was a respected official when he took the role of their… custodian. The creatures have inflicted a great deal of damage on him. They've had a corrosive effect on his personality. He's not the man he used to be. Take very great care that the same doesn't happen to you.'

'Oh, I'll take care all right,' Domecq assured him. 'It's one of my strong points.'

'If you need anything, Pryce should be able to help, but I'm online here if you wish to ask anything.'

'One thing…'

'Yes?'

'I'd like to speak to the parents, if I may.'

Tyran regarded him darkly. 'I'm afraid that would be rather difficult,' he said. 'As far as the parents are concerned, their babies died at birth.'

There was a stunned silence while Domecq gazed off into space.

'You can access full records through the med comp,' Tyran reminded him.

Domecq fixed him with a frightening look. A look that spoke of vengeance and rage. His jaw became a solid line of resentment and he seemed simply unable to put his feelings into words.

At that point Tyran was startled to see the door swing open and Zach appear unannounced.

'I said I wasn't to be –'

Tyran's anger subsided when he saw the look on Zach's face, saw how he was holding his hands in the air and stepping into the room with measured deliberation. Then he saw the blood-spattered shape of Danyal Bains follow him in.

'Just the man,' Bains said when Tyran came into his sight. He was holding two pistols, one that Tyran recognised as Zach's, and the other standard military issue.

'Now, gentlemen,' Bains announced amicably, at the same time raising the military revolver directly at Tyran. 'I think it's time for a little conference.'

The perceptual goo, thick with thoughts from foreign minds, began to clear and Anji Kapoor found a white room materialising around her. As the feelings from her own body seeped gradually back into her consciousness, she was surprised by the lack of pain. Although her memories were jumbled with others', she could still remember what had happened outside.

With great care she tried to lift her left arm, the arm she'd broken when Fitz collapsed in the storm, and was puzzled that it felt perfectly fine. There were aches and pains, as if she were just getting over a heavy bout of flu, but otherwise she felt well. She raised her head and for a few seconds simply stared at her own body as if it were something new and unexpected.

Struggling to sit up on the bed, she rubbed her face and closed her eyes tight. When she opened them again she gazed around what was obviously some kind of hospital room, although the walls were encrusted with what looked like chunks of technology out of *Start Trek: The Next Generation*. The walls were also laced with pipes and ducting which ran everywhere, including the ceiling, giving the impression that the place had been put together in a hurry and all the services added later as an afterthought. The *Star Trek* analogy went up in a puff of lo-tech smoke.

She felt the skullcap that clung to her scalp and raised her hands to inspect it gingerly. The cap consisted of a plastic harness that seemed to have tiny lumps of electronics embedded in it. Anji tugged experimentally and found that the cap peeled away with ease. Off her head it looked like a shapeless mass of colourless straps containing hundreds of what looked like old-fashioned, multicoloured, impossibly small resistors. The thing oozed in her grasp like a jellyfish. It was the sort of thing Dave might have bought her for Christmas. Your very own pet robotic invertebrate: *love it and cuddle it and don't forget to feed it or it'll die. Made in Japan.*

Out of the corner of her eye, Anji caught movement at the other side of the room, and was startled to see the diminutive shape of what looked like an alien child draped in a squalid white gown. The child simply stood gazing at her as Anji stared back with what must no doubt have been a gobsmacked expression.

The child had the body of a toddler with skinny arms and legs and a slight potbelly. But the head was a huge dome that looked out of proportion on such a scrawny physique. Tufts of wispy silver hair covered its scalp in patches, and Anji was reminded of the images on the covers of the *Space Themes* albums Dave used to buy. She was drawn irresistibly to its great black slanted eyes.

Deep in those eyes she discovered a kind of fragility, a vulnerability and childlike fear that pivoted her instantly back to her own childhood – waking to Rezaul, her younger brother, screaming in the night. She remembered the look in his eyes as he struggled to get a grip on reality and scrabble free of whatever nightmare vision had pursued him in his sleep.

As she watched, the child produced a small white ball that it was at pains to show her between the three slender fingers of one hand. It took the ball in the other hand, gazing at her all the time, and she watched as it opened the fingers to show no ball. Then it opened the fingers of the other hand to demonstrate the ball had vanished completely. Anji couldn't help but grin as the child reached up behind its ear to produce the ball again for her to see.

The door buzzed open to admit a white-smocked woman whose face contained a kind of professional determination that told Anji immediately she wasn't about to fool around with conjuring tricks. But when Anji glanced back at the child, it had gone.

'I see you're awake,' the woman said briskly, taking readings from a trolley-machine at the side of the bed.

Anji wasn't so sure. She'd felt perfectly OK until the child had vanished into thin air. The woman was nodding in satisfaction at the readings, touching Anji's forehead with the back of her fingers, grabbing Anji's wrist to take her pulse.

'I'm Dr Perón,' she said while she worked. 'You had a very lucky escape last night.'

'I don't feel too bad,' Anji told her.

'Physically you're fine,' Perón said. 'There's some bruising that hasn't healed and you have a couple of minor fractures that are only partially regenerated. Another few hours plugged in and you'll be fit as a fiddle.'

Anji realised Perón was peering with interest into her eyes. 'Do you understand me OK?'

She nodded.

'We had some concerns,' Perón told her. 'But it doesn't look like we needed to worry.'

Anji didn't like the sound of that. 'Concerns?'

'There was some unusual activity in the mid-brain. We still don't know what caused it. Seems to be fine now, though. How's your memory?'

'Like a pan of mashed potatoes,' Anji admitted, but the woman looked blank.

'Name?'

'Anji Kapoor,' she laughed. 'I can remember that all right. It's just the last day or so that's a bit cluttered.'

'Do you remember how you got here?'

Shaking her head, Anji tried to interpret the muddle of images and sound bites that constituted her recent memory. 'There was some kind of emergency,' Anji told her. 'The Doctor had to force us down in the storm.'

'The Doctor?'

Anji simply nodded. She glanced about the room, looking for the child, but there was no trace.

'Dr Domecq?'

'Doctor who?'

'You were travelling with Dr Domecq?'

Abruptly gripped by an inexplicable alarm, Anji slapped her head into her hands. She was being interrogated. This Perón woman was testing her answers. She was dressed in a white smock, but there was something not right about her. Her bedside manner was up the creak. She just wasn't friendly enough to be a doctor. Too detached. Too cold. Something wasn't right.

'I'm sorry,' Anji babbled, 'I think I'm still a bit disorientated. My head's in a tangle. I'm still experiencing hallucinations –'

'Hallucinations?'

'I saw a child –'

'A child?' That certainly piqued her interest.

Anji wondered if she should say any more, if she'd said too much already. This woman wasn't who she was pretending to be. And mention of the child had focused her like a stick of ignited dynamite.

'You saw a child? In here? Can you describe it?'

'It was standing over there. Performing a magic trick.'

Anji realised suddenly how ridiculous she sounded and shut up. But Perón seemed more enthralled than ever.

'Magic trick?'

'The vanishing Ping-Pong ball. You know…'

She tried to demonstrate with an imaginary ball but it looked a bit gawky. She never was much good with that sort of stuff.

Perón was operating the bedside machine, opening a drawer that contained what looked like packs and tubes of medicines. She pulled out a disc and placed it in the palm of her hand, peeling away some kind of cover from the outer surface. While she worked she was speaking, sounding almost apologetic.

'Sounds like you're suffering post-traumatic visions,' she surmised. 'I think it's probably wise to let you get some more sleep so we can make sure everything's in order in that little brain of yours.'

Then she slapped Anji across the face with the hand that contained the pad. Anji started to yelp with shock but the sound cut off before it had chance to get out.

And then there was silence and black.

Back in her office, Perón activated the security 'gram and an image of med-ops bloomed into the air above her desk. Streaming back through the last ten minutes, she found Kapoor waking to gaze about the room, apparently not daring to move too much. The girl eventually sat up on the bed and began to examine the skull harness.

Perón watched as Kapoor's attention was snagged by something over by the wall. The girl was staring, puzzled at first but then amused. Freezing the recording, Perón called up a secondary set of readings that she studied alongside the inert 'gram. Satisfied that there was definitely nobody else in the room with the girl, Perón cancelled the readout but left the girl suspended in freeze-frame. Fingers working expertly, she called up the record from the med unit that was keyed in to Kapoor. Running back a few minutes, Perón located a point where the girl's graphs peaked suddenly. There was an adrenaline pulse and other cardiovascular evidence that girl had been startled in this time frame. Perón ran back a few more seconds before synching the 'gram with the med record, then running both recordings simultaneously. As she watched, the girl looked startled at precisely the moment her physiology went haywire. She'd most definitely seen something in that room, though the 'gram showed only her.

Running through a few quick adjustments, Perón called up the record of Pryce and Domecq's earlier visit to cell two. The picture wasn't too clear since the cells were so dark, but she could just make out Domecq's back to camera. Keying in all the image enhancements the software could muster, Perón managed to improve the picture marginally. She could see over Domecq's shoulder that he was showing the child a small white ball. A moment later the ball had vanished, only to appear again presumably from Domecq's mouth. At that point the creature actually smiled and reached out slowly to touch Domecq's face.

Fixing the image, Perón could only gaze at it in astonishment. There was a look in the creature's eyes that made her feel suddenly very uneasy. It was a look that spoke of trust and sincerity and turned upside down all the gut reactions she'd ever felt towards the things.

The image remained suspended above the desk while Perón felt that she'd been freeze-framed herself.

Until she slammed her fist on to the desktop to cancel the

'gram. Stupid. Trick of the light. These were aberrations that had eroded Pryce's sanity. They were dangerous freaks that had no right to be kept alive. Any innocence was guile disguised. And Domecq was obviously allowing himself to be taken in by it. Perón had a job to do. A mystery to solve. The legerdemain with the ball was obviously what Kapoor had referred to as the Ping-Pong trick. But how could she know what Domecq had done in there?

How could she know?

They moved silently through the filthy realms beyond the walls, a domain of darkness and dust, of circuits and service conduits, of spiders and rats. Rigged for combat and prep'd for action, they made their advance like a city-machine, steadily advancing through the superstructure towards their goal.

Captain De-ann Foley had been charged with the task of taking Bains out, once and for all. She'd been given free rein to hand-pick her own squad, and that team consisted of Klute and Downs, with Chyan and Massey for support.

The locator on Bains's stolen gun put him in Tyran's private offices. There were no sec cams in that area, so to some extent they were working blind. Assuming that Bains kept the gun firmly in his grasp, they could get a good enough fix on him to shoot him in the head. Downs was expert enough with the detector to keep everybody else out of trouble. The dilemma was that, with his injuries, Bains could well lose the gun to somebody else, and that might mean killing Tyran by mistake. Too risky. They would have to make an entrance, obtain sight, then kill. It made the op more complex than Foley would have liked, but she was here now and it was just another job to be done.

Downs signalled on her helmet and she stopped and waited for him to catch up.

'Four bodies,' Downs hissed, crouching so that she could see the detector. 'This one here is well bizarre. Looks like some heavy-duty internal enhancements.'

'That'll be Domecq,' she said.

'Well the other three must be Bains, Tyran and possibly one of Tyran's staff. Assuming Bains is the one with the pistol, we can position ourselves here –' he pointed to an inset window on the detector – 'here, and here. These are weak points. We could drop through there and there. That should put us either side and behind him. There'll be a right old ruckus when we drop through. That should be enough to shock him for a second or two. Let's say one second and we need him down. Otherwise we could have a bit of a mess on our hands.'

Foley studied the window, assessing the layout of the structure above Tyran's office. Downs was right, of course. He'd positioned them for maximum impact. That was his job. Her job was to get them back out alive.

'OK,' she agreed. 'Tell the others. We'll drop on my signal.'

There was a curious lack of satisfaction in the act of holding a gun to Tyran's head. And, now Bains had got the man's complete attention, he wasn't entirely sure what he wanted to do with it.

After some dramatic waving of weapons and shouting of threats, Bains had Tyran standing out in the open just where he could see exactly what he was getting up to along with Zach and the stranger. Bains finally eased himself into Tyran's seat and laid one of the pistols on the desk. He was engulfed in flames of pain every time he moved, and he suspected he might have internal bleeding. He felt dizzy and a more than a bit light-headed, so he had to get this thing over with quickly before it was too late.

'I want you to stop this machine,' he announced.

Tyran was shaking his head. 'Not that simple.'

'Of course it's that simple,' Bains told him. 'You just press the right buttons and apply the brakes.'

'There are no brakes,' Tyran assured him. 'Powering down an operation of this magnitude would take twenty-four hours. Have you any idea just how big this city is, Professor?'

'Then change our course,' Bains demanded, emphasising the

gun in his grasp. 'I can't let you destroy those finds. They're infinitely more valuable than your per-capita dollars, Mr Tyran.'

'We've had this conversation already,' Tyran reminded him wearily.

'*You've* had this conversation already,' Bains corrected. 'I wasn't part of it before.' He fingered the trigger pointedly. 'Now it's me doing the talking and you doing the listening for once.'

'You're willing to take a life to protect things that are long dead and gone?'

'I'm willing to do anything to protect the secrets of Ceres Alpha –'

He let off a random shot and everybody in the room jumped out of their skins. A wall panel exploded into a shower of flying shrapnel.

'Anything at all.'

'You found archaeological evidence of a previous civilisation?' asked the stranger.

Bains recognised him from Military One. He'd been dashing out with Foley when Bains was being sensitively escorted back to the cells. Bains had never seen the man before tonight, but he assumed he was part of the military setup. If he was in consultation with Tyran, he was certainly one of the top brass, despite his attire suggesting he was some kind of lunatic.

'Trinkets,' Tyran cut in. 'A crate of worthless animal bones.'

Delving into his pocket, Bains produced the triangular stone and cast it on to the desk. The stranger grasped it before anyone had chance to stop him. Bains levelled the pistol in his direction, but he was completely oblivious to it as he gazed in wonder at the detail of the stone.

'Worthless animal bones?' the stranger said, throwing Tyran a look that shot him down in flames. 'I doubt that anything you could refer to as "animal" could create carvings like these.'

He produced an eyeglass from his pockets and proceeded to peer into the intricate detail of the stone. Then he handed both the stone and the glass to Tyran, who threw them back on to the desk without so much as a glance.

'This is immaterial,' he insisted. 'This race is long gone. This land is ours, and our need is critical. Try showing that to Earth Central and see where it gets you.'

'That's just what we're going to do,' Bains told him, dropping the stone back into his pocket. 'I know what they'll say when I take this to Earth Central. And so do you. They'll stop work. They'll send out archaeological teams to excavate your precious planet. They'll spend years digging and brushing and conscientiously investigating. And in the meantime you'll lose billions. Worse than that: you'll be exposed as the criminal you really are.'

'People are dying on Earth for lack of space,' Tyran reminded him.

'People are dying on Earth for human greed,' Bains corrected. 'We live our lives in boxes. Feed our children synthogens. Extend our lives way beyond their intended spans just to spend that entire duration inside v-worlds and hologames. You can't just keep living like that, grasping all the space you can get your selfish hands on regardless of the consequences. There isn't a real blade of grass left standing on Earth. We're worse than locusts.'

'That debate is centuries old,' Tyran said simply. 'It was argued to its limits by our fathers' fathers and they made those decisions for us. Human life is the most sacrosanct thing there is. I'd like to see you convince people on Earth that they should sacrifice their children for the sake of these dinosaur bones.'

'Sacrifice their children?' Bains yelled, ignoring the agonies his shouting ignited. 'You can't ignore the lessons of the past. You could sacrifice every life that sets foot here if you don't understand what devastated that previous civilisation –'

At that instant a million things seemed to happen at once. The ceiling caved in with a crash that lasted for ever. Bains's suffering was promptly replaced by a kind of tingling shock. Black-armoured people appeared in the room, guns raised at his head. Tyran and Zach were obviously overcome by the same shocked stasis that affected Bains. But the stranger had somehow removed a pistol from one of the falling soldiers and now he held it to Tyran's head. The soldier appeared completely perplexed, wavering in the background with his empty hands held high.

'Ah, Captain Foley,' the stranger said cheerily. 'How nice of you to drop in.'

Foley stood almost directly in front of Bains, eyes everywhere, evaluating the situation. She could shoot him easily, but she was glaring at the stranger furiously. Out of the corner of his eye, Bains saw one of the other soldiers swing his gun to cover the stranger.

'I believe this is what's known as stalemate,' the stranger grinned, seemingly having the time of his life.

Bains could see the advantage slipping through his fingers. He was holding a gun on Foley, but there were more guns on him. He sensed somebody at his rear but he didn't have a clue how many of them there were. If he fired he was shooting himself. There was a good chance he would fail to do enough damage to make medicare ineffectual, but the others were experts and they certainly wouldn't. Bains didn't know how good a shot the stranger was, however, and, since it seemed the man was on his side, that redressed the balance somewhat. It was, as the stranger had pointed out to everyone present, something of a stalemate.

'Don't be stupid, Doctor,' Foley seethed. 'Put it down.'

'You first,' the Doctor responded jovially.

Tyran raised his hands in the air.

'Captain Foley,' he said, the strain showing in his voice, 'would you please put down your arms?'

'Sir?'

'I don't want this man hurt any more than he has been already,' Tyran said, obviously meaning Bains.

'Sir?'

'Would you all please put down your arms?' Tyran repeated. 'Professor Bains is going to walk out of here and book himself into Medicare Central, and you are going to return to Military One, mission accomplished.'

'This man is dangerous,' Foley began to argue, keeping the gun level and Bains in her sights.

'Captain Foley,' Tyran said more firmly now, 'if you don't lower your gun now I'll have you sweeping floors before breakfast.'

Foley lowered with all the reluctance in the world, and the squad followed suit. There was a tangible release of tension when the Doctor also lowered his gun and handed it to Tyran. Only Bains remained on full alert, pistol raised at Foley's head.

'You'd never make it,' Tyran pointed out.

Bains assessed the logistics of his predicament, already aware that Tyran was right. The gun dropped begrudgingly and he waited for Foley to shoot him dead. As he expected, Foley's gun sprang up and she took aim swiftly.

'*Captain Foley!*' Tyran yelled.

This time Foley gritted her teeth and jammed the pistol back into her holster. She turned on Tyran furiously.

'This man almost killed –'

'*Almost,*' Tyran cut her up. 'This man is quite obviously in a great deal of pain. Just look at the state of him. I think Military One have inflicted enough damage on this particular man for one night, don't you?'

'Sir.'

'Dismissed, Captain.'

Foley's stare stayed exactly where it was for long seconds, until she finally spun on her heel to leave the room by the conventional route.

'Captain,' Tyran shouted after her.

She stopped at the door, still quite obviously fuming.

'Well done,' Tyran commented simply.

Foley gave a hasty salute, before vanishing from the doorway, and Bains found Tyran regarding him with equanimity.

'We'll talk again soon about your role here on Ceres Alpha,' Tyran said. 'When you appreciate the situation fully, I'm sure I can convince you to see things from my point of view. Zach, could you please ensure Professor Bains reaches Medicare Central in one piece without blowing anybody's head off on the way.'

The guard nodded and took Bains by the arm, leading him through the door after Foley and her entourage. As he was leaving, Bains glanced back to see Tyran raising his newly acquired pistol at the Doctor.

The winds were dying as the first purple splashes streaked the orange morning sky of Ceres Alpha. It was a short-lived effect caused by exotic combinations of gases in the upper reaches of the alien atmosphere, and it was Ayla Damsk's favourite part of the day.

Stopping the survey buggy so she could simply sit and watch the sky paint itself silly, she switched off the engine. This moment contained a sumptuous serenity that Ayla understood she was privileged to experience. She was not a religious person, but she did believe in an underlying mysticism in the universe. An indefinable sorcery that linked all things. Magic without a name, without scientific rationale, a subtle thing she'd not recognised anywhere in any of the sacred teachings she'd ever studied. But it was definitely at work here in this miracle that was morning.

Closing her eyes, Ayla listened to the receding winds and imagined the sound of birdsong in the air. She'd never heard the real thing, of course, but she'd enjoyed the virtual reconstructions. With the smell of the soil and the cool gentle breeze in her hair, with a little imagination she could send herself back five hundred years. The time when the last birds sang. The time when the last trees fell. Her grandmother had known birdsong. Her mother had not. It was sad that two generations now had been deprived of such a simple thing. But it was exciting that Ceres Alpha could be a world where birds might be reintroduced from genetic records stored on Earth Central. Ayla's children could well be the first generation in half a millennium to hear the sound of birds. She smiled at the idea and opened her eyes to survey the land.

Deciding to leave the buggy and take a short walk, Ayla grasped her analyser and set off on foot. The ground was pretty even here, fine silt deposited by the aft engines of the city-machine. About thirty or so metres away she could see the lip of a ridge. The area might need some remedial attention from the diggers that scavenged in the wake of the city-machine, tidying up 'pockets' where collapses had occurred, filling in natural hollows and working localised basins.

On the way she bent to scoop up a sample that she dropped into the analyser while she walked, enjoying the morning and the breeze and the endless nothingness that went off to meet the far distant purple-orange horizon. A blue-white forever was replacing the deeper hues in patches, asserting its supremacy. The planet was covered in vast stretches of water, like Earth, and it shared with Earth certain qualities of colour. The sky was mostly blue. The clouds were mostly white. The vegetation was mainly green, although the indigenous foliage lacked much variegation and tended to plump for a grey-green homogeneity. Not very exciting, and not in the least bit palatable, although it was nutritionally adequate for human beings to just about survive on.

Reaching the ridge, Ayla peered down into a crater that stretched some hundred or so metres off into the distance. It was longer than it was wide, and ran to about fifty metres at its deepest. There was a good few days' work here for the team, and they'd be chuffed to be handed such a big job on top of all their other troubles at the moment.

Feeding the grid reference into her com, she took an image of the site before clipping the com back on to her tunic. Then she tipped out her sample and plonked herself on the edge of the ridge to enjoy the majestic splendour of the scene. People could live out entire lives without ever seeing such vast landscapes. She felt so damn lucky to have earned her position with WorldCorp. There were days when she just couldn't believe her life, couldn't believe her good fortune.

And that was what she was thinking when her luck changed and the ground gave way beneath her. She fell rapidly, scrambled for a hold, felt the dirt sliding beneath her. Glimpses of sky – then the thick heavy stench of soil. And darkness so complete that she switched into panic mode. Thrust her hands, clawed the dirt until she saw light, gasped for air and finally sat upright in the landslide. The motion had stopped, but she knew full well the danger that it might start again at any moment.

For a while she simply sat there with her heart thudding and the adrenaline coursing through her veins. Standing cautiously, she began to cast about for the analyser, but all she could see was dirt and disturbed rubble.

Then she saw the figure lying half buried. It looked like a man, upper torso and head picked out in relief against the background dirt. If you glanced you could easily miss it. He was covered in mud, perfectly camouflaged.

Alert for new movement, Ayla made her way over with great care and dropped to her knees to inspect the body. There was a pulse, but it was weak and irregular. As far as she could tell he wasn't wearing any kind of all-weather tunic and he didn't have an obvious com clipped to him. She couldn't imagine how he'd got here. You just didn't find half-dead bodies on Ceres Alpha. You just didn't find anything except dirt and sand and storms.

Taking him by the hand, she prepared to tug him out of the muck, but as she disturbed him he made a groaning noise that could have been pain or an attempt to communicate. She leaned in close to his face. Most of the sounds were gibberish mixed with moaning, but a word bobbed intermittently on the surface of the nonsense.

'Doctor…'

'It's all right,' Ayla soothed as she got on with the job of getting him out to safe ground. 'You're gonna be OK. We'll get you fixed up. Just hang on.'

But he was a dead weight and the ground slithered hazardously under her feet. They were near the bottom of the ravine, and it wasn't going to be as easy as she was trying to make it sound.

'You're gonna be fine,' she assured him breathlessly. 'Camp's only ten minutes away… We got med facilities there… Accelerators and drugs… Get you fixed up in no time… Don't you worry… You're gonna be fine…'

As she spoke, voice packed with phoney conviction, she realised abruptly that she was prattling more for her own benefit than his.

Tyran waved the gun in Domecq's face before dropping it on to his desk.

'I'm surprised by the speed of your loyalties, Doctor,' Tyran told him, picking up his drink only to find it full of floating detritus.

'I'm afraid I automatically side with the underdog,' Domecq said. 'It's an affliction.'

Dropping heavily into his chair, Tyran surveyed the mess that Foley and her team had left. There were gaping holes where several of the ceiling panels should have been, and the desk and floor were littered with debris and fragments of plastic. He prodded the desktop speculatively, and the nearby cabinet opened.

'You seem to be plagued by quite a number of afflictions, Doctor,' he observed casually as he poured two fresh shots of whisky.

Domecq shrugged, playing the fool. 'I don't know what you mean…'

Having handed him one of the glasses, Tyran returned to his seat. 'You seem to have a propensity for confrontation, for a start.'

Domecq sniffed his glass and gazed into the amber liquid, swirling it around as he spoke.

'I love a good argument,' he said playfully. 'Don't you?'

'I find them tedious, to be honest,' Tyran informed him. 'A game gets boring when you can never lose.'

'Oh, everything and anything can be lost,' Domecq assured him, his face abruptly cheerless.

Sipping his whisky, enjoying the flames that cavorted around his tongue before leaving their aftertaste of richly blended malts, Tyran shook his head.

'I'll tell you a story that has no middle,' he said. 'Seventy years ago a baby was found abandoned in the drains of Earth Central. When they rescued him he had chunks of flesh missing where the rats had been gnawing. He was basically dead from cold and malnutrition. That's the beginning of the story.'

Tyran opened his arms. 'And this is the story so far. That child became one of the most powerful men in the seven worlds. He controls his own private army. He owns extensive chunks of Earth Central itself, either directly or circuitously.'

Taking a sip of his drink for effect, Tyran watched Domecq's face carefully. The man seemed puzzled.

'I'll leave it to your imagination to fill in the gap. Suffice to say –' Tyran fixed Domecq with his sternest look – 'I've been called ruthless. I've also been called merciless, sadistic and heartless among many other things.'

A light came on in Domecq's eyes. 'Ah,' he said, as if he'd just discovered a lost sock at the back of an old drawer. 'You're threatening me.' He seemed peculiarly relieved at his realisation.

Tyran nodded and smiled. 'I don't appreciate having guns pointed at me, and if you ever do it again it will be the last thing you ever do.'

'I'm sorry about that,' Domecq said. 'It's not something I make a habit of.'

'Professor Bains is a strong-willed man with misplaced zeal. If you can forget all extraneous distractions and concentrate on the job in hand, I think we'll get along just fine.'

Domecq nodded, and Tyran was satisfied that he'd finally got the message.

'You can taste the oak, can't you?' Domecq said. Tyran must have looked completely blank, because Domecq lifted his glass and jiggled it in the air. 'It really is very good.'

'I only ever have the best,' Tyran said.

'And now you've got me,' Domecq replied.

Perón took the call on her com as she was about to check on the girl. She recognised the callsign instantly as Tyran's, and decided to answer without visual. Clipping the earpiece into place, she scanned the corridor before replying.

'Perón.'

'Colonel,' Tyran said, his tone clipped and formal. 'There have been developments. Medicare Central is under martial jurisdiction as of now. Get your own men in there. Use civilian technicians where necessary, but keep them to a minimum. Domecq is going to work with Pryce. He's on his way back now. Give them freedom to work, I don't want Domecq alarmed by a high-profile presence, but watch what he's up to. Let me know when the girl wakes. I want to question her personally. Oh, by the way, you also have a new patient due any moment. Bains. Get him in and out as quickly as you can. He sees nothing, talks to no one.'

The line cut dead and Perón couldn't help grinning as she put in her call to Military One.

When Josef woke for work he was alone in bed. He switched off the alarm and plodded down the corridor to find Veta in the nursery. She was on her knees in front of the holographic incubator, and when he entered she jumped to her feet and grasped his hand.

'Remember the room?' she asked him in an urgent whisper, as if she were trying not to disturb the baby.

'What room?' Josef felt as though he were still asleep.

'The room where we saw our baby.' Her eyes were wild and pleading. Her breath came in little shuddering gasps.

'In medicare?'

'Yes.'

Josef nodded, perplexed by the question and her fervour. Turning to the wall beside the door, Veta stretched out her arms.

'There was a window here,' she reminded him.

'Yes,' he agreed.

'And that was the only source of light.'

Josef nodded uncertainly.

'Look.' She grasped his hand and showed him the incubator.

He watched their baby lying there lifeless and the hole inside him opened up. He fought the tears that threatened to come.

'See?'

'See what?'

'The shadows are wrong.'

'What?'

'The shadows are wrong for the light. There – round his head especially. If the light was coming from over there, those shadows should have been more round the other side. Don't you see?'

But all Josef saw was the grief in her eyes.

'What are you saying?'

'What we saw was not our baby. It was a hologram. *This* hologram.'

He felt his eyes tingling with tears that fell when he shook his head.

'Don't do this,' he pleaded. 'You're going to kill yourself… us…'

Now Veta was shaking her head emphatically, squeezing his hand so tight that it hurt.

'*Look!*' she snapped. 'It's all *wrong.*'

He tried to take her in his arms but she pushed him away in frustration and anger.

'*Can't you see?*' she screamed, swiping her hand through the 'gram. '*Can't you see?*'

And of course he could see her desperation. He could see that she couldn't let go. He could see the madness that was overtaking them both and he could see where they were heading.

Consciousness came and Fitz wished it hadn't. Bits of him were hurting that he'd never known he possessed, uncharted regions of his anatomy that cried out in suffering and torment.

He opened his eyes and the light charged in to ransack his brain, crying havoc and creating a right old mess. He slammed his eyes shut again instantly and let out a low groan. Then he tried a different tack, simply lying there, endeavouring to listen through his thumping head to the distant flapping of canvas in a breeze.

There were other sounds, too. A low rumbling of machinery mixed with a higher-pitched mutter of what Fitz took to be a compressor. There was the intermittent clang of impacting metal and the unmistakable sounds of human whistling. There were voices vastly distant and an industrial clamour that Fitz recognised as that of a building site. Completely at odds with the far-off noise, he could smell a clean, antiseptic scent, and he was lying on a firm surface that his fingertips recognised as soft linen.

Risking the eyes again, he found himself in what looked like a makeshift sickbay. Most of the walls seemed to be made of canvas but there were dark-brown cabinets and other medical-looking provisions on metal racks. Alongside these, Fitz saw chunks of nifty looking hi-tech sheets of plastic that appeared to have controls painted on them in such subtle colours that you could hardly make them out.

Sensing movement nearby, he tried to move his head and immediately regretted it.

'Hey, steady on,' said a voice.

She leaned over him, sweeping into sight like some angelic vision. A snub-nosed girl with big brown eyes and a windblown brown bob. She smelled of honeysuckle and smiled like a cover girl.

'Where am I?' he tried to ask. But his voice refused to work and he sounded like a bullfrog.

'Don't try to talk,' she told him. 'You're in fieldbase Gamma Twelve. You're going to be fine, but it'll take a while to get you back on your feet. A few hours yet, I'm afraid.'

He croaked again and she leaned in closer, pressing his lips gently with cold fingers.

'Don't talk, I said.' When she was annoyed she looked a bit cross-eyed, which Fitz found very fetching indeed. She was doing something with her hands that Fitz couldn't quite see. Perhaps sticking something in the palm of one hand and peeling it back off. He realised she was touching has face and an overwhelming need to sleep swept through him.

'I'm Ayla Damsk,' she said, her voice drifting around in his head. 'You picked up some pretty comprehensive damage out there, but you're going to be fine. You were very lucky I picked you up.'

Yeah, thought Fitz as he slid down the long dark tunnel to oblivion. *Yeah...*

Domecq went straight to the girl on his return, and having followed him on the sec cams Perón was only moments behind. He was sitting on the seat beside her bed, stroking the hair out of her eyes, peering into her face with a fierce longing. Perón suspected they might be lovers, going by the way he watched over her.

'Did she wake up?' he asked when Perón entered.

Perón shook her head. 'No. There's still quite a bit of work for the accelerators to do. I think she'll sleep for a while yet.'

'Who took off the ECG cap, then?'

He fixed her with the very same look she employed in the interrogation cells. The fact that she was thrown off guard by the question must have been written all over her face.

'Her hair wasn't like this before. Look. The cap's been removed and replaced.'

'Oh,' Perón said suddenly. 'One of the staff must have made adjustments.'

Seeming satisfied, Domecq returned to the door. She watched him standing there, momentarily torn between Kapoor and whatever else he had on his mind. He was a curious figure in those odd clothes. His shirt was still torn from his walkabout in the storm, and his coat still carried the stains from his burial. The cuts and bruises on his face seemed to be healing fast, though, despite the fact that he'd spent no time at all on an accelerator. For a man who'd just gone through so much torment, he seemed full enough of energy, and she wondered for a second where the hell he got his stamina. No doubt those internal enhancements were serving him well. Still, she thought, she wouldn't be too keen on experimenting on her own body to that degree. This man

Domecq was pushing the boundaries of medical science into the Frankenstein arena, and that wasn't a place Perón would be happy to enter, however many storms it meant she could weather.

'I need to speak to Bains,' Domecq announced.

'Professor Bains is under deep anaesthetic,' she informed him. She remembered what Tyran had said about nobody contacting Bains. 'He'll be out for most of the day.'

Domecq seemed disappointed, then contemplative. Suddenly rubbing his hands together, he looked eager to get on, as if a switch had been thrown in his head.

'Is Dr Pryce still about?' he asked.

'I believe he's in his office,' Perón told him.

Domecq gave her a questioning look.

'Down the corridor, first right, first door on the right.'

'Right… right…' Domecq repeated, following an imaginary corridor with his hand. 'Right.'

He awarded her a huge grin. And then he was off. She watched him march past the window down the corridor, turning briefly to wave at her and grin again. As he disappeared from view she wondered about her Frankenstein analogy. There was another that suited him more and came from the same literary era. He wasn't a Frankenstein monster at all, he was Dr Jekyll and Mr Hyde.

Pryce jumped from sleep at his desk when the door buzzed open. He found Domecq standing there regarding him with an apologetic look.

'I'm sorry if I disturbed you,' Domecq said. 'The door was unlocked.'

Straightening himself up, Pryce waved Domecq in.

'No, come in. Please.'

Domecq dropped into the seat on the opposite side of Pryce's desk, making himself instantly at home. He seemed relaxed and amazingly awake.

'I hope you don't mind my saying so, but you look tired,'

118

Domecq informed him.

'I'm due for a rest break. I haven't slept for nearly twenty-four hours.'

'I mean *unnaturally* tired,' Domecq said. 'Like a man who hasn't slept for... two months.'

Pryce couldn't help but look up sharply, and Domecq gave him an amiable smile.

'You called them evil,' Domecq said suddenly, sustaining the pleasant expression.

'Yes.'

'I still think that was a curious choice of word for somebody of your... professional standing.'

'I called them evil because that's what they are.'

'They are?'

Pryce fixed him with a calculating look. 'They get into your head,' he told Domecq, tapping his temple meaningfully. 'You can feel them in there. All the time. They're a disease that eats away at your sanity.'

'From what I saw in that cell, that poor child's reaction when you appeared, I'm not surprised they treat you so badly. Perhaps they were using your own animosity against you,' Domecq suggested.

Pryce stared at him, momentarily dumbfounded.

'Just look at the conditions they're kept in,' Domecq went on, his smile now gone. 'They're treated worse than animals. And you call yourself a doctor?'

Pryce thought back to the days just after the babies arrived. He'd kept the Manni baby in his own apartment for two days while the annexe was added to Medicare Central. In those two days, he remembered clearly, he had regarded the baby as just that. A baby. A strange baby, yes, but he hadn't thought of it as a creature, or evil, or anything but a human being. It was only after they were all incarcerated together that the disquiet had started.

He remembered seeing the annexe for the first time, protesting bitterly to Perón that they couldn't keep the children in such barbaric conditions. He'd argued they should be returned to their parents. Allowed the chance of a normal life.

But Perón had reminded him of his debts and implied he could lose his job. She'd convinced him that these things were aberrations and it was for everybody's good that they were caged and kept under strict supervision. Following that meeting, he'd gone to see the Manni baby in its new cell and, as he gazed at it, struggling to satisfy himself that Perón was right, a kind of subtle metamorphosis had occurred. He'd seen for the first time a darkness in the eyes of the child, and for the first time he'd regarded it as something else. Something inhuman.

As Domecq waited for an answer, a kind of shuddering realisation dawned on him at that moment. Perón had planted a seed. The children had nurtured it. And Domecq was absolutely right.

Part Three

*And I lie even among the children of men, that are set on fire:
whose teeth are spears and arrows, and their tongue a sharp
sword.*

– Psalm 57, v. 4

Josef was in the middle of a delicate operation when Veta's call came through. The air above his desk teemed with multilevel lines of code on which he was running comparative diagnostics in an attempt to expose a rogue substructural command. The call had been bleeping annoyingly on his com for a few seconds when he allowed it through and Veta's head burst into the air in front of him.

She looked tired, with her dark eyes and face full of fretful lines.

'How long will you be?' she asked.

Puzzled, Josef answered, 'Why?'

'Come home now,' she said simply, and cut the call.

Josef stared at the strings of code that had reasserted themselves in her absence. And instantly the dread hit him like a giant wave of cold water. Cancelling the readouts, he closed down his console, snatched his jacket and rushed for the door.

As the elevator swept him homeward, his head was a jumble of worries. All day he'd been haunted by the image of Veta standing in the middle of the nursery. The look in her eyes as she insisted she'd discovered subtle lies in the shadows around the baby's head. She was grasping at straws, of course. Finding meaning where there was nonsense. And it tormented him to see her like that. To watch her crumbling daily, collapsing under the strain of their loss.

The few minutes home seemed to take an age. He couldn't imagine why she'd called him like that. She never usually called him at work, and lately she didn't seem to care *what* time he came in at night.

When he opened the door to their apartment, he found it in its usual state of clutter. Veta sat on the sofa, hands on her knees, watching him with a strange look in her eyes.

'What's up?'

'Sit down,' she said, waving at the seat beside her.

He did as he was told, not bothering to take off his jacket and perching on the edge of the sofa.

'There's something going on in medicare,' she told him.

He observed the deep shadow round her eyes, almost black despite the bright lights in the room. The lines of anxiety etched into her features were even more pronounced now than they had been before. He noticed that her hands were clenching sporadically, clasping and unclasping as if she were tugging an invisible cord.

'I wish you wouldn't do this,' he told her quietly.

'I'm not making this up,' she said.

He felt the irrational anger rising inside him, threatening to engulf him completely. He stood and marched across the room, turning on her fiercely.

'What did you find?' he demanded, 'More funny shadows? Fairy dust on his pillow? Did you enhance the image to discover a nebulous reflection of Beelzebub in the incubator glass?'

'*Joe* –'

'You're turning our life upside down for a trick of the light!'

She regarded him with fury that swiftly mutated into a sorry look. When she spoke, her voice was that of a frightened child.

'It's not just the shadows,' she told him. 'It's the dreams.'

He watched her in silence, feeling the tears that had pooled in his eyes. He wanted to tell her to stop, not to look back any more but to look to the future. Heal the wounds and try to build a new life for themselves. Maybe try for another child. But he couldn't get the words out into the air. All he could say was –

'Just… dreams…'

She shook her head. 'They're not just dreams. And the shadows *were* wrong. I just needed to know the truth, Joe.'

'We know the truth,' he said. 'Joby died.'

'Maybe he did,' she agreed. 'But what we saw was not our baby.'

He stepped back and knelt in front of her, grasping her hands and peering into those unsettled eyes.

'I don't believe what they showed us was a hologram,' he told her. 'But if it was, didn't you think there might have been good reasons not to show us the truth?'

'Yes of course,' she said. 'Joby might have been badly deformed. A terrible… monster. I know they might have been trying to protect our feelings. But all that matters to me now is the truth about our baby.'

He gazed at her, not knowing what to say.

'I've been into the med comps today,' she announced. 'I did it this morning, when you left. And now I *know* something odd was going on when our baby was born.'

He felt a stab of alarm. 'You can't just violate personal records. There'll be a trace on what you've done –'

'Oh, don't worry,' she said. 'I was very discreet. Set up phantom IDs all over the place. I used substructural idiom. Closed all the gates behind me and covered my tracks. It's what we do, you and me. That's why we were employed here. Nobody does it better.'

Clutching his hands, she pulled him gently on to the sofa again at her side.

'Two months ago there were staff changes made in Medicare Central. A handful of new people were listed on the personnel roster. I did some background checks. They were all military.'

'You didn't go into the military system?'

'Dr Perón was put in charge. She's a confidante to Gaskill Tyran. And she's a colonel in Military One.'

'They're gonna drop on you like a –'

'*Gaskill Tyran!*' Veta insisted. 'Do you know what he looks like?'

Josef shook his head, and she used the remote to open the comp. A face appeared out of a buzz of holographic static, and Josef was stunned when he recognised it.

'He was the man in the suit,' he said.

'He was there in Medicare Central while Joby was being born,' Veta confirmed. 'He never said anything, kept out of the way. I assumed he was part of the management team. But that is the great Gaskill Tyran. Now why would he be hovering about in Medicare Central while our baby was being born, eh?'

Josef was dumbfounded.

'And another thing,' she said. 'Some of the records are kept offline. Doesn't that strike you as odd? Medicare records not available to medicare staff? As far as I can see they were transferred directly to Perón's personal databook.'

'Records of straight birth defects would have been left available to the staff,' Josef agreed. 'However terrible they were.'

'Well I think those records weren't left online for one simple reason.'

'What?'

'They were a military secret.'

Josef glared at her.

'There's something else,' she told him. 'The staff changes two months ago were never reversed. Military One have been in charge of Medicare Central ever since. And today there were special orders sent out to all civilian staff to report to alternative posts. The military have total control now. And that can only mean one thing.'

Josef could only shake his head in wonder.

'Whatever that military secret was – it's still ongoing.'

'Oh my God.'

'Now do you think I'm being paranoid?'

'What are we going to do?'

Veta took a deep breath. 'We're going to confront them.'

Josef shot her a startled look.

'I already called Dr Pryce today,' she said. 'He seemed very edgy. Not at all the man we met two months ago. But he agreed to see us. Now.'

'Oh, shit,' he said.

* * *

126

The sound of a growling dog metamorphosed into the voice of a growling man, and Fitz was left with a disturbing half-dream impression of a big gruff bloke with a Doberman's head as he surfaced swiftly out of sleep. His eyes were on fire so he lay there while the sounds took form in his head. The building site off in the distance. Tent flaps thrashing in a rising wind. The rumbling of machinery.

Then he heard Ayla's voice, urgent and imploring, and focused immediately on her words.

'...certainly not well enough to be bullied by your brutes,' she hissed.

'Better to strike now before he's well enough to resist,' the dog voice growled. 'All I'm interested in is the truth.'

Fitz risked a look but Ayla and the man were the other side of the canvas sheet that made up the walls of the room.

'*Your* truth,' Ayla said angrily, obviously struggling to keep her voice down as well as her temper. 'All you're interested in is your version of the truth. Oh, this is very convenient for you, isn't it, Jörgan?'

'It's very suspicious, yes,' Jörgan replied.

'Well, I'm med officer here and this man's under *my* authority until he's well enough to fend for himself. You'll get a report from me first thing in the morning.'

There was a moment of silence before the dog voice replied.

'We'll see. I'll talk to Reeves and the others.'

'I don't care what they say,' Ayla told him flatly, 'this man doesn't leave here until I say so.'

There was a scuffling of heavy-booted feet and a short silence ensued. Then Fitz heard another scuffling of boots, this time much lighter, and he found Ayla standing in the doorway regarding him anxiously. He began to struggle to sit up but a buzzing warning filled the air and Ayla rushed over to restrain him.

'Hey,' she said, 'don't try to get up. You're not cooked yet.'

'No,' Fitz croaked. 'But I soon will be if that Jörgan bloke gets hold of me, by the sound of it.'

'Don't worry about Rassel Jörgan,' she told him, forcing a smile into her face that just didn't look genuine. 'I can handle him all right.'

Fitz allowed himself to be pushed gently back on to the bunk and awarded himself the momentary luxury of simply gazing into her face as she fussed with the array of fine wires between him and the monitor. She proceeded to poke at the machine with a slight frown of concentration and he thought suddenly that this being badly injured wasn't so bad after all. There were upsides to every down.

'So why do they want to interrogate me?' he asked.

'They just want to ask you a few questions,' she said dismissively. 'Jörgan's a bit of a drama queen, you know. A lot of fuss and palaver about nothing. It does his ego good.'

'So how come he's so uptight about me?'

Ayla shrugged. 'You just don't find people out in the field. You've got no ID and you haven't got a com.'

'A com?'

She gave him a curious look and he knew instantly he shouldn't have shown his ignorance.

'I must have lost it,' he babbled, but she didn't look too convinced.

'Can you remember what happened?'

Fitz could remember the hysteria on board the TARDIS, remember the Doctor plunging into the storm with Anji while he lay in the hollow. He could remember the earthquake that swallowed him. How could he forget?

But there was a pack of hungry animals baying for his blood and his instinct was to say nothing. The Doctor would be fine, he thought. The Doctor was always fine. Fitz just needed to tread carefully until he could get back to that city and look for him. Or until the Doctor came riding out of the storm to save his skin from the rabble.

He shook his head and she gave him a sorry look.

'But I'm not a spy,' he told her.

'Oh, I believe you,' she said. 'A spy wouldn't have been so stupid.'

'Hey. Less of the "so stupid". I could be playing the old double bluff. I could be anybody.'

She grinned and he watched her eyes sparkle before her mood switched.

'Now,' she said, abruptly businesslike, 'I think it's time you got some rest.'

She prepared one of the sleep-inducing pads but he grasped her arm, bringing her hand into plain view and peeling the pad back off.

'I'm perfectly capable of resting without being knocked out,' he assured her, folding the pad with care and handing it back to her, a little lump of squishy plastic.

Sighing, she remained still on the edge of his bed, staring straight through him lost in thought.

'Promise I won't disappear,' he said.

'You're not fit to get up yet,' she warned him. 'You had some pretty serious internal bleeding that's only just stopped and there's a danger it could open up again. Another few hours on the accelerator and you'll be good as new. But if you get up now you could be dead by tonight.'

He stuck his right hand into the air. 'Scout's honour.'

She gave him another puzzled look and jumped from the bed to leave. At the door she glanced back and he threw her a wink that most probably looked like a spasm. Then she vanished and he lay there with only the sounds around him.

His impulse was to sneak straight after her, but even the thought of moving made him hurt. He closed his eyes and weighed the facts. There was a good chance that Jörgan might return with his big brusque mates, of course, but Ayla hadn't failed Fitz yet. And it sounded like she was well used to standing up to this Jörgan bloke. But then, if he came back with his mates, she might not stand much chance against a whole lynch mob of dog-headed men.

If he could only get back to the city Fitz was sure he'd find the

Doctor, who was most probably searching for him this minute, and they could all get back into the TARDIS and fix the disease. He'd certainly be glad to climb back into his own bed with a good old-fashioned pack of aspirin and stay there for a week at least. Unfortunately, as he continued to consider the option of ignoring Ayla's order to stay put, he kept meeting with her parting words –

'If you get up now you could be dead by tonight…'

So there he lay, listening to the tent flaps smacking in the gathering storm of oncoming night. And mingled in the winds he imagined the baying of mad hungry dogs.

Anji emerged from the fuzz of sleep to the equal fuzz of being awake. She was still on the bed in the hospital room, but things felt… *strange*. As if she were still in a dream. As if she were seeing through the eyes of someone else. But the bombardment of foreign thoughts had disappeared. Her head felt perfectly clear. It was hard to define. But things weren't right. It took her a while to bring the feelings into focus, and only then did she realise what the problem was.

The need.

There was a simple, overriding compulsion that made everything else subordinate. Even her perception of reality came second to it. As she gazed about the room, she realised that it was glittering. The walls were twinkling, made of pixels, like computer-animated graphics. There and solid, but at the same time only constructs of a RAM imagination. Insubstantial stuff so easily lost. She felt like Lara Croft waking in a virtual world.

Only the need.

Sitting up on the bed, she gazed at the monitor unit at her side. The intermittent beat of her heart was a giant thing. Every pulse a colossal, dull note. As if she were hearing an action replay, played back at quarter speed, the sound reverberated through her head like rolling, repeated thunder. The monitor made other sounds. Sounds she was sure should be blips and beeps. But to Anji they were attenuated cries, full of coruscating tones and competing pitches, like little voices screaming out, millions of them in chorus.

Only the need.

The need to… what? In the heart of her heart, like a primitive calling, she felt it more clearly than she felt the room around her. But it was impossible to fathom. A kind of driving force to do something, but the something was just out of reach, just beyond her understanding.

Her mother handed Rezaul to her, and she took the tiny bundle, feeling contented and privileged at the same time. He was sleepy after his feed, but still squirmed in her grasp, occasionally flicking an uncertain hand up to his chubby cheeks. He felt warm and special in her young arms. Then she caught her first glimpse of his eyes, and a love so profound bloomed open inside her. She remembered that feeling – the comfort and rightness of it.

And then it was gone.

And then she saw him standing there. In the room. By the door. The alien child. Reaching out. Made of pixels like something not real.

There was no answer at Dr Pryce's door. They pressed the com again and again, but he refused to reply. Josef shook his head in dismay as they put a call out to his personal com. It connected, but there was no answer. Repeatedly no answer.

'Perhaps he's had an emergency,' Josef said.

But Veta was busy with the com, not listening.

'Let's go to medicare,' he suggested.

The WorldCorp logo materialised in the air in front of Pryce's door, and the WorldCorp voice greeted them in helpful, ingratiating tones.

'Can I help you?'

'I have an appointment with Dr Aaron Pryce,' Veta said. 'Can you tell me where to find him, please?'

There was an almost imperceptible pause. 'Dr Pryce has not

reported for work this evening, I'm afraid. If you'd like to leave a message, I'll see that he gets it as soon as he arrives.'

'No,' Veta said. 'That's OK. I'll call him myself tomorrow.'

'That's fine,' the voice told her. 'Is there anything else I can help you with?'

'No. That's all, thank you.'

'Thank you for your call.'

The logo zipped itself up into nothing, and Veta started work on Pryce's apartment door com.

'Hey,' Josef yelped in alarm. 'What d'you think you're doing?'

'Getting in.'

He glanced up and down the corridor.

'You can't do that.'

'Of course I can. It's easy.'

'I mean… ethically.'

She shot him an obstinate look while he watched the corridor nervously.

'Ethics? He lied to us about our baby –'

'We don't know –'

'*I know!*'

'What are you going to do?'

'I'm going to see if he's left his databook lying around.'

'You can't just –'

She grasped him by the collar and glared hard into his frightened eyes. He fidgeted nervously in her grip, unable to meet her stare.

'I can do anything,' she told him. 'Anything at all to get to the truth about our baby. If you don't want to help, go back home and I'll see you there later.'

He took a deep breath, waved his arms in a gesture of compliance, and finally nodded slowly with a resigned and rather silly look on his face.

'If anybody comes, just act like we're supposed to be here. If you persist in looking so neurotic you're going to draw attention to us.'

Josef's nodding intensified. Stuffing his hands into his pockets he strolled around a bit, obviously trying to pull himself together. Then he returned to her side and continued to dance from foot to foot in a state of agitation while she worked.

'Would you stop doing that?' she asked. 'We're comptechs. Nobody's going to question us fixing a faulty door com.'

The door swept open and she awarded him a satisfied grin.

'You keep an eye out,' she hissed. 'If he comes back... do something.'

'Do what?'

'Oh, I don't know. Create a diversion.'

She left him gawking up and down the corridor and plunged inside the apartment to find it lit with dull pools of yellow illumination. As she made her way into the empty living area, she wondered for a moment if she was doing the right thing after all. Despite all the evidence she'd found about the medicare staff changes, she could be making a big mistake. Maybe there was some simple, honest explanation for it all, and for Pryce's distinct edginess when she contacted him today. Maybe, as Josef had pointed out, medicare was simply covering up a truth that was too unpalatable for them to be subjected to. Maybe she ought to leave the whole thing alone. If Joby really were dead, knowing the whole truth might only hurt them both even more.

Yet something was driving her on. Many fractured jigsaw pieces that added up to an as yet unrecognisable picture: the look on Pryce's face when she called him; the fact that Military One were not only still in charge of Medicare Central, but had suddenly intensified their grip today; and the dreams. The dreams of a child still alive.

A child still alive...

That was a possibility she couldn't shake out of her brain.

The living area was tidy but pretty much empty. It was the room of a man living alone, but a man who spent little time at home. Everything had its place, and Pryce was clearly a fastidiously tidy person. That meant that his databook should be in the study along with any other work backups he might store there. Looking at the scarcity of family pictures in the room, Veta felt that Pryce probably spent a good deal of his spare time in his study.

The layout of Pryce's apartment was similar to Veta's own, and she found the study where the nursery was situated in their apartment. The light was on and the room was bright. She felt a stab of panic when she thought suddenly that he might well be in there, perhaps working and deliberately ignoring the door. She stopped in the hall and listened, but there was only silence.

As she pushed open the door, the panic returned when she saw him slumped over his desk with his back to her. For a second she was frozen with fear, but as the panic passed she saw that he was preternaturally still. Not even the rhythm of breathing. There was no response at all to the sound of the door scraping the carpet. He didn't move a muscle.

Then she saw the blood on the desktop. The blood from his wrists that had puddled under him and dripped on to the carpet below his seat.

She continued to stand and stare, unable to propel herself into action for a moment that seemed like forever, before she stepped forward into the room and leaned over to see his face. It *was* Pryce. His eyes were open and staring, his face and lips blue. He was leaning on his arms as if resting, and the blood had soaked into his sleeves. There were claggy damp patches in his hair where it trailed into the pooled blood on his desktop. Veta could see an old-fashioned metal scalpel lying discarded by his side, and the comp light was on, although the unit had closed itself down.

She found a remote keypad on a shelf under the desk and used it to reactivate the machine. The hologram opened above the desk to reveal Pryce's usage record for this afternoon. The bottom lines of the history intersected Pryce's head, and Veta had to adjust the hologram to raise it higher into the air so she could read it. Scrolling through the log, she found his last action, and caught her breath when she realised what it was.

The last thing Pryce ever did was to take the call from her.

* * *

When Colonel Perón arrived for duty the handover crew reported that Dr Domecq had retired to rest in the hospitality suite. He'd spent the entire day on Pryce's computer, however, and she was intrigued to discover what he'd been looking at.

Pryce's office was empty when she arrived, despite the fact that he was supposed to be on duty from almost an hour ago. Activating his desktop, Perón located the machine's audit folder and opened it up. The hologram above the desk was instantly filled with lines of information, and Perón was immediately shocked at the sheer volume of data Domecq had reviewed. Surely it wasn't humanly possible for one person to read this amount of material in one day.

He'd spent the first couple of hours trawling through Pryce's prenatal records on the Manni baby. He'd looked at scans and genetic sweeps, bio-profiles and a whole lot of detailed stuff on the foetal development. After the first two hours, it seemed he'd spent the next hour and a half constructing some virtual experiments on zygotic maturation. He'd tried bombarding the cells with all manner of radiation and other influences, including some attempted spatio-temporal contortions that the comps had rejected as unprogrammable. The results that those investigations alone had thrown up would take a whole team of medical professionals weeks to analyse fully. Domecq had spent less than twenty minutes looking through them.

He'd then reviewed the hormonal correlation already conducted by the medicare comps. He'd spent seventy minutes looking at embryonic evolution in general, but another forty minutes looking specifically at one particular day in the Manni baby's in-uterine life. He'd spent some time reviewing the same day in the development of all the other eleven babies, and Perón had to assume that he'd discovered something vital on that day.

However, that was where the audit trail ended and Perón was forced to follow a tenuous string of data that took her on a circuitous route to a dump file logged in the comp's bin-memory. The file was unnamed, simply represented as a featureless blue icon. The comp warned her that she needed a password to enter, and she regarded the icon furiously as she considered what might be in there.

Domecq had spent about three-quarters of the day investigating the creatures, but what had he done with the rest of his day? Thinking back to Pryce's ridiculous acceptance of the man's identity, Perón decided that she needed to get inside the dump file, and she instructed the comp to start work on cracking the password, giving the task Priority One clearance.

Instantly, the blue icon began to dissolve with a small sound effect like a scraping, wheezing noise. After a second or so of fading in and out of comp memory, it was gone without trace. Perón simply sat and stared in surprise at the hologram above Pryce's desk, before she slammed the desktop with her fist and put a call through to Military One.

The head and shoulders of a military receptionist materialised above the desk to replace the displayed contents of Pryce's comp bin. The young man snapped to attention when he realised who was calling.

'Colonel Perón. Can I help you, sir?'

'I understand Dr Domecq has retired to hospitality. Can you tell me where he is at the moment?'

The receptionist's eyes flicked right and a faint frown line appeared on his brow. She watched his shoulders move about as he fed the request into the sec comp. The frown line deepened and he met her eyes again with a hint of distress.

'I'm sorry, sir. We don't appear to have a trace on Dr Domecq at the moment.'

'Right,' Perón said, 'let me know the moment he turns up on the system.'

The receptionist was in the middle of responding when Perón cut the call to replace it with another to Gaskill Tyran. Tyran's head unfolded almost instantaneously in front of her.

'Colonel,' Tyran said. He was smiling, looking quite pleased with himself.

'Sir,' Perón said, 'we have a probable security breach.'

'I take it you're referring to the ubiquitous Dr Domecq?'

'He's been rooting around the comp system. Deliberately covered his tracks. Seems to know what he's doing. Could have been anywhere.'

'Where is he now?'

'Unknown.'

The smile was deteriorating fast in Tyran's features. 'Can you find him?'

'I think I probably can,' Perón told him.

'I'd like you to bring him straight to me, please. I'd like to get his report on what exactly he's discovered today.'

'Yes, sir.'

'Thank you, Colonel,' Tyran said, cancelling the call from his end.

Bringing up the readings they'd taken from Domecq when he was first admitted to medicare, Perón put a com call direct to Captain Foley.

Foley's head snapped into the air beside Domecq's readout.

'Colonel?'

'Captain. Report to Medicare Central. My office. And bring a detector.'

'Yessir.'

The head snapped out of existence and Perón prepared Domecq's readings to be downloaded into Foley's device. As her fingers worked expertly among the controls, a smile wormed its way across her face.

'You might think you can run, Doctor, but you certainly can't hide…'

Bains returned to his apartment with little remaining trace of his earlier injuries except for a vague kind of rawness around the ribs and a grumbling suggestion of a headache. What he actually felt more than any physical discomfort was a sense of astonishment. Considering the knowledge he possessed, and, perhaps more to the point, his determination to expound that information at any cost, he simply couldn't understand why he was still alive to tell his tale.

The thought struck him that he shouldn't question providence. He should be grateful for his life and keep his head low. Perhaps WorldCorp was gambling Bains would reciprocate and abandon his cause, accept Tyran's pay-off and disappear to another assignment as far away as possible from Ceres Alpha. If that was the case, then WorldCorp wasn't as shrewd a judge of character as it should be.

When he let himself into his apartment, Bains was puzzled to see that the lights were on. He remembered turning them off when he'd left last night, and he was very much a man of habit when it came to conserving energy.

Hanging his jacket by the door, he stepped into the living area to find it littered with his folders, handwritten records and reams of printouts. They were all scattered across the floor in what at first appeared to be a mess, but which Bains realised very quickly was no such thing. There were heaps of diaries that he could see at a glance were stacked in date order, and the other documents seemed to be fanned out in thematic sequence. A panoramic 2-D image of the main cave he'd discovered was arranged on his sofa, and other images were dotted around the room, most of them lying on the floor, but some stuck up on his walls.

As he gazed about in bewilderment, assuming that WorldCorp was about to instigate a spring clean for him, he sensed motion at the back of the room and discovered the Doctor standing in the kitchen doorway. The man smiled warmly and swept across the room to greet him like an old friend, grasping Bains by the hand and shaking it enthusiastically.

'Professor Bains. So nice to see you again. How are you feeling?'

Bains stared at him, briefly lost for words. 'Fine, thanks. What are you doing here? How did you get in?'

'Please,' the Doctor said, all apology, 'forgive the intrusion. But you were still under anaesthetic and I really needed to make a start.'

Bains indicated the mess in the room. 'A start?'

The Doctor raised his hand to show Bains the small carved stone that Bains had thrown on to the desk in Tyran's office. Bains's hand shot to his pocket where he kept the stone at all times. The Doctor was grinning like a child.

'This is most fascinating, you know. The detail. The craftsmanship. How do you think they were able to work in such minute detail?'

Bains shook his head. The images on the stone were so tiny that you could only really appreciate them if you used a magnifying glass. But all the evidence he'd uncovered suggested a very rudimentary civilisation without technology to speak of.

'I think they didn't use their eyes,' the Doctor suggested, seemingly playing around with a theory. 'I think they may well have worked in a kind of trance state, producing these images through precise accident.'

'Precise accident?'

'But the thing that really fascinates me is the shape,' the Doctor said, moving swiftly on. 'What do you think of this shape?'

Bains shrugged as he watched the Doctor grasp the little finger of his right hand with the thumb, pressing the two outer digits into his palm. He placed the stone between the three remaining fingers and Bains could only shake his head. The Doctor was grinning again, seemingly afflicted by a bout of effervescence.

'I think it's designed to be held comfortably by someone who happens to have three fingers, wouldn't you agree?'

'I thought it was decorative,' Bains said. 'Perhaps with some religious relevance.'

'Do you know what I think?'

Bains didn't.

'I think,' the Doctor said, 'that we need to have a good look at the site of your dig.'

Bains felt as if he'd been kicked in the teeth. He was still recovering from his last attempt, and he didn't particularly feel like trying again while his ego, if not exactly his body now, was still so freshly bruised.

'If you can get my archaeology permit renewed, I'd be very glad to show you.'

Shadow passed through the Doctor's sunshine face. 'I had in mind a more... informal visit.'

'Tried that,' said Bains, making his way towards the kitchen at the back of the room. 'Doesn't work.'

'Oh, but I'm something of an expert at clandestine operations,' the Doctor informed him. 'I can get us there and back tonight before they even realise we've gone.'

Bains left him standing there in the middle of the apartment and stepped through the kitchen to prepare himself a cup of tea. As he worked, he heard the Doctor enter behind him.

'I can understand your reluctance...' the Doctor began.

Bains cut across him. 'I'm very grateful for what you did for me in Tyran's office,' he said, 'but I really don't think I can face any more confrontations like that before I've had a good night's rest. D'you mind if we talk about this in the morning?'

'I'm afraid I don't know how much time we have.'

Bains deposited two cups in the oven and programmed hot tea, determined that he wasn't going to be rushed into rash action he'd very quickly regret. He'd get his own back on WorldCorp, all right, but there was a place and a time for direct action, and right here and now weren't either of them.

'I have no doubts now that my dig will be destroyed,' he confided. 'But I've collected a good deal of evidence already to make a case to Earth Central for a full investigation. I've decided that I can only work through formal channels. WorldCorp are going to face the music, but it's going to have to be official.'

Removing the cups from the oven, he offered one to the Doctor. The Doctor gazed at the cup without taking it. After a moment's silence, Bains found the Doctor's eyes on his, and they were full of what he could only imagine to be disappointment.

'No, thank you,' he said. 'I'd better be on my way.'

As he turned to leave, Bains felt a pang of regret. 'On your way where?'

The Doctor hesitated in the middle of the living room. 'I thought you were a man of powerful ideals. I thought you'd stop at nothing to get to the truth. I'm sorry if I misjudged you.'

He marched to the door.

'Hey, wait!' Bains placed his cup on the sideboard and picked his way through the paperwork to the Doctor. They stood facing each other for an uncertain time before Bains lifted his hand to show the Doctor a tiny gap between his thumb and forefinger.

'That's how close I came today,' he said. The gap closed completely and he squeezed tight and gritted his teeth. 'That's how close I came to being dead. And I was perfectly willing to make that sacrifice. But do you know what happens to all my evidence if I die? It dies with me. I'm the only link to the truth on Ceres Alpha. And it's vital that I survive to tell my story.'

'Organisations like WorldCorp are unassailable,' the Doctor reminded him. 'Men like Gaskill Tyran are untouchable. I don't understand why you are standing here now, but I really don't think a man like you is ever going to get off this planet alive.'

Bains sighed heavily. At the bottom of his heart he knew that was true. He didn't understand why WorldCorp had seen fit to let him live this long. But preserving that advantage, however slim or artificial it really was, seemed the most important thing right now. While ever he was alive, so was the truth about his work.

'I really must go,' the Doctor said quietly. 'I can manage alone, but having you along with me would have made things so much easier.'

'Hold on,' Bains said, grabbing his jacket. 'If you really are going to the dig, you'll need an expert guide.'

Appearing gratified, the Doctor swung open the door and they were about to march out into the corridor when they stopped dead in their tracks.

'Doctor,' said Captain Foley, swinging her rifle in his direction. 'What a surprise. Going somewhere?'

There were two armed military personnel at her shoulders, both of them big enough to have trouble getting through a standard doorway.

'Captain Foley,' the Doctor said. 'A surprise indeed. We were just about to take a walk. Professor Bains here has offered to show me the sights.'

'That might be difficult at the moment,' Foley suggested, at pains to keep the gun in plain view. 'Mr Tyran wants to see you. He wants a report on the work you've been doing today.'

'Of course,' the Doctor said brightly, turning to Bains. 'Perhaps we can do our little tour later.'

'Will you be long?' Bains asked.

The Doctor redirected his gaze to Foley, who shrugged. 'That depends on Mr Tyran.'

'In that case,' Bains said gloomily, seeing another chance slipping through his fingers, 'you may be gone some time.'

'Yes,' the Doctor agreed, an oddly resigned look passing through his features. 'I'm afraid you might be right.'

'I think I'll go have an hour in For'ard Obs,' Bains told him. 'There's someone I'd like to talk to if she's there.'

'You do that,' the Doctor said, touching Bains on the shoulder in an amicable parting gesture.

Bains smiled uncertainly, and the Doctor waved a brief goodbye as Foley marched him off down the corridor.

'Dead?' Josef looked as though he were about to wet himself. 'How? Why? How come you were so long in there?'

'He killed himself,' Veta said as they swept down the corridor towards the elevators. 'Just after he took my call, by the looks of things.'

'Oh Christ.' The elevator door opened and they clambered inside. 'Did you let them know in medicare?'

'No.'

'So what were you doing in there all that time?'

Veta watched the hysteria rising inside him, saw the tightness of his face and the quickness of his eyes. He looked like a man possessed.

'Calm down, will you?'

'Calm down? You've just found Dr Pryce dead and you're strolling about cool as anything. What's going on, Veta? What the hell's happening?'

Gritting her teeth in an attempt to keep a lid on her boiling anger, Veta grasped him by the shoulders and forced him to look her in the eye.

'I don't know what's going on,' she said. 'But we're going to find out.'

'What d'you mean?'

Pulling Pryce's databook from her pocket, she saw Josef's alarm intensify a hundredfold.

'You didn't steal his databook?'

'We borrowed it,' she told him softly.

'Shit!' His arms flew up, knocking her hand from his shoulder. 'You know what you've just done, don't you?'

She was about to respond when he continued like a barrage.

'You've implicated yourself. Don't you think it's going to look mighty damned suspicious when they discover his databook on you after he's just committed suicide? Have you got any idea what you've done?'

He punched the control pad and stopped the lift, poking the panel to take them back down. Veta instantly cancelled the instruction.

'What are you doing?'

'Taking you back. We can return his databook and put a call in from his apartment to say we found him.'

Veta was shaking her head, instructing the elevator to take them to their home level.

'Too late. I already did some work from his comp. We're going to Medicare Central.'

'*What?*'

'I took a look at this,' she said, waving the databook in front of him. 'There are a lot of antenatal records but all the postnatal stuff was transferred somewhere else. Pryce doesn't have any record of what happened after the birth. Don't you find that singularly odd?'

143

'So what are we going to do? Walk into Medicare Central and ask to see all their top-secret files?'

'That's exactly what I'm going to do.'

He looked at her as if she'd suddenly turned green with purple spots. He was apparently lost for words.

The elevator door opened and they stepped down the corridor to their apartment.

'I'm assuming that the postnatal records are kept by Colonel Perón,' she said quietly as they went. 'I set up a substructural glitch on her machine. When she turns it on, her entire personal system will collapse.'

'She'll call comp maintenance,' he said.

Opening the door to let them in, Veta nodded.

'I also set up an intercept on her next call to comp maintenance. The call will be rerouted.'

'Where?'

Striding across the living area, Veta switched on the comp and Josef watched the WorldCorp logo curling through the air.

'Right here,' Veta said, slumping into the seat beside the comp.

She patted the arm of the chair and invited him to join her, but he floundered in the doorway refusing to settle. Feeling exhilarated and abruptly more alive than she had done for months, Veta grinned at him.

'All we can do now is wait,' she said.

'Yeah,' Josef said bleakly. 'Wait to be called into the lion's den.'

Having spent God-knows-how-long drifting in and out of nightmares about being devoured by the ground and savaged by legions of dog-headed barbarians, Fitz decided he'd had enough bad dreams for one day. He took a deep breath to evaluate the pain levels in his poor, racked body, and realised with some considerable relief that he felt much better than he had any right to do.

Sitting up on the bunk, he prodded experimentally at the monitor, trying to locate the off switch. The thing began to screech in alarm, and his poking intensified until it fell sullenly quiet. Alert for the sound of boots coming clomping, he was thankful to hear only silence. There was a storm brewing outside and the clamour of the nearby building site had vanished.

He tugged the sensor wires free and hung them over the machine. Swinging his long legs over the side of the bunk, he immediately regretted moving when a wave of nausea hit him. He sat with his head in his hands until it passed, then got up gingerly to assess his balance. He was a bit shaky but at least he was able to remain reasonably upright. He felt as though he'd had maybe one too many on an empty stomach, but that feeling he was equipped to cope with from long experience.

His clothes had been taken and he was wearing a flimsy white gown that would make him a tad conspicuous out in the storm. He wondered if Ayla had been the one to undress him, and his cheeks flushed at the thought. There was something improper about a woman seeing you in the buff when you weren't conscious to make excuses or sheepishly flex the muscles you possessed. He began to cast about, looking for clothes.

There was a tall locker on one wall, and Fitz discovered a work tunic hung inside. There was fresh underwear along with Fitz's old boots stacked neatly in the bottom of the locker, presumably left by Ayla.

As he dressed quickly, Fitz heard the approaching sound of a nearby machine. Lifting one of the observation flaps in the canvas wall, he discovered a tempestuous night outside. The same combination of sandstorm and every other kind of storm he'd met when they force-materialised last night. Trust the Doctor to drop them in the middle of the hurricane season. Typical!

In the swirling squall he could make out the giant lumbering shape of the most gargantuan earth-moving machine Fitz had ever seen. It was painted in that standard yellow colour that all such machines throughout the cosmos seemed to attract. It was one of those comforting universal constants Fitz had discovered that made you feel at home when you were a billion trillion light years from Earth and the twentieth century. Except that this machine was probably bigger than an office block: the biggest, most fearsome machine Fitz had ever seen. So huge that the outer reaches disappeared into the storm before his eyes could discern the shape of it.

The thing trundled past on innumerable caterpillar tracks, travelling with surprising speed for something so vast. In the machine's searchlights, Fitz could make out what looked from here like a compound full of similar vehicles. They were like crouching monsters, huddling in the fierce storm, waiting their time to advance and to conquer. With an army of those things, Fitz thought, you could vanquish worlds.

He closed the tent flap when he heard the distant clamour of raised voices. They were like phantoms in the wind, but as he concentrated they became human voices rising in argument.

Pushing his feet into his boots and strapping up quick, Fitz was about to investigate when he caught sight of himself in the mirror by the door. The bright orange tunic didn't do a lot for him. He wasn't the stockiest of blokes at the best of times, but he looked ridiculously lanky in the overall. The long straggly hair did nothing to enhance his image, and the fact that it was still caked in mud and stuck out like something you'd buy in a joke shop added to the overall sense of calamity. Licking his hands, he hastily tried to tame the wilderness above his face, before conceding that he was fighting a losing battle. He flashed himself the Sean Connery smile and decided that when he got back to the TARDIS he really must make time to get a proper haircut.

The corridor outside was short and mud-splattered. An all-canvas construction that whipped and rattled in the wind. There were dull yellow lights strung from the ceiling, dirty and under-powered, which threw up gloomy spectres on the flapping surfaces. Fitz made his way rapidly to the far end and crouched by the flap that represented another door. Beyond was a further stretch of corridor, similar in construction but much longer. It was empty, so Fitz slipped through and risked following the sound of the voices.

There was a further door about halfway down and, as he approached, Fitz could hear the arguments much more clearly. Kneeling by the door, simply a double flap loosely stitched, Fitz found he could peer through the gaps down the seams. Beyond was a large open area lined with long tables and benches, evidently some kind of meeting hall. Men in orange overalls milled about in the distance, grumbling among themselves, while on a raised platform nearby, partly cut off from his view, Fitz could just make out the great bulk of a bearded man beside the slender shape of Ayla Damsk.

Ayla was speaking, her voice raised above the muttering of the assembled rabble.

'We can talk to him tomorrow morning. He needs to rest. He's in no state –'

'We can *talk* to him tonight,' the bearded man argued, and Fitz instantly recognised the voice as that of Jörgan, who had been so keen to interrogate Fitz earlier. 'I say it's quite obvious who and what he is. Considering the problems we're up against here, there can only be one explanation – *rival agents!* That man Fitz is obviously one of them. He must have been treating the soil when the collapse took him by surprise.'

While he spoke he swept his arms with energetic gestures and jabbed the air with his finger. He was a crowd-pleaser, a showman, and a general murmur of agreement rose from the mob.

'I don't believe he's an agent,' Ayla said, her voice equally firm and emphatic. 'And if he's unable to remember *who* he is there's not a lot of good in questioning him, is there?'

'This loss-of-memory stuff is just a put-on,' Jörgan claimed. 'He's having us all on.' Fitz saw Jörgan turn his back on Ayla and point with his thumb. 'There,' he said, jabbing his own back, 'see where it's wet.'

More ugly growling. Things were likely to turn nasty, Fitz thought, and he didn't want to end up on the messy end of a man like Jörgan. He began to back away silently from the door, but it was only when he rose from his knees that he felt the hand big as a shovel grasp him by the scruff of the neck.

Perón had returned to her own office when the call came in from one of her medicare troops. She took it on her personal com and the face snapped into the air in front of her. Perón recognised the young private as Danes. He was keen and looking for promotion, hungry for recognition.

'Sir. The girl. She's gone.'

'Gone?' Perón queried. 'Impossible. I set up an alarm on her med unit.'

What the hell was going on here with these people? They were making a distinctly irritating habit of disappearing.

'Sir. The med unit seems to be malfunctioning. It's reading as if she's still here, but she's most definitely gone, sir.'

Activating her desktop, Perón tried to operate the sec cams in med-ops. But the hologram that opened up above her desk showed nothing but a hollow void of static. The static proceeded to churn and coil in on itself, finally vanishing into a swiftly developing dark centre like water down a plug-hole. Gazing in consternation at the empty space, Perón prodded her desktop repeatedly with increasing irritation. The space remained just that.

'Get a search under way,' Perón ordered, the exasperation showing in her voice. 'She's in no state to have gone very far. And report to me immediately with a bio-detector.'

'Yes, sir,' Danes responded.

Cancelling the call, Perón regarded the desktop with a brooding scowl, as if that might magically rectify all the glitches and problems she was experiencing. She tried the desk again, but the scowl had achieved nothing, so she put a com call through to comp maintenance. There was a two-second delay before they answered, and then a harassed-looking man's head materialised in the middle of her office.

'Comp Maintenance, how can I help you?'

'Ah. This is Dr Perón in Medicare Central. My comp just crashed. Can you get somebody down here pronto?'

The man paused and looked away, presumably checking schedules.

'I can have somebody there in just under ten minutes, if that's OK?'

'That's fine. Ten minutes. It's Dr Perón. Just ask anybody when you get here and they'll point you in the direction of my office.'

The man smiled but his face filled with shadows for an instant before Perón cut the call.

Dr Domecq was in high spirits as Foley marched him to his meeting with Tyran. He chatted cheerfully about the city-machine and the work on Ceres Alpha. Foley managed to keep her responses to single-syllable sentences as far as possible, but that didn't seem to dent his exuberance at all.

As they entered the elevator and she allowed Domecq to program their destination, she kept the rifle conspicuously angled for use. Domecq apparently didn't even notice she was wielding it.

'Terrible weather we're having lately,' he announced, folding his arms and regarding her with something akin to amusement.

Foley couldn't stop herself from grinning. This man had been through hell and back, gone strolling off in a squall without storm gear, spent, according to the day shift, all day working intensely in Pryce's office, managed to slip out from under their noses for the last couple of hours until Perón had arrived on duty, and now, after all that, he was full of energy and chatting casually about the weather.

'Do you *ever* stop talking?' she asked him bluntly.

'If I'm drinking, yes. Even then I can sometimes manage a soliloquy or two. I spent some time with Edgar Bergen in the sixties.'

'Edgar Bergen?'

'*The Edgar Bergen and Charlie McCarthy Show*,' he intoned jovially, fanning his fingers before wrapping them back into his folded arms. 'Featuring Mortimer Snerd and Effie Klinker.'

149

Foley looked blankly at him.

'Ventriloquist.'

She shook her head.

'Of course, it's probably a forgotten art form now,' he said without moving his lips.

They arrived on the top floor and the door swept open to reveal Tyran's vast reception area. The place was brightly lit, with a noticeable absence of the pipe and wiring conduits that snaked across the walls in all other areas of the city. Up here the dampers were exceptionally sensitive and you could easily forget that you were enduring a helter-skelter ride a kilometre or so below.

As they made their way towards Tyran's suite, the Doctor stopped to gaze into one of the enormous pictures that adorned the walls of Reception. They were holograms, stretching off into an indeterminate distance, breathtaking vistas of rolling landscapes with huge mountains and pale-blue skies. She awarded herself the temporary luxury of sharing his wonder at the view.

'It's hard to believe, isn't it,' she commented, 'that all of Earth looked like that once?'

'Careful,' Domecq cautioned. 'You're letting your sensitivity show.'

Regarding him with surprise, Foley found his diamond-clear eyes penetrating her soul. For several seconds she was speechless, until she remembered the multiphase rifle cradled in her arms.

'You don't have to be a robot to make a career in Military One,' she told him. 'Come on. We've got an appointment to keep.'

His eyes remained on her, making her vaguely uncomfortable, until she jerked the rifle and he finally let go of the moment, allowing her to march him towards Tyran's office.

The place had been completely repaired and cleaned since Foley's spectacular, unannounced entrance earlier. The vast arched ceiling had been restored, and Tyran lounged in his seat at the far end of the huge desk. There were other people present, all men: Zach, whom Foley recognised instantly, three men in full-armament Earth Central military gear whom Foley didn't recognise at all, plus another man with long blond hair. Zach and the militaries stood to attention around the edge of the room, while the blond man sat on one of the conference seats at the side of the desk. Foley took an instant dislike to him. He was too smug and far too pompous even before he opened his fat mouth. And she had a keen sense of these things.

Standing and waving them in, Tyran smiled amicably at Domecq, offering him a seat.

'Doctor, please come in. Sit down.'

Domecq took the offered seat, throwing himself into it with gusto, while Foley tried to catch Tyran's eye for a signal of dismissal. Tyran noticed she was hovering uncertainly, and smiled in her direction.

'Please stay, Captain Foley,' he said. 'I'm sure we'll have use for your talents.'

She stood to attention, lowering the rifle, and glanced across at the other three troops who she realised were observing her as if they were assessing her fitness. There was something not quite right about the situation. Something false about Tyran's manner. Either Domecq had failed to notice it, or he was simply playing along.

'Now, Doctor,' Tyran said, 'I trust you had a very… constructive day?'

'Very much so, yes, thank you,' Domecq said.

'And you found the information you wanted on our comp system?'

'Yes,' said Domecq. 'I've been looking at the developmental histories of the… the creatures. I think I found some interesting data, but it'll probably take me a short while to interpret it.'

'Interesting data?' probed Tyran.

Domecq simply nodded, refusing to elaborate.

'I understand from Dr Perón that you deliberately concealed a large part of your audit trail for this afternoon.'

From where she stood, Foley could view only a section of the

Doctor's face. She could see, however, enough of a profile to know that he was grinning.

'Did I? Perhaps it was a comp glitch. They can be very temperamental sometimes, I understand.'

'Oh, you understand a very great deal about comp systems, Doctor,' Tyran told him.

'I know you need to back up regularly,' Domecq said. 'And it's a good idea to keep your diskettes away from household items that generate electromagnetic fields.'

'Don't play games with me, Doctor,' Tyran warned, suddenly deadly serious.

'Why not?' Domecq responded as if this were some whimsical banter. 'You're playing games with me.'

'Yes,' said Tyran. 'But this time I'm the one with the guns.'

'So I noticed.' Domecq glanced around the room at the armed presence. 'They do seem to be very much in evidence today.'

Pushing himself back in his seat, Tyran watched Domecq with a dark scowl. If he'd expected Domecq to start squirming at this point, he was going to be disappointed. Domecq crossed his legs and appeared completely relaxed and at home.

'Who are you?' Tyran asked.

'We've already been introduced.'

'Then perhaps I should introduce you,' Tyran suggested gravely, indicating the blond man sitting opposite Domecq, 'to the *real* Dr Domecq…'

Jörgan was a grizzly bear of a man with an ugly face and an even uglier attitude. His broad, squashed face was rimmed with frizzy hair and a beard, and his hands were as wide as Fitz's shoulders. Or, at least, that was how he appeared to Fitz when he was thrown to his knees in front of the man-mountain.

'Found him sneaking about outside,' grunted the Neanderthal who had grasped Fitz by the collar and lifted him bodily off his feet to whisk him into the meeting hall.

Jörgan smiled and his face grew uglier still, if that was possible.

'Too ill to talk, eh?' he scoffed.

Ayla shot Fitz a fierce look.

'He should be in sickbay. He's not well enough to be off the med unit.'

'Looks all right to me.'

'He's still under my supervision.'

'Looks like he just signed himself out.'

'Look at the state of him,' Ayla argued. 'He's not fit to be wandering about.'

Fitz glanced from one to the other as if he were at a tennis match, before finally raising his hands.

'Hey, if you two want to argue it out, I'll just get myself back off to bed, shall I?'

Clicking his fingers decisively at the Neanderthal, Jörgan pointed to a nearby chair. Fitz was abruptly airborne again and landed on the seat, which was a metal thing that Fitz met with a thud. The tight grasp at the back of his neck didn't loosen while Jörgan paced about on the stage. He was six foot four, Fitz estimated, and nearly as wide as he was tall. If things were going to get physical, Fitz had about as much chance as the proverbial cat in hell.

'What were you doing out in the field?' Jörgan demanded.

'We crash-landed.'

'We?'

'Three of us. Me, the Doctor and Anji.'

Jörgan appeared suspicious at this admission, but Fitz saw Ayla's face brighten at the news.

'Where are the others?' Jörgan demanded.

Fitz shrugged. 'They were heading for the city.'

'The city?' Ayla asked, suddenly urgent.

'Anji was ill. The Doctor was taking her to the city to get help.'

Ayla grinned triumphantly at Jörgan.

'There,' she said. 'I think we ought to put a call in, don't you?'

Jörgan appeared more than a little disappointed, but he conceded grudgingly. By the time he'd reached into his pocket for his communicator, Ayla had put in the call and an animated holographic logo materialised in front of them that showed a blue sunny sky with a flock of birds in the approximate shape of an elongated *W*.

'Can I help?' the logo asked, while the birds wheeled about in their virtual sky.

'Ayla Damsk. Fieldbase Gamma Twelve. I need to talk to someone about new arrivals.'

'Hold, please.'

While they waited, Fitz gazed round at the gathered vultures. They were a mean-looking crew, like characters out of an old pirate film. He could just imagine them with wooden legs and hooks for hands. They all wore the same grimy orange overalls with the WorldCorp insignia, and they all wore the same fatigued and fed-up expressions.

The holographic logo fizzled a few times before a woman's head appeared in its place. The head looked about as unfriendly as any that Fitz had come across today, although it didn't appear as uncultured as the mob around him now. She had short-cropped dark hair and a thick jaw that reminded Fitz of a man's. Her eyes were dark stones, and she regarded Ayla impatiently.

'You were asking about new arrivals?' Perón asked.

'Yes,' said Ayla Damsk.

'Why?'

'We found a man this morning. Badly injured out in the field. He claims he had companions heading for the city last night.'

'He's conscious now?'

'Yes.'

'Put him on.'

There was a short bout of static and motion while Damsk clipped her com to the man's lapel. The com took a split second to reorientate itself, and finally a scruffy, wide-eyed head appeared in the air above Perón's seat. He was a youngish man, slim with slightly crooked features that suggested he had no money for enhancements, which suggested to Perón that he had no right being able to afford to travel to Ceres Alpha legitimately. There was a good chance that they might be able to get some information out of this one.

'You had companions?' she asked him.

'Yes. They were heading for the city when we crash-landed last night.'

'You crash-landed?'

The man appeared momentarily unsure of himself. 'Yeah.'

'How many of you were there?'

'Me, the Doctor and Anji.'

'No more?'

'No.'

'Why did you come here?'

'We were forced down. Our ship had some kind of... problem.'

'What kind of problem?'

'I'm not sure. It's all a bit technical for me.'

He was lying, and she was wasting her time over the com. Gritting her teeth in frustration, she briefly considered travelling out to Gamma Twelve, but it would take time she didn't have right now, and there were other priorities here. While she was considering her options, there was a buzz at the door and she saw through her obs window that it was a young comptech.

'Give me Damsk,' she snapped.

Loss of signal, then Damsk's head reappeared.

'I want that man questioned. I want to know who he is and what he's doing here, d'you understand? I want the truth, and I want it fast.'

Damsk looked distressed. 'But he's still under medical supervision.'

'He's well enough to talk,' Perón told her.

'He's suffering concussion.'

'He's having you on,' Perón sneered. 'Question him now and report back as soon as you know who he is and who he's working for.'

155

'No. I'm med officer here, and I say he's not fit to be questioned.'

'You're talking to Colonel Perón of Military One,' Perón said, feeling the anger boiling up inside her. 'I would advise you not to question my orders.'

'And I would advise you not to question my patient.' Damsk stuck firm. 'He'll be well enough to talk to you in the morning. I'll call you back then.'

The call was cancelled and Perón snarled, jumping out of her seat to get the door.

After a few seconds' delay, the door buzzed open and Veta recognised Colonel Perón from her military files. Perón was in dark temper, obviously fuming but trying to keep a cap on her rage.

Lifting her databook, Veta forced a smile into her cheeks that felt all wrong.

'Comp maintenance,' she announced, trying to sound friendly and official. 'I'm looking for Dr Perón.'

'You found her,' Perón said, waving Veta into the office.

It was a fairly spacious room. Bigger than Pryce's office. Veta was struck by a noticeable lack of personal possessions. Like Pryce, Perón didn't seem to need reminders of her family while she was at work.

Standing by her chair at the back of the desk, Perón was waving her hands around trying to activate the desktop.

'There. See. It's completely dead. Collapsed as soon as I turned it on today.'

'No problems recently?' Veta asked. 'No warning signs at all?'

'Minor glitches.' Perón shrugged.

Veta squeezed another smile into her face. 'There're some funny things happening lately.'

'You can say that again.'

Slumping into the seat, Veta used her security key to unclip the access panel on the edge of the desk, revealing the interface that would allow her inside the comp. Hovering at her shoulder, Perón appeared uneasy, as if she needed to be elsewhere but didn't want to leave Veta alone.

'I have one or two things to sort out,' she informed Veta at last. 'I'm going to have to leave you to it.'

'No problem,' Veta said. 'I'm sure I can manage.'

Perón was heading out the door when Veta suddenly spurted, 'Oh! Passcode!'

'Passcode?'

'I'm going to need it to even get this thing started, I'm afraid. If you're worried about security, you can always set up a new one as soon as I've done.'

Again, that look of angry frustration, as if Perón had too many irons in the fire and the fire were getting over stoked. She hesitated at the door, uncertain.

'Libra-one,' she said abruptly.

'Libra One?'

Perón spelled it out and Veta nodded at each letter.

'OK. Shouldn't be long,' Veta said brightly, forcing a confident smile into her face. 'You leave it with me.'

For a dreadful moment, she feared Perón was about to change her mind and hang around to watch, but, after a second of uncertainty, Perón gave her a brief nod before leaving.

Leaving the comptech to work on her machine, Perón stormed into Pryce's office and closed the door, checking the security light was illuminated before she tried to call Foley. The WorldCorp logo informed her that Foley was currently offline, so she put another call in to Military One. She got a green-cap receptionist, a young man who looked as though he'd just got out of school and just got out of bed. He didn't even straighten to attention when he saw her. She raised his name and rank under his image for reference.

'Where's Captain Foley?' she barked.

The young man looked aside, then back at Perón. 'Offline at the moment, sir.'

She was amazed he'd remembered to add the 'sir'.

'I know she's offline,' Perón seethed. 'I asked where she is.'

Again he looked aside briefly. 'She's in Gaskill Tyran's offices, sir. There's a call silence set up. No indication of how long it might last, I'm afraid.'

'Get a unit out to Gamma Twelve,' Perón demanded. 'They've got a visitor there I want back here. I've put a trace on Dr Pryce. He seems to have vanished off the face of the planet. His com may be faulty. Keep trying for me, and as soon as Captain Foley's back online get her to look for him and report back to me. And next time I see you, if you've not had a comb through that hair, I'll have you cleaning toilets for the next six months, Private Szymanowski.'

At last he straightened to attention as if she'd put her boot up his backside.

'Yes, sir.'

She cut the call, and another was waiting. Private Danes.

'We got a fix on the girl, sir.'

'Where is she?'

Danes shook his head, unsure of himself.

'Well this thing says she's toplevel, sir.'

'Where on toplevel?'

'According to the readings, she's outside.'

'How the hell did she get outside?' she fumed rhetorically. 'Where are you now, Danes?'

'Reception Sixteen. We're just about to go out, sir. The storms are pretty severe and the readings are a bit wild. We'll have to carry out a manual search.'

'I'm coming up. I'll meet you out there.'

'Yes, sir.'

Danes's head cut and Perón took a moment to gather her thoughts. Things were getting a bit wild, all right. And now, with more of these disappearing people arriving out in the field, there was a good chance that the situation was going to escalate. It didn't have the hallmarks of a military op, but it was clear to Perón now that they had rival agents at work all over the place.

The field troubles could only be a result of infiltration by a rival corporation, and it was becoming more obvious by the minute that the worsening comp difficulties were also linked to the same agent activity.

She really needed to get a complete security scan under way, review the personnel files and look seriously at anybody who might have links with rival organisations. That would be a huge task, but it was one that she could look at getting under way as soon as she could talk to Tyran.

For the moment, her priority was to get the girl back. It wasn't going to look too good if she lost somebody in whom Tyran had shown so much personal interest.

To Foley's dismay, when Tyran introduced the real Domecq, the impostor Domecq jumped up from his seat and rushed round the desk to shake hands. Domecq seemed as taken aback by this as everybody else, and there were suddenly more guns in evidence than ever.

'Dr Domecq,' the other Doctor said, a great grin slapped across his face, completely ignoring the Earth Central firepower aimed directly at his head. 'It's a great pleasure…'

At a signal from Tyran, Zach swept forward and grasped the impostor Doctor by the shoulder, levelling his pistol smoothly to his head. Raising his hands, the Doctor allowed Zach to guide him back to his seat. While Tyran paced about the open space beside his chair, Zach remained at the Doctor's shoulder and the gun remained firmly at his temple.

'Now,' Tyran said quietly. 'Shall we start again?'

'Start again?'

'Who are you?'

'I'm the Doctor.'

'What's your name?'

'I don't know.'

'You don't know your name?'

'It's a long, long story.'

159

'I bet it is. But one way or another, you're going to tell it to me.'

Standing now in front of the impostor, Tyran was passing from hand to hand what looked to Foley like a short rubber truncheon. She found Tyran's eyes on hers, and glimpsed in them such a profound vacuum of pity that it made her shiver.

'Cuffs, Captain Foley.'

It took a second for the command to register, but when it did she stepped forward and slipped the cuffs around the Doctor's wrists. He didn't struggle, didn't resist. She clipped them into place, but left them as loose as she possibly dared. Captain Foley had been assigned interrogation duties before, and it wasn't a part of her job she particularly enjoyed. Military combat was one thing, beating the shit out of a potentially innocent civilian was entirely another. And in her brief engagements with this alias Domecq, she'd somehow managed to forge a kind of begrudging respect for the man.

Smiling now, Tyran raised the truncheon like a gun in front of him, and Foley realised with shock and horror that it was a probe. Banned for three hundred years, it was a piece of technology that even Earth Central military didn't stoop to utilise. Its use was the only crime in the seven worlds that carried the death penalty.

'Now,' said Tyran, 'I think it's time to see what dirty little secrets you have locked away in that head of yours.'

As she caught the scent of ozone, Foley saw the Doctor spasm in his chair. The walls abruptly darkened, pulsing with thick intermingled colours. The colours swirled and combined, producing areas that may or may not have been suggestions of images. Faces appeared briefly. She recognised the girl in medicare. There and gone in an instant. The face of a man with long straggly hair. The blue wooden crate she'd brought into storage. More faces, flashing transiently through the walls like so many ghosts in flight. Memories of people he'd known. Ephemeral moments in his life.

Perched on the edge of the desk, gazing around the walls at the contents of the Doctor's head, Tyran seemed satisfied with the results. The Doctor was breathing hard, the air hissing through his teeth in short, harsh bursts. He was straining at the cuffs, his arms stiff and shoulders hunched in God-knows-what agonies. Foley felt physically sick just being there.

'Who are you?' Tyran asked evenly, almost politely.

The walls were filled with the Doctor's face, multiple images gazing at them like reflections in a shattered mirror. Eyes wide open and fingers at the lips, exploring as if seeing itself for the first time.

The Doctor gasped, arching backwards in the seat.

'Name.'

'I... don't... know...'

'Name.'

'*I... don't... know...*'

'Don't be stupid,' Tyran advised. 'This is on the first setting. I can take it up much, much further. It's your choice.'

'*John... Smith...*'

'Smith?'

'*Doctor... John... Smith...*'

'Who do you work for?'

'*I... work... for... no... one...*'

'*Who?*' Tyran shrieked.

'No... one...'

He made an adjustment to the probe. The Doctor screamed. Foley felt her grip on her rifle tighten. The other people in the room were standing there watching, expressions impassive, while the real Domecq looked on, fascinated. She felt her teeth grinding and wondered how much more of this she could watch.

The multiple images of the face were growing bigger, as if they were moving into close-up, their edges merging. For a second the whole room went completely black as the images vanished, then instantly reappeared.

'*Who sent you?*'

Tyran was yelling now, his face red with fire and frustration.

'*We... crashed...*'

'*Who sent you?*'

'*Travellers…*'

'*Who?*'

'*We're… travellers…*'

'*Who do you work for?*'

'*Innocents…*'

'*You can't hold out for ever. Tell me your name.*'

'*Smith…*'

'*Your real name.*'

'*No… name…*'

'*Name!*'

'*I… am… the… Doctor…*'

By now the images on the walls were so close up that Foley could see only the eyes. They came closer. Closer. One eye. One huge eye a hundred times over, covering the walls and the ceiling. Again the image blacked momentarily. Tyran swiped the probe, slamming the Doctor under the chin. The walls blacked. Came back. One huge eye that was blue and green both at the same time. Closer still. Closer still –

'*Who are you?*'

The Doctor slumped forward in the seat, only the cuffs stopping him from tumbling on to the floor. Zach grasped his shoulder and yanked him back. Tyran punched him in the gut and he collapsed with a roar. Zach dragged him up by the hair.

'*…mystery…*'

'*What?*'

'*…mystery…*'

The Doctor was breathing hard and fast. Tyran bent to hear what he was trying to say. Foley could just make out the words.

'*…I… don't… know…*'

The steady close-up was now focused on the pupil of the eye. The iris had gone and there was only empty black. A fathomless, frightening dark so deep that it made her skin crawl.

The first few blows were always the worst. They could be a bit of a shock to the system, but it doesn't take long before the mental shutters slide down and you close your eyes and lock your brain to the pain. After that it's pretty much plain sailing, really.

The hologram call to Colonel Perón hadn't gone Fitz's way at all. It had strengthened Jörgan's argument that the 'spy' should be interrogated without delay. Ayla had stuck to her guns, standing up to Jörgan with such vigour that Fitz had thought she'd got away with it. But the lynch mob had turned nasty, and the tide of opinion was too much for her to repel. She'd done her best, bless her. But - *hey!* - the best of the best just isn't good enough sometimes. She'd been forced to make a hasty retreat and leave him at their mercy.

Mercy! The questions tumbled over him in a barrage. Who the hell was he? Where the hell did he come from? Who the hell did he work for? What the hell were his employers doing to the soil? Why the hell…? When the hell…? Who the hell…?

Being dumped into the middle of the unknown, without cultural knowledge or identity, without awareness of even the most rudimentary mores, was hard enough when you had time to absorb some information. Fitz normally prided himself on his natural flair for pretence. For fitting in most places where people had two arms, two eyes, pink skin et cetera. But waking up in the middle of an interrogation tends to put one at a slight disadvantage. The TARDIS often magically endowed its occupants with the ability to understand and speak the local idiom, but even then it couldn't possibly instil all the knowledge you needed not to make a complete arse of yourself if you weren't ultra-careful.

So the questions came. But the answers didn't. At least, obviously, not the right ones.

He'd tried being vague, spouting stuff about the crash, about his loss of memory, about all this being an accidental incursion, but the more he spoke - the more they punched. In a state of swift-approaching delirium, he'd even tried telling them the truth. And that was when they got really pissed off with him.

Jörgan was sweating and slightly out of breath from his

exertion. He stood in front of Fitz with his fists clenched, ready to start again. Fitz tried to bend forward, to raise his hands to protect his face or his stomach, but his arms were gripped tight from behind, presumably by one or more of the Neanderthals. It was getting harder to breathe, the pain erupting inside him every time he tried. He could taste blood but he was pretty sure all his teeth were still in place. His nose was full of thick stuff that could have been anything, so he was forced to hiss through his clenched teeth.

He found Jörgan's frizzy face only half an inch in front of his nose. So close he could smell the stench of his hairy breath.

'It's simple enough,' Jörgan said quietly. 'Just start talking and you stop hurting. Savvy?'

'I told you,' Fitz gargled. 'I'm not a spy. We crash-landed.'

Eyes glinting, Jörgan smiled sweetly in his face. Fitz saw the fists clench, draw back, closed his eyes, waited for the damage –

It didn't arrive. He opened his eyes to find Jörgan's face still immediately in front of his own, but this time it was drained of all humour, stock-still, and the eyes were hard right. Fitz's arms were steadily released, and through the haze of pain he saw Ayla standing beside Jörgan with a dumpy handgun held to his head.

'No sudden, violent moves,' she said.

'Don't be stupid,' Jörgan growled.

Ayla shook her head. 'This man's in no fit state to tell you anything, Rassel.'

'He'll talk when we've got him softened up.'

'Don't you think you've done enough?'

'We're only just starting.'

'No, Rassel. You're just stopping. Come on, Fitz.'

He tried to stand, but slumped to the floor like a jelly. She helped him up, somehow managing to keep the gun on Jörgan, and slowly they limped to the door. As they were about to leave, Ayla paused, flourishing the gun for them all to see.

'Anybody tries to follow, they get flared.'

And then they were moving, every step a small eternal agony that pulsed through his legs and his chest and his poor, pummelled head. The canvas swept past him, a series of fluttering ghost shapes that seemed to be waving him over. He was leaning heavily on her, but Ayla moved quickly and expertly with him hanging on her shoulder. The idea struck him that she must have had some fire-brigade training.

Then he was sitting back on the bunk in sickbay, Ayla forcing the gun into his hand while she started hooking him up to the med unit. Switching the machine on, she fretted over the readings, making adjustments to the settings before she finally took the gun back.

He felt drunk again, the room swaying slightly, the sensation not helped at all by the shimmering shadows caused by the flapping canvas walls. The storm was intensifying, wailing in the night.

His head was raised and he discovered Ayla's dazzling eyes peering into his. She looked anxious but hopeful, he thought, as well as incredibly beautiful.

'Why are you doing this?' he asked.

The eyes were bloodshot, the surrounding tissue tender and obviously sore. He was drowsy, but probably not too badly injured to run.

'I know you're not a spy,' she told him.

'You don't know anything about me,' he said, his words not slurred at all. That told her his brain was functioning normally.

Taking another look at the readouts on the med unit, she was satisfied that the damage was mostly superficial. Jörgan must have been holding back, hoping for some information before he had his real fun. The internal bleeding hadn't restarted, but there was a possibility that it still could do.

'Before I got this geo-engineering post I worked for PlanetScape on Gildus Prime. Military surgeon. I had the job of patching up the poor souls who just happened to be in the wrong place at the wrong time when things went pear-shaped.'

Even for one who'd just taken a beating, Fitz was looking particularly blank.

'You don't know what Gildus Prime is, do you?'

He shook his head and she laughed.

'I don't know who or what you are, Fitz, my friend, but you sure as hell ain't no spy. Industrial espionage isn't for you, let me tell you that for nuthin'. Don't ever make the mistake of going for a job, will you?'

He shook his head dumbly while she searched the unit drawer for a tube of res-gel.

'I did forty years for PlanetScape.'

Fitz appeared shocked, but she ignored the reaction.

'You get to know who are the spies and who are the victims of misfortune. Course, those on the blunt end, people like Jörgan who get the job of finding the truth, they don't know... What are you gawking at?'

'You don't look...' he began, then stumbled over his words. 'I mean... you don't look... the military type.'

'That's why I left PlanetScape. That's why I retrained for a new career. The military experience is useful wherever you go, and of course the medicare credentials are useful. WorldCorp saw they could get two jobs done here for the price of one. Medicare's a bit of a non-job, to be honest. It's all med units these days. Not much of a challenge. Not much variety. Plug 'em in and let 'em cook.'

She began to apply the gel around his eyes and mouth, dabbing it with her fingertips into the small lesions.

'I wanted to be out on my own. That's what attracted me to this post. Thousands of miles of uncharted territory, and me alone with the sun coming up over an alien horizon. I always thought I'd buy me a plot and maybe help set up an avian reintroduction programme. Settle down somewhere with kids that I can show an open sky with birds wheeling around in it. Can you imagine that?'

He was nodding his head wistfully.

Throwing the gel back and closing the drawer, she frowned at the readings. It wasn't good. Not at all. But he didn't have time to hang about. She switched off the machine and removed the cables, delving into her pocket for her keys, which she presented him.

'D'you think you can manage to walk on your own?'

He appeared shocked at the question, staring at the keys as if she'd offered him a poison chalice. 'Walk where?'

'Take my bug and get away.'

'Where to?'

'I don't know. Back to the city. See if you can find your friends, if they're still alive.'

'Still alive?' Now his eyes were full of panic. 'What d'you mean?'

She watched him with pity, amazed at his naïveté. His genuine, honest, complete and utter naïveté.

'They'll be sending troops,' she told him.

'Troops?' It was a yelp as if she'd kicked him unexpectedly on the shin.

She glanced at the door, wondering how much time she had.

'Things are getting very edgy here now. They've been bad and getting worse for months –'

'That's not *my* fault…'

'Can you imagine the amount of dollars and man-hours that go into a project like this? People put their lives and the lives of their children into terraforming. It's a multigenerational pursuit. When it goes wrong, people can get very trigger-happy. If they can't find a reason, they'll find a scapegoat.'

'I have no idea what you're talking about,' he said.

'What d'you know about pedology?'

'The study of feet?'

'Soils! The chemical properties are changing. We engineer the chemistry, reconstitute the soil with our own seeds and microbiology. With the atmosphere here it should have been a simple task. We should have been growing crops since months ago. But no. The rhizosphere seems to be constantly morphing at molecular level. We've been monitoring the changes with spectrometers, but the phylogenies of the micro-organisms are just mystifying. It's as if whatever we do to the soil, it automatically reverts back to its original state.'

'I love it when you talk dirty,' he grinned.

Jamming the keys into his hand, she pushed him off the bunk. She grasped a scalpel and knelt in the corner by the wall, cutting just enough canvas to let him through. Immediately, the wind tore in through the gap, causing a small sandstorm in the corner.

Fitz dropped to his knees beside her.

'Turn right and follow the perimeter of the base. You'll see the bug on the left parked just beyond the main door about two hundred metres along.'

He was about to squeeze through the gap when she grasped his shoulder.

'You'll need my passcode to get the bug started.'

'Passcode?'

'Goldfinch.'

'Goldfinch.'

After pushing him out through the gap, she was rising when he popped back through and grasped her arm, tugging her back to her knees. He watched her with a look of confusion.

'How do I get to the city?'

'You can't miss the tracks it's leaving,' she told him, swiftly becoming exasperated.

This looking stunned was becoming a habit. He did it again. 'The city's *moving*?'

'Of course it's moving. And so should you be if you want to live.'

The realisations were obviously crowding his brain. She really ought to carry out some more ECG scans to check he was OK, but they didn't have time for that.

'*Go on!*' she urged.

He vanished, only to reappear instantly, his absurd hair now piled around his head in an even more ridiculous heap. He reached in and grasped her arm, regarding her intensely. For a second she thought he was going to kiss her.

'Thank you,' he said.

And then he was gone.

She set to work pushing the bunk into the corner to cover the slit she'd cut. Then she trundled the med unit to the top of the bunk and grasped the flare pistol. She was about to turn to sit on the bed and wait, when she felt the cold metal of another gun on the back of her neck. She dropped the pistol and raised her hands into clear view, turning to find Jörgan with his own flare gun aimed directly at her face.

'Where is he?' Jörgan demanded, eyes flashing around the room.

'Gone.'

'Gone where?'

'I don't know.'

The gun dropped and his fist replaced it, connecting with her jaw and sending her twisting back on to the bunk. She fell on the pistol and when he dragged her back up for another punch, she pushed it up under his chin and he froze.

'You're a stupid man, Rassel Jörgan,' she told him.

He lifted his hands into the air and she jerked the gun hard into his face.

'Get out.'

He turned to leave, but paused at the door, turning back with a sneer.

'He won't get far,' he snarled. She recognised bloodlust in his eyes. A look she hadn't seen in years, but a look that she'd be able to identify for ever. Jörgan left with an angry smack of canvas.

Ayla dropped back on to the bunk and leaned there caressing her jaw. Jörgan *was* a stupid man, she thought. But he was also effective and he got results. He wasn't the most subtle of souls she'd encountered on Ceres Alpha, but there were different people for different jobs and he was good at his. She knew she'd done what she could for their strange visitor, and she knew that Jörgan would kill him if he caught him. He was a man who took his work very seriously. She'd noticed his flare pistol was loaded, for example, whereas hers had been empty from the start.

The storms were getting worse, she could swear. Even wrapped in storm gear, Perón felt the teeth of the winds trying to tear her apart. The readout in her goggles that should have been pointing her in the direction of the others was a useless mess of static and fuzz. There was a crackling in her ear where there should have been a clear signal.

'Where are you, Danes?' she spat into the mike.

The crackling intensified, and Danes's voice was barely audible, although he couldn't have been that far away.

'We're just beyond chopper pad twenty. There's a…'

Interference hissed through her, making her reach up spasmodically to tug the earpiece away from the side of her head.

'Didn't catch all that,' she yelled. 'I'll try to get closer.'

The earpiece hissed nonstop as she made her way down the chopper bays and finally caught a glimpse of powerful lights sweeping through the almost impenetrable sandstorm. There was a small team of troops, she wasn't sure how many, even at these close quarters, but she could make out that one of them was holding a detector out in front of him. She made her way over and nudged him on the shoulder.

Private Danes peered through his goggles at her, and saluted when he recognised who she was. He hoisted the detector so she could see the readings.

'It's very garbled,' he said, and now she could hear his voice tolerably clearly on the system, although even right at his side there was still hiss and crackle.

'The whole damn system's falling apart,' she commented, trying to see the detector screen through her goggles.

Another voice suddenly cracked across their coms, vying with renewed static activity on the line.

'Over here. I got her.'

'Where?' Perón snapped.

'I think I'm near pad twenty-two. There's a ventilator shaft. Get a reading on me.'

'If we could get a reading on you I wouldn't have asked where,' Perón told the voice.

'Hold on… Can you see that?'

Through the wall of seething sand, they could just make out an intermittently flashing searchlight.

'Got that,' said Danes. 'Keep signalling and we'll close in.'

Following the light, they made their way forward until they could see a black oblong shape looming out of the sand. It was the entrance to a ventilation maintenance block, and there was a man at the side of it swinging his light for them to track. Perón grasped the detector from him and squinted at the reading. Less than two metres in the direction of the block. She was inside.

'She shouldn't be armed,' Perón announced. 'But don't take any chances. OK. I'm going in.'

Releasing her rifle from its locking harness at the back of her shoulder, she entered her code to open the door. The panel remained red and the door remained shut. Perón tried again, feeling the frustration curling awake inside her gut. Still the door remained locked.

Lifting the rifle, she blasted the mechanism and the door jerked ajar. She stepped aside and let the others move in to push their fingers into the gap. Then she levelled her rifle at the opening fissure while the searchlights jiggled about in the wind. Finally she could see Kapoor on the other side of the door, her frightened features gazing back at the light. As the door was prised slowly open, Perón was astonished at what she found.

'You didn't see this,' she told the others on the com. 'Tonight this didn't happen. If I hear any word of this when we get back, you'll all be on report.'

Returning the rifle to its harness, Perón stepped inside. Kapoor was standing in the middle of the small room, no more than a shed that contained a handful of maintenance tools. And in her arms she was holding one of the creatures.

As Perón approached, Kapoor backed away across the tiny space, clasping the creature to her chest and twisting in a futile attempt to stop Perón taking hold. Glancing back, Perón saw the troops behind her gathering in the doorway, bringing the lights into position so they could see what was going on. She watched one of them unclip his rifle with a single-handed manoeuvre to cover Kapoor.

When she turned back, Kapoor was cowering, grasping the creature tight enough to burst it. As she took the last couple of steps she realised Kapoor was speaking, her voice quiet and pleading, just audible above the sound of the wind.

'We don't belong,' she said. 'We don't belong.'

As Perón reached out to take the creature from her, it gazed at her out of pitch-black eyes.

And so did Kapoor.

Having spent the last twenty minutes pacing across the apartment feeling like a wild thing caged, Josef was on the verge of going after Veta. The only thing that stopped him was the fact that, as Veta had pointed out, the military were in control of medicare for a good reason, and it would look suspicious if another very anxious-looking comptech turned up looking for his wife, who just happened to be working on the most security-sensitive comp in the entire place. Not the best way to run an undercover operation.

He'd spent the first half an hour online monitoring her progress as she gained access to Perón's system and started transferring a whole load of top-level files into her databook. The whole procedure had gone smoothly, and Josef could only assume that Veta had had the considerable good fortune to be left alone to work.

But then, without warning, twenty minutes ago Veta's connection had been cut and Perón's machine had been hastily exited. Since then Josef had been walking on coals, his head full of images of Veta being caught, Veta being brusquely chucked into a cell, Veta being menaced by thugs in black Military One uniforms.

He'd actually walked out of the door three times in the last ten minutes, setting off to see where the hell she was. But each time he'd returned home to pace up and down a little bit more.

Switching on the comp, he surreptitiously checked medicare for any unusual new activity. Any reports of Veta's discovery, any recordings of her mistreatment. Nothing. He entertained the idea of looking through Military One's system, but just couldn't bring himself to violate their security. The slightest mistake could bring them down on him in no time. And right now he was just too damn nervous to be confident he could scrub every single trace.

He cancelled the comp and jumped up again, this time determined he was going to medicare. Grabbing his jacket, he swung open the door, and found Veta standing wide-eyed on the other side, obviously just inputting her code.

'Where the hell have you been?' he asked, alarmed at how high and stringy his own voice sounded.

'You know where I've been,' she told him, forcing past him into the apartment.

He shut the door and hung his jacket back up, and by the time he came back into the room Veta had already opened the comp and was scanning the information on her databook. The hologram above the little desktop was a blur of scrolling lines.

'I was worried about you,' he said, plaintively.

'Well, don't. I'm more than capable of looking after myself.'

He plonked down beside her, watching her work, seeing for the first time in God-knows-how-long the Veta he'd married twelve years ago. The shadows were still there, and she looked like a woman who needed to take a well-deserved holiday, but there was also that spark back in her eye. That drive and genius that had captivated him.

'You didn't have any trouble, then?'

'Course not. I got a copy of the stuff she'd left online, but I suspect a good chunk of the more juicy stuff has been loaded on to her 'book. Hopefully she'll plug it in at some point, then I can go raid it.'

'While she's using it? Risky...'

She shot him a look that told him to shut up.

'Well... I mean...'

173

'Will you please stop fussing?' she asked without taking her eyes off the surging data. 'I know what I'm doing. Ah!'

'Ah, what?'

No answer. Her fingers skipped across the desk, and the lines of code in the hologram were abruptly replaced by an image. It was a sec recording of a young woman waking in medicare. She lifted herself warily and reached up to pull the skullcap ECG from her head. Her attention was caught by something nearby, and she gazed in surprise at the empty wall. Then, gradually, she smiled at the same vacant space.

'What's she seen?' Josef wondered.

'That's obviously what Perón was asking when she was reviewing this 'gram.'

The scene cut, to be replaced by a foggy picture that showed the back of a man who was hunched in the dark. It was difficult to make out the detail, but he seemed to be manipulating something in his hands. Was it a small sphere? Josef strained to see, but the image was infuriatingly dim and grainy.

Then he saw it. In the shadow. The small shape watching. The shape of a child. A smooth-skinned child with bulbous head and big black eyes. The whole world froze in that instant. Time stood perfectly still. The universe stopped.

It started again only when he heard Veta's voice, just a whisper in the immense and delicate silence.

'Oh God…'

Dragging his eyes from those of the child, he discovered Veta at his side gazing into the 'gram with her mouth loose open and the tears streaming down her cheeks.

The impostor Domecq lay bloodied and crumpled on the floor.

Foley felt sick. Physically sick. Standing on the sidelines, she put all her effort into appearing impassive, but she was sure her cheeks were burning with rage and discomfort. Military training was supposed to bolster you against such emotions, but in the case of this Doctor Whoever He Was, Foley's training had somehow slipped off-track. She remembered his casual chattiness on the way up in the elevator. His childlike enthusiasm and energy. His determination out in the storm to recover his friend, regardless of the obvious danger to himself. She'd very quickly developed an uncharacteristic respect and affection for this man. It was a revelation to realise just how uncomfortable she could feel at his mistreatment.

Lucky for her that Zach plainly didn't share her esteem. He'd quite eagerly stepped forward to offer his services when Tyran had discarded the useless mindprobe in favour of more traditional methods. They'd removed and searched his jacket, finding nothing except a bag of soft-jelly sweets shaped like fat little people, some odds and ends and trinkets including a yo-yo and a monocle. Then they'd replaced the cuffs and fastened the impostor Doctor back into the chair. By this time he was more or less devastated by the effects of the probe, but that didn't stop Zach expertly and energetically laying into him while Tyran punctuated the proceedings with quick-fired questions.

Meanwhile, she'd concentrated on the real Domecq, doing her best to shut out the impostor's cries of pain and the repeated dull thuds as Zach enjoyed his job. Domecq had remained in his seat, arm curled over the back and legs crossed as if he were nonchalantly watching a game of chess. There was no reaction in his face, no repulsion, and he didn't take his eyes off the action for even a second. Her instant initial assessment of Domecq had not been off-target.

'We're getting nowhere,' Tyran announced abruptly, sneering at the pulverised impostor.

Foley felt a surge of relief.

'Get him out of here,' Tyran snarled, and she realised with a start that he was talking to her.

Clipping her rifle into her shoulder harness, she knelt by the impostor and grasped him by the arm, wondering if it was broken as she pulled him up into a sitting position. His face was smeared with blood, and there were cuts around his eyes and lips. He appeared unfocused, unable to look her in the eye, and she was grateful she didn't have to suffer the indignity of having to connect with his look.

Dragging him to his feet, she swept his arm around her shoulder and Zach took his other arm to help her carry him from the room.

'Medicare?' Foley asked.

Tyran looked brooding. 'No,' he said. 'Throw him in the cells.'

'But sir,' she began.

The look Tyran gave her stopped her in her tracks. He didn't have to say a single word. She shut up and nodded, and allowed Zach to tug her towards the door. They took Tyran's private elevator and descended swiftly to the lower levels. None of them spoke, until they reached the cells and a burly guard indicated a door near the main desk. While the guard opened up the door, the impostor managed to take his own weight and as he was about to step inside he turned to Foley with a smashed face that contained a smile.

'Remind me to take my thick cardigan next time we go anywhere together.'

She felt her lips spasm, automatically trying to form a smile that she just couldn't condone. She saw him hobble over to the bunk and the door sliced shut with that hollow, desolate clang that all such doors are designed to make.

They used the staff route to return to medicare, Perón holding the creature swaddled inside her jacket in case they came across anybody, Danes frog-marching Kapoor with his face a cold, fixed mask and his phase pistol tight in his grasp. Kapoor hadn't said a single word since repeating her strange utterance over and over. The words had stopped the moment Perón removed the creature from her, and she'd allowed herself to be brought back without resistance, almost as if she were in a trance. When they got back, Perón instructed Danes to return Kapoor to med-ops and ensure that she couldn't sneak out again.

'Sir?' Danes queried.

'I want her strapped and zapped,' Perón told him.

She saw Kapoor's eyes, which had miraculously returned to their normal human coloration, widen. She couldn't resist the hateful smirk that escaped into her features.

'If you will insist on making such a nuisance of yourself,' she told the girl, 'then you'll receive the appropriate punishment.'

But Kapoor was gazing at the bundle in Perón's jacket, lines of anxiety etched into her face.

'Don't even think about it,' Perón cautioned. 'I'm posting a permanent guard on these things. Until they're disposed of.'

Kapoor appeared anguished, but she received a rough shove from Danes that sent her staggering down the corridor. Perón was sure she was about to yell something back, until she saw Danes's pistol aimed straight at her head. Perón watched her being bulldozed out of sight, before she marched with the creature back to the cells.

The clang of rattling metal was almost deafening when she entered the holding bay. The eleven titanium doors were being reverberated from inside the occupied cells, and as she stepped down between the doors, Perón felt the hairs on the back of her neck bristling. She stood stock-still for a moment, trying to understand the reasons for her own fear. It was an irrational reaction, she knew, but one for the life of her she couldn't fathom or prevent. It was something in their air. A kind of supernatural presence. She stood there feeling like a small child alone in the dark.

Opening a gap in the jacket that wrapped the creature, she found the great black eyes gazing at her without emotion. The face was blank and expressionless, entirely void of any human response.

'Get them to stop,' she snarled.

The sound continued, and there was the sudden, dread realisation that the banging was exactly in time with her own heartbeat.

Letting the jacket fall to the floor, she grasped the creature by

177

the scruff of the neck, and watched its eyes widen with what must have been fear.

'I'm not going to warn you again,' she told it.

But the sound persisted, now getting louder and just a little bit faster, until Perón snapped and hurled the creature down the short corridor. It landed with a thud, a pile of twisted arms and legs, the ridiculous head bent awkwardly over to one side. The breath exploded out of its lungs and Perón heard the soft low sound of its voice.

The door rattling endured, and Perón swept across the tiny space to grasp the creature again. The thing's eyes were wide with terror, and Perón sensed a huge loathing inside her, threatening to consume her completely. There was a moment of stasis, a stalemate when the doors clanged and boomed through her skull while the anger boiled through her.

Then all the pent-up rage escaped –

All too aware of the pistol held to her head, Anji lay back while Danes placed her wrists and ankles into the restraint straps and slipped the bolts into place. She felt cold and confused, with only the most hazy memory of how she'd managed to get herself and the child out there in the storm. What she did remember, however, was the distinct feeling that they were all intruding. That was clear as a bell. They didn't belong here.

She'd sensed a deep bond with the child, beyond any physical attachment: an invisible connection. No words to describe it. Something inside so strong. It tugged at her soul like…

mother and child

Oh God! Anji had never thought seriously about motherhood. Not seriously. It had always been one of those Major Life Decisions she was just not quite yet in a position to make. There were things to achieve first: money to make, investments to consolidate to protect against Future Eventualities. She needed a pension, a substantial rainy-day fund, a pot to cover school fees and uni costs. The thought had crossed her mind after about eighteen months with Dave that she really ought to be planning her finances with a little more urgency if there was a chance they might want to get pregnant in their early thirties. But then he'd come home with the holiday brochures. And the urgency would somehow evaporate.

mother and child

Her only real experience of maternal longings was when she was little and Rezaul had appeared on the scene. She remembered constantly having to babysit while her mother served in the shop. She'd made a great show of resenting the loss of her freedom. But, secretly, she wouldn't have changed those babysitting days for the world. She remembered dressing Rezaul in her Cry Baby clothes and popping him in the Cry Baby buggy to take him for walks round the garden. She remembered plonking him down to tea, all propped up with pillows, and spooning baby slop into his plump face. She played mother so well she remembered being the one who woke in the night at the slightest sound. She remembered feeling…

mother and child

Danes had her arms secured and now he was wheeling the med unit into place near her head. He switched the unit on, but it refused to respond. He began to prod the controls, becoming more agitated by the second until he finally slammed his fist down on top of the machine with a crash. He shot Anji a severe look full of fury, but there was other movement on the other side of the bed. She turned to find the child, eyes wide and black and fearful. The room around him was shimmering, as if she were seeing him in a heat haze, or a dream, or a memory. She tried to reach out to him, but her arms were locked in place. He began to squirm, his hands clutching at his chest and his face as if he were being invisibly punched. She caught the look in his eyes again –

Wide and black and fearful.

Hysteria exploded inside her like an incendiary device going off. She wrenched the restraints, trying to force herself up on the bed. Danes pushed her back. She flailed and yowled and lunged with her teeth for his hand, catching him and drawing blood. He slapped her viciously across the face, so hard she was momentarily stunned. Then he was gone and she saw him rooting through a cupboard on the opposite wall. When he turned back he was holding a syringe up to the light to expel the air. He returned to her side and she thrashed and wrestled the bonds.

The child was still there, but his image was fading, folding in and out of reality like a flickering television signal. She had to get out. Had to reach him. Had to help.

But Danes leaned over her with the syringe, leering like a deranged scientist in a creaky old horror film. Gleaming eyes and gleaming white teeth. Karloff on acid. She pulled away but it was no good: her arms were fastened tight and the syringe was closing in.

His leering face swooped in and he paused to enjoy her fear. He was getting a kick out of this, the sadistic bastard. The straps burned her wrists, searing into the flesh. Closer he came, and abruptly his eyes widened further, his face froze in a death grin before he toppled forwards and collapsed on top of her. The syringe clattered to the floor. Struggling with renewed vigour, Anji felt the straps give way and her arms came free. Pushing Danes off her, she sat up on the bed and gazed about in shock and confusion.

Danes had tumbled beside the bed, and now she could see the syringes sticking out the back of his neck and the tops of his shoulders. The cupboard door across the room was wide open as he'd left it, but the entire arsenal of stock had been plunged into him. There was nobody else in the room.

Releasing the ankle straps, Anji clambered off the bed and lumbered across the room, still shaking. By the door there was a mirror and she caught glimpse of herself as she was about to leave. She looked drained and windblown, and there was something wrong with her eyes. Peering closer, she watched in cold horror as the pupils began to grow. They spread outwards like an oil slick until there was nothing left but black.

* * *

The ice in Bains's drink had melted, and now the alcohol was diluted and insipid. Which, as it happened, just about matched his mood.

For'ard Obs wasn't as busy tonight, and he'd quite easily managed to secure the same table as yesterday so he could gaze out into the tempest. It seemed these tables with a view weren't very popular, these days. Not since the city-machine had entered the stormy season. Perhaps the restlessness of an alien world made people uneasy.

After a full day on the accelerators Bains felt well, but tired. The memory of his beating at the hands of Military One was still raw, but otherwise the med unit had worked its marvellous magic and since his brief meeting with the Doctor he'd felt at something of a loose end. The Doctor's enthusiasm and urgency had stoked his stubborn old fire, but his abrupt disappearance had left Bains with a sense of disappointment.

He'd deliberately returned to the seat where Carly had approached him, hoping for a follow-up visit. But he'd been here over an hour now, and there was no sign of her. Not that he was too sure if he really wanted to see her anyway. He'd kind of remained in the comfortable old habit of being alone since Jazz. That was the way he'd wanted it to stay. Bains and his work. Just the two of them. Inseparable buddies. But Carly had sparked something off. He hadn't realised it at first, but he'd woken today from anaesthetic to discover that she'd been bothering him in his sleep. He couldn't put his finger on it, but there was a vague feeling that she'd been desperate, haunted. She certainly hadn't communicated that through her body language or manner. She'd managed to come on strong, putting herself over in a predatory role. At the time that was all he'd seen. But there was more to her than that, and now he felt they ought to talk.

A woman squeezing between the tables appeared to be heading his way, and for a second he thought it was her. But she was smiling at someone a few tables beyond, waving a greeting and sweeping on her way oblivious to his presence.

So he sipped his drink. The same drink he'd been touching to his lips for the past hour in pretence that he was actually enjoying it. And he lost himself in his thoughts…

'Penny for them?' he'd asked Jazz.

'Huh?'

She'd looked up from her meal, eyes far off in another time, another place.

'What's wrong?' he'd pressed.

'Nothing.'

'Of course it's something.'

She'd refused to talk, refused even to look him in the eye. And it had gone on for weeks before he'd come home from work to find their apartment cold and quiet and lonely. Before he'd come home from work to find his life cold and quiet and lonely. Over the years to her leaving, Jazz had become the core of his existence. All his dreams revolved around her. All his hopes. All his desires. And without her, everything crumbled to meaningless grey dust.

There was no parting 'gram, no note, no sign of what might have driven her away. He'd talked to their friends, and found them all as mystified as he was. He'd used an agency but they'd been able find nothing. For a year he'd looked, for a year he'd kept in touch with the agency, and for a year he'd feared that something terrible had happened to her.

The agency call had come out of nowhere. Jasmine Bains had been found. They sent him the 'gram by email and he replayed it over and over and over.

There she was. Jazz. His Jazz. Walking and laughing and dancing and quite obviously head-over-heals slap-bang in love with another man. The 'gram followed them, hit and miss, sometimes through areas of low-resolution graphics, until finally they arrived back at a huge ocean liner with smart white fins and invisible dollar signs scrawled all over it. The camera followed them as they ascended the ramp, and there he saw on the side of the liner, just for an instant so that he was forced to rewind the image and freeze it to be sure, the word 'Jasmine' in immaculately italicised letters.

He felt so stupid. What a dolt. There she was having the time of her life while his life had fallen apart and lay in pieces at his feet. How stupid could he be? How... stupid...?

So he'd moved on, accepting a job with SysTime that took him under the Gobi for five years. Field research that would keep him busy and take his mind off things. He sold the apartment and rented a place near his work. He took the decision to obliterate every shred of evidence he possessed that she'd ever existed. All the pictures, the 'grams, her letters and her emails. And gradually, through a great effort of will, he'd managed to forget her. Almost. Just about.

Except when he tried to sleep. Or when he tried to enjoy himself. Or when he tried to start a new relationship. Or when he...

From the Gobi he'd gone to work on campus in 'Zona. There had been many chances there to start a new life and a new serious relationship. But somehow he was never, ever in the mood. After only a year he was ready to move on, looking for work that would put him as far away as possible from other people. He worked on Gildus Prime, finding a post there that allowed him to vanish into the wilderness for weeks on end. But Gildus Prime had proven a lifeless rock that was hazardously close to a spatial anomaly. Nothing there for an archaeologist to work on. The attempts at settlement were a disaster, and the place had been finally abandoned after years of speculation. Now it contained a remote-controlled comp base and the anomaly was used to gatecrash the subether system for info-freight but nothing heavier than electrons.

A whole string of solitary jobs followed. Danyal Bains had grown happy in seclusion. He'd grown into selfish habits. He'd grown into a dour old sod.

Then, thirty whole years later, the 'gram came through. A message lodged on his answer service. One of a large batch that he almost wiped without scanning.

Christ knew how she'd tracked him down.

She'd unfolded into the air in front of him, her face lined with fear. Her eyes were everywhere, wild and terrified. The tension gripped his guts and he glared at the face he hadn't seen for three decades.

'I'm sorry, Dan,' she'd said. She was close to tears. 'I'm sorry. We need to talk. We need to meet…'

To meet! After thirty years! To meet! His reaction was understandable. He cancelled the 'gram and forgot all about it. For several minutes. Then he'd mulled over what on Earth the 'gram could mean for the next two weeks. And finally his curiosity had got the better of him and he'd retrieved the 'gram from his bin, where it had lain waiting to be wiped when he got round to it.

She'd set up a rendezvous for the following week.

So off he went. As arranged. An apartment in a block on the expensive side of the town where they first met. Her 'gram had contained a passcode and that worked fine to get him in. But he found the place deserted. At first he thought she hadn't turned up. He waited a couple of hours, using the holowalls to fill the time. Then he'd got bored and started to nose around, checking all the rooms. The master bedroom contained a wall of mirrored doors, and he found himself in front of them watching the scruffy figure he'd become gazing back out at him like a lost soul.

It was then he'd heard the breathing. Such a soft sound. Hardly audible at all above the muffled background buzz of traffic and heating and air conditioning. But he'd heard it and he opened the mirrored door to find her slumped inside.

She was as beautiful as the day they'd first met. Slim and dark-haired. But she crouched there in the bottom of the empty wardrobe, knees thrust up and hands lying loose at her sides. Her face was bent in his direction but she gazed right through him. He knelt in front of her, afraid to touch, and she didn't react at all.

184

'Jazz?'

Silence, except for the hardly audible sound of her breathing. Eyes wide open – nobody home. Autonomic pilot. Her empty eyes were the most terrifying thing he'd ever seen.

Somebody laughed. A burst of mirth that brought Bains back. The drink was still in his hand, in a state of suspended animation, frozen in the space in front of his face.

He watched a group of people in comptech uniforms sitting at a nearby table. They all looked fit to drop. Since the city had been experiencing progressively more frequent power glitches, Bains supposed they were working extended shifts trying to clear the problem.

He glanced out of the observation screen. Wind and sand and swirling night. Tumultuous stuff like he felt inside. He scanned the vast area that was For'ard Obs, trying to locate Carly. There weren't a lot of people in tonight. And Carly wasn't one of them.

Yan Leung had signed up for Military One with visions of Important Roles in civilian disasters. He saw himself as a dynamic hero dashing in to save lives where others feared to tread. He saw himself hanging by the tips of his fingers from dangerous precipices, stretching inexorably to grasp wide-eyed children from the very jaws of oblivion. He saw himself tearing across the still burbling surface of a seismic collapse, screaming through gritted teeth, face all smeared with fresh-churned mud, a man on each shoulder as he punched his legs with dogged determination towards safety and salvation. He spent long, hard hours punishing himself in the military gym, finely honing his already powerful physique in preparation for just such eventualities.

But he'd never really seen himself sitting for hours in front of a monitor with a grey and grainy little 2-D picture of a man in a box.

The prisoner was a curio. His shirt was torn and stained with what appeared to be a mixture of mud and blood. He'd received a good beating for some reason, and his injuries were being deliberately left untreated. Leung wondered what he'd done, what major indiscretion had brought him here in this sorry state. He'd heard stories of Corporate Espionage. Cloak-and-dagger figures infiltrating Ceres Alpha with a mission to snatch the contract. There were rumours that they had people in Comp Maintenance implanting virus programs. People out in the field disrupting the crop chems. And he'd heard rumours that they'd captured some of the enemy agents and tortured them in a specially built secret annexe down in Medicare Central.

Leung had hoped for a piece of the action. He'd volunteered himself for special duties, thinking he might be posted somewhere vital. Now he was disgruntled.

The man in the cell was wandering up and down, apparently forgetting he'd just been truly trounced. He gazed around, inspecting the walls with careful attention, running his fingertips over some of the welds, tapping every now and then with his ear to the surface. Turning his attention to the door, he spent a good ten minutes tapping, rubbing, listening and finally kicking in frustration. Leung watched him empty his pockets on to the bunk but he obviously found nothing of use in them. Abruptly, he was on the floor, scurrying about on his hands and knees. Same routine of tapping and listening and scrutinising every inch closely. Then he stood in the middle of the room with his arms outstretched, fingertips touching the wall at one side, apparently estimating the gap left at the other side. He scratched his head.

He moved the bunk into the middle of the room and jumped on top of it to take a closer look at the light fitting in the centre of the ceiling. After a few minutes trying to break into the high-security seal with his bare fingers, he gave up and continued with his gazing. Then he finally noticed the hidden surveillance camera and his battered face loomed large in Leung's monitor as he looked closely into it. Leung saw the man's fingers trying to prise open the high-sec seal on the camera lens, blobby white shapes probing the outer edges of the monitor. Eventually he gave up and his vastly bloated features receded. He remained in full shot, a nice close-up of his bloodied face, which was abruptly filled with a big beaming grin.

Leung watched in irritated fascination as the prisoner raised his hand to show Leung a small white sphere that he was holding between his fingers. He raised his other hand to grasp the ball. Then opened both hands and to Leung's surprise the ball had vanished altogether. He opened his lips slowly, and the ball had miraculously appeared inside his mouth.

He waved cheerfully at Leung before jumping down off the bunk and pushing it back into position against the wall. Then he threw himself on to the bunk with his arms behind his head and his ankles crossed, and he fell motionless except for the rhythmic flexing of his foot.

When the fear surged through her, Anji slammed her eyes shut tight. She *had* to get a grip. *Had* to take control. Calm down. Take stock and assess the situation. The tide of dread subsided, and she opened her eyes to find them back to normal in the mirror.

Had she imagined the spreading blackness? Or was it part of the illness she was suffering from the TARDIS? Did it have something to do with her dreamlike connection with the children in the hold? Who were they? Why were they held in such barbaric conditions? And what was going on in a hospital that was run by doctors with guns?

Had they arrived in a lunatic asylum that had been overrun by the inmates?

Too many questions. And she was in no fit state to find the answers.

What she needed was a Plan. She was drawn towards the hold. Back to the children. But Perón had said they were posting a permanent guard. Too dangerous. She had to find the Doctor. He'd know what was happening. He'd have everything sussed.

So where was he?

With a glance round the room, she saw Danes sprawled on the floor. He was dead, of course. Massively overdosed on everything going. She knew that without even checking his pulse. How did she know?

Apart from the bed and the machine that Danes had wheeled to the side of it, the room appeared to be empty. What she needed was some information. She needed to discover where she was and how to get to wherever the Doctor might be. What she needed was some nice person to ask.

Huh!

No… Not necessarily some nice person… Perhaps some nice *thing* to ask. A place with this level of medical technology would have computer systems that she might be able to communicate with. Some sort of HAL 9000. But how would she recognise it? Dave had always blabbed on excitedly about miniaturisation and computers getting everywhere. About how she'd be able to talk to her microwave in years to come to set up her business meetings.

She tried the medical machine. Tugging it across the room to avoid Danes's body, she poked a couple of the buttons experimentally.

'Hey,' she said. 'Anybody there?'

No answer.

The machine eventually buzzed into life under her haphazard ministrations. Its business area filled with lights and tiny screens, like windows passing around and through one another.

'Can you hear me?'

It couldn't. Obviously. So she continued to press and poke until the machine died to darkness.

There were large panels on the walls that looked at first glance like sheets of Perspex with vague areas of translucent colour sprayed on the other side to show through. Art? Or computer interfaces? Who could tell? The sheets appeared to be completely at aesthetic odds with the untidy conduit-covered walls. Maybe they were there for decorative purposes, to draw the eye away from the bad workmanship.

Approaching one of the sheets, she tried stroking it to see what happened. She was slightly surprised and extremely gratified to see the colours on the other side of the Perspex move and merge in response to her touch. A bubble of holographic animation materialised in the air by her head. A blue sky with a jolly great sun shining off to the right, and a flock of birds wheeling about in the top half of the image.

'Hello?' she tried.

'Can I help you?' the hologram asked. It was a sexless voice that could as easily have been male or female, but it had a friendly enough intonation.

'I don't know,' she admitted. Unsure if she was talking to a human operator or the machine itself, she needed to be careful. 'I wanted some information.'

'How can I help you?'

Come on, Anj, take the plunge. 'I'm looking for someone.'

'Name?'

'The Doctor.'

'Which Doctor would you like?'

'*The* Doctor. That's his name.'

'I'm sorry. We have no one registered by that name on the records.'

Pause. 'OK. Can you tell me where new arrivals report to?'

'New arrivals?'

'New visitors...' An idea struck her. Knowing the Doctor, it was worth a try. 'Is there a VIP suite?'

'The VIP suite is situated by Central Offices.'

'And where are those?'

'Level Ninety. Median region.'

Great. Where the hell was that?

'Can you give me a map?'

The holographic sky vanished to be replaced by a three-dimensional schematic diagram that looked like a map of some mad architect's worst nightmare. There was a pulsing red dot somewhere in the centre, and near the top was a pulsing green dot. It took Anji a few seconds to work out that the red dot was her, and the green dot was where she wanted to be. And in between was a whole damn lot of messy schematic: millions of hair-thin lines intersecting one another mostly at right angles, but many of them taking tangential detours. It took her another few seconds to work out that the lines were colour-coded, and that most of them were probably ventilation shafts and maintenance access tunnels that she could ignore.

'Can you show me the standard route I'd take?' she asked.

Ninety-nine per cent of the lines promptly vanished, leaving only a skeletal map showing a few corridors and lift shafts with truncated offshoots to help her get her bearings. Anji suddenly had a better idea.

'If I wanted the... maintenance route,' she said, unsure of exactly how to put this without hearing alarm bells and sirens, 'in order to check the...' (*the security of the grommets and sky hooks?*) '...main power lines between here and the VIP suite, could you show me that?'

'Main power lines?'

Oh I don't know! The way nobody will see me... the tradesman's entrance... let me up your back passage...

'I want to check the security of the...' (*telephone lines? washing lines? ley lines? wiggly-whatsit lines?*) '...communications channels.'

'Com channels are monitored entirely by comp systems.'

'The ventilation system?'

'Manual vent maintenance is not necessary.'

'But can you show me the ventilation system between here and the VIP suite?'

The skeleton-map reconfigured instantly. A to B by a different route. But still lots of aborted branches that she imagined could be hugely confusing if she tried to memorise even a small portion of the route.

'Thank you. Can I have a printout?'

'Printout?'

'Can I take this picture with me?'

'I'm sorry. Your com is inactive.'

'Com?'

'Please activate your com.'

Com... Com...

Dashing over to Danes's inert body, she turned him over and unclipped the small badge from his chest, clipping it to her own chest. The badge was simply a disc of transparent plastic with splurges of colour slopped on the wrong side, but she knew now what the technology around here looked like. How to get the badge to work, on the other hand, was another thing entirely.

She tried pressing it in the centre.

'Com active,' the hologram announced, and the map vanished, only to reappear again instantly at her side.

'Com active.' Anji grinned. 'It's good to talk.'

The night had teeth. Big vicious sharp teeth that it was keen to sink into Fitz. He scurried down the perimeter of the base as Ayla had indicated, but he could see only a few yards ahead in the terrible conditions. Only a couple of hundred metres, she'd said. Metres equals yards plus a touch. For all the years he'd spent with the mostly metric Doctor, his mind still insisted on working in imperial.

It took him a good few minutes to reach the main door, and just beyond, as Ayla had promised, were the landbugs. They were like three-wheeled bikes with giant thick tyres and odd-looking boxes attached that reminded Fitz of those sidecars he used to see a lot when he was growing up.

There were four of the bugs, huddled together as if they were trying to protect one another from the squall. He began to take a closer look, trying to decide which one might be Ayla's, when he saw that each bug had an emblem painted on the side. The one nearest to him had a picture of a tree, the next one along a skull. He moved round the other side and saw that one had a picture of a bird painted on it, and decided that was probably Ayla's.

Fumbling for the keys she'd given him, which in actual fact were a set of small discs like coins all fastened together on a thin chain, he knelt across the bug's seat and inspected what he took to be the dash board. It was simply a panel of dark plastic that seemed to have splodges of dim paint spilled under it. Separating out one of the 'keys' at random, he began to search for a slot but failed to find one. As he leaned closer, however, the panel glowed into life and he saw that it now contained a screen with little animated windows sliding about inside it.

In the sparse, flickering light he could see a tiny slit on the edge of the panel. He pushed the disc into the slit and a word appeared in one of the windows on the dash.

PASSCODE?

Another window suddenly contained a qwerty keyboard and he used it to input the letters 'G… o…'

A shout went up nearby. There was the sudden clamour of voices and Fitz saw dark shapes shifting in the swirling weather. Lights danced about in the gloom, some of them falling directly on him.

'…l… d… f…'

'Get him,' somebody yelled.

'…i… n…'

With a burst of air exploding from his lungs, Fitz was sent sideways off the bug and hit the ground with a crash of shoulders. Somebody heavy landed directly on top of him with a grunt and the stench of sweat. There were more voices and lights flailing about in the winds. A long moment of confusion before Fitz got an intense light straight in his face. He brought up his arms to shield his eyes. As far as he could see there were two dark blobs moving about in the fierce illumination, plus the roughneck who'd landed with him.

He felt himself being dragged to his feet and manhandled past the bug. Then he was held tight while the lights explored him and the surrounding area. He saw one of the black blobs yank the keys out of the bug and hurl them in a long wide arc through the air. Fitz watched the keys get swallowed up by the storm, and saw his hope of freedom go swiftly with them.

Perón's hands were shaking as her fingers manipulated controls on the desktop, first renewing her passcode, then calling up the scenes she'd recorded last night when Pryce had attacked the creature. The image was fuzzy, a grey ball of static with barely definable areas of light that she could only just make out to be Pryce. She rechecked the readings, as she had already done last night, to trace the fault. Nothing.

She'd assumed when her machine broke down that yesterday's bad reception had been a warning glitch in her system. Now the repairs had been carried out by Comp Maintenance, the system should be clear.

Scanning the sec log, she found the point at which she'd entered the hold with the creature. There were three multipic lenses in the corridor outside the cells, and that should allow her to obtain excellent images from various angles. What she found, though, was another grey ball of fuzz. The sound was also nothing more than an annoying hiss through which she could only just make out the clanging of the cell doors.

She watched herself enter the hold, listening to the bang and clatter, the trepidation evident in her face. She watched as she dangled the creature by the neck in front of her. The crackle was now louder than ever, too noisy for her to make out her words. The picture failed and almost instantaneously resurrected itself. She watched as she threw the creature across the bay and it slammed into the far wall, a crumpled ball of arms and legs. It lay there looking stunned.

The picture blacked out completely, and the volume of sound became abruptly unbearable. A deafening hiss of noise. And suddenly she heard them. The voices. Talking much faster than she could possibly comprehend, but the sound now she'd recognised it was unmistakable –

Thousands of muttering voices.

'She's in,' Veta said urgently, almost startled at the realisation that the warning flag she'd set up was finally glimmering.

Josef watched over her shoulder as she worked furiously on the substructural code around Perón's machine.

'We got the new passcode,' Veta announced triumphantly. 'The databook's plugged in. I'm going into it... *now*!'

The hologram seethed with lines of data, flowing like a raging river. File headings surged and spun in its depths, whipped up by the furious currents of information. The room was filled with a resounding hiss that sounded to Josef like water gushing.

As they watched, the hologram flickered uncertainly, off and on again in an instant.

'What was that?'

Veta checked the system, hurling a bubble of test programs into the main hologram. It bobbed and sank and resurfaced. Veta shook her head.

'Nothing wrong as far as I can see...'

Again the system failed for an instant, and now the hissing was getting louder. Veta cancelled the test bubble and launched a stabilising program to replace it. The dataflow continued to flicker, but the information was still managing to get through.

'What *is* that interference?' Josef demanded.

'I don't know. Never heard anything like it.' Veta was biting her nails, gazing absently into the stream.

The 'gram crackled and fizzed and finally collapsed altogether to leave a solid black orb hovering above the desk that reflected the light ominously.

'What the hell happened then?'

Veta rebooted and the 'gram opened up. She ran a brief diagnostic that failed to find anything wrong.

'Did we get the info?' he asked.

She checked the log, nodding uncertainly.

'Quite a list,' she said. 'But certainly not all of it.'

'Looks like we got some big holorecs,' he commented, poking his finger into the middle of the 'gram.

She took a deep breath and he found her eyes full of disquiet.

'So,' he said. 'D'you wanna see one or not?'

She was a million miles away, fingers pulling and poking at her chin. She'd got exactly what she wanted, but now couldn't face the truth.

'You do it,' she urged, jumping out of her seat to let him in.

Josef took her place in front of the 'gram and caressed the desktop with his fingertips, drawing down a file that had been recorded a month ago. Somebody, presumably Perón, had given it a title:

EXPT 71

With an unsettled look at Veta, he opened the file and projected the 'gram full-scale. The apartment was instantly inhabited by ghosts. Perón stood over by the kitchen, partially embedded in the wall, while Pryce rummaged in a cupboard that was suspended in midair on the opposite side of the room. By the side of Perón was one of the children, like the one they'd seen earlier in Perón's scratchy recording. This time the picture quality was better, and they could see the child clearly. It was noticeably younger, but still possessed a large, bulbous head and was impossible to sex from its facial features. As it observed Pryce across the room out of its great, black, slanted eyes, Josef saw with revulsion that the child had been strapped by its wrists and ankles to a gurney. Perón made some adjustments to a wall comp, presumably keeping an eye on the recording, while Pryce eventually found what he was looking for in the cupboard. Josef saw a laser scalpel briefly visible before it disappeared into Pryce's pocket, and Pryce left the room.

Continuing with her adjustments, Perón ignored the restless fidgeting of the child on the nearby gurney. The child was tugging at the restraints, trying to release its long spindly arms. It gazed up at Perón, but if she noticed she ignored it. Instead she busied herself checking the other side of the room, which Pryce had just left. After a moment of fumbling with the wall comp, a full-size image appeared in the space Pryce had left. It was a small cell that contained a bunk, a toilet and one of the children. The child cringed as Pryce opened the door and came inside. He closed the door behind him and that half of the room fell dark, illuminated only by a single dim light in the ceiling. Removing the laser scalpel from his pocket, Pryce advanced on the child, who was cowering in the corner by the toilet.

Perón cancelled the image and Pryce vanished.

The child on the gurney was becoming more agitated, jumping up and down and making hysterical squeaking noises. Perón simply stood impassively watching without the slightest compulsion to soothe it. After a few seconds, the squirming and jumping had become a furious struggle to escape its bonds, as if the child were in paroxysms of pain. A second later, the image vanished completely, and Josef found Veta standing there with the remote control.

Her eyes were full of tears, her face was full of pain, and her voice was full of certainty.

'I'm going to kill her,' she said.

The call had come through from Military One just after Foley had seen the impostor locked in the cells. A message from Colonel Perón to locate Dr Pryce and report back to her. Foley had tried the usual channels, putting a call through herself to his com, asking Military One to trace him. But it seemed that Dr Pryce had vanished himself into thin air.

Putting a call in to Medicare Central, Foley had discovered that Perón was out of her office, and that there was still no sign of Pryce. She called Comp Maintenance and spoke to a frazzled-looking operator, requesting a comptech to meet her at Pryce's apartment.

The comptech who turned up was a wiry man with a thin face

and long nose: a nervous, twitchy type. He refused to break Pryce's code until Foley had gained express permission from Military Security and his boss had come online to confirm the order. But finally she was in.

Pryce's apartment appeared to be empty. The place was silent. No sign of life. He'd left the lights on low in the living area, but he'd also left the door open at the back of the room and she could see a bright light shining beyond. She stepped towards the light and saw that it was coming from one of the bedrooms.

The bedroom in question actually turned out to be Pryce's study. She found him slumped across his desktop in a pool of congealed blood. They hadn't been the best of buddies, Pryce and she. They'd had more than their fair share of run-ins over the last few weeks since Military One had set up their tense semi-residence in Medicare Central. But it was still something of a shock to see him like that. Perhaps it was the influence of the Domecq impostor, but her mask slipped and she felt suddenly sorry for Pryce. Then she slammed up the defences and told herself not to be so feeble. She had a job to do here and feelings didn't come into it.

The position of the body and the injuries made it pretty obvious what had happened here. The room was immaculately tidy, devoid of any sign of a struggle. It was a fairly sure bet that Pryce had committed suicide. Foley felt she could safely risk six months' wages on it.

She was about to com Perón to deliver the news when she stopped. Some blood had pooled on the carpet at his feet, dark red and thick. It formed an almost perfect circle. Except that one edge contained a slight indentation. Kneeling to take a closer look, Foley could see that the indent had been caused by somebody touching the very rim of the puddle. Going by the drag pattern and the lack of nearby blood trail, she guessed that whoever had stood in the blood had done so quite a long time after death, when the blood had almost dried.

The disturbance was so slight that whoever had been in here

probably hadn't even realised they'd left a clue to their presence.

Scanning the shelves around and under the desk, Foley couldn't be sure if anything had been taken or moved, but Pryce had a good collection of databooks and it was quite possible that one or more could have been taken. The only way to be sure was to look through them and check the sequence of dates. It might take a while to establish for certain whether any were missing.

Deciding that this wasn't a job for her, Foley touched her com.

'Perón.'

Captain Foley's head arrived in the air nearby.

'Sir, I found Pryce.'

'Where is he?'

'In his apartment. He's dead.'

The words were a simple statement of fact, empty of compassion.

'Dead?'

'Suicide.'

This wasn't a surprise to Perón, of course. She'd been observing his slide for weeks, seen the psychosis building inside him, watched him disintegrate. She had a file on her databook that followed him down his dark little hole to oblivion, and the culmination of the Pryce Experiment had been staring her in the face for weeks. Now she could close the file with her summation: mental trauma inflicted telepathically by the creatures.

'Right,' Perón said. 'Get a clean-up duty in there. Keep it high-security. I want all his databooks bringing to me. I'll make you responsible for their safe return, Captain.'

'Sir. There may be a security leak.'

'What d'you mean?'

'There's evidence that somebody was in here some time after Pryce died.'

'Evidence?'

'I think somebody stepped in the blood on the carpet. It was considerably congealed when that happened, sir.'

'In that case, get his apartment sealed off. Get our forensics in there. If anybody saw him after he died, I want to know who, when and why. Report back to me as soon as you've got something to tell me.'

'Yes, sir.'

Cutting the call, Perón returned to her comp. The auto-shut had closed down her 'gram and replaced it with the WorldCorp animation. For a moment she gazed into it as if hypnotised, watching the birds curling through the air into the distance and back again, forming and losing and reforming the loose and extended 'W'. In the animation, the sky was a clear deep blue without a hint of pollutant clouds and the sun was a bright yellow disc that always shone.

If only.

It took a while to get the hang of the hologram thing, but Anji finally realised that pressing the com just about anywhere would activate it, and the rest she could do by simply talking to the resultant hologram. Presumably the com was somehow linked into the main computer system, so she decided to use it as little as possible just in case somebody somewhere stumbled across her usage and thought they might check up on it.

It turned out that the vent system had a nifty little network of lifts running along parallel to most of it for the purposes obviously of human inspection. They were one-man open-cage affairs that were thick with grimy dust, and evidently hadn't been used in years. But it saved having to clamber up what looked like interminable miles of stepladders that also followed the vents in the cramped and only intermittently illuminated superstructure.

Every so often she had to bring her lift cage to a clanging halt in order to get her bearings and check her progress. There were several intersections on her journey that meant she had to climb out of the cages and push her way through filthy hanging wiring harnesses that ended at junction boxes which looked to Anji like laptop computers. She'd poked at one experimentally, and it had thrown a small hologram into the air that contained multiple windows of computer code that were completely meaningless to her brain, despite the fact that she'd trained for years to grasp at a glance the intricacies of multinational balance sheets.

She located another lift cage in the gloom and operated the hologram, delighted to see just how close she'd managed to get to the VIP suite.

'Can you give me a close-up of the last section?' she asked.

The hologram performed a neat little pirouette and expanded to show her that she had only a few levels left to climb. The lift cage should take her to the correct floor, and there was an inspection hatch that should allow her to get back out and have a nosy around. In the weak yellow illumination of the nearby light, she checked her clothes, which had been filthy enough before she set off, but now looked as if she'd taken a mud bath in a scrapyard.

She'd have to keep a low profile. Perhaps try to find some fresh clothes along the way. Hopefully, she'd find the Doctor and he could get her back to the TARDIS.

There was movement nearby in the dark. For a second she thought she'd imagined it. But there it was again. A shuffling shadow keeping low. A clump of nearby wires swung around as the thing brushed past them, and Anji jumped into the cage and pressed the button to take her up.

The cage refused to budge. She tried again, peering into the shadows trying to locate the movement, but again the cage remained stubbornly inactive.

Then she saw it, this time more clearly as it sauntered into a local pool of light. A rat the size of a cat. It shuffled about, sniffing the air and coming closer. Anji froze. She'd seen rats. One or two. But never so close, and never in such intimate conditions. And never one so damned huge. The creature stopped in the middle of the puddle of light, gazing up at her in the cage, and the hairs on the back of her neck stood on end. The breath emerged from between her lips in coarse rasps, and she became terrifyingly aware of a mind-numbing fear that made it impossible to move a muscle. The rat opened its mouth and emitted a long hiss. It observed her out of its little black beads-for-eyes, and they shared a moment of inertia.

Forcing herself to reach up, Anji clasped a rung of the nearby ladder. As soon she moved, the rat stopped hissing. What the hell did that mean? Was it preparing to pounce? She caught a brief glimpse of yellow teeth and a lapping pink tongue, before the rat suddenly lunged forward into the shadow and the cage around her shuddered and clattered.

In a furious explosion of arms and legs, Anji shot up the ladder as fast as her limbs could project her, not for a second looking back. Lungs pumped. Heart thumped. Her whole body afire with fear. She heard the cage behind her clang and rattle, and had a fleeting vision of the rat clambering after her.

At the top of the ladder was an intersecting floor. She threw herself on to it, tumbling painfully. Burning with adrenaline, she gawked about in the dark. She had no idea where she was, but she could see a service hatch nearby and she scrambled on hands and knees to get to it.

Hurling herself through and slamming the door behind her, she found herself in a storage cupboard lined with metal shelves. The shelves were crammed with packets of cleaning products, and there were several large buckets piled up against one wall.

As the fires inside her began to die, she stood and tried to calm herself, taking deep breaths and keeping a wary eye on the hatch.

On one of the shelves she noticed a heap of folded overalls. She grasped one and flapped it out to try it against her for size. The garment was big but would fit well enough to disguise her filthy appearance, so she thrust her legs into it before she poked her head out into the corridor.

Nobody home. It looked like a rarely used backwater of a big hotel. Pulling her head back inside, she pressed the com to get her bearings. The red dot that represented her had now converged with the green dot that represented the VIP suite. Bingo! Grasping a bucket and cloth, she strolled out into the corridor and hesitated uncertainly before marching off to try some of the doors along the sides.

All she had to do now was find the Doctor.

The search party was marching Fitz back to the main door when the lights hit them. They came curling out of the storm, swooping down from high in the sky, the roar of the engines competing with the roar of the winds. There was a moment of confusion, and Fitz saw his chance.

The man with the gun raised his hands to protect his eyes from the swirling light and gushing dark. The others were momentarily surprised by the arrival of the chopper.

Fitz snatched the gun and levelled it at them, putting several paces between himself and the goons. They raised their hands in unison, looking dismayed and stupid. But the chopper was probably loaded with troops arriving to pick him up. Fitz probably had only seconds before they dismounted with rifles and marksmen. For an instant he considered what the hell he could do, then he had an idea.

Swinging the gun, he took a shot at the nearby landbugs. They erupted into flames with a roaring explosion, and his legs erupted into frantic motion.

Suddenly he was lost in the storm, the wind ripping at him and the sand and rain battering his sore skin. He kept running until the fear that he could get himself completely lost overtook the fear that they might catch him.

Lungs searing, he came to a halt and looked back to see the dying flames of the fire he'd started. He could also see vague splashes of light washing through the agitated darkness, probably the troops searching for him. He could hear voices yelling above the sound of the squall, and the lights began to spread out around him. Then there were more lights and more screeching voices as the damage he'd inflicted brought more of them out after him.

Trying to get his bearings in the impossibly wild darkness, he set off in an attempt to reach the compound where he'd seen the giant earthmovers earlier. There would be cover there, and hopefully somewhere to hide and gather his thoughts.

Out of the storm came a pulse of bright pink light and the ground exploded near his feet. They'd spotted him. He forced on, hoping the storm would give him cover, and a second pulse of light went yards astray.

Behind him, the voices and lights were becoming more agitated and more concentrated as his hunters converged. He could see the compound ahead. The fence picked out in mad spatters of the pursuers' lights. Then another flash of pink sent him flying. He crashed to the ground, lungs filled with dank earthy air. He heard them closing in. The lights were crashing about him. The storm screamed in his ears.

A flare went off in the distance, way off target, and suddenly there was even more confusion as the lights swept this way and that. Fitz took the opportunity to run, scrambling for the compound fence and clambering up and over and collapsing to the ground on the far side. He scrabbled on his hands and knees until he reached a nearby earthmover, and managed to hurl himself behind one of the giant caterpillar tracks before the lights caught up.

Gasping breaths that shuddered through him, he lay in the grease-stinking dark and peered out at the chaos of winds and voices and churning lights. They'd reached the other side of the fence but the sand had obviously already covered his tracks because they were milling about in bafflement muttering to one another.

Fitz was about to crawl further under the giant machine when the lights picked out something that snatched his attention. A stack of boxes over by the fence where the searchers were congregating. The boxes were black metal things with white lettering sprayed on the sides. And the lettering was the thing that had grabbed his attention –

EXPLOSIVES

Things were happening far too fast. Perón's com was operating constantly, buzzing her like an annoying fly. The guard she'd posted on the hold called, his head appearing in the middle of her comp 'gram so that he was fused with the report she was working on. He was sufficiently stressed for the lines of anxiety to show through the lines of data.

'Sir. Permission to allow entry to the hold?'

'Don't be stupid. You know what I said. Who the hell wants to get in?'

A second head appeared beside the first, watching her with evident impatience.

'Mr Tyran,' she said. 'I'm sorry. I didn't realise…'

'Glad to see you're taking security so seriously,' Tyran told her dryly, and she was unsure whether he was being complimentary or caustic.

'Let them in,' she told the guard, feeling the tension building inside her.

'Yes, sir.'

'Thank you,' Tyran smiled, and both heads vanished together.

Switching to the sec cams, Perón watched them enter the hold. The picture was a mess, full of noisy sibilant static as it had been before, but above it all she could hear the clanging of the doors. There was a tall blond man accompanying Tyran, a man she didn't recognise, and the two of them were talking too quietly for her to hear the detail of their conversation. They entered one of the cells and Perón switched to observe them. Tyran looked like he was explaining something, pointing at the creature and swinging his arms around. Then she saw he had something in his hand. A stubby black instrument of some kind. Maybe a short truncheon. Both he and the blond man seemed to be considering its use on the creature.

The door com buzzed and she cancelled the sec image to discover Captain Foley waiting outside.

Colonel Perón appeared very edgy. Her eyes were wild and staring, and the woman was momentarily lost for words.

'I brought Pryce's databooks,' Foley said.

'Ah. Yes. Thank you, Captain. Put them over there, would you? Any news from forensics?'

'Nothing yet. They got some suspects, but it'll take a while to get anything conclusive.'

'Suspects?'

Foley handed the datadisc over.

'They gave me this. There were a few people caught on the elevator cameras who got out near Pryce's apartment today. They're working through the records now trying to match names and faces.'

Perón pushed the disc into her desktop and the 'gram came alive with images, angled shots of people in the elevators. Hard to make out and sometimes grainy. Perón watched the faces flash by. Suddenly she stopped the flow, retraced her steps a few frames until the 'gram showed two people, a man and a woman together in the lift. Perón was staring in disbelief at them.

'You know these people, sir?'

'Damn right I know them,' Perón muttered angrily, her fingers racing across her desktop. 'This woman is a comptech. She was here earlier today. And when I put my call into comp maintenance, that's the man who answered. What the hell's going on here?'

The 'gram was teeming with data. It flowed faster than Foley could follow, until abruptly the lines disappeared to be replaced by two more images. Perón had a positive ID. And now she looked more shocked than ever.

It was amazing, the anonymity bestowed by cleaner's garb. There were people about, but the few that Anji passed looked straight through her rather than at her. Nobody even noticed the state of her clothes underneath the overalls as she pottered about with the bucket, opening doors willy-nilly and gazing around. One or two of the doors were locked, but most of them were open and empty. Obviously due to a deficiency of Very Important People at the moment.

Making her way swiftly down the corridor, she came to a door that took her through to a large open hall that seemed to be some kind of assembly area. The place was deserted and unnaturally quiet. The constant hum of machinery and slight grumbling motion of the city was almost entirely absent in this area. The walls were adorned with a staggering series of holographic vistas that took Anji's breath away. They appeared to be computer-animated graphics of mountain ranges and stunning lakes. All of them had perfect clear blue skies and wonderful sunny days, with wispy clouds and occasional birds the only reminders that they were actually animated at all.

She headed past a series of elevators towards a pair of impressively large doors at the far end of the hall. Pressing her head up to the doors, she could hear only silence beyond, so she tried one of the handles and found the door to be open. It swung ajar and she discovered a further huge room, this time with a giant table dominating the centre. The décor was strangely discomforting: grey walls laced with white lines that appeared to deliberately mimic an immense spider's web. Around the table were dotted numerous padded seats that reminded Anji of those she'd sat in around innumerable boardroom tables.

And slung over the back of one of the seats was a scruffy-looking bottle-green coat.

Dashing over, she picked up the coat to see instantly that it was mud-spattered and stained with dark patches that might well have been blood. There were a few items scattered nearby on the table. A yo-yo, monocle and a crumpled little white bag of sweets. Snatching the assorted bits, she began stuffing them back into the coat.

So. He'd been here. But where was he now?

As she was refilling the pockets she noticed the marks on the floor and gasped. The carpet was a dark beige colour so it was difficult to be sure, but the marks appeared to be blood. And they were sprayed in various patterns around the chair that had contained the Doctor's coat.

The lights dimmed unexpectedly. There was motion nearby. One of the children waving its arms. She saw it for an instant –

Then the voices hit her. And the hysteria. A shock sensation that came from nowhere to consume her entirely. As blackness zoomed in she had the impression of muttering whispered voices and a kind of searing dread that made her fingers tingle –

The lights began to flicker and Leung checked the monitor to find the man in the cell suddenly jumping to his feet. The monitor was dying with the lights, fluttering on and off and filling with flashes of static. Punching the keyboard to initiate a systems analysis, Leung watched the cell while he waited for the results.

The prisoner was staring at the door. Or maybe at something in front of the door, although there was nothing there to see. He seemed frozen for a moment, then a ball of furious motion, slamming his fists against the door. The room was filled with the banging, as if Leung were sitting inside a gigantic bell. It made the hairs stand up on the back of his neck. That and the lights dancing crazily.

The cell door was shuddering under the prisoner's repeated impact, and Leung could hear his muffled voice yelling and screaming. Trying to bring the sound online, Leung was shocked by the hissing static that resulted. Trying to cancel the sound, Leung found it impossible. The noise rose to a swift crescendo, forcing him to cover his ears.

As he gritted his teeth against the onslaught he could swear for a moment that the static was actually thousands of sinister whispering voices –

Veta was screaming, hands to her head. She was staring wide-eyed into the middle of the empty room and Josef could do nothing to calm her.

In blind panic he shook her, then found her eyes full of so much emotion he couldn't begin to read it.

'What's wrong?'

'Didn't you see him?'

'See who?'

'Oh my God!'

'What is it?'

'*No!*' she cried, collapsing in tears. He took her in his arms but she pushed him away, glaring at him in terror and desperation.

'They killed him,' she gasped in disbelief. 'Oh my God, they killed him…'

Part Four

Ye fathers, provoke not your children to wrath.
    – Ephesians ch. 6, v. 4

Voices. Muttering. In the black. Voices she knew and yet they were strange. They curled through the dark inside her head, growing closer and louder and far more distinct.

Her eyes flicked open and Anji was momentarily fazed to find herself on the floor, face pressed against the blood-spattered carpet. Her brain felt thick and muzzy, thoughts misfiring like her dad's old car. The room around her was also misfiring, flickering dull and bright in a commotion of light.

The voices in her head mingled with the voices outside as she clambered to her feet and gazed about in confusion. There were people approaching. Very near. Two men arguing. No escape. Nowhere to hide. She was going to be found. Blood on the carpet. The Doctor's coat. Fast getting closer and nowhere to run –

Tyran swept open the door and waved Domecq inside.

'Take a seat,' he offered, indicating the desk vaguely while he rushed over and tried his comp.

The WorldCorp logo fizzed into the air above the desk, distorting and fading but just about managing to remain recognisable. Tyran explored the controls, using the comp to connect to Comp Maintenance. The logo was replaced by a human head that wavered and sparked with little blasts of light.

'Mr Tyran!' the head said, its voice cracking and spitting.

'What the hell's going on?' Tyran demanded.

The head shook and shimmered. 'Same as before, sir, only worse. The whole substructure of the comp system seems to be collaps-' The voice and head dissolved and returned.

'…monitoring and repairing as fast as we can but it's difficult to keep up with the damage. It's accelerating faster than we can –'

The head snapped out of existence and Tyran scowled at Domecq, who sat with infuriating insouciance on the other side of the desk.

'See?' Tyran appealed. 'We have to act *now*!'

'There are larger issues at stake here than building a planet.'

'There *is* no larger issue than building a planet,' Tyran almost yelled. 'We need this world. The situation on Earth's getting severe –'

'No doubt the strain on WorldCorp's finances is also getting severe –'

Tyran regarded Domecq with subdued fury. The man sat there with his arm hooked over the back of his chair looking smug and conceited. The failing light made him look like a fading hologram, and no doubt he felt he was just as untouchable.

'Don't play games with me, Dr Domecq.'

Domecq returned his stare with equanimity. 'Don't play politics with me, Mr Tyran.'

Gritting his teeth, Tyran forced the scrambling demons back down inside. He'd felt increasingly exasperated by Domecq's attitude since the man arrived. Tyran couldn't help feeling things would have been easier if the real Domecq had been delayed just another day or so and WorldCorp had been able to use the impostor Domecq as their tool and scapegoat. But now Tyran could feel the reins being tugged from his grasp by this self-possessed tinpot bureaucrat.

'If Ceres Alpha turned out to be another Gildus Prime,' Tyran told him, 'it would be disastrous for everybody, not just WorldCorp. Your precious Earth Central Administration is not exactly in a position to be able to afford the luxury of procrastination. People need room.'

'We need to tread carefully with this situation,' Domecq announced levelly. 'We need to understand these creatures. There's a time for destruction, and there's a time for caution.'

'We don't *have* time for caution. Work here is already months behind schedule.' He waved vaguely at the room around him. 'There's a real danger that this entire project could collapse completely.'

'We need answers –'

'Forget answers!' Tyran slammed his fist on the desk. 'Destroy them. *Now* –'

'Very dangerous tactics,' Domecq warned. 'We don't understand where these creatures came from, what the full extent of their power is, what they're capable of…'

'I don't *care* what they're capable of. Kill them and they're capable of nothing.'

'Not that simple.'

'Of course it's that simple.' Tyran felt the blood boil in his veins. He clenched his fists in frustration. 'These things aren't immortal. I just proved that.'

'And look at the results,' Domecq argued. 'For all we know the damage they've instigated could be irreversible when they're gone. While they're alive, there's a good chance to get this situation back under control…'

'Two months!' Tyran shouted. 'Two months you've had us playing the waiting game. Experimenting on them. You had all the sub-ether reports. You knew what damage they were inflicting here. What harm they've caused. If we'd destroyed them at the start like I said, we'd have none of this trouble now.'

'Might I remind you, Mr Tyran, that you are here only under licence by Earth Central?'

'What's this all about, eh, Doctor?' Tyran demanded suddenly. 'Don't tell me Earth Central are concerned about the welfare of these creatures, or of WorldCorp. These things have been kept alive for a reason…'

Domecq said nothing.

'You're hoping to somehow harness their powers, aren't you?'

Still, the steely silence. It spoke volumes.

'You bastard! You want to have your cake and eat it. You want Ceres Alpha *and* these creatures. And you're willing to risk every life on this planet to get them.'

'I wouldn't say there was risk to life, Mr Tyran…'

'Tell that to Dr Pryce. Those things sucked his mind dry.'

'Dr Pryce committed suicide. From what I've seen of your reports, he was potentially unstable from the start. That's why you were able to use him as you did.'

'The comps are dying!' Tyran seethed. 'We can't grow crops! Does Earth Central expect us to live like savages here?'

Domecq wallowed in a short silence. Then he stood and walked about the back of his chair lost in thought. When he spoke again, his voice was reconciliatory.

'I'm going to be candid with you,' he said. 'We think these creatures are a new weapon, somehow implanted here probably by one of your corporate rivals. We don't know how, and that's what I've been sent to discover. It's quite possible that they pose a threat greater even than mind-probe technology. Imagine – telepathic technology! A brand-new kind of psycho-warfare. The talents these creatures possess are only just developing, just beginning to make themselves known. We can't risk not discovering the truth about them.'

Tyran shook his head. 'You're playing with fire.'

'We may well be playing with fire,' Domecq agreed evenly, 'but someone else has got the matches.'

Tyran considered what Domecq was saying. He'd felt all along that his troubles on Ceres had to be the result of corporate espionage. He'd thought they'd somehow managed to install their people at every level and in every area of his organisation. He'd carried out clandestine security sweeps on even his most senior personnel and had been constantly mystified at the complete lack of results.

How much simpler to implant twelve creatures that could affect all aspects of the terraforming without even lifting a finger. Telepathic manipulation at molecular level. That would explain the substructural comp breakdowns, and the swift evolution of the micro-organisms that was hindering germination in the soil.

And embryonic implantation or some form of foetal engineering would most probably result in these creatures, these *weapons*, being nurtured and cared for and protected.

But things had gone wrong. The med comps had picked up on the abnormalities and recognised the pattern even though it was so widely dispersed. That would explain why the human agents were now showing themselves. They'd been forced into the open to rectify their plans.

The modus operandi pointed to an organisation that would regard genetic enhancement and bioengineering as their playground. And that pointed to the impostor Domecq and the girl. Although the girl showed no physical signs of enhancement, her psychic processes certainly did. According to Perón, Kapoor had displayed clear signs of telepathic ability, particularly in connection with the creatures.

Trying his com, Tyran received only a continuous hiss of static. He cancelled the call in annoyance and jumped up from his seat.

'I think we better try talking to our impostor again,' he said, already heading for the door. 'Don't you?'

Domecq held back, shaking his head. 'Even the mind probe failed on him. He's a man of immense enhancements. His outlook has probably been fundamentally altered by his employers. He'll die before he talks. I have an impeccable instinct for these things.'

'Perón said he showed uncommon affection for Kapoor,' Tyran said. 'Perhaps I can prove he's not quite as resilient as you might imagine.'

As they left, the room fell into silence. A moment later, the silence fell into a state of disrepair as one of the seats toppled over and Anji emerged from under the desk, crashing her head as she clambered out.

The other Domecq, they said. Dr Perón had asked her if she'd been travelling with Dr Domecq. The conversation above the desk, coupled with the Doctor's coat, emptied pockets and the blood-spattered carpet, had supplied enough clues for her to paint a sketchy but probably accurate picture of what had happened to the Doctor.

Typical! You turn your back for one minute and the guy's poking his nose into all kinds of trouble: getting himself interrogated, subjected to mind probes and generally crudely abused. The Doctor had an unenviable knack for dropping them into the smack dead centre of calamity, and she'd begun to wonder if the TARDIS had some kind of bad-situation sensor in its guidance system.

The lights were dimming sporadically, conjuring shadows and pools of darkness into the room. The whole place was falling apart and they were, natch, taking the rap for it all. She had to get to the Doctor. Find out what was going on. Maybe grasp him from the jaws of adversity. Or something. One thing was sure – the two men on their way to see him right now were not going for a friendly chat.

She dashed for the door and peered cautiously out to see one of the lift doors closing. The vast reception area was still empty, so she risked rushing across to the door and watching the little digital counter that showed which level the lift was descending to. The counter was flickering on and off like the rest of the lights, but the numbers were just about managing to hold on by the skin of their teeth. Finally the descent stopped. Level twelve. She waited to make sure, watching the display fade and fizzle, before finally calling the next lift.

If the Doctor was on level twelve, then that was where she was too.

When the monitor finally died, Leung had spent a few minutes attacking it with repair programs, before reverting to attacking it with his bare fists. Where the software fell sadly short of expectations, he was gratified to see that his fists achieved the desired results. The monitor stabilised, but Leung frowned at what it showed. It was simply black, although the dialogue told him it was active and fine.

Trying his fists on it again, he failed to get a picture. With a sigh, he stood and marched over to the door, preparing his pistol before unlocking the cell to peer inside.

He was baffled to find the cell empty. The bunk was in position, crumpled where the prisoner had been resting, a pair of shoes and socks left neatly at the side. Otherwise – nothing.

Stepping inside to jab his pistol under the bunk, Leung was mystified to find the space completely clear. Then he was winded. The prisoner dropped from above. The pistol went scuttling out of his grasp. His head hit something hard. There was a flurry of wild moments. Then his own pistol a centimetre from his face as the prisoner bent to collect his shoes and socks.

The man was smiling out of his battered and tired face.

'It's been a pleasure,' he was saying. 'But I'm afraid I really have to go now.'

Immediately after Veta's vision, the lights had fouled up and now the comp system was refusing to respond. Veta perched in front of it looking distressed but determined, while the 'gram flared and hissed and cackled at her.

'It's no good,' Josef said.

'We can't stop now.'

'You're never going to get any sense out of it while it's acting up like that.'

She ignored him, continuing to trawl the lines of code with a dozen or more stabilising programs proving less than useless. She'd miraculously managed to open a couple of files and skim through the information they contained, but it was tortuously slow going and the information was highly corrupted. Like trying to read a book whose pages had been crumpled into little balls.

'There – look,' she said suddenly.

'What?'

'They built an annexe. It's been basically bolted on to the side of Medicare Central. Twelve cells.'

'How do you get to it?'

'It's near Perón's office,' she said, pushing her finger into the

217

shaky 3-D plan. 'I recognise the layout.'

'Twelve cells,' he said, remembering the image they'd witnessed of Pryce entering the darkened cubicle containing the child.

'That's obviously where they're being kept. So that's where we're going.'

'We'll never get in,' he complained, feeling the fear gripping hold even at the thought of an attempt.

'Course we will. There's a major comp disruption. There'll be technicians everywhere. Come on.'

She was already halfway to the door, not even bothering to cancel the comp. As she swept open the door he grabbed his jacket. He was twisting into it, following her out, when he crashed into her and realised she'd come to a dead stop.

There were six of them in the corridor. Black combat gear and multiphase rifles. The rifles were aimed at Josef and Veta.

'We seem to have a comptech problem,' said Colonel Perón.

It happened as they made their way towards the cells to check on the prisoner. The lights went out, and Tyran found himself in pitch-black quiet. Even the motion of the city-machine had finally stopped. There was a sound he hadn't heard in months, not even in the plush apartments of his own private suite. Something that sent a shiver down his corporate spine and meant the end of absolutely everything.

Silence.

The lift was plunging smoothly when the lights went out. Then all hell let loose as Anji crashed and tumbled and came to an abrupt, bone-wrenching halt. As she lay waiting for the emergency lights to ignite, feeling a bit like a pebble in a cement mixer, she realised that her slightest movement was making the lift shift and creak. She had a flash image of the lift jammed against a narrow ledge in the shaft, holding on with only millimetres of movement between safety and oblivion below.

She could hear the sound of her own ragged breathing. Her

adrenaline-soaked body wanted to run, to yell, to thrash about wildly. But she could only lie there feeling her battered bruises, not knowing how badly injured she'd been in the fall, not knowing if movement would dislodge the lift from wherever it had jammed.

Even after a pause long enough for her eyes to get accustomed to the dark, she could see absolutely nothing. No vague areas of light and shadow. Not even the faintest glimmer of illumination anywhere. Such a profound and perfect darkness that she wondered if she'd been knocked blind in the fall. Her breathing intensified at the idea, rasping fast and shallow out of her lungs.

Forcing herself to remain calm, she told herself that she *wasn't* blind. She *wasn't* badly injured. The lift *wasn't* going to plummet into the depths. The lights *would* come back on. In a minute. Any minute now. Any... minute... now...

She closed her eyes and tried to picture herself in a crumpled ball in the corner of the upturned lift. She'd worked with a trader who used Eastern methods of visualisation to combat what he called 'the pressures of life in the city'. He was mid- to late thirties so he'd had a good few years of 'pressures' to deal with, including the late eighties, so she'd forgiven his pseudo-mystic leanings. Now she remembered him sitting there with his eyes closed when one of his more adventurous portfolios spectacularly crashed leaving his *numero-uno* client high and dry, several hundred thousand pounds adrift. She smiled to herself. The pressures of life in the city? If only he could have known. If only...

She wished she had her bag. There was a torch in her bag. But of course the Doctor and Fitz were blokes and they just didn't recognise the absolute necessity of a girl's handbag.

At last she felt able to move her arms cautiously. She shifted her weight so that she was supported in a semi-upright position against the wall, or floor, or ceiling, or whatever she was resting against when the lift clattered to its halt. Running her hands over her body, she felt bruised but not seriously damaged. After a while she felt confident enough to try to stand. Her legs were like jelly and so was her head, but at least the adrenaline had dispersed from her system. She vaguely remembered reading somewhere that an adrenaline pulse would last normally only a few brief seconds before the chemistry was depleted.

As she clambered to her feet, the lift creaking and moaning around her, she stopped abruptly to listen. There was another sound mixed with the groaning of the lift. A sound she couldn't hear distinctly at first, but which swiftly grew clearer to make the adrenaline burst through her veins again.

A scurrying, scuffling kind of a sound.

The explosive charges looked like slender sticks of dynamite with small digital timing mechanisms fixed to one end. Each mechanism consisted of a tiny red switch and what looked like a remote-control antenna. There was a miniature screen on the end of each stick, which Fitz presumed was a communications device.

Stuffing a handful of the sticks into his overall pockets, he gazed into the storm to keep an eye out for approaching lights. The hubbub of voices had receded, and he could see pools of flashlight illumination bobbing about in the mid-distance.

He'd formulated a plan, of sorts, but it was full of holes and potential disasters. Ideally, he just needed to make a run for it in one of the giant earthmovers. In theory, that was an easy plan. In practice, however, he had no idea how to drive or control one of those things. The others were much more expert and they would easily catch up with him. Besides, even if he did manage to, say, smash up all the controls in all the pursuit vehicles, then there were still the troops on his tail and they had real fire power and some sort of flying machine that could cut through the storms.

So, all in all, his chances if he made a run for it weren't really all that good. What he needed was time to think, and maybe somewhere to wait out the storm. Maybe let them think he'd gone away, and make his dash for freedom bright and early in the morning when there was nobody about. There was certainly enough cover in the storm to hide. He could probably even ge some sleep if he could find somewhere on the construction site to get his head down. As he cast about for ideas, the lights hit him.

'*Got him!*' somebody yelled on the other side of the fence.

A chaos of voices suddenly growing nearer. Fitz set off at full pelt towards the skeletal structure that he could just see looming out of the squall. As he made his way towards the building he could hear the fence rattling behind him. They were close, their lights sweeping about him like wild things.

There was a platform nearby. As Fitz was clattering across it, he realised abruptly that it was a materials lift obviously for the purpose of getting stuff up into the structure. There was a simple mechanism with buttons on the side, and he punched it frantically.

The platform rattled and shuddered, and finally began to rise with an infuriatingly unhurried momentum. The lights were getting swiftly nearer, coming together out of the storm, crowding nearby and flashing at him sporadically. Fitz considered jumping off and letting them *think* he'd gone up on the platform. By the time he'd made his decision it was too late. There were shapes surrounding him on the ground.

He was just out of reach for them to jump on after him, and he watched them gazing up out of their ferocious light, dark blobs shuffling about, considering what to do next. Then more lights appeared. Sharper, more focused beams. Probably the troops. There was movement among the black blobs, but he couldn't make out what they were doing or what they might be saying.

Then the platform ground to a halt and Fitz felt his legs buckle beneath him.

Damn! Remote control. Probably a safety cutout in case of accidents. The platform remained momentarily stationary, the wires that controlled it whisking about and clattering in the wind. Then he was moving again. This time down. Back to the lights and the troops and the guns.

At last he could see their faces. Quite a reception committee. There was Jörgan, a handful of his Neanderthals, and three black-clad figures with helmets and goggles and stubby rifles which Fitz presumed were standard military issue around these parts. The combat crew lifted their rifles to cover him, and he raised his hands where they could see them. Then he saw Ayla among the Neanderthals. Her hands flashed up to cover her eyes. She held up the fingers of her free hand. Five fingers… Then he noticed she was holding one of the squat pistols that the fieldbase personnel used. Four fingers… It was a completely different design from the military rifles. Three fingers… Some kind of flare pistol? Two fingers…

Jörgan watched the prisoner descend and just couldn't stifle the grin that spread across his own smug face. Now they were getting somewhere at last. Now they had real rifles, real firepower, and they had the prisoner back in their grasp.

As the platform descended, the prisoner lifted his hands into the air in a gesture of defeat. The troops moved in, rifles trained, and now the platform was only a few short metres off the ground. Then –

The scene turned white. An instant of panic and blindness. Then the flare had gone.

And so, it seemed, had the prisoner…

She was moving fast, the wind ripping through her hair, the breath bursting out of her. Fitz was limping badly, holding on for dear life. They made their way together into the depths of the structure, tumbling over rough ground they couldn't even see below them. The agony of their flight seemed to last for ever, until finally, gradually, they slowed to a full stop and she leaned him against one of the giant support pillars.

He collapsed to the ground, wincing in pain, struggling to catch his breath.

She peered back through the forest of beams and girders, and only in the furthest distance could she make out the confusion of lights behind them.

'We need to keep moving,' she gasped.

'Give me a minute,' he said, his voice as ragged as the wind that cut through the framework around them.

'One minute,' she agreed, collapsing beside him so they leaned against each other in shared exhaustion.

'Maybe five,' he rasped.

His legs were afire. His lungs were screaming for air. He couldn't face running again. He'd just been through far too much in the last twenty-four hours. He knew he was capable of only so much, and after a day like today he'd just about reached that limit.

He felt Ayla pressing against his shoulder, felt her heaving, heard her breathing deep and hard. He wanted to grab her and thank her. Maybe plant a big sloppy kiss on her lips. Without her he'd be dead. He was perfectly aware of that. She'd dragged him out of the mud, cleaned him up, got him back on his feet. Then she'd saved him from the pack.

'Why are you doing this?' he asked.

She huffed. 'I told you. I did forty years for PlanetScape. Military Arm. We were on Gildus Prime and there were problems. People were dying all over the place, and the crops we'd got established all withered in the space of three days. They said it was corporate infiltration. There was a witch hunt. Everything just went stupid. There was so much hope and so much money ploughed into that project. Now I can see the same thing happening here. History repeating itself. And I knew a lot of good people who died on Gildus Prime.'

He reached across and grabbed her hand. Squeezed it tight and found her face turned towards him. Found her big beautiful eyes peering into his, smiling. Then there were lights. Combing the area. Sweeping around and disrupting the cosy shadows around them.

'We need to get moving,' Ayla said, tugging him back to his feet.

He grasped the girder for support as he felt his legs begin to give way beneath him, and only then did he see the figure in black. She was a young woman with storm goggles raised above her eyes. She was watching them with the beginnings of a smile curling through her tight lips. Fitz sensed Ayla moving nearby. The woman jerked her rifle and Ayla's movement stopped.

'Now,' the trooper said softly. 'Turn round and get your hands in the air.'

Emergency lighting ignited at last, and Tyran tried his com. Still inactive. The corridor was barely illuminated, full of bizarre shadows and pools of deep dark. Domecq's face was picked out in the curious gloom like an apparition, his blond hair glowing slightly under the yellow lights.

'We're going to get this sorted once and for all,' Tyran told him, stalking off in the direction of the cells. 'Our impostor friend has got some urgent questions to answer. We'll take him to the girl and use her to get the truth out of him.'

But when they arrived the guardroom was empty. Tyran had given specific orders that the prisoner was to be watched closely, and nothing left to chance. So where was the guard? Trying the monitors, Tyran found all the surveillance equipment out of action.

He tested the door com to cell one and found it unresponsive. He punched in his master code hopefully, but the door remained stubbornly shut. Removing the emergency cover below the com, Tyran reached inside and tugged out the manual lever. Pumping furiously, they watched the door slide slowly ajar. The cell beyond was completely dark, except for the wedge of yellow light that sliced in from the anteroom. By the time the door had opened a few centimetres they were just able to see the figure on the bed gazing back at them with hope and fear and a whole mixture of other emotions on his fretful face.

A figure in the black uniform of the Military Guard.

As the scuffling and scratching intensified around the lift, Anji found it impossible to see a thing. She wondered if they could smell her fear. If they could sense her vulnerability. She grasped herself tight, unable to stop the shivering that had taken over her entire body.

Then the light came on. Not the soft-glow white panels that had illuminated the lift originally, but a pathetic yellow light embedded in the ceiling, like an inexpensive torch with dud batteries installed. But at least now she could see.

The sounds of scuffling abruptly cut. Anji remained still and silent, listening for them coming back, waiting for their courage to return. But the silence was complete and, it seemed, permanent.

The lift had remained roughly upright, but now it was tipped at a slight angle that meant the doors were leaning about ten or fifteen degrees forward at the top. She tried the door button optimistically, but wasn't surprised at all when it failed even to mutter in limp response.

OK. Don't panic. Where there's a will there's an escape route. Emergency trap… Emergency trap…

On the ceiling, by the light, she could make out the faint lines of a panel. Pretty well disguised unless you were stranded and in bordering-on-the-hysterical-mode. There was probably about a foot of empty air above her, but when she leapt she was able to push the panel askew. A trail of black dust swept down towards her and she jumped back, coughing.

Achieving a fissure in the ceiling gave her hope and trepidation. Whatever she'd heard scratching outside could well still be there, biding its time, waiting for her to get desperate. She experienced a flash memory of the enormous rat she'd disturbed on the way up. Remembered its black little eyes and lapping pink tongue. She'd never been comfortable with rats. Not rats. Shortly before she left Earth with the Doctor and Fitz, Earth at the very beginning of the twenty-first century, she'd heard a news bulletin that not a single living soul in Britain was ever more than twenty feet away from a rat. She'd shivered when she heard the item, just an 'and finally' tagged on to the end of a report, and now she was shivering again. It wasn't a phobia. No. She didn't suffer phobias, as such. But her dislike of the filthy, disease-ridden creatures did sometimes border on the irrational. And when she found herself alone in a darkened lift and the only way out was through a roof hatch and possibly a whole herd of huge rats (they were too big to constitute a mere pack, she decided), then she felt she was allowed the luxury of senseless terror.

Listening for signs of motion outside, she heard only silence. Throwing herself into the air again, she managed to dislodge the panel completely, this time sending it clattering into the blackness outside. She stopped and listened carefully. Nothing.

Taking a deep breath, she launched herself at the open hatch, grasped the edge with her fingers, and managed to haul herself out into the gloom. Perching on her elbows with her legs still dangling below, she gazed about in the shaft. There were metal ladders on the walls, and, about five or six metres above, she could see what looked like a pair of doors set in the wall. Unfortunately, the only source of light was that in the lift, and it was almost impossible to see any detail so far above. She would need more light.

Dragging herself on to the roof of the lift, she found the emergency light and pressed it with her fingers. It moved under the pressure, and she found that it was screwed into place from this side. After quickly unscrewing the fitting, she pulled out the lamp and positioned it beside her, trying to aim it roughly towards the doorway above. Better! Now she could –

The light extinguished. There was movement in the black. A quick commotion she could hear but couldn't see. She jerked the light and it came back on. Used it to pierce the dark. Found nothing. Her heart thrashed about in her chest, threatening to burst free any minute.

A moment of quiet. A moment when she thought she was going mad and imagining everything. Then she saw it nearby. The sleek black fur and glinting black eyes. Only a metre or so away.

Instantly she was scrabbling up the ladder. She could hear the scuffling behind her, and she was certain now that there were more than one. Far more. She could hear them making low squealing noises, hear them chattering and hissing and scurrying about. But she didn't look back.

She found a handle by the pair of doors, and discovered that the doors would open slowly when she turned the handle furiously. Lots of turning for very little opening. And the chaos of sound behind her was getting closer. It took a few seconds to open the doors just about enough to see through. Out in the corridor beyond she could see thick ochre light that contained people dashing about. They seemed panic-stricken by the collapse of the power. There were hushed and frightened conversations nearby.

Then she felt the tugging. Something pulling at the hem of her smock. Something remarkably strong. And big. And black.

And the scream finally tore out of her throat –

Trying to race down the service stairs to Medicare Central, Tyran found himself in a crush of emergency patients who were shouting and arguing, pressing the harassed-looking staff for treatment. There were people with cuts and small wounds, people who had obviously been in the middle of something when the lights cut. The whole reception area was in turmoil, and when Tyran tried to get through he was accosted by an overzealous civilian medic who wanted to know where he was going.

'I'm here to see Dr Perón,' Tyran told him, doing his best to sidestep the man.

'You'll have to join the queue, I'm afraid,' the man said, pushing Tyran gently back.

Brushing the man's hands aside, Tyran glared at him furiously.

'I'm Gaskill Tyran,' he yelled, forcing the man out of his way and barging with Domecq towards med-ops.

They left the medic watching after them with a dumbfounded look, and Tyran slammed open the door to let himself and Domecq through to the deserted corridor beyond. They found Perón's office empty. Tyran slammed his fist into the window in mounting frustration. The whole operation was falling apart.

With a furious snarl, he led the way to check on the Kapoor girl, and that was when they found the body of Danes on the floor by the bed. While Domecq checked the body, Tyran glared about the room in silent wrath. This was one young woman. Perón had the entire might of Military One at her disposal. What the hell was wrong with these people?

Domecq looked up from the body. 'He's been dead a short while.'

Marching for the door, Tyran was astonished when it crashed shut in front of him. He tried the handle, only to find it secure. The comps around the room were glimmering with life, colours swirling and merging. A voice filled the air. The voice of the WorldCorp hologram.

'Danger,' it warned them flatly. 'Biological hazard. Secure this area. Biological hazard. Area secure. Please wear your masks. Biological hazard.'

Tyran saw Domecq jump up from his position by the bed, startled and alarmed. He backed away with his hands raised, and abruptly Tyran saw why. Danes's corpse was rising on its arms, its blue face animate but its eyes completely blind. It raised a hand in Tyran's direction, pointing accusingly. Then the thing spoke, its voice a rasp of cold air from its throat.

'*We don't belong!*' it hissed.

Then the body slumped back to the ground and Tyran found Domecq's eyes wild and staring.

'*He was dead!*' Domecq assured him, almost screaming.

Slamming his fists into the door, Tyran felt himself tumble helplessly off the edge of a steep precipice into delirious rage.

The doors jerked open and she felt fingers grasping her wrists, tugging her out through the narrow gap into the corridor. Then there was a face, close-up, peering into hers with concern and puzzlement.

'Are you all right?' the woman asked.

Anji fought for air and light, jumping to her feet. The corridor was in a state of yellow-tinted gloom that she took to be emergency lighting. There was a general air of panic, people talking in furious whispers. She was attracting attention from others in the corridor. A tall thin man observed her curiously. The woman who had pulled her out of the lift shaft gazed down into the abyss behind her.

'What was that?'

'Rats,' Anji gasped. 'Bloody big ones.'

'Did they bite you?'

She was middle-aged, Anji guessed, kindly-looking and harmless enough. One of those busybody women who want their nose firmly inside your business.

'No. I don't think so.'

'You ought to report to medicare,' the woman said.

'No,' Anji yelped before she knew what she was saying. 'No. Really. I'll be all right. Honestly. I'm fine.'

There were soldiers further down the corridor who appeared to be trying to calm the panic. They were making their way towards Anji. One of them caught her eye. They were probably just coming to check if she was OK. Probably nothing to do with Perón and the medicare lot. But she didn't want to take that risk. She had to get moving. Get on her way. She could lose herself in the confusion. It would give her cover while it lasted.

'You look a bit peaky to me, dear,' the woman told her confidentially. 'Look at the state of you. What were you doing down there?'

'Trying to get out,' Anji told her in all seriousness.

'Why don't you come in for a minute?' the woman asked, indicating an open door nearby.

She meant well, Anji knew, but she felt exposed among these people. She didn't have the clothes to fit in. Wasn't *au fait* with the social customs. There was a good chance somebody might report her to the authorities. She had to keep moving.

'No,' she said. 'Really. Thank you.'

The woman accepted her refusal and let her go with a gentle tap of her arm. Anji wandered off down the corridor, pulling the

Doctor's coat tight around her shoulders, feeling vulnerable and alone. Her Plan had been derailed. The Doctor was in trouble and she didn't even know where *she* was now, never mind where *he* was. She had to get to him. Had to tell him about the children in the cells. About her link with them and about the awful waking vision she'd had of one of them dying in horrible pain. If anybody could make sense of what was happening to her, it would be him.

Glancing back, she was relieved to see the soldiers being accosted by a short dark-haired man who was shouting about the lights in his apartment. The one who had caught her eye was still watching her curiously, so she quickened her step and tried to lose herself in the crowd.

Bains had lost track of the time he'd spent in For'ard Obs. He'd been so consumed in his own head that time had become meaningless. But he was brought back to reality when the lights blacked out and people began to scurry about with flashlights. There was a turmoil of light and black that lasted a few minutes, along with an outburst of excited comments. The comptechs on the next table were on their feet immediately, dashing for the doors, only to find them jammed. They'd had to use the manual release, and it had taken them over a minute to get through.

Bains waited in his seat, watching the swirling storm through the observation panel. He remained still and thoughtful until the emergency lights ignited. Then he decided to make his way home in the semi-darkness and the bustle of people returning to their families.

The lifts were out of operation and they were all forced to take the service stairs. Pretty much swept along by the flow, it still took Bains a good thirty minutes to get home to his apartment, and then he found his door com resolutely defiant. Using his key to unlatch the emergency handle, he pumped the door open manually and finally stepped inside, automatically trying to switch on the lights. They refused and the apartment remained drenched in shadow.

Somewhere, he had a flashlight. Somewhere among all his equipment in the study. It wasn't something you normally needed in the city. Not something you usually had to keep to hand unless you were out in the field. He made his way across the living area, tripping over books that the Doctor had left piled all over the place earlier. He fumbled towards his study, and when he opened the door he stopped abruptly.

There was somebody there. In the dark. No sound at all. Not even the sound of breathing. But he knew for absolute certain that there was somebody in the room.

Then the light hit his face. His hands shot up to cover his eyes. He squinted back, trying to make out who the bloody hell was trying to blind him with his own flashlight. There was motion. Black blobs moving about beyond the edge of the bright white sheet. The light moved, swept round, and finally Bains saw a grotesquely uplit face gazing at him from across the room, thick shadows in all the wrong places making the thing appear frighteningly horrific. The phantasm spoke. Its voice was cracked and strained.

'We wondered where you'd got to,' the Doctor said.

Veta and Josef were marched at gunpoint back to Medicare Central. They took the staff route to avoid contact, and they were nearly back in medicare when the lights had gone out. Instantly, the failsafe flashlights built into the military armour flared into life, and any chance the prisoners might take to run was quashed.

Perón followed them up at the rear, letting the others have all the fun with the guns. Since hearing the whispers in the static she'd felt decidedly uneasy, particularly when the lights and coms had started acting up. There was something in the air. An unspecific threat that her military training was alerting her to. Nothing definite, but a feeling as if a sniper were watching her back, waiting for an opportunity to pick her off. When the lights went out she was ashamed at the yelp of alarm that escaped her, but Veta and Josef had also cried out and she'd managed to get away with it in the momentary hubbub.

They continued on their way using the flashlights, having to manually operate all the doors en route, but finally they got the prisoners into one of the isolation rooms. The door was locked and a guard posted where he could keep a close eye on them through the inspection window.

Perón watched them pacing about in the darkened room like a pair of caged animals, and she was lost for a moment in thought. She was suddenly sure that this was the same room in which the falsified projection of their dead baby had been shown to them two months ago. She felt a pang of remorse when she caught the woman's shadowed eyes gazing back at her, and for a split second she remembered glimpsing a precarious humanity in the eyes of one of the creatures.

Slamming down the mental shutters, she snapped at the guard.

'Don't let them out of your sight.'

Then she marched back to her office, trying her com repeatedly while she went. As she tramped down the corridor she became aware of a ruckus ahead. A handful of men in black uniform crowded around the door to med-ops. As she approached, she saw that they were frantically winding the manual door mechanism to release somebody from inside.

Tyran burst out of the room, closely followed by Dr Domecq. She noticed they were both ashen and Tyran seemed to be wiping perspiration from his face. When he saw her approaching, his eyes locked on to hers and she saw his teeth clench.

'Colonel Perón,' he said, clearly struggling to keep his anger under control. 'Is it too much to ask that you keep one young girl locked in one room for one single day?'

She didn't have a clue what he was talking about, until she positioned herself by the door and saw Danes's body slumped by the bed. She glared at Tyran.

'I gave specific instructions that she was to be –'

'I don't care what instructions you gave, Colonel, they were obviously not carried out. And I just found one of your so-called guards locked in the cell which should have contained our prisoner. What the hell kind of operation are we running here, Colonel?'

'Sir, you have no idea what –'

'I have a very good idea what you've been up against, Colonel. And, although you have my sympathy, you also carry full responsibility when your people fail in their duty.'

'Yes, sir.' She became acutely aware of the troops nearby.

'D'you think you could find Kapoor and the prisoner and bring them to me?'

'With the comps offline, sir, it will take some time under these conditions. We can't access the biodata to trace them using the detectors.'

A head materialised into the air in front of Tyran at that moment. It was full of static, but it was just about succeeding to remain discernible.

'Mr Tyran,' the head hissed and spat, 'we've managed to get some services back online. They're erratic, but coms and comps should be just about usable.'

'Very good,' Tyran said. 'Keep me informed.'

'Yes, sir.' The head was sucked into a fizzling pinprick in the air.

'Looks like you got your detectors back, Colonel. If I were you I'd make the most of them while you've got the chance.'

'Yes, sir,' Perón snapped, turning on her heel to the nearby men. 'Come on, you lot. Grab some detectors and get Kapoor's biodata inputted. I want every available man on search duty.'

The men jumped to attention, saluting and dashing off down the corridor.

When Perón turned back, Tyran was already stomping off in the opposite direction, taking Domecq towards the creatures' cells. Uncertain whether to follow or not, she decided to let him stew and return to her own office to check on the state of her comp. She needed to get some security 'grams set up. There were just too many things to watch and not enough staff to delegate responsibility to. She could really do with some help down here, and there was one person she could trust to supply that help. She jabbed her com as she swept down the corridor.

A head materialised at her shoulder. It was difficult to make out, but she could just about recognise the features.

'Captain Foley,' she said, 'could you report to my office, please?'

Everything was happening at once. The impostor Domecq had vanished into thin air along with the girl, and suddenly the whole city-machine had ground to a halt. It was obvious to Tyran that it would take more than two people to cause such widespread havoc, and the only explanation was that the creatures were exacting revenge for his killing of one of them.

'I don't want them harmed,' Domecq told him as they sped down the corridor towards the hold.

'I don't care what you want,' Tyran said. 'If these things really are the cause of everything, if they really are the psychic weapons you suspect, I'm going to have them deactivated any way I can.'

He swung the mind probe at Domecq as they marched.

'We don't have much time,' Tyran said. 'Our comptechs are fighting a losing battle. While we've got the comps online, I'm going to take whatever they've got in those evil little minds.'

Domecq grasped him by the shoulder and swung him to a halt in the middle of the corridor.

'You're not sanctioned to take this action,' Domecq warned him, his face dark with meaning.

'I just sanctioned myself to take whatever action I deem necessary to keep my crew here safe.'

Tyran snatched his hand away and stomped off.

'Earth Central will destroy you for this,' Domecq shouted after him.

'Earth Central can try to do what the hell it wants to me,' Tyran yelled back without missing a step.

This time the guard snapped to attention when he saw Tyran approaching. Tyran threw him a brusque salute and indicated the door to the cells.

234

'No problems?'

'No, sir.'

But, as he passed through the storeroom into the hold, Tyran knew immediately that something was wrong. Last time they were here the doors had rattled and slammed and there was a subtle but definite sense of tension in the air, as if the creatures had sensed their purpose.

Now the short corridor was silent, except for the howling wind outside that sounded as though it were clawing at the walls to get in. Pushing his key into the nearest lock, Tyran tugged the door to find the cell dark and cold…

…and empty.

Fitz raised his hand into the air but didn't turn his back on the trooper. He saw immediately the smirk disappear from her face when she saw the explosive he was holding.

'Cyclotol concentrate,' Ayla said somewhere behind him. 'Develops a detonation pressure of about fifty thousand atmospheres a square centimetre.'

The trooper was drip-white, Fitz noticed, and he felt the colour abruptly drain from his own face too.

'If it goes off it'll take everything within a quite a few square metres,' Ayla continued. 'Very instant. Very painless.'

The gun was wavering now in the trooper's hand, and Ayla stepped through a slow wide arc to take it from her. With a sigh of relief, Fitz lowered the explosive stick and regarded it with a new respect bordering on reverence. The smirk had transferred itself from the trooper to Ayla.

'Tranquilliser pellet,' Ayla said, matter of fact and businesslike.

The trooper reached carefully into a pocket and removed a small blister pack that contained a row of tiny pills. Popping one of the pills, she slipped it into her mouth at great pains to keep every movement clearly visible. A few seconds later she slumped to the ground and Ayla was fussing over her comatose body, snapping a pair of the trooper's own cuffs around the wrists and grasping the woman's flashlight.

Fitz was gingerly tugging the sticks of explosive out of his pockets where he'd stuffed them.

'I was kidding,' Ayla said.

'Hmm?'

'It's not really cyclotol concentrate. It's old-fashioned TNT. We use it to excavate sometimes. Keep hold of it.'

'We've got a gun now,' he pointed out. 'Seems a bit stupid running about loaded up to the eyeballs with this stuff. One spark and I go off like a box of fireworks.'

'Keep it,' she said, grabbing some of the sticks from him and proceeding to stuff them into her own pockets and pouches. She tapped him on the chin with one and grinned. 'We're going to use it in our daring and nail-biting escape from the very jaws of death.'

'Oh,' said Fitz. 'Righto.'

The chopper was being hurled about like a kite in the storm, and visibility was down to the windscreen. But the Doctor refused to give up the controls and let the autonavigation system take them in.

Bains had strapped himself into one of the side seats, but the children were all crouched on the floor huddling against one another for stability. He found them peering at him intermittently out of huge black eyes, skinny hunched shapes like primates. They'd been nervous of him at first, but the Doctor had soothed their fears, introducing Bains as their friend, and finally they'd seemed to accept him as such. One of the girls had taken his hand, pulled him down to her level, and stroked his face with cold, spindly fingers. In an instant he'd understood there was a trust between them. Not just himself and the girl, but all of them.

The dead child was still shrouded in the makeshift sling that the Doctor had carried strapped to his back, and now it was fastened into the seat beside Bains. He could just see the top of its head through an opening in the material, a few loose strands of wispy silver hair curling out from the folds.

Again, he felt the chopper suddenly dip and swerve.

'Where the hell did you learn to fly these things?' Bains asked the Doctor over his shoulder.

The Doctor didn't look back. 'I watched Captain Foley last night,' he said. 'The principles are fairly elementary.'

Of course, Bains didn't believe for an instant that the Doctor had trained by watching Foley last night, but he let the comment go, as he had done most of the Doctor's comments over the last hour or so.

Their escape had been effortless. Unlike Bains's earlier miserable failure. The Doctor had led them up through the superstructure in a series of cagelike lifts that apparently maintenance crews used in emergencies. They'd reached toplevel unhindered and unseen except by a few rogue rats. They'd emerged through one of the ventilation maintenance blocks out into the vicious storm and made swift progress to the chopper pads.

The Doctor had entered military codes to release the chopper, and in no time at all they were on their way. When Bains remarked on the smoothness of the operation, the Doctor had waved a hand dismissively.

'I'm something of an expert at escape attempts,' he'd said, adding, 'and besides, I've had all day and unlimited computer access to plan this one.'

The expansion of the word 'comp' jarred. But it was only one of many, many small mysteries that this man seemed to carry around with him.

And some of the other small mysteries that he carried around with him were the children. He'd given Bains only the sketchiest explanation on their way up in the cages. The Doctor didn't know who or what exactly they were, but he was sure they were somehow linked to all the troubles that WorldCorp were experiencing on Ceres Alpha. He also suspected – something to do with connections he'd made between what he'd read on the medicare comps and what he'd read in Bains's journals – that they were something to do with Bains's dig. Bains had lost the strand of the conversation at this point, but the Doctor had said that hopefully things would become clearer if they could visit the dig.

The chopper dipped abruptly, and the storms parted in front of them like a curtain.

'There,' Bains said. 'That's the area. There's an entrance to a cave system.' He pointed. 'Just follow that rim. About a hundred metres. You can put us down just outside it.'

The chopper swooped and the Doctor brought them in for a perfectly executed touchdown, unhooking himself and opening the door before the propellers had even had time to stop. Bains tumbled out after him, and found the Doctor standing nearby gazing up into the sky. The effect was stunning. There was a kind of void in the storm above them, an opening through which they could see a star-filled sky. Around the perimeter of the opening was a frontier where the storm was a grey blur, and beyond that it quickly became an impenetrable wall of sand and wind.

'We seem to be in the eye of the storm,' the Doctor noted.

'I've never seen anything like it,' Bains admitted.

'Fascinating…'

'Bloody amazing…'

Without warning the Doctor was moving again, heading back to the chopper where the children were helping each other out, landing one at a time in the dirt. Bains watched their huge black eyes widen as they gazed about in wonder.

Then he saw one of the children bend and scoop up a handful of loose soil, lifting it for the Doctor to see. The child gazed expectantly into the Doctor's face, and the Doctor knelt to examine what the child was showing him. Then the child spoke, its voice soft and quiet, barely a sound at all.

'Home,' it said. 'We belong.'

Tyran answered the com call and Perón's head appeared in the air above his desk. The woman looked exhausted, the stress now very evident in her features.

'Yes?' Tyran demanded, his voice a whip-crack sound.

'Sir, we have a fix on the girl. We're moving in now. But we've done a complete sweep for the impostor and for the children. Nothing.'

'Nothing?'

'No, sir. If we can trust the comp readings, then they've left the city completely.'

Tyran was beginning to consider the significance of her words when she continued.

'I've also done a scan for Professor Bains. He wasn't in his apartment so I used the biodata readings we took from him today and ran a city-wide scan with them. He's also gone.'

Now Tyran was finally beginning to see the pattern in the apparent chaos. 'Get a chopper out to Bains's dig,' he told her.

'I've already done that, sir. Captain Foley is on her way right now.'

'Excellent.' Tyran grinned. 'What orders has she got?'

'Bring them all back alive, sir. Or as alive as they need to be to answer questions.'

'Slight adjustment to that order, Colonel. Patch it through to Foley, would you? I want them all back here all right, but I don't want a single one of them alive. Got that?'

'Yes, sir.'

'Oh, and Colonel…'

'Yes, sir?'

'Destroy everything in Bains's apartment, would you?'

Perón nodded. 'Yes, sir,' she said, and her head cut cleanly out of the air.

'We seem to be getting our comps back online with these creatures off-city,' Tyran pointed out to Domecq, who sat alongside him at the huge desk. 'I think the answer to all our problems is staring us right in the face, don't you?'

Jörgan was sticking close to one of the troops. If anybody was going to find his prisoner, it was going to be the professionals, not his ramshackle army of brutes.

The trooper was using a detector, but the readings were all over the place because Jörgan's rabble was darting about here, there and everywhere. They'd tried to use Damsk's medical readings for the man, but they'd found all the records deliberately sabotaged, presumably by Damsk. So the trooper was reverting to more old-fashioned scanning techniques, looking painstakingly for patterns of movement that might indicate the pursued rather than the pursuers. It was not going to be easy, but Jörgan felt it was still probably more effective than his men.

'There!' the trooper said suddenly. 'We got one body not moving. He's resting. Ground level. He's found himself a hidey-hole. Looks like he's planning to lie low.'

The trooper marched forward, keeping an eye on the readings, raising her rifle with her spare hand in readiness.

'Twenty metres… Eighteen… Fifteen… Viczinski, can you read me? Close in on my position… Viczinski?'

Jörgan was gazing into the forest of girders and huge thick beams, watching the light from the trooper's torch zooming in on their prey.

'Ten metres… Viczinski? Where the hell are you?'

There was a central strut-array up front, cross-linked with braces that created a cagelike effect with a hollow core. There was just enough room for a man to squeeze inside, and when the trooper's light got close enough to pick out the detail they could see that the middle of the struts was piled high with packaging. They could also see a boot protruding from underneath.

The trooper stopped dead only a metre away.

'All right. Come on. Let's have you out of there.'

No response.

She nudged the boot with the muzzle of her rifle.

'*Move it!*'

Again, nothing.

Keeping the gun up front, she reached in to tug at the cover, revealing the body beneath, and her voice was suddenly full of defeat and fury.

'Viczinski! You stupid –'

A roar from behind them cut off her voice. Instantly they were running. Galloping back towards the entrance. Jörgan was breathing hard and fast, not quite able to keep up with the trooper, who was lighter and more agile on the rubble-strewn surface.

Out in the open, with the winds ripping round them, they saw one of the giant machines crashing through the perimeter fence. It grumbled with a commotion of sound and a stench of exhaust gases out into the field, and was quickly consumed by the storm. Jörgan watched as the surrounding machines were started one by one, preparing for the chase. He was about to clamber up the ladders into the nearest one when the trooper grasped his elbow.

'We'll take the chopper,' she said, snapping her goggles back down over her eyes and dashing off into the dark squall.

Close on her heals, Jörgan was launched suddenly off his feet by the huge explosions that followed. He crashed to the ground, a confused heap entangled with the trooper.

'What the –'

More detonations. He was showered with dirt and flying debris. The trooper let out a scream and Jörgan saw her grasping her leg. The blasts continued, one after another, rolling like thunder, until finally all that was left was the sound of the screeching winds.

Raising his head, Jörgan looked back to see the remaining earthmovers immobile, their caterpillar tracks ripped like canvas, immense chunks of mangled metal.

'They rigged the tracks with dynamite,' Jörgan hissed, still struggling to catch his breath.

The trooper was scrambling to her feet. He followed her as she set off limping into the squall. Making their way round the side of the base camp, they both cluttered to a halt when they saw the military chopper sitting in the churned mud, its nose poking upwards and the rest of the body a mass of lumpy smashed parts.

Veta sat with her back to the window, and Josef slumped on a small stool opposite. He watched the guard and the guard watched him back. For a second, Josef thought the man was asleep on his feet. His eyes seemed to glaze over, going completely out of focus as if he were staring into the space above Josef's head. Then Josef saw him run a hand through his hair and realised that he was inspecting his own reflection in the glass.

'We got systems back on line,' Veta said softly, her fingers flickering with almost imperceptible motion across the surface of the remote control. 'They're very patchy. All the resources are being put into military security. They've got full shielding on all their communications.'

'Watch they don't detect you.'

He received a flash of her shadowed eyes and she didn't need to utter a word.

'Where are you?' he asked.

'I got access through Perón's system. We got her passcode and her security. I've set up a cloak to stop anybody looking at what I'm doing in here.'

'What *are* you doing in here?'

'I'm going to use the same trick on them as they used on us.'

'Uh?'

'Is he still looking?'

'Yeah.'

'Does he look suspicious?'

'Just looks like he's doing as he was told. He looks bored.'

'Anybody else about?'

'No. Wait. Yes. Somebody talking to him.'

'Is he still looking in here?'

'No. Yes. No.'

Josef was moving. Unexpectedly flying through the air. They landed together in the shadow of an incubator.

'What *are* you playing at?' he hissed, gazing anxiously back at the window to see the guard looking into the room again.

Then he saw himself and Veta still sitting there talking. In the middle of the room. On their little stools. Then Veta's hand grasped his ear and she dragged him back under cover of darkness.

'He'll see you,' she said. 'Keep down.'

'What are you doing now?'

'Just shut up.'

He did as he was told, trying to get a view of what she was up to in the corner of the room. There was a repeated low rattle of metal against metal, then Veta fell backwards and he saw that she had a vent grille in her hands. She pushed it over to one side and began to feed herself into the hole in the wall. Then she was gone with a shuffling sound, and he poked his head in to watch her disappear into the suffocating blackness.

'Are you coming or what?' she whispered, her voice echoing slightly in the enclosed space.

Scrambling on his hands and knees, he set off in pursuit, concentrating on the soles of her feet moving ahead of him with a quick rhythm. She stopped and he heard another clatter of metal and a new source of dim light entered the confined space as Veta extricated herself from the vent. He followed, poking his head out to find himself in another room very similar to the one they'd just left.

Except, of course, that this one didn't have a guard on it.

The Doctor had asked Bains to excavate a small hole. With his digging equipment stored in the caves, it was a simple enough task. He'd piled the loose soil each side, then, as the Doctor had requested, left a single shovel to fill the hole back in.

He found the Doctor and the children back at the chopper in sombre mood. They were sitting cross-legged on the ground, arranged in a circle like a class of schoolchildren and the Doctor the teacher. In the middle of the circle was the small shrouded shape of the dead child.

As Bains approached, the Doctor clambered to his feet and met him with a face full of starcast shadows.

'I thought it was only right to devise some sort of ceremony,' he told Bains quietly.

Bains saw that the children were touching one another gently, pointing across the circle and muttering.

'What are they doing?'

The Doctor smiled, but it was a smile full of sadness. 'Speaking their names.'

'Sorry?'

The Doctor grasped him by the shoulder and pulled him away. They walked a small distance and the Doctor's hand remained on Bains's shoulder.

'They didn't have names,' he said, stopping and lowering himself and Bains to the ground. 'They were just given numbers. The numbers of their cells. It's all that was needed to differentiate them for the purposes of the experiments.'

Bains watched him with a mixture of shock and horror, but the Doctor avoided his eyes. He was watching the children as they ceremoniously pointed to one another, and his face was dark.

'The naming of kids is a difficult matter,' he said softly, his voice just audible above the strange cries of the nearby winds. 'It isn't just one of your holiday games.'

They shared a short silence.

'They named themselves, you know,' he said suddenly. 'Quaxo, Coricopat, Rum Tum Tugger, Mungojerrie, Rumpelteazer, Bombalurina, Mr Mistoffelees, Macavity, Asparagus, Bustopher Jones, Skimbleshanks, Jellylorum.'

'Those are names?'

'Oh yes,' the Doctor said quite earnestly. 'Particular. Peculiar. Dignified.'

Another reflective silence.

'I suggested Old Deuteronomy. But they wouldn't have it. They said *I* was Old Deuteronomy. "Old Deuteronomy's lived a long time; He's a cat who has lived many lives in succession." They understood. They understood so much. The poetry is almost a thousand years old. And I didn't give them anything except a handful of names. Dr Pryce was right when he said they get inside your head. But he was wrong about them being evil. Look at them.'

The children remained cross-legged on the ground, still pointing at one another simply speaking their new names. They looked slightly ridiculous in the clothes the Doctor had put on them. He'd raided Bains's wardrobe and adapted anything he could find. Jumpers that were far too large. Shorts tied with string that came down to their toes. Coats with strategic knots. Shirts torn in two. They were smeared with dirt from their ascent in the city superstructure. Dark marks that streaked their pale faces. A motley band of ragamuffins if ever he saw one. But they also looked solemn, reverent and entirely and wholly innocent, thought Bains.

'Have you ever conducted a funeral?' the Doctor asked him suddenly.

'I'm sorry?'

'A burial. Have you ever conducted the service for one?'

Bains was gawking at the man. 'No.'

The Doctor looked disappointed. 'I don't know if I'm the right person to do it,' he admitted.

'They seem to look up to you,' Bains said.

He emitted a delicate laugh. 'They do, don't they?' Then he looked sombre, his eyes abruptly distant.

'It's difficult,' he said finally. 'I lost somebody. A good friend. He died out in the storm when we landed. I should have been there for him. I let him down.'

'No,' Bains told him. He didn't really know the man at all, but he knew beyond all doubt that what he was about to say was the truth. 'You don't let people down. It's not in your nature.'

She had a rendezvous with death, and Foley wasn't looking forward to it one little bit. The chopper bucked and lunged through the storm and she would normally be shouting orders and abuse at Klute who was in the driving seat. But the words just wouldn't come. The anger was no longer there.

The mission had started out as a straight search-and-retrieve. But a few minutes after they were airborne Perón had amended her

245

instructions, obviously a command from Tyran. They were to bring them all back dead.

It was a simple enough instruction. *All back dead.* Three syllables. The kind of order the military mind was trained to understand. No frills. No complicated long words to fluff the meaning or give rise to any misunderstanding. No room for any kind of personal bias. Dead. Simple.

She'd risked her skin to save this man. She'd felt physically sick to see him interrogated. She'd realised with a wrench that she'd developed quite suddenly a very great respect for him. These were feelings she was completely unfamiliar with. Her duty had always been very clear. No grey areas. Just black and white. Orders were orders and the enemy was the enemy, even if you knew full well he didn't deserve to die.

If she deserted, if she tried to help him, she'd be hunted down and treated no better than he had been.

So, then. A simple choice. Ultimately, either way, her rendezvous remained unchanged.

Using ropes, Bains and the Doctor stood either side of the grave and lowered the body into the ground. The children huddled nearby watching with sombre faces. No tears. No nothing. Just blank expressions. The Doctor had said they were only two months old. Although they appeared much older, perhaps they had no concept of what death really meant.

While Bains removed the ropes the Doctor prepared to say a few words. He appeared ill at ease, gazing off into the distance trying to sort his thoughts.

'It's difficult,' he said at last, 'to lose a friend. We can all only really deal with loss in our own… private way.'

A pause of quiet sorrow.

'Some of us…' he began again, but the words stumbled to silence and he stood there with tears in his dark eyes, unable to speak and unable to meet any of their expectant gazes. One of the children took him by the hand, and he tried to force a smile into his lips that refused to come. His face a muddle of pain and memories and regrets, he shook his head and Bains saw a solitary tear roll down his cheek.

'I'm sorry,' he muttered in a broken voice.

The girl pulled him down to his knees in the dirt. She stroked the side of his face and the Doctor grabbed her suddenly, scooping her up and hugging her tight.

Then he bent and returned her to her feet, offering a handful of soil. She watched him in puzzlement, and he took a handful for himself and tossed it on to the body.

'To say goodbye,' the Doctor explained, his voice barely a whisper.

She did the same, and so did the others while the Doctor stood by gazing deep into space and time and himself.

Bains gathered the children together and led them off towards the caves. There was no need for words. They knew where they were going. They knew the Doctor needed time alone. As they picked their way over the uneven ground, Bains heard a single sharp stab of the shovel behind them.

The wind was full of strange distant cries. He looked up through the tunnel above them into the black-blue depths of space and stars, and realised he'd never before seen the night sky on Ceres Alpha. There had always been storms that came with the dark. He'd never seen the stars from this world. And now there was a window on them and they looked crystal clear and lovely. He discovered one of the children tugging at his sleeve and bent down to see what he wanted.

'Twinkle twinkle,' said the boy.

'Little star,' one of the others continued.

'How I wonder,' said another.

'What you are,' somebody finished.

He smiled at the simplicity of it, but it was a smile tinged with gloom. Funerals were terrible things. A child's funeral doubly so. The universe was so very full of might-have-beens. So very full of grief.

247

'*Bains!*' the Doctor screamed. '*Bains! Help me!*'

When he looked back, the Doctor was gone. For a split second there was only blind confusion. Then Bains saw the dirt flying and set off at a run.

'*Bains! Help me!*'

Falling to his knees at the side of the grave, Bains peered over to see the Doctor frantically swiping the dirt from the small corpse. He looked up with wide mad eyes.

'*He's alive!*'

The body was pushed up to him, and Bains took it with a numb sense of unreality, laying it on the soft soil to see that it was indeed moving. He saw small fingers grasping at the edge of the material, pulling it aside. Then a face spattered with mud.

The other children were gathering round, helping to tug the shroud free.

'Oh my God!' uttered Bains.

'I've never seen anything like it,' the Doctor gasped.

The dead child was sitting up, opening his eyes groggily, reaching out to the others and finally smiling. The others were watching him in wonder, touching and stroking his frail naked arms.

'Bustopher Jones,' said one of them. 'Bustopher Jones.'

They all began to chant the name, as if it was some ritual incantation, their voices eerie low whispers in the still night air.

'*Bustopher Jones Bustopher Jones Bustopher Jones Bustopher Jones…*'

'How I wonder,' said one of the girls, her voice louder and suddenly out of step with the others, 'What you are…'

Having made her way down to level twelve via the stairs, Anji very quickly realised that she had no idea at all where she was and where the Doctor might be held. Fortunately, level twelve, the immediate vicinity at least, seemed to be well and truly deserted. She'd emerged into a wide corridor that was poorly illuminated by the same dreary yellow lighting that the rest of the city was using. She'd tried her com badge, but it merely spat and fizzled at her in a not very friendly way at all. The place was obviously falling apart at the seams.

Not far down the corridor was a wall panel like the ones she'd used in medicare. Checking for activity, she set off and tried touching it.

'Anybody there?' she asked, trying to keep her voice low and confidential.

In response she got the same holographic logo as before, except this time it was weak and the voice was high and stringy.

'Can I help you?'

Now… How to phrase this… There wasn't a lot of option. Not many ways she could frame a question like this. Alarm bells or not, she took the plunge.

'Where are the prisoners kept?'

'Prisoners?'

Damn.

The VIPs who just had the crap kicked out of them, she wanted to scream. But instead she said, 'Is there a prison section? Are there any cells nearby?'

'I'm sorry, I'm not sure I understand your question. Please be more specific. Do you wish to see the Doctor?'

She glared at the thing in astonishment. How did it…?

Then she saw them at the far end of the corridor. Three black figures walking towards her with their rifles raised. One of them was grinning, talking into a little microphone that was suspended in front of his mouth.

'In that case perhaps I can help after all…'

The cockpit of the earthmover was amazingly sumptuous and serene. Fitz was impressed by the huge array of holographic screens that swam around the driver's seat. He was also immensely impressed by the way Ayla operated the controls with practised ease. After they had left the fieldbase in tatters, she'd spent a few minutes feeding it instructions, then she'd sat back to enjoy the ride.

He'd thankfully taken a back seat to lick his wounds. He was in a mess. His long legs ached, his chest had taken about as much of a battering as it could manage, and his arms felt fit to drop off.

He found Ayla watching him from her position up front, a look of distraction on her face.

'What's up?' he asked.

'I was just curious,' she said.

He grinned. 'I'm a real mystery, I know. I'm sorry. It's not easy to explain.'

'Try me.'

'I travel with a man called the Doctor. We travel through time and space in a blue crate that looks just like a twentieth-century wooden police box, but which is in actual fact a multidimensional time ship that's the product of an infinitely superior alien civilisation.'

She raised her eyebrows dismissively at him and turned back to face the controls.

'It's bigger on the inside than it is on the outside!'

She ignored him.

'I told you it's not easy to explain,' he said.

So they remained silent for a good long while until the holograms started to cackle and shimmer. Then a distorted face appeared in front of Ayla. It was a young woman with long blonde hair tied up in a bob. Quite smart, thought Fitz.

'You wish to make an approach?' the face asked.

Wouldn't mind, Fitz thought.

'We're coming in for repairs,' Ayla told her.

'I'm sorry. We're experiencing some difficulties here at the moment. I can't open the bay doors, but we're also stationary right now so you could park outside and come in on foot. I'll extend a boarding tube for you. Please let me have your controls and I'll position you from this end.'

Ayla relinquished the controls and the machine began to grind and shake. Fitz glared at her in alarm.

'She's not a smooth operator like you,' he complained.

'They're moving us into the aft zone. The ground's pretty unstable here. Just hold tight.'

Finally the creaking and jerking calmed, and Ayla led him to the escape door, where Fitz now found a long kind of enclosed gangplank where there should have been ladders to the ground. She led him across and they emerged into an immense holding area that was as big as any aircraft hangar Fitz had ever seen.

The place was badly illuminated, full of geometric shadows and hideously enormous blocks of darkness. It was constructed of gigantic beams with what must have been thousands of interconnecting metal-grid walkways. It looked to Fitz like a nightmare vision from one of those old German films about the future. Off in the dim distance he could see a row of parked earthmovers, some of them with their tracks dismantled. The scale of the place took his breath away and, as he gazed down into the huge open area below, so did something else.

Grasping Ayla by the arm, he pulled her to the railing and pointed down into the hold. It was some distance away, couched in shadow, but his eye had been drawn towards it as if by some strange invisible attraction.

'There,' he announced triumphantly. 'I told you... A twentieth-century wooden police box.'

The three choppers emerged from the storm unexpectedly, swooping down like vultures into the open area around the caves. They moved with military precision, landing in a tight triangle in front of Bains and the others. The three side doors sprang open and black-uniformed shapes spilled out, rifles raised at the small group.

The Doctor stepped forward under the intense glare from their searchlights. Bains saw one of the figures flick up her goggles, then reach round to peel off her helmet. Even with the full glare of the lights behind her, he recognised Captain Foley.

She was watching the Doctor with a curiously vacant look in her face, pausing as if she were uncertain what to do next.

Bains wrapped his arms round the children, and saw her eyes flick from the Doctor to them. The troops were gathering into tight formation around her, guns ready.

Foley was shaking her head, arms held in front of her in a strangely pleading gesture. She was gazing straight at the Doctor now, and Bains could see the twinkling of tears in her eyes.

'I'm sorry, Doctor,' she gasped.

And Bains saw their grips tighten on the rifles.

'I did tell you,' Fitz said, finding it hard to keep the smugness out of his voice.

Ayla was standing there with her mouth wide open, gawking at the impossibly vast interior of the TARDIS. The console room was still in a mess from the Doctor's earlier mad panic, and the floor was littered with all manner of instruments from sonic wrenches to bent paperclips. But despite the chaos, and despite that fact that the TARDIS may well remain a useless heap of transdimensional scrap, Fitz felt an overwhelming sense of relief to be back.

'But it's impossible,' Ayla was saying as she tumbled down the steps into the room and then sustained the full impact of realising there were even more ludicrously gigantic areas leading off from the central control area.

'That's what they all say,' Fitz told her, running his hands over the centre console like a man stroking his prized Lamborghini.

'I just knew there was something about you,' she muttered as she performed a slow pirouette on her heels, trying to take in the sheer scale of the TARDIS interior.

'I can be a surprising man,' he told her, putting on the Connery slur.

She didn't react at all. Just kept on turning and gazing and looking utterly gobsmacked, obviously far more impressed by the hardware than the man. Uh-huh. OK. He still had one or two cards left up his sleeve.

'I'm going to take a shower,' he told her.

No answer.

'An antigrav shower,' he explained.

She turned and nodded.

'It's very stimulating.'

She was smiling now and shaking her head.

'Well,' he said, finally resigned, 'there's a kitchen through there. You're very welcome to make yourself at home.'

'I will,' she said. 'Thank you.'

He found himself standing there like one of those naff nodding dogs. The situation dragged on for a whole ten seconds before he finally squeezed a big stupid grin into his face and made his embarrassed retreat.

He was holding a short black truncheon up to her face. She simply gazed back at him with all the determination she could muster. But her arms were tied and she was feeling queasy and achy and she really didn't know how much more of this nightmare treatment she could withstand.

'Who do you work for?' he asked, getting more agitated by the minute.

Anji was aware of Perón standing nearby, watching her with an intense stare.

'I don't work for anybody,' she told him for the umpteenth time. 'We're just travellers. We crash-landed.'

'Explain how you just happened to travel hundreds of light years into the middle of nowhere when we didn't have a single residue of hyperspace drive when we scanned after your crash.'

'We don't travel through hyperspace.'

'Liar!'

He jerked the truncheon in her direction and she felt her head explode with light and pain. The sensation died and she found the man glaring at the truncheon with gritted teeth.

'Get me some power to my comp,' he yelled, his face crimson with effort.

He tried again, pointing the device close to her face, his eyes wild and manic.

Again, the light burst into her head. This time dimmer but more sustained. She could feel it burning the backs of her eyes, as if her brain had erupted into flames. She screamed but the man was screaming back.

'*Tell me!*' he cried. '*Tell me!*'

Then there was calm. A cool breeze of air. The fires died out and she gazed dizzily at the room full of people who were like things in a dream, wispy and not quite material. And on the walls around her she saw the image. The picture they'd ripped from her head. Distorted and repeated dozens of times as if she were in the heart of a hall of mirrors.

A picture of the TARDIS.

Foley's apology seemed such an inadequate thing for the murder she was about to commit. The Doctor watched her with pain in his eyes, and suddenly all she could see was the glitter of starlight through tears. She sensed Klute and Downs either side, rifles primed and ready to fire. They awaited her order, fingers already squeezing the triggers. She sensed a deep dark space open up inside her and out of it came a sorrow so huge that she found it impossible to stifle the sobs as she raised her own rifle and fired –

The explosions were immense and simultaneous. The whole world turned in all directions at once, spinning and crying and howling, until Bains landed with a thud in the dirt. He opened his eyes to find he'd been thrown a good few metres, and the children were scattered around him, rising groggily from the ground to gaze back at the flaming inferno that used to be choppers and troops.

The Doctor was scrambling to his knees in the churned mud nearby, and a moment later Bains saw the anguish in his face as he stared back at the children, his eyes flashing from one to another. Framed against the burning backdrop, the Doctor appeared to Bains like a dark avenging demon, hair a disorderly pile above his ferocious face.

'You could have simply jammed their weapons,' he shrieked.

The sudden appalling realisation hit Bains hard. The children had somehow caused the rifles to backfire, destroying the troops and the whole area around them in one tremendous fireball. His view of the innocents took a sharp swerve and he regarded them with new horror.

The Doctor tramped over, grabbing one of the children seemingly at random and dragging it up by the scruff of the neck. He glared into the child's eyes, and the child scowled back. For long moments they were locked in conflict. Then the Doctor's chin fell to his chest, and when he looked up again the anger had declined.

'I know they were going to kill us,' he said quietly. 'But it's no reason to kill them.'

The child, one of the boys, reached out to touch the side of the Doctor's face, a look of puzzlement clear in his features.

'It's not easy to explain,' the Doctor told him. 'It's just that... life's just... too *precious*.'

There was an unspoken moment of understanding between them, Bains could swear, while in the background the flames curled and writhed, sending thick black clouds of smoke to obscure his new view of the stars.

They'd tried cutters and explosives, locksmiths and comp scans, everything that they could think of yet there it remained. Obstinately locked. Tyran touched the surface of what appeared to be a flimsy wooden door and found it vibrating slightly. The city-machine was still stuck in a state of immobility despite their most strenuous efforts, so the vibration was nothing to do with their motion.

The Kapoor girl appeared from the shadows and Perón shoved her with such force that she came skidding across the grimy floor to his feet. He watched her for a minute writhing in pain, her hands still cuffed to her back and her face now grazed and bloody.

'Stand up,' he snarled.

But she could only lie there feebly, breath coming shallow and frail.

Perón stepped forward and wrenched her to her feet. She winced and cried out in more pain. While Perón held her tight, Tyran pushed his face close to hers. Her eyes were unfocused, but she was watching the blue box behind him with what he could swear was a degree of yearning.

'What the hell *are* you people?' he growled.

She didn't, or couldn't, respond.

'Get this thing open,' he ordered.

'Can't,' she whispered.

'What?'

'Can't… Only the Doctor…'

'Only the Doctor?'

'Key…' Her voice was nothing but a breath.

He reached out and fingered the chain around her neck, and she pulled back, her eyes abruptly more alert.

His face swam about in the thick goo in front of her. She felt him trying to tug the key from round her neck and instinctively tried to pull away. In response she got a greatly bloated leer.

'So only the Doctor has a key, does he?' The words swam about in her head. She tried to grasp them one at a time. They were wriggling fish.

There was a sharp scratch at her neck and the key came free. The Doctor had told her… the key would only work for her… '*Only you…*' he'd said. '*Only you…*' His face filled her head. His voice filled her head. *Only you…*

The man tried the key in the door. He pushed and twisted and slammed it and… *Only you…*

Then the man turned back, his face full of rage. He threw the key to the floor and she saw his mouth working with fury… His eyes were wide and wild… His face was red and raging… She saw him reach behind her. Her head was full of noise thick as treacle… Stodgy and sickly sweat sound… It oozed through her brain… The words now had gone and there was only glutinous sound…

A gun… He waved it at her… His face still furious… The Doctor's voice came back, bursting on the surface of the thick noise in her head, a bubble of unexpected clarity…

Only you…

The gun jerked. Went off. Sound stopped.

The girl collapsed at his feet and Perón plunged to check her carotid. She shook her head, letting the body fall lifeless to the floor. Tyran could only stare in numb silence. What had he done? Perón was standing again, taking her rifle back from him, and uttering confirmation of what he already knew.

'She's dead.'

Corporal Vanburgh was getting bored. He had no idea what he'd done to deserve such a godawful post, but he'd been here over an hour now and the couple in the isolation room had hardly even moved. They sat chatting on little stools in the middle of the room, the woman with her back to him and the man occasionally glancing to meet Vanburgh's eye.

There had been some activity up to about half an hour ago, people passing by, people to talk to, small distractions to take his mind off the monotony. But in the last half an hour he hadn't seen a soul and now his patience was wearing thin.

Then he caught it out of the corner of his eye. The incubator had appeared from nowhere. One minute the corridor was empty, he could swear, and the next the thing was there. He did a double take and simply stared at it for a few moments before his brain alerted him to go and check it out.

As he approached he saw that it contained a sleeping baby. A small, naked thing with arms outstretched and eyes closed. He stood in front of it, peering into the nearby empty room where the equipment must have come from. There was nobody about. The room was empty.

'Hello?' Vanburgh tried.

Nobody.

As he reached out to push the incubator back into the room, his hands passed through the plastic sides and Vanburgh was taken momentarily off guard. What happened next was too fast and puzzling for his mind to grasp. The woman who was sitting in the next room talking just a second ago, the woman whom he'd been watching closely for the last hour who hadn't moved a muscle, was standing in front of him smiling. Her hand came up to meet his face and swift oblivion gushed up from nowhere to engulf him.

After killing the girl, Tyran had forced a hasty retreat back to his office. His lair. He poured himself a quick whisky and slumped in his seat at the head of the desk. A supernatural silence and stillness permeated the room. Although the lights and comps were returning to normal, there was no sign at all of the city-machine getting on its way again. He'd received engineering reports that spoke of immense physical failures caused by a barrage of infinitesimal substructural glitches. Gears ground in places to dust. The glitches had come from nowhere. No traceable path. The equivalent of a man giving himself major body traumas by simply believing on a whim that he'd sustained them.

Major body traumas...

Tyran experienced a startling instant memory of Danes's rising body. Blue lips speaking. Cold air emerging from already dead lungs.

He tried to take a gulp of whisky, but as he lifted the glass he realised with a small cold shock just how much his hands were shaking. Slamming the glass back on to the desk, he then realised how cool the room had abruptly become.

Then he saw the wall panels. Darkening as something surged with swift fluidity down the other side. Thick liquid, like oil. It came from above, in the middle of the ceiling, the centre of the huge web design. The darkness oozed with a terrifying rapidity down towards the floor all around him.

There was a dripping sound, and he found great globs of thick red liquid dribbling from above on to his desk, quickly creating a spreading pool that surged outward, stretching with terrifying speed towards him. He found suddenly that he was frozen, completely unable to move his hands as the fluid flowed around them, oozing cool and viscous between his fingers.

Then there was movement and he saw them with a gasp of sheer horror. The people sitting around the desk. Crowds of corpses that glared at him out of sightless sockets-for-eyes. Among them he recognised the Kapoor girl and the creature he'd killed earlier. Then he recognised others. One after another, flash recollections of people he'd killed. People who'd got in his way. Barriers he'd overcome in his drive for the top.

More bodies were emerging through the walls. Looming like ghosts until they were solid. Many he didn't even know. The room was full of milling dead people, passing around and between and gazing at him from out of dark holes.

Many he didn't even know...

He'd reviewed the reports from Gildus Prime. There were immense hazards from the local anomaly, but the phenomenon came and went without warning. PlanetScape were plotting to undermine his operations. There were boardroom manoeuvres to take down the upstart WorldCorp and leave the company no more than scattered stardust. So Tyran saw his chance. He made changes to the engineering reports and people who had worked on them simply vanished. The reports were published without mention of the anomaly. PlanetScape, exercising its financial might to acquire key people in Earth Central, took the contract. The rest... The rest was history...

He felt hands sliding down over his shoulders, stroking his chest. Palms still fixed to the desk, he flicked back his head expecting to find Carly, but the real shock was yet to come.

'Oh Christ,' he heard himself say as the breath burst out of him in tight spasms.

The woman gazed at him out of sightless eyes. He knew instantly who she was. The face he'd never forgotten. The first person he'd ever killed. He'd sucked out her mind for leaving him dead. And now she was back. Returned from the grave.

'Mother…'

'That wasn't a nice thing you did,' she said. Her breath smelled like earth.

'What you did was worse,' he told her, appalled at the thick sound of fear in his own voice. 'Leaving me to die in the gutter.'

'I told them where to find you,' she said, her hands sweeping around his chest in a perverted, sensual motion, leaving thick trails of blood in their wake.

'You abandoned me!' he spat. 'The rats got me first. I was lucky to live. While you went chasing the sun. Digging for gold. You're nothing but a prostitute, you callous, evil bitch.'

Trying to yank his hands from the desk, he found them still fastened firm.

'Qualities to die for,' she purred, her hands rising higher until he could feel her damp fingers wrapping round his neck, 'in such a material world.'

The fingers were getting tighter. His ragged breath rasped and gurgled through his constricting throat. The dead people watched in gruesome fascination.

'Qualities,' she said, 'you inherited from me.'

Domecq had been charged with a task. It was an elementary thing, and he brought with him all the authority of Earth Central to help him carry it out. But events on Ceres Alpha were getting swiftly out of hand, and Domecq sensed authority slipping through his fingers in the face of Gaskill Tyran's bloodlust. Now, he'd learned from his sources, the man had murdered the girl, having failed to get inside the mysterious blue box in the hold. The box may well have contained vital clues to the mystery of the creatures. They were obviously dealing here with a number of brand-new technologies. But, once again, Tyran had destroyed his only means of moving forward in his investigations.

Barging into Tyran's office unannounced, Domecq found Tyran slumped alone at the head of his desk. His head shot back as Domecq came in, and Domecq found his eyes full of dread fears, dark and manic and haunted.

'Oh Christ, did you see them?' Tyran demanded, his voice a terrified whisper.

Domecq shook his head in puzzlement. 'See who?'

Eyes flashing about the empty room, Tyran gasped for no reason at all, then seemed to come to his senses, gathering his thoughts and waving Domecq over to the desk. He looked drawn and tired, black eyes deep with shadow. For a moment, Domecq saw him as a small figure behind the far-too-huge desk. Just a man, whose power wasn't as absolute as he had imagined.

'I've submitted a sub-ether report,' Domecq informed him.

Tyran smiled a crazy kind of smile and simply pointed to the glass in front of him.

'Join me,' he said, voice still plainly quivering. 'In a drink to absent friends.'

The chopper bounced through the winds with near-zero visibility and Bains sat with his fingers crossed. He checked his harness for the fiftieth time. The bumpy ride didn't seem to bother the children. They were huddled together again on the floor, arms entangled for mutual support.

After the weapons had exploded killing the troops outright, the Doctor had bulldozed them all back into the chopper and insisted they get back to the city. As soon as it was learned that the troops had been killed, there would be more sent after them. A bigger force with bigger weapons, and the children were too young to understand, the Doctor said.

'If they're harmed they'll lash out. We've got to get them safe. Away from the military.'

'Why go back to the city if you want to get them away from Tyran and his nutters?' Bains had asked, nonplussed at the

Doctor's perverted logic. 'You're walking right into his hands.'

The Doctor had merely smiled one of his mysterious smiles that Bains was fast beginning to find more than a bit irritating.

'I know a place we can find sanctuary,' he told Bains enigmatically. 'We need some time to calm the situation. I can get the children safe and bargain with Tyran.'

'Bargain with Tyran?' Bains had blustered. 'You must be joking.'

'It's our only chance. You saw back there what these children are capable of. Their powers are growing all the time. If we're not careful this thing will end up in a bloodbath.'

The chopper dipped abruptly and for a second Bains thought they'd lost control, but when he looked out through the screen he found he could see little yellow pinpricks of light.

'Where are we?'

The Doctor was maintaining a stationary position, running scans on the forward sensors, somehow managing to keep them stable in the face of the buffeting storm.

'We're outside the hold where the heavy equipment is stored and maintained.'

Watching over the Doctor's shoulder, Bains suddenly realised that one of the chopper's plasma missiles was being armed and aimed. The comp system informed the Doctor that the area was safe, and that no personnel had been detected in the immediate vicinity.

'What the hell are you playing at?' Bains demanded.

'Getting us in,' the Doctor said, glancing back with a smile while he shot off the missile and the wall of the hold exploded in a blast of glittering metal and fire.

Then they were moving. Plunging through the flaming hole, the chopper swooped low, a metre or so off the ground, and Bains ducked when he saw the beams and walkways skimming over the top of them. Then Bains saw the small blue box ahead, and the half a dozen armed guards around it. They were levelling their rifles as the Doctor touched down in front of the box. The chopper searchlights flared and the troops were blinded and confused. As the door buzzed open the Doctor let off a round of shells that sprayed harmlessly into the distance but caused so much racket that the troops were sent diving for cover.

In no time he was out at the blue box and Bains saw the door swing open. The children were moving fast, diving into the gap that had opened up. Was this the Doctor's sanctuary? Was this man completely bonkers?

The Doctor was yelling at him to get a move on, and Bains stumbled out of the chopper as the first shots were fired by the surrounding guards. Diving for cover into the dark opening, Bains was utterly perplexed when he arrived in a wide-open space that seemed to be the interior of a completely different city.

'This is impossible,' Bains gasped.

'That's what they all say,' the Doctor shouted, dashing past him to pull a lever on a mushroom-like control console in the centre of the room.

What had been a thin wooden door was actually a pair of sturdy white doors from this side, and they swung shut at the Doctor's command with an electronic warbling sound.

Ayla was drinking tea in the kitchen when she heard the commotion outside. Returning to the control room, she found the place suddenly populated by a strange mix of people. A man in torn shirtsleeves was checking the instrument panels on the central console, while another, older man was wandering about the perimeter of the room looking as baffled as she'd been when she first came in, and then there were children everywhere.

And then she saw them properly. Children, yes. But very odd children indeed –

'Can I help you?' The man in torn shirtsleeves was gazing at her in astonishment.

'I was just about to ask you the same thing,' Ayla said.

At that moment Fitz arrived back and he too was gazing in astonishment at the man in white sleeves.

'Doctor!'

'*Fitz!*'

They crashed in a tangle of limbs, and Fitz looked completely taken aback at the Doctor's enthusiasm.

'Doctor,' the older man was saying in the background, but the Doctor was too enthralled in his reunion with Fitz to hear.

'Fitz Fitz Fitz Fitz Fitz,' the Doctor was stammering, looking happy and sad and entirely confused. 'I'm so sorry. I thought… Well… I thought…'

'*Doctor!*' the older man repeated, his voice now urgent.

Still grasping Fitz by the shoulder, the Doctor turned to see what he wanted, and Ayla saw that the children had collapsed to the floor. They were deathly white and torpid, struggling to sit up and reach out for help, as if the life had been abruptly sucked out of them…

Medicare seemed to have been completely abandoned, and they'd reached the cells without seeing a soul. Veta was like a missile, locked on to her target with fierce determination. She was hugging the rifle in the crook of her arm and Josef had no doubt whatsoever that she wouldn't hesitate to use it on anybody who might be unlucky enough to get in their way.

The cells were unguarded. Veta swept through the cleaners' storeroom and hesitated only a moment to work out the secret door disguised with stacks of cleaning cloths. Then they were in, Veta slamming each door in turn to discover every cell empty.

Josef finally caught up with her in the last cell, where she was standing in the dark looking lost and afraid. There was the distant howl of wind, the buffeting of sand and rain against the outer walls. The cells were freezing cold, tiny spaces without any source of light except for that from the connecting corridor outside. The air was rancid with the stench of uncleaned toilets.

He reached out to take Veta in his arms, and discovered her shadowed eyes gazing off into the blackness where there was nothing at all to see. There were hairline cracks appearing in her new resolve.

'We don't know they're dead,' he said, reading her mind like an open book.

Then he saw the tiny opening in the ceiling. The gaps around a rough square hole that he guessed had been cut from outside. The hole would have been just wide enough to take the bulk of a man, and the removed section had been quickly and very clumsily welded back into place.

Sensing his excitement, Veta saw the repaired hatch and the determination took up residence again in her features.

'I think we ought to review Perón's security 'grams,' she said, hoisting the rifle in her arms. 'Don't you?'

Gaskill Tyran was quite mad, Domecq was absolutely sure. It had probably been an insidious thing, creeping through him for the last few months while the Ceres project steadily collapsed. It was likely that the complete breakdown of the city-machine and the incident with Danes had both helped tip him over the brink. The insanity may well have had something to do with the influence of the creatures since Tyran had always been ultimately responsible for their treatment, but it was difficult to be certain, and now they might never find out. His casual murders of the girl, the impostor and the creatures were irrational moves they would all regret.

'I think your work is finished here,' Tyran told him flatly.

'There'll be a full enquiry,' Domecq said.

Tyran's eyes flashed full of wild thoughts.

'I have two armed ships in orbit,' Domecq said quietly, tapping his com. 'An open channel since I arrived. My men have strict instructions. Don't think you can silence me the way you've silenced so many others. Earth Central were determined to get those creatures. You've squandered an extremely valuable opportunity –'

'The valuable opportunity is Ceres Alpha,' Tyran insisted.

'We could have had both –'

'The creatures were halting the work here. It was them or the planet. You *couldn't* have both.'

The argument would go round and round in circles. It was a moot point now the creatures were gone.

A call came through on Tyran's com. He pushed back in his seat and took it immediately. The head that materialised above his desk wore a military cap, but it wasn't one of the people Domecq recognised.

'Sir,' the head said in a state of obvious excitement. 'We're down in the hold with the alien box. I think you should get down here straightaway.'

'What's happening?'

'The impostor, sir. He's back. And so are the creatures.'

'I'm so stupid,' the Doctor was ranting as he scurried round the centre console flicking switches and taking readings. 'Stupid stupid stupid.'

'They're getting worse,' Bains said from his position kneeling by one of the strange children.

The Doctor was growing more frantic by the minute, and now there were more troops than ever crowding round the TARDIS. Fitz watched them on the scanner as they milled about in confusion, some of them preparing their rifles nervously, as if they expected the door to open and some giant force to come suddenly rushing out.

'I think they're dying,' Bains said.

'I think you're probably right,' the Doctor agreed as he continued to work.

'But why?'

'I have a theory that fits the facts,' the Doctor said, attaching a small television-like box to the centre console. 'I think the whole biosphere of this planet is one giant sentient entity. A kind of Gaia principle taken to its extreme. You uncovered clear evidence that there was a previous civilisation here. I think they suffered a huge catastrophe, like you've had on Earth. Maybe a giant meteor strike. It was an apocalyptic event. All life almost wiped out.'

He was banging the top of the little attachment until it flared into operation and gave him some more readings that cast a green glow over his face, making him look sinister and alien.

'But the planet is rebuilding itself. Life is evolving and taking hold. It's in the process of repairing the damage. Since humans arrived the biosphere has been screaming out in the only way it knows how but nobody listened. It's been trying to reject you. To stop you interfering with the process of...' The Doctor searched for the word he needed. 'Regeneration.'

The screen had obviously given him bad news. He yanked it from its housing and dropped it with a clatter to the floor, then knelt beside Bains and began to examine one of the children, lifting it gently and gazing into its closing eyes.

'At your dig I think you disturbed a dormant psychic force. The life force of the planet's original sapient, powerfully telepathic inhabitants. Your discoveries came at the same time as these children were moving from the zygote into the embryo stage in their mothers' wombs. I think that force entered the nascent embryos and hijacked them, producing a bridge species in order to communicate with the humans who were ravaging the world.'

He lowered the child back to the floor with a look of despondency.

'These children aren't evil,' he said. 'They're not genetic monstrosities. They're emissaries.'

Bains glared at him.

'But why are they dying?'

'The TARDIS forms a protective envelope. In here we're completely cut off from the outside world. We've stepped into a different dimension. We've cut them off from the planet. They can't survive without that intimate link. It's an elemental, crucial bond for them. You saw the effect it had when we buried Bustopher Jones.'

Fitz watched the monitor as two men arrived who weren't in military uniform. One of them was dressed in black with short black hair. He seemed to be in charge. Behind him was a taller man with blond hair who was suddenly arguing with the man in black. They were both staring and pointing at the TARDIS.

'I think the bigwigs are here,' announced Fitz.

The Doctor jumped to his feet and came to see, his face now more despairing than ever.

'I can't risk a short hop. The TARDIS isn't healed yet. We could end up anywhere, anywhen.'

Fitz found his eyes full of pain as the Doctor moved to the centre console and pulled the door lever.

And suddenly the TARDIS was crawling with troops.

The med unit blipped satisfactorily while Perón brought the windows online to check Kapoor's vitals. The phase rifle had caused massive internal trauma, stopping the heart and disrupting even the autonomic centres of the brain. Tyran had killed her in a fit of rage, but then instantly regretted it and gave Perón the job of reviving her. She was now the only link they had with the enigmatic alien box.

If it were up to Perón, she thought sourly, she'd have let her rot. The infiltrators were perfectly willing to kill people to get what they wanted. They didn't deserve to live. The box might be a loose end that Tyran was keen to tie up, but if it were up to her she'd take it out and bury it deep along with the impostor and the rest of his associates –

Unexpectedly, Kapoor gasped and her eyes snapped open. Perón was stunned to see they were completely black, flashing about, then settling directly on her. Perón remembered with a shiver the pitch-black eyes of the creatures.

Kapoor was muttering under her breath, most probably delirious, suspected Perón. But suddenly she grasped Perón by the lapel and pulled her down to her face. The black eyes seethed with a fury so fierce that even Perón felt terrified in the face of it.

'*Stop them,*' Kapoor hissed.

Perón pushed her back to the bed and slapped her hard across the face, using the transient shock to force one of Kapoor's wrists into a restraint strap.

'*No!*' Kapoor screamed, fighting with her free arm.

But Perón was too fast. She had both arms secure before Kapoor had chance to escape.

'*Let me out,*' Kapoor screeched, thrashing about wildly on the bed, sending equipment clattering and dislodging her sens-cables so that the med unit whined in alarm.

'*They're dying. Let me out.*'

Perón grasped the girl's jaw tight in the fingers of one hand, sneering into her hysterical face, deep into her oily black eyes.

'*Shut up!*' Perón screamed.

The convulsions gradually subsided, and Kapoor watched her with gritted teeth and shuddering breath.

'I know you,' Perón told her fiercely. 'I know you. I've seen those eyes before. I've felt them trying to get into my head.'

There was a scalpel on the med unit, and she grasped it suddenly, sweeping it in front of Kapoor's quivering face. The blade glinted in the soft yellow light.

'Tyran might need you alive,' she hissed. 'But he doesn't need your eyes.'

Kapoor looked horrified as the scalpel edged closer.

'*If thine eye offend me,*' Perón hissed with sick humour, manic grin stretching across her hot face.

Then she saw the muzzle of the rifle. A centimetre from her head.

'Move back.'

She did as she was told, and found the Manni woman observing her with a face entirely vacant of emotion. Her eyes weren't black, but they might as well have been. The rifle went off and Veta's merciless expression was the last thing Perón ever saw.

They'd been roughly ejected from the safety of the TARDIS, and Fitz found himself once again a man with far too many rifles being pointed directly at him. The Doctor had tried to help the soldiers with the bodies of the children, but for his efforts he'd received a bloodied eye from the butt of yet another rifle. Fitz and the others were herded into lifts that soared upwards with a velocity that made him feel sick. Finally they were thrust into a vast office which contained a huge desk big enough to hold a meeting of the rulers of the universe.

The room was full of guns and men in smart black tunics. Fitz was constantly amazed at the Doctor's capacity to drop them continually into such deep and desperate trouble. They seemed to spend their entire lives racing from one giant catastrophe to another without a moment to catch their breath in between.

The bloke in expensive-looking clobber with uncommonly dark eyes – Tyran, the Doctor had called him – perched on the edge of his gargantuan desk while the scary-looking bodyguard stood only a few feet away pointing a stubby black pistol straight at the Doctor's head.

Fitz was on the other side of the desk along with Ayla and Bains, right where the handful of military types with rifles had told them to stand. There was a palpable tension in the room.

Tyran was holding a short truncheon, slapping it repeatedly into his hand, smiling amicably in the Doctor's direction.

'I'm not going to waste my time with the mind probe,' he announced. 'I know how extremely resistant you can be to its effect.'

He hurled the instrument on to the desk and it landed in the middle with a thump. Fitz noticed that the Doctor followed its progress with a little relief.

'I think we'll just… chat,' Tyran said, for all the world as if he were a friend catching up on old times. 'Perhaps you'd like to start by telling me where you got this… TARDIS from,' he suggested.

'I made it,' the Doctor said. 'From old washing-up bottles and some odds and ends I had knocking about.'

'I'll tell you what I think,' Tyran said, ignoring the Doctor's little joke. 'I think you're working for another organisation who've stumbled across some alien technology. And I think you're going to tell me all about it.'

'You're very wrong, Mr Tyran. I told you before, we're simply travellers.'

'Then perhaps you could explain to me how you managed to crash-land here on Ceres Alpha at this particular moment in time?' Tyran asked politely.

The Doctor ran a hand through his hair and gazed off into space lost in thought. Fitz could almost see the cogs going round in his head. Then he could almost see the light bulb appear above it.

'*Of course!*' the Doctor erupted suddenly. 'Of course... of course... *yes!*'

He jumped to his feet and began to pace up and down, taking the bodyguard by such surprise that Fitz thought he was going to shoot the Doctor dead there and then. When he stopped pacing he started rambling, the words crashing out of him one after another in a furious barrage that Tyran listened to with growing irritation.

'The children were all born simultaneously, despite the fact that they were spread right across the planet. It was a combined effort that brought them into the world, and the shared birth trauma would have been immense. They're part human but part... *indigenous*. The indigenous part has powerful telepathic abilities. The TARDIS has telepathic circuits. They're mostly redundant at the moment. I really need to get round to looking at them, one day. We were travelling through the local vortex. There must have been a colossal psychic blast that wreaked havoc in the only telepathic receiver in the vicinity. The TARDIS. The blast would have ripped through, causing immense damage. That might explain the viral manifestation in the TARDIS systems.'

'That might explain,' Tyran said suddenly, 'absolutely nothing. *Sit down*, Doctor.'

The Doctor did as he was told, but he continued to look excited, perched on the edge of his seat as if he were on the brink of jumping up again.

'Who do you work for?' Tyran repeated.

The Doctor shook his head, and Fitz saw the look on his face. The look of a frustrated schoolmaster who's just explained a beautifully elegant theory to the school bully, only to be asked when rugby practice begins.

'We…' the Doctor said, the exasperation now obvious in his voice, '…are… travellers.'

Tyran straightened up on the edge of his desk, and Fitz caught a quick glance that passed between him and his bodyguard, who stepped forward to press the muzzle of his gun to the Doctor's temple.

'"I am a passionate, obstructive man",' Tyran said quietly. 'Your own words, Doctor. Obstructive, certainly. Now let's see how passionate you can be, shall we?'

He stood and made his way round the desk to take a rifle from one of the troops in front of Fitz. The others moved into position with their weapons raised either side, while Tyran swung the rifle from Bains to Ayla to Fitz, gazing across the desk at the Doctor still slumped on the little seat with the bodyguard's gun at his head. As Tyran's rifle bobbed about in front of them, Fitz saw the anguish in the Doctor's eyes. He recognised the look of hopelessness in his friend and then he saw the rifle settle on his own chest.

There was a brief pause of silence, then the Doctor roaring for all he was worth –

'*Nooooo…*'

Domecq had arranged them on specially erected lab benches in Tyran's private rooms. The creatures now were barely alive, but he hoped he could still retrieve vital information from them. He was particularly interested in the grey matter contained in their skulls. If he could get open access to one of the brains, it might be possible to run in-vivo tests that could reveal the secret of their telepathic abilities. There was most probably a specialist area in the brain that dealt with those powers.

Choosing one of the creatures at random, he unfurled a pack of medical instruments on the bench beside it and set up his com to record the operation.

He would start by peeling away the scalp. A simple circumferential incision should reveal the bone structure in the top of the head. If the children were only two months old, the fontanelles should still be soft enough to allow very easy access into the cranial cavity without producing too much distress.

He had thought about anaesthetising the creature for the op, but it was so weak he didn't want to risk losing it before he'd started. Better to seize what information he could as expeditiously as possible while they were still holding on to life.

Reaching into the pack of instruments, he chose a scalpel and leaned over the creature to make his first cut. He could feel its soft warm breath on his cheek as he neared it. Testing the skin on its forehead with his fingers, kneading it to check elasticity and density, he touched the scalpel to the surface but stopped before he applied any pressure.

He'd become abruptly aware of a distant susurration. Like a thousand far-off voices whispering all at once. He checked his com for interference, and was certain the com wasn't the cause. Then he heard a scratching sound behind the walls, mixed with the hissing whispers.

He felt the touch on his sleeve. Hardly a pressure at all. He found the creature's eyes locking on his. Found he couldn't tear his gaze away. The whispering was getting louder and the black eyes were oozing like slicks of oil.

Then the sheer terror took him from nowhere, gushing through him like freezing cold water.

As the Doctor's scream echoed to silence, the lights abruptly dipped and flared. Tyran pressed the trigger again, but still the rifle refused. He indicated one of the soldiers, who stepped forward to execute Fitz, but his gun was jammed as well.

There was a fray on the other side of the desk and Fitz saw the Doctor standing with the bodyguard now pinned on the end of his own pistol. The man raised his arms in the air.

The lights were flickering wildly now. Then Fitz heard the hissing, like he might get from a radio that was miles off-station.

There was movement on the far side of the ceiling. Dark shapes scurrying across the panels. They looked like rats as big as cats.

Then the panels began to glow and Tyran began to scream, grasping his head and stumbling about the room, falling across the desk and scrabbling for the mind probe that he'd discarded earlier. He'd almost reached it when he shrank into a tight little ball, screaming louder than ever.

The ceiling panels were alive, quick-scurrying shadows passing behind them and images flickering across their surface. Fitz saw hundreds of faces in quick succession. People screaming, people writhing in obvious pain, people with their hands to their heads, people with tears in their eyes, great thick shapes of human suffering.

'It's Tyran's mind,' the Doctor said. 'It's taking his memories.'

Fitz saw Bains stumble beside him, grasping the desk for support as he watched one of the images that was being repeated over and over in the centre of the ceiling –

Bains was stunned. He'd witnessed Carly's death, whisked up among the many others, but there was much worse. There at the core of all the images he saw one of his own memories. There was Jazz in the bottom of the wardrobe where he'd found her all those years ago, her face vacant of feeling and reason. *Eyes wide open – nobody home. Autonomic pilot. Her empty eyes were the most terrifying thing he'd ever seen.* But the wardrobe swung shut and Bains found himself staring not at his own reflection in the mirrored door, but at a reflection of Tyran. He was holding a mind probe loose in his grasp, lost in his own emotionless gaze. The image of the eyes began to grow as the rest of the ceiling surged with other people's deaths. And Bains found that he couldn't take his eyes from Tyran's.

The image bloated, growing slowly bigger until only the eyes filled the entire expanse of the great arched ceiling. Finally there was just one huge eye in close-up, the pupil a black hole at the heart of an enormously exaggerated iris full of delicate swirling colours.

Tyran killed Jazz. *What did it mean?* He remembered her call, her last desperate cry for help. She'd been terrified of something, somebody coming after her, and it was something she desperately wanted to tell Bains about. *What did it mean?* Then he remembered the cat-and-mouse games with Tyran. How baffled he'd been that Tyran hadn't simply killed him outright. *What did it mean?*

The whispering voices filled his head, took hold of his thoughts and moulded them. And abruptly he knew. He knew what Jazz had wanted to tell him. Why she'd been so desperate for them to meet after thirty years apart.

He knew, as if in a flash of divine inspiration, that Gaskill Tyran was his son.

The lift had reached toplevel when the lights started to fade and flare. The doors jammed half open, and Josef grasped them desperately as they began to jerk shut again. Managing to force them apart, he allowed Veta through first with the girl, before tumbling out himself into the vast reception area outside Tyran's offices.

The whole city-machine had begun to reverberate, as if the engines were striving to grumble into motion. The huge holowalls showing idyllic vistas were flickering crazily, the pictures oscillating between 3-D and 2-D, as if the distant horizons were being flipped forward to slap Josef in the face. The effect was disconcerting but fascinating. There were shadows dashing behind the walls. Scurrying dark shapes. They flashed by one after another, running in all directions like things in a state of frenzy.

The girl in Veta's arms collapsed with a groan and Josef helped to lift her up.

'Where are they?' Veta demanded.

The girl gazed about deliriously, her black eyes strangely devoid of reflection.

'Near,' she gasped. 'But we're not going to make it.'

Dragging the girl to her feet, Veta grasped her by the scruff of the neck and shook her violently.

'*Where are they?*' she shrieked.

The girl's head tossed from side to side, as if she were listening to a thousand conflicting messages that nobody else could hear.

'It's coming,' she gasped. 'Oh God, it's here.'

'What's coming?' Veta yelled.

'The dark –'

The holowalls exploded with a huge crash of shattering glass. The area was flooded with dark rushing shapes. Hundreds of rats like a river of black fur. The lights flared. The girl screamed. Josef gave in to the sheer tide of terror that had been clawing at his throat.

With a final agonised cry, Tyran fell still, his lifeless body sprawled across the desk. His eyes were wide and vacant.

The boom that had been gradually building for the last few minutes suddenly detonated into an ear-splitting crash as the entire ceiling burst in on them. There was a series of deep explosions that rocked the city. As Ayla ducked for cover, she felt the clatter of detritus on her back, then the brush of warm fur on her hands and the side of her face. Something snatched at her hair and she opened her eyes to find the floor seething with rats. Blind hysteria ripped through her, then she felt herself being carried, swept towards the door through the turmoil of sound and dark motion.

She was being supported by Fitz, then by the Doctor, as they crashed through the door into the reception area outside.

'Where the hell did those things come from?' she asked as the rats ran amok at her feet.

'They're constant companions to the human race,' the Doctor replied. 'They go everywhere you go. They used to share sea voyages with the early mariners. They're a species every bit as devious and adaptable as human beings.' The man was actually grinning in admiration at the tide of black fur. She found his eyes sparkling enthusiasm in his pummelled and still-bloody face.

Then there followed a chain of confused events that battered her like a storm. The Doctor and Fitz crying out in recognition of Anji. The woman supporting Anji hysterically yelling about the children. Anji falling into the Doctor's arms, muttering senselessly. The Doctor grasping her by the face, forcing her to look into his eyes. The lights were flaring and dimming. The rats were tugging at her ankles while the whole city was shaking and breaking up. Ayla was certain that underneath all the surface commotion, she could hear the murmur of thousands of whispering voices.

'Show me,' the Doctor's voice was soft but intensely compelling as he spoke to Anji. 'Concentrate... Come on... Show me where they are...'

Then they were moving. Forcing their feet through the thick carpet of screeching rats. Fitz with his arms tight around her. Doors swept open in front of them. As they progressed the tumultuous chaos seemed to be dying, the rats dispersing, the whispering voices spluttering into silence.

Then they were in a large room filled with temporary benches. There were great dark holes where there should have been ceiling, fast-moving shapes as the rats dispersed. Ayla sensed everybody round her standing in awe and then she saw what they were looking at.

The floor crunched underfoot as he stepped into the room and Fitz was stunned at the devastation. On the benches lay the lifeless grey shapes of the children, picked out in dull yellow light. They were covered in fallout from the shattered ceiling, jagged lumps of debris and dirt that layered everything.

Straight ahead in the centre of the room, where two huge ceiling joists intersected, was the body of Dr Domecq. His arms were pinned out sideways, fixed to the beams with what looked to Fitz like a pair of scalpels through the palms of his hands. Dark blood dribbled from the wounds, and his cheeks were traced with trickles of blood from his eyes.

As he stared in rapt fascination, Fitz became vaguely aware of the Doctor moving nearby, clattering through the detritus to bend over one of the children. He grasped the child's hand and gazed into the huge black eyes, and when it came his voice was less than a whisper.

'Macavity, it's me,' he said. 'Can you hear me?'

Macavity briefly raised his hand, but it was too much effort to sustain. The hand fell limp by his side and the Doctor abruptly lowered his head, his brown hair falling like a mane to obscure his face and his emotions.

He didn't straighten up, didn't turn to face them, didn't say a word.

Josef couldn't bring himself to enter the room. From the doorway he watched the small group that had gathered there speechless and inert. The Doctor stood with his head bowed in silence, refusing to look them in the eye. And then Josef became aware of Veta nearby. Despite her closeness to him, she stood alone in a void of sorrow.

Weeping softly.

Bains could see Macavity's eyes from where he stood. He saw them glaze as the hand fell limp. And he knew they were too late. The other children were exactly the same. Corpses. Small things still and silent.

Abruptly the Doctor was an outburst of frantic motion, scooping Macavity up in his arms and stomping over to grab one of the others as well.

'Help me,' he yammered. 'Bring them all. Follow me.'

Bains and the others rushed forward to pick up the remaining bodies, finding them light as empty shells, and the Doctor led them all from the room, hurtling up the maintenance stairs until they emerged on to the city roof. Bains was stupefied to find the storms completely calmed and the sky above full of clear silver stars.

'Quick,' the Doctor yelled, making a dash for the chopper bays. 'I don't know how much time we've got.'

They loaded two choppers with the children and adults, and the Doctor and Bains jumped into the cockpits. Bains fired up the engines and the monitor asked for his passcode. He glared at it for a moment frozen in horror. Then he found the system overridden by an emergency protocol, accepting messages from the Doctor's chopper that allowed Bains to lift the craft into the air and follow the Doctor down to the surface.

They touched down in the dirt and frantically scrambled out with the corpses, the Doctor and Bains leading the way and the others helping with the bodies.

The Doctor was frantically digging with his bare hands, clawing the soil until he'd created a shallow cavity. Veta watched him with a numb sense of bewilderment as he laid one of the children into the recess and pushed the loose soil back around the corpse, not burying it but leaving it protruding out of the ground.

He scrambled back to the chopper to bring out another body, yelling as he went.

'Help me,' he gasped. 'Get them into the ground.'

There was a bustle of activity as the others did what he ordered, but Veta found it impossible to move. The entire universe spun on this perfectly still moment, whisked about her in its furious fire of activity. She could only gaze through her tears at the small pale shape that the Doctor had covered in dirt. She dropped to her knees in the mud, and a tornado of emotion raged through her as she reached out with quivering fingers to touch the boy's face. She was sobbing helplessly, tears flowing freely down her cheeks. She began to trace the outline of the body, feeling it cold to her touch. They were such frail little things. Slender arms and delicate hands with three fragile fingers like twigs.

Lifting the small hand out of the soil, she wrapped the fingers around her own, bending them and holding them tightly in place. Months' worth of sorrow and fear were surfacing, bubbling up and forcing their way out of her throat.

Then she felt the small fingers spasm round hers, saw the head jerk in the mud. The chest heaved, and as she looked on in wonder the eyelids flickered open. She saw large black eyes underneath.

Eyes she suddenly understood that she'd known for ever.

The lips twitched as their eyes met.

A fragile smile.

The mouth opened.

She heard a small breath of air that carried a word.

'*Mama…*'

Epilogue

The meadow was brimming with wildflowers, and over at the distant horizon the sun was sinking at the end of a lovely day. A day full of nothing. A day full of rest. A hazy, lazy, Sunday kind of day. Somewhere, there was a skylark singing. Somewhere else, there were cattle lowing and goats bleating. Somewhere, perhaps far off in the back of her mind, in the depths of her dreams, in the quixotic corners of her soul, she could hear Bill Withers singing.

A door opened nearby, and beyond she briefly caught sight of a TARDIS corridor that reminded her where she was. The Doctor stepped on to the meadow and the door sliced shut behind him to become a tall slender sapling that oddly never moved in the breeze.

He came over and plonked by her side with a smile.

'How are you feeling?' he asked, scanning the improbably beautiful landscape.

'Better,' she said.

He peered into her eyes and nodded a satisfied nod.

'You *look* much better, I must say.'

'How's the TARDIS?' she asked.

'Getting there,' he said. 'To be honest I'm just leaving the old girl to it. She's pretty good at repairing herself following that kind of damage.'

'You've still no idea why I was affected so badly?'

He frowned. 'I think those children were crying for a mother, somebody that could understand them intimately,' he said. 'I think the overwhelming psychic blast from the birth trauma was diverted to the only person on board who might be capable of receiving that kind of signal. It's possible that somehow or other the *TARDIS* inadvertently caused the damage to your latent telepathic centres. Or perhaps it was the signal itself…'

'You don't know, do you?'

'I'm not certain, no,' he admitted begrudgingly. 'The TARDIS is a very complex entity. It'll take time to understand her completely. If ever. I don't know everything, you know. I'm not perfect. I'm only –'

He cut off mid-flow, head tilted, listening carefully.

'What is it?' she asked.

'Can you hear somebody singing?'

She shook her head. His eyes narrowed, squinting into the empty sky.

Then he began to croon softly, '*A lovely da-a-a-ay…*'

Some extraordinary facts about the author...

Steve Emmerson has got two hearts. He was born in 3691 on an airless, inhospitable world. In his garden he has an ordinary-looking shed which is infinitely bigger on the inside than it is on the outside. Steve has travelled as far as the Dark Vortex and he sings Venusian lullabies. He knows what aikido is and he's scientific adviser to UNIT. A man of remarkable dimensions, he's even been seen speaking to animals. He's quite surly. Claims he's a Time Lord.

I'm sorry, I'll read that again –

Some extra, ordinary facts about the author...

Steve Emmerson has got two lungs. He was born in 1963 on an NHS hospital ward. In his garden he has an ordinary-looking shed which is infinitesimally bigger on the outside than it is on the inside. Steve has travelled as far as Blackpool and he's read *Venusian Lullaby*. He knows where Ikea is and that's where he buys his kitchen units. A man of remarkable dementia, he's even been seen squeaking to animals. His wife Shirley says he's a slimeball.

http://www.steveemmerson.com

Acknowledgements

Many, many thanks go to a few people this time:

Friends at the BBC –
Justin, for trust and confidence in me. And, once again, for suggestions and nudges that helped create a better book. Jac, for all the twiddly bits that go into getting a book like this finally on to the shelves.

Friends in the wider world –
Dave Tulley for the past XX years of *Who*, bacon butties, and general mutual baiting. Susan O'Neill for feedback and encouragement on the *DP* first draft.

Friends at home –
My most major thanks this time to Whirl for amazing support way above and beyond during the writing of *Dark Progeny*. Special note of thanks to Angie Towler, for Gibran and general thought provocation. And thanks to Ben, just for being so damned wonderful and inspiring.

BBC DOCTOR WHO BOOKS
FEATURING THE EIGHTH DOCTOR

DOCTOR WHO: THE NOVEL OF THE FILM by Gary Russell
ISBN 0 563 38000 4
THE EIGHT DOCTORS by Terrance Dicks ISBN 0 563 40563 5
VAMPIRE SCIENCE by Jonathan Blum and Kate Orman
ISBN 0 563 40566 X
THE BODYSNATCHERS by Mark Morris ISBN 0 563 40568 6
GENOCIDE by Paul Leonard ISBN 0 563 40572 4
WAR OF THE DALEKS by John Peel ISBN 0 563 40573 2
ALIEN BODIES by Lawrence Miles ISBN 0 563 40577 5
KURSAAL by Peter Anghelides ISBN 0 563 40578 3
OPTION LOCK by Justin Richards ISBN 0 563 40583 X
LONGEST DAY by Michael Collier ISBN 0 563 40581 3
LEGACY OF THE DALEKS by John Peel ISBN 0 563 40574 0
DREAMSTONE MOON by Paul Leonard ISBN 0 563 40585 6
SEEING I by Jonathan Blum and Kate Orman ISBN 0 563 40586 4
PLACEBO EFFECT by Gary Russell ISBN 0 563 40587 2
VANDERDEKEN'S CHILDREN by Christopher Bulis
ISBN 0 563 40590 2
THE SCARLET EMPRESS by Paul Magrs ISBN 0 563 40595 3
THE JANUS CONJUNCTION by Trevor Baxendale
ISBN 0 563 40599 6
BELTEMPEST by Jim Mortimore ISBN 0 563 40593 7
THE FACE EATER by Simon Messingham ISBN 0 563 55569 6
THE TAINT by Michael Collier ISBN 0 563 55568 8
DEMONTAGE by Justin Richards ISBN 0 563 55572 6
REVOLUTION MAN by Paul Leonard ISBN 0 563 55570 X
DOMINION by Nick Walters ISBN 0 563 55574 2
UNNATURAL HISTORY by Jonathan Blum and Kate Orman
ISBN 0 563 55576 9
AUTUMN MIST by David A. McIntee ISBN 0 563 55583 1
INTERFERENCE: BOOK ONE by Lawrence Miles
ISBN 0 563 55580 7

INTERFERENCE: BOOK TWO by Lawrence Miles
ISBN 0 563 55582 3
THE BLUE ANGEL by Paul Magrs and Jeremy Hoad
ISBN 0 563 55581 5
THE TAKING OF PLANET 5 by Simon Bucher-Jones and
Mark Clapham ISBN 0 563 55585 8
FRONTIER WORLDS by Peter Anghelides ISBN 0 563 55589 0
PARALLEL 59 by Natalie Dallaire and Stephen Cole
ISBN 0 563 555904
THE SHADOWS OF AVALON by Paul Cornell ISBN 0 563 555882
THE FALL OF YQUATINE by Nick Walters ISBN 0 563 55594 7
COLDHEART by Trevor Baxendale ISBN 0 563 55595 5
THE SPACE AGE by Steve Lyons ISBN 0 563 53800 7
THE BANQUO LEGACY by Andy Lane and Justin Richards
ISBN 0 563 53808 2
THE ANCESTOR CELL by Peter Anghelides and Stephen Cole
ISBN 0 563 53809 0
THE BURNING by Justin Richards ISBN 0 563 53812 0
CASUALTIES OF WAR by Steve Emmerson ISBN 0 563 53805 8
THE TURING TEST by Paul Leonard ISBN 0 563 53806 6
ENDGAME by Terrance Dicks ISBN 0 563 53802 3
FATHER TIME by Lance Parkin ISBN 0 563 53810 4
ESCAPE VELOCITY by Colin Brake ISBN 0 563 53825 2
EARTHWORLD by Jacqueline Rayner ISBN 0 563 53827 9
VANISHING POINT by Stephen Cole ISBN 0 563 53829 5
EATER OF WASPS by Trevor Baxendale ISBN 0 563 53832 5
THE YEAR OF INTELLIGENT TIGERS by Kate Orman
ISBN 0 563 53831 7
THE SLOW EMPIRE by Dave Stone
ISBN 0 563 53835 X

PRESENTING

DOCTOR WHO

AN ALL-NEW AUDIO DRAMA

Big Finish Productions is proud to present brand-new
Doctor Who adventures on double CD!

Available from August 2001
PROJECT: TWILIGHT

A four-part story by Cavan Scott & Mark Wright.
Starring **Colin Baker** as the Doctor
with **Maggie Stables** as Evelyn Smythe.

*In the renovated docklands of South East London, on the bank of the river
Thames, the doors of the Dusk are open for business. Bets are called, cards
are dealt and roulette wheels spun. As fortunes are won and lost, an inhuman
killer stalks the local avenues and alleyways –
a killer with a taste for human flesh.*

*And what connection does the apparently sleazy Bermondsey casino have to a long-
buried government initiative known as Project: Twilight? The Doctor must form uneasy
alliances where the line between friend and enemy is blurred…*

If you wish to order this, please photocopy this form or provide all the details on paper.
Delivery within 28 days of release.
Send to: PO Box 1127, Maidenhead, Berkshire. SL6 3LN.
Big Finish Hotline 01628 828283.

Other stories featuring the Sixth Doctor still available include:

BLOODTIDE   THE SPECTRE OF LANYON MOOR

For more details visit our website at
http://www.doctorwho.co.uk